DEEP WATER, THIN ICE

Kathy Shuker was born in Wigan, England. After training and working as a physiotherapist, she studied design and went on to work as a freelance artist in oils and watercolours. Now writing full-time, she lives in Devon with her husband.
Deep Water, Thin Ice is her first novel.

To find out more about Kathy and her other novels, please visit:
www.kathyshuker.co.uk

DEEP WATER, THIN ICE

Kathy Shuker

Published by Shuker Publishing

All enquiries to kathyshuker@kathyshuker.co.uk

ISBN: 978-0-9928327-1-1

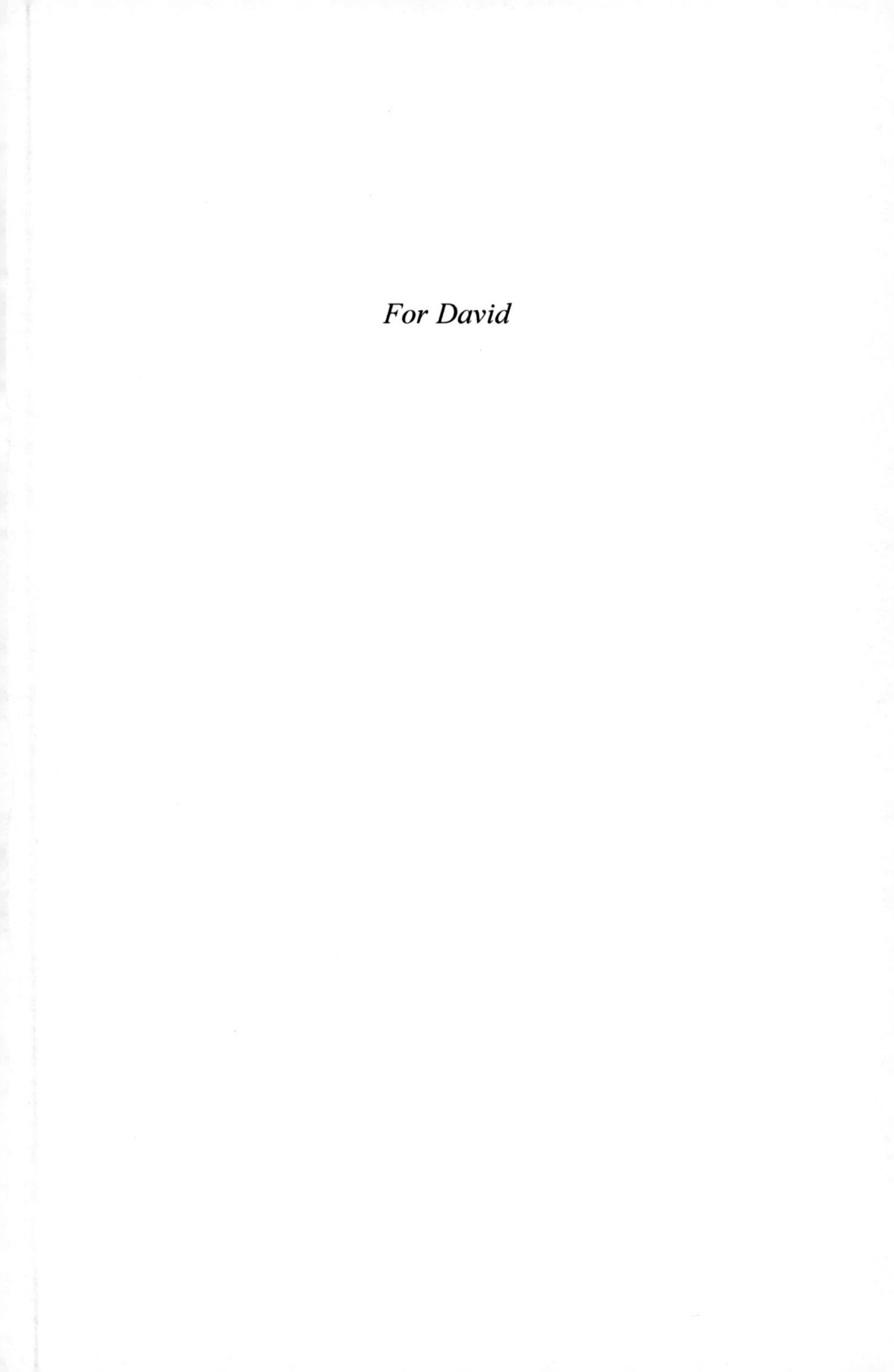

For David

Prologue

He found he was on Regent Street but couldn't actually remember getting there. He must have been walking for ten minutes already since leaving the restaurant, maybe longer; he'd lost track of time. Twice he'd looked round, with the flesh-creeping feeling that he was being followed, but he'd seen nothing to confirm his suspicions. It was autumn but the day was surprisingly warm and sunny, sultry even, the streets of London choked and sweaty with the multilingual cosmopolitan crush of tourists and shoppers: women in sleeveless tops and cotton dresses, men in t-shirts and cropped trousers, and office workers on late lunch breaks, their jackets abandoned and formal collars loosened. There were children too. Maybe it was half-term; he couldn't remember. But everyone, it seemed, wanted to make the most of this unwonted last farewell to summer.

Simon felt himself carried along by the press of people, unable to pin his thoughts down any more than he felt he could control where his feet led him. He moved with the flow of bodies - like a stick tossed into a river, he thought. The image brought back a rush of memories he'd tried hard to forget and he pushed them away. They wouldn't have come to mind in the first place if he hadn't had to meet that man for lunch and he was angry suddenly that they had been thrust back at him after all these years. Damn the man. Damn him to hell. Why did he have to surface now? Though if he were honest Simon knew he'd been waiting for it, that it had always only been a matter of time. And yet there was nothing he could do about it now. All the regrets in the world wouldn't change anything. The anger dissipated to be replaced by the stealthy heaviness which had become so familiar to him of late. Regrets. So many regrets. These last weeks had been a struggle. His life was starting to unravel and he felt as if he'd lost control.

He reached a large junction and stopped, hesitating a moment and trying to clear his mind, but someone collided with him from the rear and he felt himself moved forward and was swept along and then down, descending the steps into Oxford Circus tube station. Yes, he would get on a train and get away from the bustle of town. He'd purposely left the afternoon free; maybe he would go home, listen to some music, calm himself down and try to put it all away from him again. He queued for a ticket, passed through the barrier and headed for the platform, not really registering what he was doing. He knew the way well enough though he rarely used the tube these days, preferring to walk or take a cab.

The platform was surprisingly quiet; a train must just have left. Simon moved on. The crowd built up steadily behind him and he kept to the front – he'd never been the sort of person to hang back. Again he had the uncomfortable sensation of being watched and glanced round nervously, only to find himself looking into the indignant and challenging eyes of a young woman. He quickly looked away.

A snatch of a tune had come into his mind and he began to hum it. It wasn't his usual sort of music and he struggled to identify it. Then he realised what it was: 'Moon River' from *Breakfast at Tiffany's*. That was it. Alex had been singing it while she was packing just before she went away. Alex. She often sang it; it was one of her favourites. She'd sung it to him on their honeymoon he remembered now. How could he have forgotten that? His throat thickened with long suppressed emotion.

The rumble of the next train echoed distantly down the tunnel and he felt the first whisper of cold air flicking his hair. Everyone shuffled a little forward as more bodies weighed onto the platform and the rumble grew and swelled. Simon found himself looking down at the tracks, mesmerised by them as the sound echoed in his ears and the wind whipped against his face. His eyes swam with tears though he never cried. The tracks looked so close; all he had to do was step out and it would be done. Over with. Just like that. No more regrets. No more half truths and covering up and trying to forget.

'Moon River' drifted into his head again. Alex.

He lifted his head, dragging his eyes away from the track. He should have talked to her, should have told her everything but he'd never found that sort of thing easy. And surely it was too late to do it now. He'd pushed her too far away. He thought of phoning her; he'd like to hear her voice. But what would he say on the phone? He had no idea. It was pointless.

He turned his head as the train roared into the station and suddenly he was falling forward, out into empty space. He heard the screeching of brakes, someone screaming, and then all was silent blackness.

Chapter 1

Her sister was flirting again. Through a gap in the sea of bodies which straddled the room, Alex could see Erica talking to a young man of lean build and animated expression. The pose and mannerisms were unmistakeable and Alex inwardly smiled. It was a familiar and comforting sight in a world which now felt suddenly quite unreal.

She turned as a woman to her right remarked on what a lovely service it had been and expressed her sympathy. Alex immediately thanked her and tried to place the woman's face but couldn't. A lovely service. Was it? She couldn't remember much about it, only the music.

'You'd think that they'd have gone to more trouble with the music, wouldn't you?' Simon had once complained, as they'd left the funeral of an elderly musician friend. 'I'm sure he'd have preferred to go out in a blaze of strings and brass. I know *I* would.'

'I'll bear that in mind,' Alex had responded flippantly. 'What would you like? Shostakovich? No, Beethoven? Or what about the 1812?' She'd laughed at him then. They hadn't long been married and she didn't take the comment seriously. He was just thirty-one at the time and she was twenty-eight; she hadn't yet reached the stage of considering their mortality. Simon was a talented conductor and a rising star in the classical music world; she had a successful singing career. The future looked bright. 'Perhaps a little composition of your own?' she teased.

'Not a bad idea at that,' he said, grinning. 'If you can't get your music played at your own funeral, when can you?'

Now, here she was, barely ten years on, listening to a small chamber orchestra - friends and colleagues scratched together at short notice - playing a selection of Simon's pieces. She was standing in the function room of a large hotel in northwest London, still clasping the untouched plate of food Erica had pushed on her, feeling dislocated from the event as if she were trapped inside a transparent bubble.

'Alexandra,' said a booming voice to her left. She turned as a big man wearing a black bow-tie, his chin-length hair parted crisply down the centre of his scalp, put his arm round her shoulders. He was a violinist – pompous and difficult to work with, she remembered Simon saying - but she couldn't bring his name to mind. 'You poor girl,' he continued. 'What you must have been through. I've been reading the papers. Pure conjecture to sell copies. Don't pay any attention to it, that's my advice. I presume the police are happy that it was an accident?'

'They said they haven't closed the case yet. There's going to be an inquest.'

'Is there really? I suppose they have to. But of course it was an accident. He seemed happy enough to me. And he thought the world of you; always singing your praises – no pun intended of course. Speaking of singing though, I thought that last recording you made of those Bach cantatas was wonderful. Such vibrancy and yet such lightness of touch. So many sopranos make heavy weather of it. I suppose you'll be wanting a break from singing for a while but don't leave us for too long will you?' He released her shoulder, picked up her free hand and ostentatiously kissed the back of it before moving off.

Alex watched him go, his comments still echoing round her head.

'Mum says aren't-you-going-to-eat-any-of-that-you-haven't-eaten-anything-all-day,' intoned a young voice, the words tumbling out all on one breath. Alex looked down into the intelligent eyes of an auburn-haired boy beside her and smiled. It was Erica's ten-year-old son who looked not remotely like his mother.

'I'm afraid I'm not hungry Ben,' she said apologetically.

'Mum said you'd say that. And I'm supposed to say…' He paused and screwed his eyes up in concentration. '…It doesn't matter whether you're hungry or not; you should eat.'

Alex grinned in spite of herself.

'I'll bet she did.'

'Please Aunt Alex,' Ben pleaded in a resigned voice. 'You know what mum's like. You'd better eat something or we'll both get into trouble.' Alex sometimes thought Ben was old for his years. Living with Erica would do that to you.

She glanced across the room again but her sister had disappeared. Erica had been a rock ever since Simon's accident. As Alex had frozen into numbed inactivity, Erica had taken charge, taken all the organisation on herself and done what she always did best: made herself indispensable. Alex had chosen the music and readings for the service and Erica had done everything else. It had been slick and grand. 'It should be a statement,' Erica had said. 'A celebration of his life and achievements.' Simon would have approved. Though often introspective at home, he was a natural performer; he liked occasions. Of course Erica had been right and Alex was immensely grateful to her sister for all the trouble she'd taken. But if she'd been free to organise it as she would have wanted, if Simon hadn't seemed in some way to be public property, Alex would have gone for something more intimate and casual, maybe even one of those natural, woodland burials. There were too many people here she barely knew and she didn't find polite conversation easy at the best of times. There again, if she'd had to do it herself, feeling as stupid as she did at the moment, the whole thing would probably have been a shambles.

She glanced down at the delicate, cordon bleu finger food on her plate, caught Ben's eye watching her, his young forehead puckered into a frown, and forced herself to pick a rolled salmon canapé up and pop it in her mouth. She crinkled her eyes up into a smile for his benefit.

'Just keep chewing and swallowing,' Ben said. 'Like I do with mum's steak and kidney pie. It goes down in the end. Trust me.' Alex tried to oblige but her mouth was dry and it took a while to swallow. 'I'm thinking of becoming a vegetarian,' he confided. 'Lots of naturalists are vegetarian. It makes sense really.'

'Oh?' Alex looked at the remaining food on her plate. Under Ben's watchful gaze she picked up a frighteningly orange-filled vol au vent. 'Have you told your mum?'

'I mentioned it. She said it wasn't healthy while you're still growing but then she doesn't know anything about it. She'll come round with time. I'll work on her.'

Ben slipped away again and Alex replaced the vol au vent on her plate as another succession of people came up to pay their respects.

It was the back end of November and already more than four weeks since Simon had died. Alex had been in Vienna, doing a series of concerts at the Kursalon when Erica rang her late one afternoon to tell her that Simon had fallen under a tube train on the Victoria line in London. 'He's alive,' Erica had said, 'but badly hurt. You should come quickly Alex.' She'd left Vienna on the first available flight.

But Simon had never regained consciousness and was dead long before she could get to the hospital. Then there'd been the official identification of the body and a brief interview with the police. It had been a few days later when the police had asked to see her again. There were 'inconsistencies in the witness statements' the Inspector said. They needed to 'clarify a few things'.

'Were you happy together Mrs Brook?' was his opening gambit.

'Of course.' She frowned. 'Why?'

He grunted and then glanced at his notes before raising questioning eyes to her face. 'Or should I call you Miss Munroe?'

'I use my maiden name for performing…well, for most things really. It's easier.'

'I see.' He said everything as if it had some significance but she failed to see what it was. 'You spent a lot of time apart I understand?'

'It was the nature of our jobs. We have…did…occasionally work together – that's how we met in the first place - but inevitably not that often. You have to go where the work is.'

'I see. And you have no children?'

'No. We were…no.'

He paused and lifted his eyes slowly to her face. 'And there wasn't anyone else involved?'

The question took her completely off guard.

'No. No…of course not.'

He raised his eyebrows and sighed.

'I'm afraid, Miss Munroe,' he said in a gentler voice, 'there's reason to believe that your husband may have committed suicide.'

'Suicide? I thought it was an accident?'

'Some witnesses said it looked as if your husband stepped out purposely as the tube train came into the station. Of course the platform was very crowded and it was difficult to see but they said it seemed very sudden. Did your husband have any problems Mrs. Brook? Was there anything the matter in his work? Were there any money worries perhaps?'

Dazed, she shook her head. She and Simon were blessed with money, a nice home in Hampstead and a comfortable, albeit hectic, life.

'You'll forgive me for pressing the point,' the Inspector persisted. 'But in the circumstances I have to ask: you don't have a lover? It isn't possible your husband recently found out about it?'

'No, for God's sake, no.'

He nodded, slowly.

'And you haven't found a note?'

'If I had, I'd have told you,' she said crisply.

'Good…Well, if you do, you will inform us, won't you?'

She stood up to go, angry and upset, but he hadn't quite finished.

'And do you think your husband had any enemies, Miss Munroe?'

'Enemies?' Alex frowned, genuinely confused. 'No. Not as far as I know. Why?'

'There was one witness who said she thought he'd been pushed. I understand you were out of the country when it happened?'

‘Yes. I was in Vienna. Why? What are you suggesting?’

‘I’m not suggesting anything. But it’s important we check everything. I’m sure that’s what you would want us to do as well. Thank you for your co-operation. We’ll be able to reach you at this number in London I assume?’

Now, as she looked across the room and saw the last of the funeral guests speak to Erica before leaving, Alex found the policeman’s questions circulating in her head once more. She dismissed the idea that Simon might have any enemies who wished him dead as unthinkable. But what had taken him down to the station that day? He hated the underground. She was incessantly haunted by the implication, barely disguised in the policeman’s remarks, that she was responsible in some way for his death.

*

With the funeral reception over, Alex returned to Erica’s house in Ealing, reluctant to go home. She had stayed with Erica and Ben since her return from Vienna. Her own home was frighteningly quiet and empty on the inside while, by her gate, a crowd of journalists waited expectantly for news or comment. She couldn’t face them.

She stood inside the patio doors at the back of Erica’s terraced house and watched Ben pottering round his newly dug pond. The long strip of garden had been the deciding factor in Erica’s choice of the otherwise unremarkable property some two years before; Erica knew how much pleasure the garden would give Ben though it had pushed her to the upper limit of her budget. But, in an effort to satisfy Ben’s interest in wildlife, the pond was an even more generous move on her sister’s part. As a three year old child,

Erica had fallen in a child-minder's pond and nearly drowned. Alex, two and a half years older, had pulled her baby sister out covered in slime, insects and beetles. Alex had often attributed her own fastidiousness to that event. Certainly Erica's fear of water could be blamed on it; she'd had nightmares about it for months afterwards.

'It seemed to go well,' said an impersonal voice behind her. 'Very smooth.' There was a pause. 'Didn't you think?'

Alex came out of her reverie and turned. Her mother, Victoria, was sitting on the sofa, legs elegantly crossed, hands resting in her lap. Like Erica, she tended to plump rather than slim; unlike Erica, it never seemed to bother her. As a successful barrister she had always worn smart, fitted suits which expressed, as did everything else about her, her determination to be business-like and get the job done. Recently retired, little had changed. Her energy had simply been diverted into writing and the support of a number of good causes. Her clothes still suggested her gritty determination to win whatever project she chose to espouse, however long it took and whatever the cost. A driven woman with a greater dedication to professional success than family life, she was looking at Alex with the expectant expression her daughter knew well. Alex had spent her whole life, she thought, failing to live up to that expectation.

'I suppose so,' said Alex. 'Very smooth. I'll go and see if Erica needs any help in the kitchen.' And she left the living room, carefully closing the door behind her.

Erica was just pouring tea into china mugs. A plate of biscuits had already been put on a tray and she was half way through eating one, her short fair hair neatly styled into place.

‘Why did you invite her back here?’ muttered Alex, coming up beside her. ‘She hardly knew Simon and didn’t like him. I was amazed she even came to the crematorium.’

Erica finished pouring and put down the teapot with a thump on the stand.

‘I thought she quite liked Simon,’ she said, popping the rest of the biscuit in her mouth.

‘No, she didn’t. She *tolerated* him because he was successful. When she first found out he was a musician she thought he was a loser and a ‘bad prospect’, the same as all musicians. She didn’t want to know.’

‘Once bitten, twice shy,’ chanted Erica and then, with a glance towards the living room door, dropped her voice. ‘Well, whatever, I thought I ought to ask her. I thought she should be there. It’s about time the two of you buried the hatchet.’

‘It’s already buried. We just don’t talk much. We’ve nothing in common. Anyway she makes me feel so…’ Alex shrugged. ‘…inadequate. She always has.’

‘I know.’ Erica laid three mugs on the tray and looked at them doubtfully before raising her eyes to meet Alex’s. ‘She’ll think they ought to be china cups.’

‘Does it matter? Mugs are fine.’

‘I suppose. Anyway, try and be nice to her will you? I think she’s trying to be supportive. Well, you know, in her own way.’

Alex gave her sister a brittle smile.

‘You’re right. I know. You always did try to bring us together. I’ll try.’ The smile dwindled into nothing. ‘You’ve been great Ricky. Thanks for everything. What would I have done without you?’ Tears threatened and Alex gave her sister a quick, fierce hug.

'Oh, I'm an absolute angel,' said Erica dryly, accepting the hug rather stiffly. She picked up the tray. 'Will you give Ben a shout before you come through and get him to come in? His drink's on the side there. He's got homework to do yet and he'll stay out till it's dark given half a chance. Anyway, mum'll want to see him before she goes.'

Alex walked down the garden instead to speak to Ben and to look at the embryonic pond. When they got back to the house, she sent him upstairs to wash and then paused outside the living room door which stood slightly ajar.

'I don't know who he was,' Erica was saying. 'I've been through all the pew cards. There are no names that ring any bells.'

'Perhaps he didn't fill a card in,' said Victoria. 'Not everyone does.'

'I suppose not. Strange though.'

Alex pushed the door open and walked in.

'What's strange?'

Erica hesitated.

'*There* you are,' she said. 'Your tea's going cold.'

'Erica said she saw someone at the funeral who looked like Simon,' replied Victoria, apparently oblivious to Erica's preference to drop the conversation. 'She was wondering if he was a relation. Were you expecting anyone?'

'He hasn't got any relations...alive,' said Alex in a flat voice. 'Not close ones. He's...he was...an only child. You know that. He never mentioned anyone anyway.'

'What was this man like?' Victoria asked Erica.

Erica glanced at Alex before replying. Her sister's face, usually so expressive, was blank.

'I'm not sure exactly,' she said. 'I didn't speak to him. I saw him the other side of the room. Like I said he looked a bit like Simon. He had fair, wavy hair, short though. But he was tallish and perhaps a little broader. But then I got talking to someone and when I looked back, he'd gone.' She looked up at Alex again. 'Obviously you didn't see him?'

Alex shook her head and took her tea to the armchair on the other side and sat down. Even had she seen him it would have meant nothing. Over the last few weeks it had happened to her regularly. She would see Simon in the street or driving a car; she'd hear the phone and assume it would be him; she'd even sometimes see him on television, in programmes she watched just to distract her mind. She had regularly projected Simon's features onto strangers who, on closer inspection, bore scant resemblance to him. She'd feel the familiar rise in her heart before she remembered what had happened and the cold pall of reality settled on her again.

Victoria's gaze came to rest on Alex and she considered her, much as she might have viewed a stubborn defence witness.

'I know your taste in clothes is…individual,' she remarked, as her eyes flicked over the long red and purple vividly patterned dress her elder daughter wore, 'but I was surprised you wore that outfit for the funeral.'

'Simon liked this dress,' Alex said quietly.

'Yes…well. You know you mustn't *dwell* Alex,' Victoria said sternly. 'Keep yourself busy; get back to work…' She paused and Alex wondered if she was musing on whether singing actually qualified as work. '...Sitting around is the worst thing you can do.'

'I know,' said Alex grimly without looking up. 'Work is the answer to everything.'

'And Erica tells me you have no plan to bury the ashes. Is that wise? I mean, don't you think burial would give you more closure?'

'I'm not ready.' Alex's voice was small and tight. 'I haven't decided what I want to do with them yet.'

'Well, keeping them seems rather macabre to me. It's not healthy.'

There was the sound of running footsteps down the stairs and a minute later, having grabbed his drink from the kitchen, Ben came in to the room, looking excited.

'There's someone sitting in a car across the street,' he said. 'I think he's watching the house.'

'Oh God, it's probably a reporter,' groaned Erica, wandering to the window and gingerly pulling back the net curtain. 'Where?'

Ben joined her and stared out.

'He's gone. He was over there.' He pointed.

'Thank God,' said Alex gloomily. The adrenaline she'd needed to get her through the service and its aftermath was rapidly fading. She felt exhausted and indescribably bereft. Tears threatened again.

'They'll have found another more interesting story soon and you'll be forgotten.' Victoria put her mug down on the table and rose to her feet. 'Don't let them get you down.' She glanced at her watch. She still gave the impression that her time was carefully apportioned and that it was imperative that she keep to her schedule. 'I'd better be off.' She looked down at Alex who was staring sightlessly at her mug. 'Remember Alex, keep busy. And...if you need anything, well, you know where I am, don't you?'

Alex dragged her eyes up to her mother's face and nodded. If you happen to be in, she thought, and it's convenient.

*

Alex didn't need telling to get back to work; it was a relief to have something to do and she threw herself back into it like a thing possessed. She caught up with recordings she'd missed and travelled to fulfil concert dates, returning, between times, to her home in Hampstead. As Victoria had predicted, the press had lost interest and it was quiet once more. When she wasn't working she repeatedly cleaned the already spotless house or went out walking till she was weak with exhaustion. Anything was better than sitting still and thinking.

Her usually spirited and lively personality tipped into extreme highs and lows. She would laugh exaggeratedly at programmes she'd never found funny before or weep uncontrollably at sad news stories. Where normally her temper would rise quickly and then rapidly dissipate leaving her contrite and apologetic, now a wave of anger came upon her which seemed to hover just beneath the surface, permanently waiting to erupt. She felt angry with everyone - sometimes for quite trivial reasons - and struggled to contain it, even when she knew she was being unreasonable. Even her sister and her friends came under fire when they tried to be helpful and the remorse and confusion she felt at her behaviour only added to her despair. Several times a week, usually late at night when she was alone, frayed nerves, frustration and utter hopelessness would overwhelm her and she'd sob with tears until she thought she had no tears left to give, nothing left to feed this unendingly greedy worm of grief.

The nature of Simon's death troubled her deeply and she couldn't forget it. It had been so sudden and completely unexpected. There had been no illness or injury, serious and intractable, which had warned of her forthcoming loss. She hadn't even been there when he'd died and that upset her badly. And the worst thing of all was the thought that he had taken his own life when she had had no idea that he was so unhappy. What kind of person did that make her and what sort of relationship did that mean they had shared? Guilt was her constant companion, a heavy weight which she dragged round with her during the day and which nearly crushed her at night.

Christmas and New Year came and went and still she worked. Then, slowly, the anger burnt itself out and she struggled to get up in the morning. At the beginning of March, in the middle of a solo in Handel's Messiah she shuddered and fell silent. She was aware of several hundred pairs of eyes fixed on her, waiting. The orchestra kept playing, glancing uneasily at each other and then across at her but she was frozen. The other soprano soloist came to her rescue and took up the part allowing Alex to feign a bad cough and retire from the stage, distraught and mortified. Afterwards she didn't dare go back. She was terrified of doing the same thing again.

'You don't want to let it bother you,' Erica said. 'They probably all thought you'd got the flu. You'll be fine next time. You've always been nervous before performing. It was just a bad night.'

'No,' said Alex, shaking her head. 'You don't understand. It wasn't like normal. I was...was...' Even thinking about it made her break out in a cold sweat. 'God, it was awful. I can't describe how terrible I felt...like I couldn't breathe and everything was crowding in on me. I could hardly move.'

She shut herself away. But as the days drew into weeks and her torpor and misery threatened to deepen into depression, Alex remembered an old house Simon had inherited from his wealthy widowed mother some six months before he died. An old ramshackle place, he'd said dismissively, which had been let out off and on over the years; a house which would eat money if you let it, near the sea in Devon. She wasn't sure what made her think of it in the first place but the idea grew in her mind: to get away from the oppressive memories of London and the press who hovered expectantly again outside her gate. The thought was too appealing to be ignored.

Hillen Hall, the house was called, and when probate came through she asked the solicitor all about it. It had been empty for months, he said, told her the little he knew and gave her the keys. She took them out from time to time and weighed them thoughtfully in her hands as if they might give a clue to the nature of the house whose doors they unlocked. Early on the morning after the inquest finished – an equivocal 'open' verdict was finally recorded - she crammed her estate car with clothes, linens, personal items, Simon's cello and the casket containing his ashes, grabbed a map, the keys to Hillen Hall and the solicitor's vague directions, and headed west.

Chapter 2

Hillen Hall stood on the side of a hill above Kellaford Bridge, a small seaside village on a rugged part of the south west coast. After a long journey with too much time to doubt the wisdom of what she was doing, Alex got out of the car and stared at it with dismay. Built of pale blue-grey stone, it had the compact proportions of a medieval manor house though it had been extended, apparently more than once, in a quite arbitrary way. More recently, it seemed, it had simply been left to decay. A huge old wisteria, not pruned for years, grew rampantly across the eastern side of the front elevation and elsewhere ivy coated the walls, its roots and tendrils drilling into the mortar and sucking it dry and friable. The flower beds were weed-ridden and unkempt, the shrubs rampant and shapeless, and the grass long enough to make hay with.

Alex struggled with the lock of the canopied front door and let herself in to a flag-stoned entrance hall from which stairs rose to the first floor. An oak-boarded door led into a cosy room to the right. To the left, a similar door opened into a large sitting room, the original Great Hall she guessed, which was as depressing as the outside. The curtains were rotten and shredded from the sun, the carpets worn and marked and the furniture stained and broken. The beautiful stone fireplace had had a succession of fires and never been cleaned with the resultant ash spilling out over the hearth, smeared and spattered by rain falling down the chimney. Weary from the driving and the procession of black thoughts and misgivings accompanying it which the radio hadn't been able to dispel, she could have cried.

Simon had never talked about the Hall; the first she'd heard about it was when his mother died.

'I went there on holiday once when I was a kid,' he'd said when questioned.

'So what's it like?' she'd responded, intrigued.

'Can't remember much about it. It's a long time ago.'

'But it's let out, you said?'

'Yes...I think so. An agency deals with it. Look, darling, do we need to go into this now?'

He was still grief-stricken and she'd reluctantly let the subject drop. To her, the inheritance of a house by the sea was a novelty. The Munroes were of humble origins; property was something you lived in. Victoria's present wealth was the relatively recent product of cleverness and hard work – as she had often pointed out - whereas the Brooks were rich and Simon's father had been a successful businessman. Simon didn't squander money but he took it for granted. When his mother had died and her house in Knightsbridge was sold, despite her various and sometimes generous bequests, he had benefited from a substantial inheritance. Looking around Hillen Hall now, she wondered that he hadn't put this place up for sale too, given how little interest he seemed to have had in it.

She wandered on. From a tiny rear lobby behind the sitting room another staircase, built of stone, twisted round upon itself in a circular column to the upper floor. Beyond it stood a large shabby kitchen and, via a utility area, access to an attached but self-contained annexe. Next to the sitting room, a dining-room extended forward in front of the rest of the house. Upstairs there were five bedrooms and a large, creaking bathroom.

But there was something about the house which Alex liked. An aura of faded charm still managed to percolate through the grime and mouse droppings and its very neglect struck a chord with her. She especially liked the end bedroom above the cosy room she thought of as the 'snug' downstairs. It had a window to the side looking out towards the river and another to the front. There she paused to take in the view, out down the valley towards the sea. Over tree canopies, the church tower, and the hotchpotch of village rooftops way below, away in the distance a shimmering sea reflected the clean light of the April sunshine. She pushed open the window and breathed deeply, drinking in the fresh, clear air. Somewhere in the village a car started up and then slowly negotiated the narrow, winding road out, its engine labouring up the steep incline from the harbour. On the far off horizon she thought she saw the vague, hazy shape of a ship. She felt herself slacken a little, as if a corset strung too tightly round her body had been eased out for the first time in months.

She took out her mobile to ring Erica but there was no signal. Then her eye fell on the rotten wood of the window frame coated black with mould and the desiccating bodies of dead flies on the ledge. Her lip curled in disgust and she turned away and went downstairs and outside. There had to be somewhere in the great outdoors where she could make a phone call.

*

Alex had been in Devon little more than a week when Theo Hellyon arrived in Kellaford Bridge. He swung his red Alpha Romeo over the old Roman bridge which spanned the River Kella, turned the bend and drove the sunken, banked lane a short distance towards the village before turning off right and following a pock-marked road back up the hill to The Lodge. He parked the car outside a small, high-gabled house, slid out of the driving seat, stood up and stretched. Nearly forty, of more than average height and strongly built, his skin bore the rich, even tan of someone who regularly worked outdoors. A light breeze off the sea flicked the fair, wavy hair from his forehead to reveal the beginnings of a receding hairline. He leaned back into the car, pulled out a package, and let himself in through the front door.

Sarah Hellyon was standing at the side window of her sitting room, a cut glass tumbler in her hand, when she heard the key in the lock and Theo's familiar call. She turned as he came into the room, left the glass on the window sill, and crossed the room to meet him. They embraced warmly. The smell of whisky on her breath mingled with her favourite perfume and he glanced over her shoulder at the remaining drink in her abandoned glass. He released her and held her away from him, looking her over. She was in her early sixties now, her once blonde hair now died to look the same and neatly cut into a bob, a matronly waist inexorably replacing the hourglass figure of her youth. She was as immaculate as ever but had a slightly worn look, like a favourite jacket, its colour faded and its sleeves thin and fraying.

'Theo darling,' she said. 'I'm so glad you're home. But you should have told me you were coming. I'd have got more food in.'

'I wasn't sure when I'd make it and I didn't want to raise your hopes needlessly in case something went wrong.'

'Your hair's longer.' She put a hand up to finger it. 'It's gone curly.'

'Mm, hasn't it? I've been letting it grow out. Do you like it?'

'I'm not sure.'

'You'll get used to it.' He smiled and let go of her. 'Wait there. I've got something for you.' He darted back into the hallway and returned with his gift-wrapped parcel. She took it from him with a girlish smile and sat down to unwrap it, pulling back the layers of paper and tissue to reveal a long shawl of ivory lace.

'It's from Gozo,' he said. 'We stopped off there on our last trip.'

'It's beautiful. But you shouldn't waste your money on me.' She stroked it admiringly and then draped it round her shoulders and walked to the mirror above the sideboard to examine her reflection in it.

'I don't consider it a waste.'

Theo watched her fondly. He didn't see his mother as often as he would have liked. Or at least he hadn't until now.

As his mother moved away from the mirror, carefully removing the shawl and replacing it in its tissue, Theo walked to the window she'd not long left and looked out. Partly obscured by overgrown shrubs and trees and standing higher and further round the hill, it was just possible to see Hillen Hall. He was still staring up at it when she joined him, putting her arm around his waist. He put his hand down to cover hers.

'There's someone there,' she said. 'I saw a car go past about a week ago and it stayed there. It was a woman, I think.' He looked down at her and their eyes met. He grinned.

'I know who it is,' he said, unable to mask the note of triumph. 'I've got news. Hey, don't look so worried. It's good news. Make me some lunch and I'll tell you all about it.'

*

Theo sat across from his mother at the table in her tiny dining room, eating canned tuna sandwiches on thin-sliced white bread, watching her face as she tried to grasp what he'd been telling her.

Sarah Hellyon, born Sarah Fearnly-King, was the youngest child of a much-decorated and well-heeled army colonel who'd retired to Gloucestershire. Brought up to the county life and rather spoilt, she'd married Richard Hellyon expecting to continue the lifestyle to which she had become accustomed. But her life had not worked out the way she'd planned for the Hellyon money and estates were already in decline. Sharp but not bright, she had never got over the disappointment of her choice. Even so, and despite her sometimes waspish moods, she still possessed a naïve and ingenuous quality which normally Theo rather liked. At this moment however he was finding her lack of understanding frustrating. Her increasing isolation wasn't doing her any good, he thought; she was drinking too much and becoming vague.

'So she was Simon's wife?' Sarah was saying now with a frown.

'That's right, but she still uses her maiden name. She's a classical singer, known for singing sacred and baroque music apparently. Was even on one of the BBC proms a couple of years ago. Here, I can show you a picture of her.' He got up and walked out into the hall. When he came back he had a CD in his hand and gave it to his mother and stood, leaning over her shoulder as she stared at the cover photograph. 'See. Only wears her hair up like that for concerts as far as I can tell. But she made a fool of herself a few weeks ago and hasn't appeared in public since. She's completely gone to pieces since Simon died, left London and bolted down here.'

'Her nose isn't quite straight is it?' Sarah remarked a little disdainfully. 'Striking I suppose but not what I'd call attractive.'

'What she looks like isn't really important,' Theo said dismissively, walking back to his seat and throwing the CD on the table. 'What's important is that since Simon inherited Hillen Hall from Aunt Felicity, now he's dead, Alexandra Munroe is the only heir to his estate.'

'Really? Are you sure? Aren't there any children?'

'Not a one. And certainly I'm sure. I've made it my business to find out.'

Sarah nodded slowly. 'So you think she's going to live here?'

'Yes. For the time being anyway.'

Her shoulders sagged.

'You're disappointed?' Theo asked.

'Well yes, aren't you? I suppose I thought that when Felicity died, that somehow the hall would come back to us. It's not as though Simon ever showed any interest in it. I thought that maybe Simon would…' Her voice drifted off.

'What? Give it back? I rather hoped he might too. But it was foolish of us mother.'

'I suppose so. But it should never have been his, should it Theo? And now she's got it. And even if she wanted to sell it, we couldn't afford it.'

'Maybe we could.'

Sarah frowned.

'How? Even in the state it's in now, it'd still be worth a fortune. Sea and river views, land, all that history to the house; have you seen the prices houses like that go for round here Theo? Don't think I haven't looked. I don't have any money…and you spend yours like water.' She leaned forward and stared at him as if willing him to contradict her.

Theo shrugged, a smile playing across his lips.

'I might have the means,' he said. 'There are all sorts of ways to pay for something. I suspect, in her case, there may be something she wants more than money.'

*

The bathroom, which stood next door to Alex's chosen bedroom, was as clean as she could make it but it was still a mess. The floor was covered in cracking cork tiles and the elderly shower produced a tiny trickle of water. The oil tank which fired the boiler was empty though at least the immersion heater worked. Alex sank back into the bath of sudsy hot water, closed her eyes and tried to ignore the patches of black on the tile grout. She was too tired to care anyway, exhausted from another bad night punctuated by vivid and upsetting dreams. The outstanding issues surrounding Simon's death lingered tauntingly at the back of her mind and wouldn't let her rest. How naïve, she thought, to think that I could leave them behind in London along with my furniture. Some mornings she felt so oppressed by it all that she didn't even bother to get up.

In her bedroom - the only other room she'd thoroughly cleaned - she'd put a large framed photograph of Simon on top of the chest of drawers and in front of it she'd laid the casket containing his ashes. His cello in its case was propped up against the wall alongside. Every time she passed it images of Simon came to mind: his signature curly hair flopping up and down when he conducted; the way he ran the end of a pencil round his lips when he was sitting at the piano, composing; the intense way he played the cello, especially when he needed to work something out of his system. It had often been easier to tell what mood Simon was in by the kind of music he played than by what he said – or didn't. She touched the casket every time she passed and often talked to him too. Victoria might think it macabre but Alex found it comforting.

After a long soak in the bath, Alex slipped on her dressing gown and drifted down to the kitchen. She put the kettle on to make a mug of tea and opened the fridge. It was bare and she remembered that she'd finished the last of the stale bread the day before; she'd been putting off going shopping for days. Half an hour later - wearing the dark glasses which had become habitual for trips outside since that disastrous concert - she drove down to the village for the first time.

Kellaford Bridge was perched on the higher ground between two rivers, with just one access road over the old Roman bridge from the east. To the west, the River Grenloe was silted up and slow and meandered through marshy ground before trickling over a sand and gravel bar down into the harbour; hidden beyond scrubby woodland, it was largely forgotten. To the east of the village, the River Kella was a busy waterway, especially in summer, and wound down from the southern slopes of Dartmoor, cut a deep valley parallel to the road in, and was tidal for nearly two miles inland. It swelled out by the sea into a bowl-shaped harbour flanked on one side by a quay and a large car park. Alex parked the car and went in search of food.

In a small square set back from the front behind a pub and a hotel, she found The Stores, a long, narrow shop laid out as a mini-supermarket. There, eyed with frank curiosity by the woman behind the counter, she stocked up with food, toiletries and cleaning things and retreated back to her car. Before getting in she wandered to the harbour wall and looked out over the water where moored boats were rising on the tide. The sound of rubbing and scraping drifted down from a sailboat sitting on a huge cradle at the chandlers further up river and the halyards on the boats in the harbour pinged melodically in the breeze. At the largest of three floating jetties a small, brightly-painted flat-bottomed passenger boat was moored, its decorative bunting dancing in the breeze. A couple of people were just getting on and an old, slightly bowed man stood on the pontoon, a battered peaked cap on his head, watching.

'We'll be leaving for Suth'll in a couple of minutes if y'want to go,' shouted the ferry skipper when he saw her watching. She quickly shook her head and turned away.

Back at the Hall, putting the shopping away, Alex noticed that her hands and knees were shaking. Then she caught sight of herself in a mirror in the rear lobby and stared at her reflection in dismay. The face that looked back at her was pinched and pale. Her clear blue eyes were dimmed by puffy eyelids above and smudgy hollows below. Her long dark hair, always slightly wayward, had a lank, flat look. She was gaunt more than slim. She'd never thought of herself as pretty but now she looked awful.

'Oh God,' she murmured. 'What are you doing to yourself Alex?'

*

'You're as stubborn as a…as a whole beach full of donkeys,' Victoria had once exclaimed in exasperation when Alex was a child. As an image the young Alex had found it hard to picture. Victoria had never taken her daughters on beach holidays; she believed in 'educational trips'. Still, there was some truth in the statement though it wasn't entirely fair. Alex could be obstinate, but her mother always brought out the worst in her. Victoria, dogmatic and certain of her own opinions, completely failed to understand her elder daughter whose imaginative and artistic disposition was so at odds with her own. So in response to her mother's constant and often high-handed attempts to make her conform, Alex progressively dug her heels in and the battle lines became permanently drawn.

But it was Alex's stubbornness which now started to bring her round. The image of what she had become shocked her so much that it brought her up short. Haunted as she was, she had too much self-respect to allow herself to crumble in this way. And if she had inherited nothing else from Victoria, she had at least acquired her work ethic. She needed to occupy herself; she needed a focus. And the obvious place to start was with the house: it needed attention and it was emotionally undemanding.

She started with the kitchen and utility room, clearing the cupboards of half-used sticky jars and bottles and throwing packets of congealed washing powder into bin bags along with rusty cans of polish and sprays, scrubbing cupboards and washing out dozens of mouldy wine and beer bottles. Next she worked on the snug, a room about four metres square with a ring-marked wooden table at the back and a window to the front. Two tidy easy chairs sat either side of a small inglenook fireplace housing a wood-burning stove. After cleaning it she re-laid the stove with kindling and wood from one of the cobwebby stone stores to the rear of the house. With a newly connected phone line she arranged internet access and then used her laptop to order a new washing machine. The present one shook and sounded like an elderly plane about to take off; it left her washing sodden. At the same time she ordered new mattresses and pillows for the beds, preferring not to think about what lived in the old ones.

The following week she began on the sitting room, pushing aside the furniture which was beyond repair and cleaning up what appeared to be worth keeping. She vacuumed the threadbare carpet, washed the woodwork and cleaned out the fireplace. It had the potential to be a beautiful room, she thought, redecorated and with new furniture. Against its back wall stood a handsome long case clock with a mellow walnut front, the finest piece of furniture in the house, an anachronism given the condition and quality of the rest. The case was simple and unadorned, the hood topped with a simple straight cornice. It was a craftsman's piece with a warm patina to the wood, a glowing brass dial and a silvered chapter ring. Alex lovingly dusted and polished it but the mechanism wasn't working. At the centre of the dial was a keyhole but the key was missing. She searched for it in vain and then gave up. It was a shame; the house was echoing around her and a ticking clock would be a kind of company.

The renewed activity started to work. She got a little stronger, had more energy and was eating better. She drove down to the village again for shopping and it was easier. A couple of days later, standing at her bedroom window, she saw a woman walking up the hill, a basket looped over one arm, disappearing into a dip of ground and then reappearing only briefly before passing out of sight, presumably heading for the small gabled house on the road up to the Hall. According to the solicitor The Lodge used to belong to the estate but had been sold off years before along with much else. Four acres of land Hillen Hall had now, more or less, which sounded a lot the solicitor had said, but really just meant the immediate garden and 'the park' – the rambling ground around the house on all sides. And clearly there was a footpath over it down to the village.

May came in, grey and damp. On the first fine morning, Alex stood looking out of her bedroom window at the sea, blue and broken only by the white sail of a yacht. It had been a particularly bad night. She'd dreamt of Simon again, falling under the train and calling her name. He kept calling her and she couldn't get there; she could see him but there seemed to be an invisible barrier which stopped her from reaching him. Even now, his voice still seemed to echo in her head and a shiver made her hug her arms tight around her body for comfort. She turned away, grabbed a cotton sweater and the dark glasses and went out, desperate to clear her head.

A ten-minute walk from the rusty wrought iron gate in the front garden wall, over an overgrown shale path, brought her past the churchyard and the village hall with its mound of grass and car park to the edge of the village square. To her right was a small children's playground and beyond it a new estate of modern houses. Straight ahead, a rising path between buildings brought her out by the harbour.

She leaned on the harbour wall and looked out. The sandy floor of the harbour had been deserted by the tide and was ridged and damp. A gull was asleep, standing on one leg on the back of a tilted dinghy. To the right of the harbour mouth three massive stones stood at odd angles out of the water. On a previous visit she'd heard a yachtsman on the quay refer to them as The Dancing Bears. It was hard to see why.

She turned and wandered aimlessly along the road away from the harbour, past a line of terraced fishermen's cottages, labelled Harbour Row, then a large detached house set back in a leafy garden. Where the gritty road petered out into a footpath between trees, she saw a sign which read: *To Longcombe Beach* and restlessly followed it.

*

It was mid-afternoon by the time Alex returned along the harbour road. Her jeans were torn at both knees and down one shin, and blood had seeped into the fabric which stuck to her skin in places. Her hands were grazed too and she had sand in her hair. She limped a little as she walked.

A woman stood at the gate of the detached house as she passed and called her name in a kind but insistent voice. 'Miss Munroe? Miss Munroe?' Alex stopped and turned. The house had an elegant, Georgian front, narrow but tall, with windows let into the roof, a lovingly tended garden, and a hanging sign which read *Captain's Cottage: B and B.* The woman had opened the gate and was beckoning her. She was wearing yellow rubber ankle boots and large green gardening gloves.

'Are you all right dear?' she repeated as Alex approached. 'You've obviously had a fall. Can I clean up those scratches for you?' With the back of a glove, she pushed a curly lock of grey hair back from her face, leaving a dirty smudge of soil behind.

Alex shook her head and offered a weak smile.

'Thank you but I'm fine really. It's nothing.'

'It's no trouble. Let me look at them for you. It'll only take a minute.' The woman peeled off a glove and held out her hand, smiling warmly and creasing up the floury soft skin of her cheeks. 'I'm Elizabeth Franklin. Call me Liz. What happened to you?'

'I fell asleep on the beach.' Alex took the proffered hand, feeling foolish. 'I'm Alex by the way. The tide came in while I was asleep and I was cut off. I scrambled up what looked like a path but it was very rocky. Stupid of me wasn't it?'

'Happens all the time,' Liz said comfortably. 'Coastguard's always busy round here.' She turned as she spoke and began to walk back up the long brick path to the house. 'Come in, come in. I was just about to make some tea,' she called over her shoulder and after a moment's hesitation, Alex felt obliged to follow.

Twenty minutes later, her wounds washed and dressed, Alex was shown into the sitting room where she perched awkwardly on the edge of a sofa. After so many weeks of self-imposed seclusion she felt obscurely ill at ease at having this company thrust upon her. Liz had talked at her almost incessantly from the moment she'd arrived. She was a widow too apparently, having lost her husband Bill eight years before, four years after moving into the village. And it seemed the whole village knew who Alex was and what had happened to Simon courtesy of the receptionist at the hotel who 'likes a bit of classical music.' Alex shuddered to think what else they'd been saying about her.

Liz came through and Alex forced herself to chat over tea and home-made fruit cake. Determined to avoid any probing personal questions, she asked Liz about a dog she'd seen on the beach - a black and white border collie with mismatched eyes.

'Sounds like Mick Fenby's dog: Susie. She's often on the beach. But you don't see much of *him*. He keeps himself to himself. Lives in an old railway carriage down along the Grenloe.'

'The Grenloe? The stream that runs over the bar?'

'Yes. Where that little bridge is. It's a river really but it's been so silted up for years that now it pools behind the bar in a long, wide stretch of marshy ground. It's been like that as long as anyone round here can remember. There's a rough stone wall reinforcing the bar now.'

'Yes, I saw…but I don't remember seeing any sign of a railway.'

'Oh not now. It used to come right down to the harbour where they loaded the tin into boats – oh centuries ago.' Liz grinned. 'Local history was a big hobby of Bill's, you see, so I'm a second-hand expert. They used The Grenloe originally to move the tin but the mining up river caused it to silt up so they laid the railway instead. But I don't think there's much track left now. Tin mining stopped donkey's years ago. Price fell out of the market. Have another piece of cake why don't you? No? Are you sure?' Liz put the plate of cake down again.

'So why is this Mick Fenby living in a railway carriage there then?' Alex felt her curiosity piqued for the first time in months.

'God knows. Why do any of these people live like that? Asserting their independence? Cocking a snook at authority? I don't know. New Age Travellers – what does that mean anyway? But there's only him so far as I know. He arrived there about a year before Bill died. There was talk...you know, everyone expecting trouble. But then no-one ever saw him and he caused no bother so everyone stopped talking about him. You see him at the shop every now and then, briefly, in and out. People call him The Birdman. He carves birds in wood apparently and sells them round and about.' Liz picked up the teapot and smiled expectantly. 'More tea?'

*

Walking home, her torn and bruised legs increasingly stiff, Alex felt relieved to have got away and then guilty for thinking it. She meant well, Elizabeth Franklin, quite obviously. She was a nice woman. But her helpfulness and endless talk had begun to feel more and more oppressive. At the point at which she'd started to give Alex advice on how to cope with bereavement and the importance of getting out and meeting people, and was she thinking of getting back to her singing before long, Alex had made her excuses and left. Before Liz had allowed her to go however, she'd insisted on pressing a couple of foxgloves in plastic pots on her, assuring her that they could go straight in the ground. 'They won't mind a bit of frost.' They were biennials, she said, and these were second year plants so they should flower soon. 'Right...thanks,' Alex had said, feigning enthusiasm. She had no idea what Liz was talking about.

Alex dumped the pots on the ground by the back door and let herself in through the kitchen door. After all Elizabeth's kindly chatter the house felt bloated with silence, as if it were holding its breath. Nervous suddenly and unsure why, Alex paused a moment, listening, then shrugged it off and went upstairs and ran a hot bath to soak her aching bones and muscles.

Afterwards, walking back into her bedroom in her dressing gown, she glanced towards the corner of the room and frowned. Crossing to the chest of drawers, she reached out her hand to touch the frame of Simon's photograph, then checked herself and left her hand hovering there. It had been moved, she was sure of it. It was a good eighteen inches from where she'd left it. She always put it back in the same place...didn't she? Someone had been in and moved the photograph.

Then a sound on the landing made her heart hammer and she froze for a moment before forcing herself to creep to the door and look out. The landing was empty. She looked back at the photograph and shook her head. The doors had been locked; there was no sign of forced entry. She must have made a mistake.

Chapter 3

Mick Fenby knew all the back roads and paths in Kellaford Bridge which meant he could get from one place to another without meeting too many people. And he generally moved around during the quietest times of day: early in the morning, last thing at night and that short still spell in the middle of the day when, except in the height of the season, most people were inside getting their lunch. It was just such a time that he chose to visit the new gallery which had opened on the main road down into the village. The previous business, a pottery which had been there for years, had finally closed its doors the summer before, starved out by the difficult seasonal nature of trade in the remote seaside community. Mick made a point of noticing things like that. It wasn't just that he looked for places to market his carvings. He made it his business to know who was who in the village, what their names were and what they did. Like a bird which always checks an area out thoroughly before choosing a nesting sight and then keeps an eye out for predators, Mick watched his back. If there was going to be a problem he wanted to know which direction it would be coming from.

He rarely spoke to anyone, and generally he was ignored - he was the man in the scruffy clothes who smelt of animals and wood smoke and sweat - but that suited him fine. He'd learnt long since that people's good opinions were brittle, their friendship fickle, their loyalty when things went wrong unreliable. He kept his eyes and ears open though, noticing signs and planning permission notices, overhearing odd bits of gossip in the shop, walking slowly, his dog at his heels, past men standing outside the pub, smoking their fags. People had become so used to ignoring him, they sometimes seemed to forget he existed.

So he knew that a well-known singer, recently widowed, had come to live in Hillen Hall; that Theo Hellyon had returned from a long spell of itinerant crewing work to live with his odd and condescending mother at the Lodge; and that there was a new harbourmaster in the village, an outsider called Bob Geaton. Bob, it was said, was ex navy and was throwing his weight about a bit, keen to assert himself in the job. Mick had seen him patrolling the harbour or standing outside his office on the quay. He was broadly-built, his grey hair smartly cut and clipped, the increasing fleshiness of his cheeks not yet ruining his handsome features. He was affable when approached but officious when crossed, and it was his wife, thirty-something and 'rather vain and full of herself', who had now opened the gallery.

Mick stood outside the window and looked in, his dog at his heel. In the display behind the glass were a couple of paintings on table easels, one oil, one acrylic, a few hand-painted scarves and some pottery. Hand-made greetings cards were fanned out, flat, on the ledge. Further inside he could see more paintings on the walls, decorated mirrors and a display case of jewellery. Everything looked sleek, polished, and shiny. It had new and trying to make a good impression written all over it. 'Mm, smart,' he murmured. 'What d'you think Suse? Worth a go?' It was raining and the water pooled on the brim of his waxed hat and then dribbled down onto the window sill as he leaned forward to peer inside. All the display lights were on and a figure moved around at the rear of the shop. 'Nothing to lose,' he told himself with more determination than conviction, ordered Susie to 'stay', pushed the door open and went in.

Helen Geaton turned round as the bell over the door tinkled and Mick walked in. She had shoulder-length blonde hair, hazel eyes and a clear complexion. Her mouth was shapely and lightly coated in a glossy pink lipstick, her long eyelashes enhanced with mascara. But the smile on her lips shrank at the sight of him and her expression became stony. She glanced down at the water which was dripping off him onto the shiny new oak-boarded floor and then transferred her gaze to the bin bag he was carrying under his arm.

'Good morning,' she said tersely. 'Can I help you?'

Mick didn't reply but put the bag on the floor and began to peel back the black plastic to reveal two newspaper-wrapped bundles.

'Actually,' she began, 'I'm not taking…' She stopped as he pulled the newspaper off an exquisitely carved wooden bird with long, fragile-looking legs and a curved beak. She walked over and picked it up, examining it as he unwrapped the second one and set it on the floor.

'This is lovely.' She fingered its swooping lines and the fine detail around its face.

'It's an avocet,' he said. 'That's a wood sandpiper.' He pointed to the one on the floor. 'In case you didn't know.'

'Uhuh.' She nodded, put the first one down and picked up the second. She nodded again. 'They're good.'

'Can you sell them?' said Mick.

'I might be able to,' she said cautiously. 'What do you want for them?'

'Whatever you can get.'

'I take a commission.'

'How much?'

'Thirty per cent.'

'Twenty-five.' You never got anything unless you asked, he reasoned.

'Thirty.'

'Aw, come on, what do you have to do, stand them somewhere? It's not a lot of effort for twenty-five per cent.' He paused, raised his eyebrows at her and smiled. He sensed her wavering. 'They don't need polishing or even feeding. And if they don't sell, you've lost nothing.'

She relented and sighed.

'All right, twenty-five. This time anyway.'

Mick nodded and bent over to pick up the newspaper and plastic bag.

'I'll call in now and then,' he said, 'to check if they've sold. Can I have a receipt?'

'Of course.'

She walked to the glazed oak counter, put the carving down on it and rooted in the drawer underneath for her receipt pad. Mick rammed the wrappings in the huge pockets of his fraying canvas jacket and came to stand nearby.

'Ah, here it is,' she said with a flourish, and then looked up at him through her eyelashes. 'You don't trust me,' she said with a coy smile.

'Not especially, no. Write the terms down as well, will you?'

The smile faded.

'What's your name?'

'Mick Fenby.'

'And your address? Or a phone number?'

'Like I said, I'll call in.'

Helen Geaton scribbled on the pad, tore off the fair copy, and handed it to him.

'And tell me, if anyone wanted you to do one to commission, would you do that?' she asked.

'No,' he said abruptly, pocketed the paper, turned and left.

*

But for the day of Alex's walk to the beach, the first two weeks of May stayed intermittently showery. The two foxgloves Liz Franklin had given her sat outside the back door and reproached her every time she went out. Apathy was still a problem and the flurry of cleaning activity was burnt out. She read a little and watched television with disinterest. The books had been there when she arrived, shelves of them with dusty covers and foxed paper, and the television was ancient with a set top box to convert the digital signal. Reception was erratic and the picture quality poor. She toyed with ordering a new television over the internet and maybe a DVD player – she'd always loved films, especially old ones - but kept putting the decision off.

Then a bout of restlessness hit her and she made another effort at cleaning, attacking the dining room and a couple of days later, one of the other bedrooms. The foxgloves parched and began to turn yellow, the rain barely touching their surface. When the bottom leaves went brown she threw water over them from a mug filled at the kitchen tap. Then the showers finally stopped and the sun came out in earnest and she thought perhaps she should try to find somewhere to plant them.

'Do we need to do something about the house in Devon?' Alex remembered asking Simon when his mother had died but he'd shrugged the question off. 'My mother had it all worked out,' he'd said dismissively. 'It runs itself. It'll be fine.' But it had been obvious from the moment she'd arrived that the garden had had little more than superficial attention in years. She'd found evidence of an old walled garden, set down in the bank to the east of the lawns, which still had espaliered fruit trees along one of its two remaining walls, and a bench underneath them. Some of the lost wall stones were visible further over in the grassy bank. And in a westerly loop of the winding path down the hill, set back among overgrown shrubs, she'd found a large stone basin with a statuesque water nymph tipping a jug over it. At one time it must have been a water feature, fed perhaps from an underground spring, long since dried up. There were little waterways everywhere round the village; you could hear them gurgling even when you couldn't see them. One of the nymph's hands was broken off and the features of her face were badly weathered. Alex ran a finger over it sadly, thinking how charming it must have been at one time. She wished she could do something about putting it all right but didn't know where to start. The garden she had in London was tiny and gardening had never featured in her hobbies; she didn't know a pansy from a petunia.

But now, in an effort to stop the foxgloves dying, she wandered with them round the garden. The only flower beds which had apparently received any recent attention were the ones edging the front lawns though what flowers they had once possessed were now choked with weeds. One of the sheds round the back of the kitchen was full of rusty tools and Alex picked her way in through the cobwebs and undisturbed grime, brushing silken tendrils off her hair and flinching in disgust, picked up a heavy spade and trowel, and escaped into the fresh air again. Making a mental note to clear the shed out and clean it, she set off with her tools to sort out the flower bed.

*

The following Saturday, some four days later, with the sun already high and warming her back, Alex, in cropped trousers, a sleeveless t-shirt and white canvas shoes, was washing the front door, a bucket of pine cleaner by her feet, a pair of yellow rubber gloves on her hands. Behind her the hard, sandy earth of the front path, its fine gravelled surface long since reduced to a few hard granules, looked as if it had been polished. The beds between the shaggy lawns and the paths had all been weeded too. Few plants had survived but everywhere there was bare, turned earth, and shrubs cut back within an inch of their lives. In one place near the path the two foxgloves had been pushed into the earth and drowned with water. Once she'd started, Alex had been driven to continue.

Now, as she rubbed at the dirt and bird droppings on the door, she was struck by the quietness. All she could hear was the wind in the trees, the calls of the gulls over the harbour and, perhaps, with a little imagination, the distant sound of surf on the beach. It was the hottest day of the year so far and the sun glinted off the white paintwork and brought beads of sweat to her upper lip as the midday temperature soared. Memories of the honeymoon she and Simon had spent in Italy came to mind. They'd divided their second week between Florence and Verona but the first week had been quiet, like this, and hot, under a fierce and burning sun. They'd spent it in rural Tuscany, cycling from one remote small hotel to the next. Simon had studied music at Cambridge and cycling had become a bit of a hobby for him. Alex was less adept and fell off more than once on the hilly roads. She smiled for a moment, remembering him standing over her laughing, shaking his head in mock despair, and then hauling her to her feet. He'd immediately fussed over her, looking for bruises, tickling her and teasing her until they were laughing and then kissing…

Footsteps intruded on her thoughts and she looked round. A man was approaching her carrying a large bunch of white chrysanthemums. She turned to face him, the cloth still in her hand.

'Yes?' she said cautiously. She'd heard no delivery van and couldn't imagine who'd be sending her flowers there anyway.

'Miss Munroe? My name's Theo Hellyon. I know you don't know me but we have met before, sort of. Well…here, these are for you.'

He awkwardly thrust the paper-wrapped flowers at her and she took them on a reflex and then frowned down at them.

She looked back up at his face.

'We've met…? I'm sorry. I don't remember.'

'No, well. It was at the funeral.' Theo looked down at his feet and shifted his weight uneasily from one large foot to the other. Alex was reminded of Ben when he was doing something polite Erica had told him to do.

'The funeral?' Alex tried to cast her mind back but she could recall little of it now. It had passed in a haze.

'I'm Simon's cousin. We hadn't seen each other for a while but we were very close once. I'm so sorry Miss Munroe. It was a terrible thing to happen.'

Alex looked into Theo's face, mouthing his name, the furrow in her brow deepening. Did she know of him? She couldn't remember Simon saying anything about him.

'Thank you,' she said automatically.

She stared at the man in front of her. It was uncanny. He had the same mellowed public school accent and his hair was so similar: dark tawny, receding just a little, a little curly, not as long of course…

'It looks like you've been gardening,' Theo said, breaking the silence. 'The poor old place needs a bit of attention I dare say. It hasn't been loved in years.'

'Mm?' Alex forced herself to concentrate on what he was saying. 'No. It looks like it.' She glanced round the garden. 'Actually,' she said apologetically, 'I have absolutely no idea what I'm doing. But I started to clear a patch of ground to put a couple of plants in and I got carried away.'

Theo grinned. He had an infectious smile.

'I've probably pulled out all sorts of important plants,' she said, smiling back. 'And I found a few muscles I didn't know I had. I couldn't walk the first day after the digging.' Theo's grin widened. She thought he had kind eyes. And there was something in the line of his mouth and the way his shoulder twitched before speaking which reminded her of Simon. There it was; she couldn't deny it. He reminded her of Simon, in look and mannerism. 'Would you like to come in?' she heard herself ask and some part of her wondered why she was doing this.

'Well, perhaps just for a minute. I don't want to disturb you.'

'You're not…really. I could do with a break.'

She pushed the door open again, picked up the bucket and led the way inside, taking him left into the sitting room.

'Take a seat. Can I get you a drink? Tea, coffee?'

'Coffee, thanks.'

'I'm afraid it's instant.'

'Instant coffee would be fine.'

Alex dumped the bucket in the utility room, peeled off the gloves, brushed herself down and made their coffee. Apart from the delivery men who'd brought her new washing machine and the mattresses – and she didn't think they counted - this was the first time she'd had anyone actually in the house since she'd been there. She returned with a tray bearing two mugs of coffee and a small jug of milk.

'I've no sugar, I'm afraid,' she said. 'I don't take it and never thought to get any.'

'It doesn't matter. Here, let me take that.' He took the tray from her and put it on the coffee table.

She handed him a mug, the best she'd been able to find in the cupboard, and they sat down opposite each other. There was a brief awkward silence.

'I believe you're a singer,' Theo began hesitantly. 'I know your name of course but I can't pretend I know anything about your music, I'm sorry.'

'That's all right.' Alex looked down at her hands and rubbed the palms together. She noticed she'd still got soil stuck under her nails and she'd already scrubbed them till they'd nearly bled.

'Are you preparing for a concert or anything now?' he asked politely.

'No.' She answered almost before he'd finished and looked up at him with a defiant expression. 'No…I'm having a break.'

Theo smiled warmly.

'Good idea. And you've come to a great place to have one.'

Alex was surprised. He was the first person who seemed to think she was doing the right thing.

Theo sipped his coffee and flinched.

'You *do* take sugar,' she said. 'I am sorry.'

Theo shook his head.

'It's good for me. No problem.'

Alex picked up her mug and settled back in her seat. She caught herself staring at him.

'I don't want to be rude,' she said slowly. 'But I didn't even know Simon had a cousin.'

'Oh?' Theo laughed, nervously she thought. 'Well I suppose he was living a very different life and we all seemed a long way away.'

'So that's why his mother had this house down here? He has family in Kellaford Bridge? Do you live nearby then?'

Theo looked embarrassed and replaced his cup in the saucer.

'Look, I should probably tell you before someone else in the village does. You obviously know nothing about the family background and it'd be better coming from me. We – that is my family - used to live here.'

'Here? In Hillen Hall? I don't understand.'

'Why would you? My parents owned the house and grounds but, to be honest, it was always a struggle to manage the place. My father didn't inherit any family money to speak of when my grandfather died, just the house and the family antiques business. The business wasn't that strong either. My brother Julian died when he was young and with me growing up I think my parents felt they were rattling round in it. Anyway, my father wanted more money to put into the business so he sold the house and grounds to his sister Felicity, Simon's mother. She had married into money and was pleased to have the house. My parents kept the Lodge and its garden and moved in there. You've seen the little house on the drive? It worked out well for everyone.'

'Oh.' Alex nodded. 'I see.' She hesitated. 'Then, this is kind of strange: I'm entertaining you in your own house.'

Theo shook his head.

'Not at all. Really. It's not like that. I was a child when we lived here. These days I travel a lot with my work. I don't stay anywhere long.'

'What do you do?'

'Anything to do with boats really. I love them. I'm a marine engineer by training but I often crew yachts for people who have money but no sailing experience. It's good money and I get to see the world. Between times I do a bit of boat design and building.'

Alex nodded.

'I suppose that's an obvious career choice when you grow up somewhere like this,' she remarked politely. 'I haven't had much experience of boats myself.'

'Well, you'll get plenty of opportunity round here,' Theo said with a smile. 'You'll need to take the ferry to go upriver to Southwell – they call it Suth'll locally; it takes ages by road. And it's the nearest place that's got any half decent shops.'

There was silence and Alex cast about for something else to say. 'I'm sorry about your brother,' she offered.

'Thank you. It's a long time ago now.'

'And you say you were...close to Simon at one time?'

'When we were children. Simon used to come here to spend his summer holidays. Aunt Phil couldn't cope with having him round the house all the time and used to pack him off here. He was pleased. It meant he could run around more. Phil was so protective.' Theo rolled his eyes and grinned. 'Well, you must have met her so you'd know.' He finished his coffee in a long gulp and put the cup down on the table. 'Thank you for that.' He stood up. 'Anyway I must be going. It was good to see you again.'

Alex stood up, slightly confused.

'You say Simon came here a lot?'

'Every summer for a while. Why?'

'Oh nothing.' She hesitated. 'I'm sorry I didn't remember you from the funeral. Thank you for the flowers. I must put them in some water.'

She showed him to the door, opened it and he stood a moment, then turned and rested a hand lightly on her arm.

'I remember what it was like when Julian died,' he said softly. 'He was a couple of years older than me and I idolised him. Difficult times.' He squeezed her arm very gently. 'I do understand. Be gentle on yourself, that's my advice. Oh, and if you need to know anything or maybe need a hand with something, give me a shout. I'm staying at the Lodge with my mother at the moment. She's a widow now and likes the company. Here...' He pulled a paper till receipt out of a pocket. 'Have you got a pen?' She went inside, grabbed one from by the telephone in the hall and gave it to him. 'Here's the number,' he said, scribbling on the paper against the wall.

He thrust the paper in her hand, smiled and was gone, taking the path back to the drive in long strides. He turned at the corner to give her a brief wave before disappearing out of sight.

'Simon came here every summer,' Alex muttered to herself as she walked back into the drawing room and began to clear away the coffee things. 'I wonder why he didn't say?' But Simon was a composer and a talented musician who lived on a different plane to most people. He was always listening to music or making it, or even just humming to himself. He probably didn't think it was important.

She put Theo's phone number by the phone. 'So you're Simon's cousin,' she murmured to herself. 'Nice.'

Chapter 4

'I won't be able to come down before the beginning of the school holidays. Our neighbours have got that house in Lowestoft you remember? And Ben gets on quite well with their son Graham. Anyway, they've offered to take Ben along too. So I'll see you then and you can show me this fancy place you've inherited.'

Alex was silent. The false brightness and throw-away manner of her sister's voice did nothing to disguise her agenda. Ever since her arrival in Devon, Erica had pestered her about when she was going back to London. There'd been veiled hints at first and then frank questions and barbed comments about Alex's damaged career. But Alex wasn't ready to go back. Spring was moving smoothly into summer. It was the beginning of June and she thought maybe she'd got past the worst now. She'd got a routine of a kind, she knew where things were, she was even starting to get to know people. A couple of times she'd taken the ferry to Southwell - it navigated its way upriver for a few hours either side of high tide - and caused amused comment locally by the number of bags she'd carried back and struggled with over the quay to her car. She couldn't pretend that she always felt good; she didn't. There were still days when she struggled to get out of bed. But she was coping and the last thing she needed was Erica – loyal and loving and compulsively overbearing - breezing in and trying to organise her. Her sister had all the tact and sensitivity of a journalist scenting a controversial story.

'No,' she said quietly but firmly.

'No? What do you mean, no?'

'I mean no. I don't want you to come here. Not yet.' There was a hurt silence and Alex almost faltered. 'I need more time to myself Erica. Please understand. I'd love you to come but not yet.'

There was silence again.

'So what are you doing with yourself there?' The ice in Erica's voice chilled the line between them.

'This and that. Walking. I've even done a bit of gardening.'

'Gardening? You?' Amused disbelief caused a slight thaw.

'I quite enjoyed it. You know I like the outdoors. Well, now I've found I like gardening too.'

Alex didn't need to see her sister to know what look she had on her face.

'And...I suppose you're making friends down there?'

'Not really. I told you Erica, I need time to myself. I'm not just trying to keep you away.'

'But my visit's still weeks away.'

'Yes but it's pressure. I need more time.'

'I don't think it's very nice to call your sister 'pressure',' Erica said plaintively.

'Please Erica? Don't start. You're sounding just like mum.'

'Gee thanks. If I want a character reference I'll know where not to come. Actually *she* told me she thought you were wallowing. I didn't say that.' Alex was frozen into silence. 'I'm only trying to help,' Erica added crossly.

'Of course. And I'm sorry. Really I am. But helping means not trying to organise me, OK?'

Erica sighed. 'All right. Well you take care of yourself. And keep in touch. Love you.'

'Love you too.'

Alex closed the call and stared at the handset. There had always been something relentless and demanding about her sister's devotion. Erica was intelligent and able and yet lacked initiative. As children it had always been Alex who came up with ideas for what they should do, Erica who insisted on tagging along. If Alex liked it, Erica loved it; if Alex wanted it, Erica needed it more. There had been occasions, especially during the spiky years of adolescence, when Alex had found it really irritating. 'Don't you have anything you want to do of your own?' she remembered complaining one day. 'Why do you have to follow me round?' Erica had been upset and inevitably Alex had felt guilty.

Then, when she'd left school, Erica had followed her mother into law and managed to get her degree, but a succession of boyfriends and a lack of application meant she'd never passed the Law Society exams and so failed to qualify as a solicitor. Victoria had made little effort to disguise her disappointment. Now Erica worked as a legal executive, juggling her work as best she could around Ben.

We've both been a disappointment to our mother, thought Alex, and we've both tried to pretend we don't care. But where Alex's response had been to pursue her career almost obsessively in an attempt to prove Victoria wrong, Erica had increasingly hero-worshipped her sister, fascinated by what she thought was Alex's more interesting and exotic life. There had been a spell when, as she found a working niche for herself and then had Ben to focus on, she'd seemed more content. But since Simon had died, Erica was fussing over her again. Part of Alex desperately wanted to see her sister and felt bad about keeping her at bay; the other part couldn't face the inevitable conflict it would bring.

With the discordant mood of the conversation still clouding her mind, Alex drifted restlessly into the sitting room and then paused for a moment in front of the clock. The key to the mechanism had turned up at the back of one of the drawers in the kitchen just the day before though she was convinced she'd already looked there. The clock had started as soon as she'd finished winding it and had filled the house for a while with its loud tock and melodic chimes on each quarter hour. Now it had stopped again and she glared at it reproachfully.

She wandered through into the kitchen to put away the shopping she'd bought that morning from The Stores and saw the large packet of liquorice allsorts on the table. She hated them but they had been Simon's favourite; she'd bought them automatically. She swore, hit the table with frustration, and burst into tears.

*

Theo Hellyon walked into The Armada and sauntered up to the bar. When he was a youth the old inn had had a separate bar and lounge; now it was all open plan. Dining tables, each with a plasticized menu and silk flowers in a vase, had taken over the floor area. Dominoes were frowned on and the dartboard usually locked up. But Theo remembered the first time he'd sneaked in to buy a drink when the flagstoned floor had been strewn with cigarette ends and the best food on offer was 'chicken in a basket'. Home from Harrow for the summer holidays, he'd been barely sixteen but he'd been big for his age and was pushing his luck. The landlord had served him a pint but he wasn't fooled; he was just turning a blind eye. At that time everyone in the village knew how old Theo Hellyon was. They might not have had a title but the Hellyon family had been the leading family of the village for centuries.

But the landlord of The Armada had changed several times since Theo's youth and the make up of the village had changed too. Most of the property with water views had been bought by incomers either as holiday homes or for retirement. There were just a handful of people now who knew much about the Hellyons' place in the history of the village. Most people saw Theo Hellyon as a local boy with a smart education and a glamorous job; his mother was just an eccentric woman with amusing pretensions.

When home, Theo regularly visited the pub, regaling the bar with stories of his adventures. He was gregarious, entertaining and quick to buy a round of drinks, though he rarely stayed long. Women found him charming and flattering, men looked on him as 'one of the boys'. He liked to be seen as a familiar face. He was aware that in a village the size of Kellaford Bridge, the pub and the shop could provide more relevant local news than any time spent searching the internet. They were useful both for acquiring and disseminating information.

Now it was lunch-time and quiet. Theo stood next to Eric Ladyman, a retired fisherman with a full grey beard and a dry sense of humour, who these days drank his cider in halves to please his doctor. Theo nodded first at him and then at the man behind the bar. The current landlord, Hugh Darrecott, was a big, paunchy man with wispy grey hair carefully combed across his pate. He was known to have a roving eye and a nagging wife though opinion varied as to which had provoked the other. Theo ordered a pint for himself, another half for Eric and invited the landlord to have one himself. They passed several minutes in idle conversation about Theo's work and his suggestion that he'd had enough travelling for the time being and might stay around and work locally for a while. 'Maybe I'll get back into design and build again for a while,' he remarked.

Theo waited till he was half way down his pint before bringing up the subject of the new gallery in the village.

'It won't last will it?' said Eric. 'They never do.' He laughed. 'Have you seen the prices?'

'Expensive is it? I saw some blonde woman in there the other day. Is she the new owner then?'

Eric nodded.

'Yes. Well, her and Bob Geaton,' he corrected. 'She's the harbourmaster's wife.'

'Is she indeed?' Theo nodded without apparent interest. 'So do they live in the flat above the shop then?'

Eric nodded and tipped another mouthful of cider in.

Hugh finished serving a couple of holiday makers and came back up the bar and stood wiping glasses nearby.

'I heard you'd had a run in with Bob Geaton,' he said. 'Didn't he get your car clamped for being parked in the wrong place on the quay?'

Theo could feel his blood rise again with the memory. He forced a grin.

'Yes, the bastard. Apparently the places nearest the pontoons are 'for people on harbour business only'. The bugger's made that one up himself hasn't he? It's a poor look out when someone who's lived here all their life is told where he can park and not.' Theo paused and then added, with a studiously offhand air: 'I've seen him in here a couple of times but I don't think I've ever seen him with his wife.'

'You wouldn't,' said Hugh, setting a glass down and picking up another. He glanced up and down the bar. 'There's a bit of friction there it seems.'

'Oh?' said Theo, raising his eyebrows. 'Why's that then?'

Hugh shrugged and then glanced towards the kitchen where his wife was working. He gave Theo a pointed look.

'That's married life for you. He likes to relax when he's not working; spends most of his spare time off fishing. Very keen he is. She's got other plans I hear. Conflict of interests mebbe.'

'That's what 'appens when you marry a younger woman see, Theo,' teased Eric. 'After a while they get bored.'

Theo grinned. 'I'll bear that in mind Eric.' He downed the rest of his pint in one and laid the glass down firmly on the bar. 'Thanks Hugh, Eric. Be seeing you.'

Theo wandered out onto the quay and went to lean on the wall for a few minutes, looking out at the rising water in the harbour. Then he turned away and casually walked back upriver towards the boatyards. He glanced briefly towards the harbourmaster's office to check he was there and carried on, past the chandler's and then looped round and back through to the main road and up to the gallery. He stood at the window for a minute, as if studying the display, then pushed the door open and went in.

Helen Geaton was sitting at the counter on a high stool, looking something up in a catalogue as he came in. She looked up, said: 'Afternoon,' and then he felt her eyes on his back as he slowly worked his way round the displays. Eventually he paused in front of a large painting of a naked woman. He turned suddenly to look at Helen and smiled.

'How refreshing to find something other than insipid little watercolours of the harbour. We haven't had a decent gallery in Kellaford for…actually I'm not sure we've ever had one.'

Helen came out from behind the counter and walked up to stand beside him.

'So you're local then?'

'Yes, though I've been away a lot.'

She wasn't a tall woman; the top of her head only just came up to his shoulder. A floral perfume emanated from her as well as something more electric. Perhaps a desire for something to happen to break up the day.

'You don't sound local,' she said, teasing her mouth into a sensual smile.

'That's what public school does for you.' Theo smiled again and then looked back at the nude: a large oil on canvas of a woman reclining on a chaise longue. There was something of Manet about it but the pose was less direct and more indolent, which made it all the more suggestive. 'I'm surprised you can get away with this in Kellaford Bridge without censorship,' he quipped. 'It's not a very liberal sort of place.'

'There have been remarks,' Helen said primly. 'But I don't pay attention. It's art.'

'Of course. Is the artist local?'

'Not far away.'

He studied the painting quite closely and stroked the tip of one finger slowly across his upper lip. He glanced at Helen briefly to find her eyes on him, transfixed. She flushed and moved away.

Theo stepped back, still looking at the picture, nodded and then sauntered across to the counter where Helen was staring sightlessly at the catalogue again. She put it down as he came close and looked up at him, meeting his eyes.

'Interested?' she said coolly.

'Certainly am.' He raised his eyebrows and still she held his gaze. Eventually, he slid his eyes down and allowed them to look her over, her shapely figure trapped in a low-necked clinging v-neck top and a tight skirt. He gently picked up her left hand and fingered her wedding ring.

'Married I see,' he said, looking up into her face. 'I'm Theo Hellyon,' he said. 'And your name…?'

'Helen. Helen Geaton. Yes, I'm married,' she said with a weak attempt at dignity and pulled her hand away. 'My husband's the harbourmaster here.'

'Oh yes, I know him, or rather, we've met.' Theo glanced round the room again. 'I go away a lot,' he added. 'Travelling with my work.' He returned his eyes to her face. 'Life in Kellaford can get a bit dull sometimes, can't it?'

'Oh yes,' she said quickly and then for a moment looked wrong-footed. 'Travelling must be fun.'

'It is. I suppose you're home a lot. Does your husband travel?'

Theo looked at her with innocently raised eyebrows, his eyes wide and inviting.

'He likes to go away fishing on his days off, sometimes for the weekend.'

'Sea-fishing?'

'No, river. Inland. He's got a friend he goes with.'

'And you're not interested I suppose?'

'Hardly.' She failed to keep the contempt out of her voice.

Theo leaned forward onto the counter and dropped his voice silky and low, his breath making the hair framing her face quiver.

'Then I think you deserve some entertainment too, don't you?'

Helen appeared to be almost holding her breath as she nodded. Theo suddenly stood up straight and moved away from the counter just as the shop door opened and a couple came in.

'Thank you Helen,' he remarked pleasantly. 'Lovely gallery. I'm sure I'll be in soon.'

He closed the door behind him and was confident that Helen was watching his every step as he walked away.

*

Alex had begun to spend money on the house. She replaced the cracked and stained crockery, invested in a range of new kitchen equipment, and finally got round to having a new television and DVD delivered. She looked into the options for replacing the rotten windows and contacted an oil company to fill up the tank for the boiler. She'd managed to get the clock going again – she wasn't sure how – only to have it stop again the same evening. So she'd had a clock specialist out to the house to look at it. He'd serviced its movement and had declared it in remarkably good order. 'So why does it keep stopping?' she asked. 'I'm not sure,' he replied, sounding disinterested. 'They can be a bit temperamental.' He had a bushy head of grey hair and he stooped as if he had all the cares of the world on his shoulders. He only needed the long white beard, thought Alex, to be Father Time himself. 'If you were more than two hundred years old,' he continued laconically, 'You'd probably creak a little too.' He'd glanced round the room. 'Maybe it's not quite level, not quite balanced. Try moving it a little.' He'd quickly left with her none the wiser. 'Move it a little,' she muttered to herself. 'On my own?'

And in between, she just kept walking. The apathy had largely gone leaving only the nervous agitation which drove her on and wouldn't let her settle. She wandered round the churchyard, taking in the local Devon names, reading the stones like a potted history of the parish. She sometimes sat in the church, her bottom getting numb on the hard wooden pew. She'd always loved singing sacred music but her faith was more vaguely spiritual than formally religious. Still, imagining Simon waiting for her in some after life was appealing and she clung to the idea much as a capsized sailor clings to his boat. Leaving the churchyard one day by a different gate, she came across the Hellyon family graves and saw the one for Julian, recently dressed with fresh flowers. He'd been born the same year as Simon she noticed and had died late one April, just fifteen years later. *Lost to us too soon*, it said. *But never forgotten.* She quickly moved on.

She walked all the streets of Kellaford Bridge, such as they were, even walked into the new little housing estate near the square, its boxy houses seeming to have been imported from some suburban settlement further east like so many monopoly models, the gardens little more than paved parking spaces. When locals tried to engage her in friendly conversation she was happy to exchange pleasantries but resisted any efforts to involve her in the social life of the village; she didn't feel ready for coffee mornings, quiz nights or the local history society.

And she walked alongside the River Kella too, round the boatmakers' sheds, on and up onto the footpath which snaked the muddy margins of the estuary. Oystercatchers patrolled the oozing mudflats, their piping calls echoing eerily between the tree-lined banks as they skittered away from her. The trees on the farther side of the Kella stretched unbroken up the hillside. Round a bend of the river and out of sight of the harbour, the low tide revealed a line of tall stepping stones leading to the opposite bank and a path winding away into the trees heading for the coast. But even at low tide the river ran determined and fast round the base of the stones and she didn't venture to cross them.

Most commonly however she walked down through the village, over the Grenloe to the coast, where she would stand on the cliff top, feeling the wind in her face, or kick her shoes off and walk Longcombe Beach barefoot, watching the rollers break and hiss onto the sand.

It was a sunny Wednesday morning in the middle of June when Alex saw the odd-eyed collie on the beach again. The dog brought a stick for her to throw. 'Susie,' Alex said, remembering what Liz had told her and the collie put her head on one side, then brought the stick a little closer. Alex smiled and threw it for her. A minute later Susie was back with the stick and followed her up the sand, insatiably playful. When Alex left the beach the dog pushed in front of her up the path and waited for her on the cliff top, tongue hanging out, eyes bright and expectant. As Alex reached the top, Susie skipped away again and trotted ahead, tail waving, but by the time Alex reached the footpath which led inland by the Grenloe, the dog had disappeared. Alex walked to the end of the path and looked up through the trees. She'd seen an exquisite carving of a bird in the window of the gallery in the village. *Avocet, by Mick Fenby* the label had said. Liz had called him 'The Birdman'. Some sort of eccentric artist, Alex assumed, mildly intrigued.

About to turn away, the glint of sunshine on metal caught her eye, a few feet inland along the path. Going forward to investigate, she found a man's watch, solid, old and scratched with the initials M.F. inscribed on the back of the case. Alex glanced up the path again and then, weighing the watch in her hand, followed it.

The path was little more than a slight wearing of the ground, a track where the vegetation was less inclined to grow. It wound in and out of the trees and branched confusingly with similarly obscure paths. The noise of the village and the constant ping of the boat halyards had gone to be replaced by a wild cacophony of birdsong and the occasional gurgle of trickling water. There was no sign of Susie. Alex, increasingly lost, wished she'd left the watch where it was.

She stopped to get her bearings but everywhere she turned, the view looked the same. Then she heard a dog bark and tentatively followed the sound. The ground opened out, the trees thinned to occasional scrub, and she finally came out in a clearing. To her right stood the old railway carriage, painted a rich racing green, a short run of wooden steps up to a door at each end. Originally an old Pullman car with timber doors and windows, its faded air of gentility looked out of place in this patch of wilderness. Just beyond it stood a large wooden kennel and stretched between trees, farther off, grey washing blew in the breeze. There was no sign of life.

Alex hesitated and then walked up the nearest steps. She knocked three times on the carriage door then peered through the semi opaque oval of glass. She saw no-one and there was no response. The windows were unapproachably high so she walked round to the rear where, beyond a run of wooden sheds, ran two small grass enclosures. Startled hens in the second of them lifted their heads at her approach. Further beyond again she could see the blades of a stainless steel wind generator spinning in the breeze. Turning back, to the rear of the Pullman, was a series of water butts and lengths of tubing, a Calor gas bottle, a couple of metal bins and a pile of chopped logs covered with tarpaulin. But no human and no dog.

She returned to the front and wandered round the clearing, stopping as the ground became increasingly springy and then soft. In front of her was a vast swathe of reeds, swaying and whispering in the breeze, broken in places by banks and areas of scrubby land, the whole stretching inland along the wide, flat bed of the old river. Clinging to the top of one of the reeds nearby was a small brown bird which warbled as it swayed to and fro. From a little way off came an answering song. Two shelducks flew in to land on an open spread of water to Alex's right, parping as they shuffled their wings and settled. A damsel fly flitted past and swooped low over the water. Alex thought she had had never been anywhere which exuded such a sense of peace.

'What the hell do you think you're doing?'

She spun round. A man was bearing down on her carrying a saw in one hand and an axe in the other. He was wiry and grizzled, wearing torn, dirty jeans and a sweater covered in wood chippings. Susie left his heels and trotted forward to greet her.

Alex reached a hand down to the dog's head as the man stopped in front of her.

'Mr Fenby?' she said uncertainly, disconcerted.

'What's that to you?'

Alex frowned.

'It was a polite question.'

The man shifted his lower jaw sideways and stared at her. She kept her head up and held his gaze. She was wearing the dark glasses and a small straw hat; her linen dress was plain and long (Why are you wearing a sack? her mother would have said), her feet in flat canvas shoes, her hair braided loosely into a thick plait down her back. A gold treble clef hung from each ear. She stayed completely still while he silently swept his eyes up and down her. While there was nothing sexually invasive about the look, there was no doubt he'd recognise her again.

'I'm Mick Fenby,' he said eventually. 'Who's asking?' The voice, with a slight northern brogue, was more educated than his appearance had led her to expect.

'Alex Munroe.'

'Ah.' He nodded as if that made sense. 'How do you know my name?'

'Elizabeth Franklin told me.' His expression registered nothing so she added: 'From the B and B by the harbour.'

'I know who you mean. What did she tell you? That I receive visitors on Wednesdays?' He sneered and she felt like slapping him.

'Well she didn't tell me that you were rude.'

Mick Fenby's face registered surprise for a second and then became stony.

'So what do you want? You do realise this is private land.'

'It doesn't say so.'

'Yes it does. Perhaps you should look more carefully next time. Take the sunglasses off for instance.'

'Perhaps you should make the signs more obvious?'

'Perhaps I should. Or maybe, to stop intruders, I should fence it off completely?'

Alex clamped her lips together to control her temper and stretched out her hand in front of her. She opened her fingers to reveal the watch.

'Is this yours?' she asked coldly.

Mick Fenby looked at it and then picked it off her palm taking care not to touch her. He turned it over and then looked back at her.

'Yes. Where did you find it?'

Alex jerked her head back towards the harbour.

'On the path just near the bar.' She paused. 'I assumed you'd want it or I wouldn't have nearly got myself lost or maybe drowned…' She waved a hand at the reed bed. '…trying to return it to you.'

'They're not that deep. The deepest ditches are about one and a half metres. Still it could be dangerous' He hesitated and then added: 'That's why it's private.' He looked at her with a flicker of interest. 'It seems you've already made friends with my dog.'

'With Susie? Yes. We met on the beach. She brought me a stick to throw.'

He nodded. 'She would.'

Alex glanced back towards the kennel.

'Don't you ever let her in the carriage?'

Mick followed her gaze and then looked back at her. There was the suggestion of a twitch to the corners of his mouth.

‘Sorry for the dog now. Think I ill-treat her do you?’

‘No, I didn’t mean that. There’s no need to be so aggressive. I just thought, if I had a dog, I’d want her company inside, with me.’

‘She does come in sometimes.’ He hesitated. ‘I’m not all bad.’

He had dark eyes, deep and unfathomable. There was a strained silence and then Alex turned away.

‘I’d better go. I wouldn’t want to trespass any longer.’

‘I’d better come with you…so you don’t get lost.’

Or to make sure I’ve gone, thought Alex.

But the walk back to the cliff path seemed much shorter than it had coming.

‘You should fix on something when you walk places like this,’ Mick told her, apparently less hostile now that she was leaving, ‘so you can always mark where you are in relation to it. Like the sun…’ He turned and pointed, ‘…or that big oak over there. Then you won’t get lost.’

‘All the time watching where you put your feet,’ Alex said caustically. ‘So you don’t fall into a ditch. Thanks. I’ll remember that.’ But she couldn’t imagine why she’d ever need the information. She had no intention of going there again.

Chapter 5

Alex pressed the bell push of the Lodge and listened. The bell echoed in the hall beyond but there was no response and she fidgeted uncomfortably on the doorstep. Sarah Hellyon had invited her over for coffee. There'd been no phone call, no informal conversation down at the shops. Alex had come downstairs the previous day to find a hand delivered letter on the mat, her name written in a neat round hand on the envelope. Inside, on matching ivory paper, Sarah had suggested, politely but rather formally, that she might call round at ten thirty. To Alex it had felt like a summons and her first reaction had been to refuse.

But, the previous Friday, desperate to move a big piece of furniture, she'd rung Theo to ask if he would mind lending her a bit of muscle. It had been nearly three weeks since his visit to see her but he'd responded as if he'd seen her just the day before and came round late the same afternoon. 'No problem,' he'd said, and had seemed to mean it. 'Have you got anything else you need moving? Sailing gives you muscles.' And he'd pushed the sleeve of his polo shirt up his arm and flexed it to reveal a bulging biceps. 'See?' he'd grinned. Disarmed, she got him to help her adjust the position of the grandfather clock and then admitted that she'd arranged a bulk rubbish collection for the following Monday morning. 'I've got to get it all outside ready and I'm not sure how I'll manage.' 'I'll come Sunday,' he'd immediately said, and had spent part of his Sunday afternoon hefting the furniture Alex didn't want – cheap modern pieces which looked as though they had been bought especially for letting – out onto the drive of the house. He'd even managed to get the shower to work. Afterwards she'd opened a bottle of white wine and they'd shared it, sitting outside on old white painted wrought iron chairs she'd found in one of the sheds and cleaned up. Theo had talked about the house and the village, told stories about his childhood with his brother and included odd memories of Simon. Alex had felt more engaged than she'd been for months. He'd even managed to make her laugh.

Having shunned so many people, Alex was surprised at her pleasure in his company. Theo was easier to be with however. Unlike her friends and family, he didn't overwhelm her by trying too hard. But in any case, she'd already found there was nothing simple or linear about getting through bereavement. For while one minute she wanted to be left in complete isolation to pick over the sores of her grief, the next she felt acutely vulnerable and bereft, desperate for human contact and support. Had she actually progressed in any way? It was hard to tell for her anguish seemed to ebb and flow like the tide.

Now Alex turned hesitantly on the Lodge doorstep and considered leaving. Why had she come? Because it was kind of Sarah Hellyon to ask her? Partly. Because Sarah was Theo's mother and the courtesy of the visit thanked him in some way for his kindness? Undoubtedly she'd thought that too. But since there was no answer, Alex felt justified in leaving. With a sense of relief, she turned away from the door just as it opened soundlessly behind her.

'Alexandra Brook?'

She jumped and spun round.

'Oh, Mrs. Hellyon, you're there.'

'Yes. Have you been waiting long? I'm so sorry. Won't you come in?'

'Thank you. It's Alex, by the way. People call me Alex.'

Sarah was wearing a fine tweed skirt and a silk blouse. On her feet were neat court shoes; her hair was immaculate, her apparently casual blonde bob set into position with hairspray. She was smiling but it was as if the smile was fixed on some point slightly behind Alex's head.

Alex was shown into the sitting room and offered a seat on the chintz-covered suite. Sarah disappeared to the kitchen to make coffee and Alex, ill at ease, wandered to the front window to look out. The view was a lower version of the one from the side window of her bedroom, over the drive and down towards the river Kella. She wandered across the room to the south window and found herself looking out over the gently rising ground towards her own home. An empty lead crystal glass had been abandoned on the window sill. Her unease thickened.

'Are you settling in?'

Sarah entered bearing a tray and Alex quickly turned.

'Yes…thank you.' She hesitated. 'Theo's not here?'

'No. He's just started a job at a boatyard in Dartmouth, working for an old friend. Didn't he say?'

Alex shook her head and moved to sit on the sofa, regretting the remark. She'd made it sound too important to her.

Sarah sat erect on the edge of her armchair and poured coffee from the percolator into china cups, inviting Alex to help herself to milk and sugar. She offered beautifully arranged biscuits from a matching plate and took one herself, nibbling it daintily. The offered hospitality was thorough and yet appeared to require effort. Conversation was slow and stilted. Sarah had the light, high voice of a teenage girl which seemed at odds with her prim clothes, aloof manner and considered phrases.

Was Alex thinking of staying and perhaps doing Hillen Hall up? Sarah eventually asked, her hazel eyes fixed on Alex while she waited for her response. When Alex admitted she would like to improve the place – it must have been a charming house and garden at one time – Sarah immediately fetched a photograph album and came to sit beside her. Alex glanced at her curiously. She must have been very pretty once, she thought. She had fine even features and the remains of a good complexion. But now, visible through her make-up, she had dark shadows under her eyes and a sallow colour. And, as Sarah leaned over the album at Alex's side, the smell of whisky mingled unmistakably with coffee on her breath.

The photograph album was large and leather bound. There was one foxed sepia photograph from 1914, the family sombrely posed on the lawns in front of the Hall, their servants, equally severely lined up behind them. Time jumped on to the twenties: smaller groups, fewer servants, more informal poses and more casual clothes. Then the servants disappeared from the photographs and the family stood alone.

'So, these would be Simon's - what? – grandparents?' said Alex, staring at a photograph of a sober couple standing erect, their two children in front of them.

'Yes. That was Jonathan Hellyon and Frances, his wife. And that is Felicity…' She pointed at the girl in the picture. 'And that was Richard, Theo's father, taken during the war.

Everything changed then. Richard was only four when war was declared but he remembered them having some injured soldiers billeted here. He found it all rather disturbing I think. He was a sensitive boy.'

Alex glanced surreptitiously at Sarah's face. There'd been something in her voice suggestive of disappointment. She studied the photograph again. The girl was noticeably taller than the boy.

'But Felicity was older than Richard?'

'Yes. There were three years between them.'

'So why did Richard inherit the Hall?'

'Oh, it was part of the terms of the trust,' Sarah said dismissively. 'It was thought important to keep the family name at the Hall so, for centuries, Hillen Hall went to the oldest male child.'

'That seems unfair.'

'Do you think so? Well, it was quite usual in important families at the time.' Sarah gave a thin smile. 'In any case, Felicity never showed a great deal of interest in the Hall. As you probably know.'

'I never really knew Simon's mother. She came to our wedding but she wasn't in good health. I didn't see her often after that and she was never well.'

'No. Indeed. So she always said.' Sarah lifted her chin a fraction.

Alex turned the page. There was a succession of photographs of soldiers with crutches and bandages smiling for the camera, each with a cigarette in hand.

'It was Frances who started this album,' said Sarah. 'I think she was proud of her war effort in putting these chaps up. Not sure why she needed to put them in here though. Still, I suppose it's part of the history of the house. Oh here,' she said, becoming more animated. 'This is a good picture of the Hall. See how the roses used to grow up the front there. And look at that hydrangea. It was wonderful then wasn't it?'

Alex paused politely and turned another page.

'And this is you with Richard? And that's Felicity. I never met Simon's father. He died before we started going out.' She stared at the photograph. Jonathan and Frances stood immediately in front of the main door to the house with Felicity and her husband Brian on one side and Richard and Sarah on the other. Both women held a baby. 'What a coincidence that you should both have your first child around the same time.'

'Mm. We joked about who would produce first. Of course with a first child it's hard to get the dates right. Phil spent a lot of her pregnancy lying down. Whether that was necessary or not, I couldn't say.' Sarah's tone changed and she added, in a rare moment of flippancy, 'Anyway, I won. Julian was born four days before Simon.'

The photographs continued to show the march of time. Richard and Sarah stood with their two sons while, at their side, Felicity and Brian posed with Simon standing casually just in front. Though still very young, Alex thought the resemblance between Simon and Theo was striking even then. Sarah had shoulder-length hair and a fringe, was heavily made up, wore a tight short-sleeved sweater and a skirt which finished above the knee. She looked stylish and, as expected, very pretty but Alex was more interested in Simon.

'When was this taken?' she asked.

'Mm?' Sarah leaned over and stared. 'To judge from the age of the boys, mid-seventies I would say.'

'I'd never realised,' murmured Alex. 'They were like brothers then?'

'Not exactly.' Sarah hesitated. 'I mean, Phil and Brian lived in London. We only saw them occasionally.'

It wasn't till the last filled sheet of the album that Alex found another picture of Simon. At the top of the page was a larger full length photograph of the three cousins, all wearing shorts and open-necked shirts. They were significantly older. Julian had grown rapidly and had the gawky limbs of adolescence; Simon had yet to catch up. Theo was the chunkiest of the three.

'When they were older Simon came to stay a lot,' said Sarah. She hesitated. 'Then I suppose they did play together a bit like brothers,' she relented.

'It's a nice photograph,' remarked Alex, unable to keep the wistfulness out of her voice.

There was a chilled silence and then Sarah began to prise the picture from its mounts.

'Here,' she said, almost brusquely. 'You can have it if you like.' She arranged her mouth into a smile.

'Really? Don't you want to keep it?'

'No, no. I have other photographs of the boys. I'll put something else in its place. Take it.'

'Well, if you're sure. That's very kind. Thank you.'

With the album completed, the conversation rapidly dried up. Alex thanked her hostess and left, clasping the photograph like some hard-won campaign trophy. Casual photographs of Simon were precious – most of the ones she had were posed and formal. Still, as she looked at it again before propping it up in her bedroom, she couldn't help but wonder why he'd been so secretive about his holidays at Hillen Hall.

*

It was a passionate affair, our relationship, Alex thought defensively, as if she were countering an argument someone had presented to her. Passion in love and passion in anger. She and Simon had started having arguments almost as soon as they were married, arguments which were never resolved as such, they just stopped. Simon would retreat into his music, perhaps start playing the piano or the cello, and she would storm off.

She sat now at the scrubbed pine table and watched Liz Franklin as she pottered round the kitchen. A few days after having coffee at the Lodge, Liz had rung up to invite her for lunch and Alex had been surprised at how pleased she'd been to accept. After agonising for ages about what gift to take with her, she'd settled for predictable and brought flowers: roses, alstroemeria and gypsophila. Liz had been talking about Bill, prattling on comfortably the way she did, about their life together and their children. It sounded a genuinely domestic and harmonious scene. *Too* perfect, Alex thought bitterly, and inevitably drew comparison with her own marriage.

But what did she and Simon fight about anyway? Stupid things mostly. There'd been last minute job offers, accepted in haste, causing conflicting diary dates; they'd both been guilty of that. And Simon hated her to clean or tidy his study; his music always had to be left in exactly the same place. She'd complained once that he obviously didn't even want her to go *into* his study, he was so precious about it. Then there'd been the time she'd been asked to sing somewhere at short notice and had forgotten a charity concert he was doing – he thought she'd slighted him. Then she'd been furious when he got so involved in composing one evening that he forgot to meet her for dinner after her concert, or the time he'd wandered out of the house, head in some symphony or other, forgetting to lock up. For God's sake, how trivial it all seemed now. But did it all get to him, this constant string of pointless dissensions? Did he brood on it all and she never knew?

Liz brought quiche and salad to the table and Alex tried to distract the direction of her thoughts. She'd covered this ground so many times before and these questions led her nowhere.

'Who are the elderly couple I see on the beach sometimes,' she asked, 'walking hand in hand?'

'You must mean Minna and Harry Downes.' Liz handed Alex a piece of quiche on a plate. 'Help yourself to salad and bread, dear.' She cut herself a slice and sat down. 'They're my neighbours at this end of Harbour Row. They've lived there ever since they were married I think, and that's been more than fifty years. The rest of the Row are holiday cottages. But Harry's not so well these days. He's got Alzheimer's you know, but they muddle along.'

'Really? He doesn't seem too bad. I've exchanged a few words with them a couple of times. He seemed quite friendly.'

'He is. Well, they both are. But he has good days and bad days and Minna hides quite a lot you know. And she gets ...well, shall we say...a bit touchy sometimes.'

Alex raised an amused eyebrow. Touchy? She suspected a genteel euphemism here.

'She worries that someone will say she can't manage,' Liz went on, 'and insist that Harry should be taken into care. But they aren't likely to do that, are they? It costs too much.'

'Have they got children?'

Liz shook her head and her wobbling chins gave an echoing denial.

'No, they couldn't apparently. Minna used to work up at your Hall, you know, as a cook, oh years ago. Then she worked at the school for ages doing lunches.'

'At the Hall? Was that for Sarah Hellyon?'

'I'm not sure. I suppose so. Minna never says much about it. Doesn't seem to want to talk about it.'

'Why's that?'

'No idea. Still it's a long time ago. Of course Sarah Hellyon's your neighbour now isn't she? I can't say I know her that well.'

They both fell silent for a few minutes, eating.

'So what did Harry do?' Alex pulled a piece off her crusty bread. 'I see him sometimes down by the ferry.'

'He used to be the skipper of the ferry. And he was a keen fisherman and sailor too. Worked long hours, especially in the summer. More quiche dear? No?' Liz paused while she took more bread. 'Minna says he misses it. Sometimes he wanders off and she often finds him by the quay, watching the boats. She doesn't like to leave him alone much…well, you know…she's nervous of where he might wander. He's remarkably nimble on his feet considering, whereas poor old Minna's riddled with arthritis and stiff as a board. I've offered to stay with him sometimes if he's having a bad day and she needs to go out but she doesn't often take me up on it.'

'Isn't there some sort of medication that would help?'

'They've tried various tablets I think but nothing's worked. And the doctor offered her some help at home too but she doesn't want it. She thinks if she lets them in to help it'll be the thin end of the wedge.' Liz gave a sad smile and leaned back in her chair. 'He forgets where he is sometimes, or thinks he's a child again and talks about his mother as if he's still living with her. The next day he can be clear as anything and hold a reasonable conversation. But sometimes he mixes his words up which can make it a bit confusing.' She glanced across at Alex's plate. 'All done?'

Liz stood up, clearing the plates in a swift, easy movement and walking through to the kitchen. She returned a couple of minutes later bearing two bowls of strawberries and then went back for sugar and cream.

Alex frowned thoughtfully as she poured thick cream over her fruit.

'Do you happen to know what happened to Sarah Hellyon's elder son?' Liz looked blank. 'Julian, I think he was called. He died young.'

Liz shook her head. 'I know there was another son that's all. I assumed he'd succumbed to one of those childhood illnesses.' She regarded Alex thoughtfully while she swallowed a mouthful of strawberry and cream. 'So tell me,' she began. 'Are you keeping yourself busy? Have you thought of joining the WI? Oh and I've got some more plants for you. Perhaps you'd like to join the gardening club?'

Alex's heart sank.

*

It was early on a cloudy Saturday evening and, as the tide turned to come in, it brought with it a stiff breeze off the sea and the suggestion of rain in the air. Theo cut along the footpath over the bank from the road and walked down the side of the River Kella towards the village. His mind was full of Alex Munroe. He'd been trying for weeks to find out as much about her as possible but what he really needed to know he would only find out by being with her, watching her, talking to her. He needed to know what made her tick, what ignited her passions, what she loved and hated. Coming home from work the evening after their shared coffee, he'd asked his mother how the meeting had gone. Her answers had been frustratingly vague.

'All right I suppose. How should it have gone? I showed her the photographs of the house and the family like you suggested. You're right. She doesn't seem to know anything about what happened.'

'I told you. So what did you think of her?'

'All right,' she said again. 'She's *quite* attractive, but she's too thin.' She frowned then. 'And she seems a bit headstrong to me.'

Headstrong? Was she? he wondered now. From what he'd seen of her, Alex Munroe was certainly no fool. But she was very vulnerable, that much was obvious. She had a fragile, damaged air. If he could just win her confidence…

Theo reached the quay and turned his attention back to the potential pleasures of the evening ahead, pausing by one of the boat builders' yards to look around. There were few holiday makers left out and the yards were all closed up; the ferry, which ran short trips along the coast in the summer when the tide was too low to go upriver, had finished for the day. It was quiet. Theo moved swiftly round the back of the chandlers and tried the latch on a gate in a high wall at the back of a detached square building. It wasn't locked and he entered the yard beyond and closed the gate silently behind him. The courtyard had been made over into a garden with a little shrubbery, a pot-strewn patio, and baskets of flowers hanging from the walls.

He paused, half-hidden by the fronds of a buddleia and glanced up at the neighbouring properties: on one side a hairdressers with a flat above it and on the other a holiday home. The gallery stood on the bend at the bottom of the High Street and the buildings to either side were set on slightly different angles; no window looked directly down on him and there was no-one visible. A small single-storey extension jutted out from the rear of the gallery. He slipped soundlessly down the path towards its back door.

A gentle but insistent knock brought no response so he picked up a handful of fine gravel and threw it at the first floor window. When a curtain twitched and Helen Geaton's face appeared, he pulled the bottle of champagne he was carrying out of its bag and held it up to show her. Her head disappeared and a few minutes later she opened the back door. Her manner was cool but there was the unmistakable scent of freshly applied perfume and she was breathing heavily. She held the door with one hand while the other fingered her hair into place.

'Helen,' Theo said in a smooth, soft voice. 'I thought you might be lonely.' He held up the bottle again. 'I brought us champagne to celebrate.'

'To celebrate what?' she said pertly.

'Our new friendship.'

'And what made you think I might be lonely?'

'A little bird told me your husband had forsaken you for fishes again.'

'Did it?' She hesitated. 'You've got a nerve creeping into my garden like that.' There was a faint attempt at indignation but it failed and she just sounded weak.

'I suppose I have.' Theo looked slowly round and nodded. 'Very pretty.'

'Thank you. I've been working hard at it.'

'Aren't you going to show me how much you've done to the house?'

'Suppose someone saw you come in here?'

He grinned and shook his head.

'Do you have so little faith in me? The boatyards are closed.' He looked up as the moisture in the air turned to a fine soaking drizzle and then looked back at her with a shrug. 'It's raining. There's no-one around. I checked.'

'Bob might come back.'

'Oh come on. You know as well as I do, he's away for the weekend. We can be as long as we want.' He reached out his right hand and stroked it round her ear and then down under her chin, slowly sliding it down to the exposed cleft of bare skin on her chest. 'Don't you want to get out of these tight clothes?'

Helen glanced up the yard, looked back into his eyes, then stood back and let him in.

Chapter 6

Alex pulled at a piece of wallpaper and ripped it off the wall in a satisfyingly long piece.

'Yesss,' she declared emphatically and threw it on the floor, turning to grin at Theo who was scraping at another wall of the bedroom.

'You've picked the best wall,' he said, aggrieved. 'It's welded onto this one.'

'No, it's all in the wrist action. Are you ready for coffee yet?'

'I thought you'd never ask.'

Alex went downstairs to the kitchen, musing on how strange it felt to have Theo in the house, helping like this. It was nice though. Waiting for the new filter coffee maker to run through, she looked out of the kitchen window. It was a Saturday morning in early July and the sun, already high in the sky, streamed across the parkland grass painting it pale cadmium yellow.

She'd intended to pay a professional decorator to do the spare bedroom near her own but no-one had been available at short notice. Theo had been at the Hall trying to sort out a defective light when the last of the decorators on her list called back to say he couldn't come. He'd immediately offered to help if she wanted to do it herself and she'd been unable to resist the offer. A few days before, on the phone to

Erica, she had apologetically asked her sister if she wanted to come down after all. With Erica's visit just two weeks away Alex wanted the spare room looking good. It was important that the house made a good impression, essential to avoid giving her sister any leverage.

She glanced round the kitchen as the water hissed and sputtered through the filter and thought again about replacing the shabby, scratched units. She had the money; she had an embarrassment of it and it only seemed to deepen her sense of guilt. Not only had she lost Simon, but she had all his money too. Her own earnings had been as nothing compared to his and then of course there was his family wealth. The security had been welcome but there was enough to keep her more than comfortable and then more besides. She felt she should do something useful with it but wasn't sure what. She'd been toying with setting up a trust fund for Ben but she hesitated to mention the idea to Erica, unsure how to broach the subject. Her sister was touchy about the disparity in their income and sometimes dropped envious remarks about it. But when Alex had offered to help out financially a couple of years before, Erica had been offended.

The last drips of coffee fell into the jug and she put it on a tray with two mugs, milk and sugar and took them upstairs. Theo had proved to be a breath of fresh air: he was naturally buoyant and enthusiastic, a constant source of energy and of diverting stories. That morning he'd been telling her about fighting off pirates in the seas near Somalia, and, on another trip, diving from the transom of a boat into Caribbean water striped red from the sunset. Her initial reservations about letting him help had gone. There was no pressure from him; he genuinely seemed happy messing around in the house in his free time. 'Gets me away from my mother,' he'd explained, pulling a face.

'Great,' he said now as she appeared in the room with the coffee. 'An excuse to stop.'

They sat on the floor to drink it and there was silence but for the mewing of a herring gull sitting on the roof.

'We ought to put some music on,' Theo suggested.

'Music?' she said doubtfully. She'd been avoiding it wherever possible, knowing it would bring back a string of memories, either of Simon or of that last painful concert. 'What sort of music?'

'I don't know. Oasis, Genesis, the Manic Street Preachers, the Beatles maybe. I could bring something tomorrow. Who do you like?'

She relaxed.

'Oh...pop. To be honest I'm not really into pop music. I'm sorry. I'm sure that sounds really pompous but I'm afraid I just don't get it.'

Theo shrugged.

'Don't apologise. Each to their own. So what would you listen to for relaxation? Or can't you listen to music for relaxation?' He grinned. 'Is that a contradiction?'

'Not at all. I love Sinatra and Ella Fitzgerald. I've always liked jazz, swing, old show tunes. I like old films too so maybe I associate the music with them.'

Theo shuffled his bottom back so he could lean against the wall and took another mouthful of coffee.

'I like old films too,' he said. 'When you think what small budgets some of them had compared to today and how atmospheric they are. Look at *Casablanca*, that's a great film. So what's your favourite film then?'

‘I don’t know...*High Society* maybe, or *Breakfast at Tiffany’s*. Brilliant. I love *Sleepless in Seattle*; it’s not that old but it’s got a great soundtrack.’

‘Ah, sloppy romance. I couldn’t possibly admit to liking those. I think my favourite would have to be, let me see, *Kelly’s Heroes*. Does that qualify as ‘old’? – it’s much more manly, anyway.’

Alex laughed and drank a little coffee. Theo was wearing old cropped jeans and a faded t-shirt. There was a slight bulge in the fabric of the shirt over his breast-bone and her eyes were irresistibly drawn back to it.

‘What do you wear round your neck?’ she asked.

‘This?’ Theo put a hand to the bulge and then flicked it out. He undid the chain and handed it to her. It was a piece of solid polished silver, swollen at one end with a design cut into its flattened base.

‘What is it?’ Alex turned it over and stared at the design.

‘It’s a seal. You know, an identifying mark they used to press into wax to seal letters. It’s the Hellyon seal, more than three hundred years old. Hillen Hall is in the design, inside the H.’

Alex stared more closely at it.

‘Fascinating,’ she murmured. ‘So this came to you when your father died?’

‘No, it’s always been mine. Father wasn’t bothered about it and neither was Julian. I’ve always loved it so father gave it to me when I was a kid.’

Alex handed it back to him then picked up the coffee jug. ‘More coffee?’

‘Sure. Top it up.’ She filled his mug and her own. ‘So...this sister who’s coming to stay,’ he said. ‘What’s she like? Like you?’

'Like me?' Alex's eyebrows shot up and she laughed and shook her head. 'No, not like me at all. She's my half-sister actually. We share the same mother, different fathers.'

'But you're close?'

'Yes, mostly. Very close. My father left before I was even one. He was a violinist; nice voice too. Couldn't cope with the demands of family life apparently.'

'That's what your mother said anyway.'

'Quite. More likely he couldn't cope with her. Anyway, soon after, she met someone else, whirlwind romance, another marriage. That didn't work out either but by then my baby sister Erica was born.'

'I see. So do you see anything of your father?'

'I did…once or twice, but it was Erica's dad who turned up most often when we were kids. My father had a fit of conscience when I was twelve and got in touch. He took me out a couple of times.' She stopped and drank some coffee.

'And…' he prompted.

Alex shrugged.

'And nothing really. I wasn't sure what to make of him. I hardly knew him. And he'd got his own life then, a new wife, other children.' She shrugged again, staring at the coffee. 'I went to see him perform once though,' she said, her expression brightening. 'He was good, really good.'

'And Erica? Sorry, I'm asking too many questions.'

'No, it's OK. You want to know about Erica?' Alex gave an indulgent smile. 'Erica's everything I'm not. She's a natural born organiser. She saw mum's example and decided that no way was she going to be left in the lurch by any man. So she refused to get married, lived with a chap for six years, then – just the same - he went off and left her with a son. Hasn't stopped her having a succession of unsuccessful romances mind you. She's great but she's a control freak and hates the fact I'm here. She'd like me back in London where she could keep an eye on me.'

'So you want to impress her that the house is fine, that you're fine, that everything is just fine? Hence the decorating.'

'Exactly. Then, hopefully she'll stop worrying and leave me to it.'

'And this is where she's going to sleep?' he asked, looking round.

'Yes.'

'Nice room. But surely you should have this one; it's the biggest?'

'I preferred the room the other side of the bathroom. It's big enough and there's a window looking out to the river as well as the sea.'

He nodded.

'Of course,' she said. 'You know them well. I keep forgetting.'

'I did once. So we'll have to do that one next.'

Alex laughed awkwardly.

'It's a kind thought but I can't keep taking up your precious time. Don't you have a girlfriend or someone you should be spending your spare time with?'

She'd rehearsed saying it, keen to make it clear she wasn't looking for that kind of relationship with him. But it came out wrong and she thought she'd given quite the opposite impression, as if she wanted to know if she had any competition. She flushed with embarrassment.

Theo was shaking his head casually.

'No, I've never been good at settling with anyone. Too restless my mother always says. Perhaps I've just never met the right person.'

'Maybe. I used to think I'd never settle with anyone. Then I met Simon.' She bit her lip and looked away.

'Alex?'

'Mm?'

'I hope you don't mind me asking but...I've been wondering ever since the funeral: did you bury Simon's ashes or scatter them?'

'I haven't done anything with them.'

Theo frowned.

'I don't understand.'

'I've still got them. They're in a casket in my bedroom.'

Theo turned his head, as if he'd be able to see them through the intervening bricks and mortar.

'Here?'

'Yes.'

'What...I mean, aren't you going to bury them? Sorry, forgive me asking but...you know...'

'You think it's unhealthy?' she said, bridling. 'That it's not normal? No, you're right,' she answered herself in a clipped voice. 'That's what everyone says or at least thinks.'

'I wouldn't have put it that way.'

'No? Well my mother did. I *will* do something with them. I just haven't decided what yet. I'll maybe scatter them somewhere...or bury them sometime – if I can decide the right place to do it. I don't know.' She stood up abruptly. 'Have you finished your coffee? Shall we get on?'

*

So Erica was coming to stay and Alex was glad. She didn't regret having come to Devon; she'd needed the space it gave her and she felt better for it. But, argue as they might, she loved her sister and missed her. She also recognised that she'd maybe spent too much time alone of late which sometimes made it difficult not to let things prey on her mind.

After a succession of incidents, she'd become convinced that there was something strange going on in her bedroom. Things would move, icy columns of air would develop erratically and then disappear again, she would find the door open when she was sure it had been closed. The photograph Sarah had given her had been on the bed when she'd come back home the other day and she certainly hadn't left it there. She'd stood staring at the picture, her skin prickling with fear, sweat forming in a cold band down the middle of her back. She looked round the room, barely breathing and listened to the house for sounds of movement but she heard nothing. There was no-one there.

It had been in the early hours of the following morning, unable to sleep, that the idea had come to her that perhaps it was Simon who was doing these things. His ashes were in the room with her, couldn't his spirit be there too? In the dark hours of the night it had seemed a completely rational and even comforting thought. She finally drifted off to sleep but when she woke the next morning the idea appeared altogether more far-fetched and not a little disconcerting. She was reluctant to think too much about it. So maybe she needed a dose of Erica's down-to-earth and pragmatic company after all. Her sister had always, in that dry way of hers, been accustomed to toning down what she described as Alex's 'extreme flights of fancy'. 'Entertaining idea Ali,' she often used to say when they were younger, 'but *come on.*'

Erica was the sort of person who buzzed with restless energy. In an effort to better her life she constantly read magazines looking for ideas for the house, for her hair or clothes; fleeting enthusiasms had her doing classes in upholstery or keep fit or hat-making, each hobby abandoned before much had been achieved; and she fretted over Ben too, looking for ways to enhance his education and skills, desperate to ensure his future success. She was naturally suspicious, often jealous, and yet never let a week go by without checking on her elderly neighbours in case they were ill or needed anything.

She and Erica were an odd pair, Alex thought. Like those married couples who marry and divorce and remarry because they can't live together and yet can't live apart: devoted to each other and yet completely at odds. But despite their differences, they'd always looked out for each other. When Victoria had tried, with considerable vehemence, to stamp on Alex's singing ambitions, it was always Erica who'd stood up for her, Erica who made sure she was at all those early performances when Alex was wracked with nerves; when Erica's latest romance failed it was always Alex who'd agreed what a bastard he was, who'd hugged her sister while she cried and told her there'd be a better man for her one day. A shared history created quite a bond.

But Erica hadn't been at Hillen Hall above half an hour when Alex began to wonder if she'd done the right thing. Her sister had come to stay for three nights and, with all her bags shifted inside, Alex gave her a tour of the house. They'd seen all the downstairs rooms and were now in the guest bedroom where Erica stood at the window looking out at the sweeping views across and down to the sea.

'So, what do you think?' asked Alex.

'What do I think?'

'Of Hillen Hall?'

'It's a surprising place,' Erica hedged. 'Certainly an amazing view. Nice garden too.'

'Thank you. I've done quite a bit but, you know me, I know nothing about plants. Anyway I've managed to find a gardener called Tim Prentice to come twice a week. He cut the grass down for me and keeps it all under control.'

Erica turned round to look at Alex and smiled. 'And the room looks lovely. I detect the slight smell of paint. You've been busy.'

'You like it?'

'Of course. But you didn't need to go decorating for me.'

'You wouldn't say that if you'd seen it before. Anyway, I quite enjoyed it.'

'Really? So where do you sleep?'

'Next door.' Alex began to lead the way onto the landing, past the bathroom and on to her bedroom. 'I haven't got round to doing this yet so don't be too critical.'

'Would I?'

'Ha! Yes.'

Erica followed Alex in and stopped at the sight of the oak casket on the chest of drawers and Simon's cello propped up in the corner beyond it. Alex turned to speak to her just as Erica's eyes moved to the framed photograph of Simon, meticulously positioned just behind. A look of discomfort crossed her face and she looked away.

'So you've got the view too,' she said, walking rather self-consciously to the front window.

'And a view of the river out of the other one,' said Alex. 'You can only see bits of it now with the trees in leaf.'

'So there is,' said Erica, moving across to look out of the side window. She turned and her eye fell on Simon's photograph again. She reached out to pick up the loose photo propped up against it.

'What's this?'

Alex came to stand by her and looked over her shoulder. She was a good couple of inches taller than her younger sister, partly because she stood well. Years of voice training and having her back ruthlessly tapped by her singing tutor - 'stand *tall* girl; give your lungs room to expand' - had made her stand ramrod straight. Like a shop window mannequin, she had sometimes thought, and with a similar lack of grace.

'That's Simon at fifteen,' she said, pointing. 'And that's his cousin, Julian – he sadly died not long after apparently. And that's Theo, Julian's younger brother.'

Erica frowned.

'I didn't know he had a cousin.'

'Neither did I till I came here.'

'So where did you get this?'

'Simon's aunt still lives in the village. She asked me round for coffee and showed me some old photos of the house. It seems Simon came on holiday here a lot when he was a child and the cousins were all quite close. Anyway when she saw how much I liked the photograph, she gave it to me.'

'You didn't tell me,' said Erica accusingly.

'On the phone? No.' Alex turned away and moved to sit on the edge of the bed. 'I saved some things to tell you when you came to stay,' she said easily.

Erica grunted and stared at the picture again.

'They're remarkably similar aren't they?' she said suddenly. 'Simon and his younger cousin. I was going to ask if you were sure that he *was* Simon's cousin but the resemblance speaks for itself doesn't it? I suppose that often happens with children and then they grow out of it.'

'Yes, but they still are…were.'

'Oh? You've met the cousin too?' Erica slowly lifted her grey-green eyes to Alex's with a challenging look.

'Yes.' Alex was determined to keep her tone casual, well aware that Erica's mind was working overtime. 'He's living in Kellaford Bridge at the moment.'

'At the moment? Doesn't he normally?'

'Well it didn't take long for the inquisition to start,' said Alex lightly. 'His work has him moving about quite a bit.'

'Oh?' Erica replaced the photograph against the other one. 'You must tell me all about this cousin then. What's his name?'

'Theo Hellyon.'

Erica frowned. 'Never heard of him.'

'Neither had I. But don't go getting all suspicious. You look for problems everywhere.'

'And you, my dear sister,' said Erica, grinning and tapping Alex lightly on the shoulder, 'are too trusting. You'd probably have been the only adult to follow the Pied Piper.'

Alex laughed. 'Maybe.'

Suddenly Erica shivered. 'Gosh it's cold in this room isn't it? Considering it's supposed to be summer.' She looked round at the windows but there was just one small casement open at the front. 'It must be because you're so exposed up here.'

'Actually…' began Alex, and stopped.

'Actually what?'

'Actually I'm going to open some wine. You sort yourself out up here and come down when you're ready. I've done some serious cooking in honour of your visit.'

'Ooh. I can't wait.'

As Alex went downstairs to the kitchen it occurred to her that trying to talk through her daft ideas about Simon's restless spirit with Erica was going to be impossible. She should have known better.

*

In fact, the visit proved to be a struggle with an unaccountably taut atmosphere between them. What's the matter with us? thought Alex. Is it me? Have I really become that difficult? Or was it Erica, whose protectiveness seemed to have cranked up a level from just irritating to interfering and oppressive? The inevitable result was that Alex became increasingly defensive. By the time they went to bed the first night their speech had become unusually stilted, the atmosphere between them heavy. Their arguments over the years had been fiery at times but always brief; most of the time they harmlessly bickered but were easy together. Now they seemed to be unable to relax with each other, behaving like two animals of the same species put in the pen of a zoo together, expected to get on but circling warily. Maybe I've just forgotten how it always was, thought Alex. Perhaps I've been alone so much I've lost the knack of coping with her. I'm taking it all too seriously.

Over dinner and wine that first night she'd tried too hard, giving Erica a glowing description of Kellaford Bridge, its rocky cliffs and long sandy beach, its little ferry up river to 'the serious shops in Southwell – imagine getting a boat to go shopping', and joking about her foolishness at getting trapped by the tide and having to clamber up the cliff. She'd asked about Erica's work, asked if she'd seen any more of the IT service engineer who'd been chatting her up at the office, and wanted to know all about Ben - 'You must bring him here, he'd love it.' But the conversation had been strained and it had only been a matter of time before Erica brought up the subject of Theo again. When Alex was vague about him – she didn't know him that well anyway and found she didn't want to talk about him – Erica had immediately launched into a lecture on being careful – 'You're very vulnerable right now. And being here all alone like this. It's not wise is it?' Alex lost her temper, Erica sighed and drank too much and by the time they went to bed they were barely talking at all.

Morning had brought no particular improvement. Now they were sitting outside the Blue Anchor Café on the quay. The sun was out and a stiff breeze flicked the escaping tendril of Alex's hair from her plait and made the awning over the café entrance flap noisily. Erica pulled her cardigan more tightly around her and stirred sugar into her coffee with a pinched expression. She'd already demolished two croissants and had watched with barely disguised frustration as Alex pulled her pastry into a thousand pieces before eating it. It had been the same when they were young: in times of stress Erica always comfort ate, whereas Alex's appetite dropped in direct proportion to her misery.

'So Theo's been helping you a lot has he?' Erica said suddenly, unable to leave the subject alone, like someone scratching a rash knowing it will make it itch more.

'Not a lot, but some.'

Erica fidgeted a glance up at her sister's face. She'd got the dark glasses on again.

'I hate it when you wear those. I can't see what you're thinking.'

'Don't be ridiculous; you can never see what I'm thinking – which is just as well sometimes.'

'Oh very funny. So what's he like?'

Alex sighed.

'I told you. He's very nice, helpful.' Alex's tone hardened. 'This isn't going to be a repeat of last night's: '*watch out for treasure seekers, men who prey on wealthy widows*' advice again is it? He's not short of money for a start; he gets well paid crewing yachts for rich people…I can't believe I'm saying this as if it's an issue. You're just suspicious of him because you don't know him, didn't introduce us. I can pick friends for myself you know. I'm a big girl now.'

Erica pointedly looked away, out towards the quay where Andy Turner, the ferry skipper, was drumming up custom for the next trip upriver. Alex's anger dissipated as rapidly as it had come.

'Look, please don't make a big thing out of it,' she said, trying to build bridges. 'Theo knows the house well. He's at a bit of a loose end at the moment and he offered to help. That's all there is to it. He's easy to be with, easy to talk to.'

'Easy to talk to? So what have you been saying to him?'

'What are you driving at?' Alex shook her head. 'I don't understand why you're making such a fuss. Theo's good company. He's told me all sorts of things about when they were all kids together. It...helps.'

'What sort of things?'

'I don't know: games they played, places they went, stupid nicknames and bad childhood jokes.'

'Are you sure about how true this all this? I mean, you didn't even know the cousin existed.'

'Why shouldn't it be true? You've seen the photograph of them together. What's this all about?...You're jealous aren't you? Jealous that I'm happy to spend time with him when I've been keeping you away?'

'Nonsense.'

'Is it? So what is it then?'

'Oh nothing. Forget it.'

'Don't say nothing like that when quite clearly there's something.'

'I just don't want you to get hurt, OK? When you said last night that Theo reminded you so much of Simon...well, it made me worry.'

'Now I know what this is about: you *never* liked Simon.'

'That's not true.'

'Yes it is. You told me when I first started going out with him that he seemed a bit spoilt; very la di da and didn't he think the world revolved around him.'

'That was years ago,' said Erica in a pained voice, flicking the crumbs across her plate. 'It's not fair to bring that up. I didn't know him did I?' She fidgeted in the chair. 'Anyway the point I'm trying to make is I don't think you should get involved with someone too soon.'

'Involved with someone? For Christ's sake Erica, I'm not involved with the guy. It's only nine months since Simon died.' Alex's pale complexion flushed with hurt and anger. 'I can't believe you said that. I mean… how…' She stood up suddenly, knocking her coffee cup over as she did so. The spoon fell on the floor and she bent abruptly down to retrieve it. 'Shall we get the ferry up to Southwell?' she asked briskly. 'It'll be going in a minute.'

Erica nodded and got to her feet. They walked to the ferry in silence.

Chapter 7

Erica's visit heralded the beginning of the holiday season in earnest and Kellaford Bridge was as busy as Alex had seen it, the narrow road down to the village regularly blocked with reversing cars, the quay parking full. She heard locals in the Stores wishing loudly for September but, though on nodding and casual conversational terms with some of them, she still mixed little. However the idea of completely renovating Hillen Hall had taken root in her mind and she'd begun collecting catalogues and samples, checking out local traders, suppliers and builders. Alex guessed Erica would have said that she was just planning an even bigger shrine to Simon. The night before she'd left for London, over a bottle of wine, Erica, in an unguarded moment, had remarked on Alex's collection of 'Simonabilia' in the bedroom, and it had been the start of their most heated argument ever.

'I don't think it's wise Alex,' Erica had said. 'You can't keep him here with you.'

'He is here with me.'

'Don't be absurd, Alex, he died. You've got to accept it. Move on. Pick up your life again. You're going to let him ruin it and you're too young to do that. I know I sound hard but it's for your own good.'

'Any minute now you'll be telling me to meet someone new, start again.'

'Well yes, sometime you should.'

'And weren't you the one who was telling me to beware of getting involved with Theo?'

'Yes, but that was different. I was scared that you might like him just because you think he's like Simon.'

'Oh, give me some credit Erica.'

There was a pained silence.

'Why do you have to be so controlling?' Alex muttered resentfully, running a finger round the top of her wine glass. 'Everything always has to be examined, compartmentalised and planned. And you always know better. Everything has to fit in with your idea of how things should be.'

'That's not fair,' said Erica hotly. 'And if I am controlling it's because that's how I get through. I'm a single working mother and that's not easy. But then you wouldn't know about that, would you? You do everything on a whim, as and when you feel like it. It's always been easy for *you*.'

Alex looked up then.

'What do you mean by that? I've always worked hard. I never used to stop.'

'No, but that was because you wanted to. Simon wanted children but you were too interested in your career.'

'How do you know that?'

'You told me. It's true isn't it?'

'No. Not really. I *did* want children. I just wanted to establish myself properly first. I couldn't afford the time off.'

'Exactly. But now, because it suits you, you've walked away from it. You've always been spoilt Alex, you know that? The talented child protégé with the amazing voice and people queuing up to help you on your way. And even when you got Simon it wasn't enough was it? You weren't really happy?'

Alex stared at her sister, mouth open in horror.

'That's simply not true,' she retorted. 'None of it. If it hadn't been for Francine I'd never have made it. Spoilt? You think it was easy coping with Victoria's damning opposition all those years. And if she was disappointed because you didn't become a solicitor, it's nothing to the failure she thinks I am. She thinks I'm a waste of space. Always will. Is that what you call spoilt? You spent your whole childhood saying how you wished you were me. Do you know how much I hated that? And don't tell me you're controlling now because you've got a tough deal. You were controlling when you were two, for God's sake. And you *chose* to have Ben didn't you? He wasn't forced on you. Well he's great. Look at your life; think about him. You've got so much. Stop with the self pity will you?'

'You're a fine one to talk about self-pity. You've been moping in it ever since Simon died.'

'Yes, and now I haven't got children and I haven't got him either so that should make you happy.'

There was a stunned silence while they both took stock of what they'd said. Then Alex muttered that she felt tired and went to bed.

After a long night, their parting the next morning had been polite but strained. They'd both apologised and they'd hugged but their relationship was damaged, their angry remarks standing like a barbed barrier between them.

They'd barely spoken since. Erica had been swept up into organising the summer holidays for Ben, juggling her work, plotting trips and clubs for him and Alex was relieved to be alone again. The depth of Erica's jealousy and resentment had shocked her and she wondered if she'd been staring at it for years without seeing it, too wrapped up in her own plans and schemes. Spoilt? Was she? Her sister's damning assessment gnawed at her uncomfortably.

She tried to put the argument out of her mind and threw herself into her plans for Hillen Hall, taking advantage of the fine weather of July to walk the garden and grounds, looking for the signs of features she'd seen on the old photographs, considering how much would be feasible to reconstruct. She worked out the layout of the old walled garden, talked to Tim Prentice about what would be involved in restoring it and looked up local landscaping companies though never actually contacted them. She planned a lot but did little that was concrete. The worst of the windows had been replaced and she got professionals in to decorate her bedroom, reluctant to impose any further on Theo, and yet refused to admit to herself that Erica's comments had affected her. But she went no further, struggling to commit herself too heavily.

The long case clock had become a personal battle. It had started again after being moved and ran until the mechanism wound down. She rewound it, relieved that the problem was now solved. But that night, she'd woken in the early hours, convinced that she'd heard someone moving around downstairs. There was no phone line in the bedroom and her mobile had no reception so she crept to the top of the stairs and listened in the dark, straining to hear who was there, her heart hammering. She heard nothing. When she eventually plucked up the courage to put the lights on and go downstairs, there was no-one there. But the clock had stopped again.

She stood in front of it, perplexed. The hands were stuck at twenty past eight. And yet she was sure that the clock had still been ticking when she'd passed it before going to bed. That had been around eleven o'clock.

She looked round and spoke Simon's name and it fell bleakly into the empty room like a drop of water onto sodden ground. 'Is it you?' she breathed. 'What are you *doing*?'

*

The next morning it was barely eight o'clock when Alex neared the clearing by the Grenloe and Susie began to bark, high warning barks that someone was intruding and then ran forward to meet her, whining. By the time Mick Fenby threw the carriage door open, Alex had reached his doorstep, panting heavily. She was cradling a large cardboard box in her arms.

'What the hell…?' he began, walking down the steps.

'Here', said Alex, thrusting the box at him. 'I didn't know where else to go.'

He looked at her suspiciously and then down into the box he was now holding. A terrified hare cowered in the bottom. When he looked back at Alex, she was bent over, catching her breath.

'What's this all about?' he asked brusquely and, when she didn't answer he lowered the box to the floor and crouched beside it.

'It was in the park.' Alex straightened up. 'Injured. A fox had it and I scared it off. I thought perhaps you could help it.' She'd been up early, unable to settle after the events of the night before, and had gone out to get some fresh air and clear her mind. She'd noticed a fox running away on the far side of the park and had seen something flailing on the ground. When she'd gone to investigate she'd found the injured hare. Theo had gone away the day before to help someone he knew crewing a yacht down the coast of Italy and wouldn't be back for a fortnight or more. In any case, Alex guessed Mick Fenby would be more likely to know what to do with a wild animal. She'd found a box to put the hare in and had come down directly. '*Can* you help it?' she said now.

'I doubt it,' he said. 'An injured hare hardly ever survives. And I'm no vet.'

He continued to crouch by the box though, one hand slowly running over the creature's flanks, feeling for damage, checking for wounds. Susie walked over and gently sniffed at it and then lay down, ears pricked, watching fixedly. Alex came across and crouched down beside him. He glanced up at her.

'He's beautiful,' she said. 'We must do something.'

Mick's eyes lingered on her. He grunted.

'I suppose. Let's take a look at him.' He picked up the box and took it round to one of the sheds at the back of the carriage. 'Flick that switch there, will you?' he asked and soon the spotlight suspended from a hook in the ceiling glowed brightly. He carefully lifted the hare out of the box and laid him on a dusty table while Alex stood beside him and watched.

'Doesn't look as though the fox did much damage,' he said, at length.

'But he's hurt?'

'Mm. Looks as though he's been hit by a car. Where did you find him?'

'Over towards the trees at the other side of the park. Near the road. But he'd never have got there himself. He couldn't move.'

'No, but the fox might have found it injured by the side of the road and taken advantage. Looks like you disturbed him just before his hearty breakfast. It's young. I don't think he's quite fully grown. One of this year's leverets I imagine.'

'What can we do?'

It was the second time she'd said 'we', and he turned to look at her quizzically.

'Should I have rung a vet?' she asked.

'He'd probably have put him down.'

'Oh no. That would be an awful thing to do.'

'Not really. The poor thing's suffering and terrified. His chances of survival are slim. It would be a kindness. Sentiment has no place in the care of wildlife.'

'Is that why you spend so much time caring for it yourself?'

He stared at her again, eyes narrowed.

'Do you ever go anywhere without those bloody sunglasses on?' he said inconsequentially. When she didn't answer he looked back down at the hare who was staring unfocussed at the wall, his eyes opaque and dry.

'I can't feel any broken bones though I can't be sure,' he went on. 'But he's had a nasty knock so he's badly bruised at the least, maybe the joint's badly sprained too and he's lost a bit of flesh here. Plus the fox's teeth have punctured him here and here. If we clean him up, fix him up a comfortable bed and try to keep him warm…well, that's the best we can do. If he'd eat anything that would be a bonus but I doubt it. He's too shocked. If he were younger we'd maybe have got him to suckle milk from a bottle but…' He shrugged as his speech petered out and turned to look at her. He wasn't a tall man and they were almost face to face. She could clearly see the deep furrows in his heavily weathered skin where he'd regularly screwed his eyes up against the sun. 'He's unlikely to make it through the first night,' he added. 'You do realise that?'

'But we should still try.'

'All right.' He didn't sound convinced. 'I've got some things here which I keep for emergencies but it won't be what a vet would have.'

'No, but, as you said, a vet would put it to sleep.'

'That's right. A vet'd have more sense than to try. Get that bottle over there and the bowl from that shelf. There are gauze swabs in that food container. I'll go and wash my hands.'

Three quarters of an hour later, with the hare cleaned up, Mick placed him gently onto a bed of straw in what remained of the box. At his instruction Alex had cut the front of it down and they put a dish of water and some freshly pulled grass shoots and dandelion leaves within easy reach.

'We should leave him to rest. He'll be safe in here, quiet and dark.'

He flicked the light switch and they stepped outside. The sun was well on the rise; it was a clear day and the light seemed very bright. They stood in silence.

'Thank you,' said Alex, and then stretched out her hand. 'I didn't know where else to go.'

Mick looked down at her hand in surprise, took it and gave it a brief shake. 'Thank me if he survives.' He let go of her as if she might stick to him. 'Did anyone see you bringing the hare here?'

'I don't know. Why?'

'Think about it.'

Alex had managed to park at the back of the square. She reran her movements in her mind. 'No. It was still early so it was quiet. A couple of people going for newspapers but they'd gone by the time I got the box out of the car.'

'Good. I don't want people to think they can just come and go here.'

'Why not?'

'I don't like to be disturbed. Neither do the birds.'

'I really don't think people will be flooding here with injured animals.'

'Even so, don't tell anyone.'

Alex said nothing.

'Promise,' Mick insisted.

'OK, I shan't tell anyone,' she said impatiently. She hesitated. 'But I will walk down tomorrow to see how he is.' She nodded in the direction of the shed.

She waited for Mick to answer but he just turned, walked away and disappeared up the steps into the carriage.

*

Alex rose early the next day and was down in the clearing by eight thirty, unable to wait. Susie's welcoming bark brought Mick immediately round from the direction of the sheds.

'Is he still alive?' she immediately asked, careless of the courtesies.

'Sort of,' he said, and she followed him back to the shed where the injured hare appeared to be oblivious to their presence. The rise and fall of its chest was just visible with each shallow breath.

'Has he eaten anything?'

Mick shook his head.

'Don't think so.'

'I'm sure there are less dandelion leaves there.'

'You want to think so. Anyway, I thought I'd try to get him out onto some grass. It'd be more natural for him and less intimidating. He might graze a little.'

'Will he do that?'

Mick shrugged. 'I doubt it. He's very weak, very shocked. We can try. If he lives till night, I'll put him back in the shed for safety.'

'You think he's going to die?'

Mick looked down at the hare again and then back at Alex.

'Don't you?'

'You're very callous,' she said. 'How do you manage not to care?'

'Practice.'

Alex blinked, unsure how to take him. 'Can I help?'

'If you want.'

Mick carried the box through to the empty grass pen next to the hens and took it in while Alex held the wooden gate open. He left the box in the far corner of the pen and came out, bolting the gate behind him.

'Aren't you going to get him out?'

'He'll get out if he wants to enough. Let him get used to the place first.' He squinted at her as if she were a species of bird he'd heard of but never seen before. He appeared to be trying to come to a decision. 'Do you want tea or coffee or something?' The question seemed to cost him. 'I was about to have breakfast.'

Alex hesitated, aware of the dryness of her mouth; she'd swallowed half a mug of tea before coming out.

'All right,' she said. 'Tea…thanks.'

Mick didn't move for a minute; his face expressed surprise. Then he led her back round to the Pullman, left

Susie in her kennel and took Alex up the farther run of steps. He awkwardly ushered her through a tiny kitchen with some home made units and a small gas stove, then down two steps through an arched opening into the living room. To her right stood a narrow wood-burning stove, its flue rising up through the roof, and an old armchair positioned close by. Home-made bookshelves and cupboards lined the walls and, by the front wall stood a wooden table with a bench each side. A barely-started carving was wedged in a vice clamped to the table-top, a chisel and a pile of wood shavings lay alongside. There were open books, abandoned post and old newspapers everywhere; a pile of tools had been dumped on the floor. A thin film of wood dust covered every surface. But for the pile of dirty clothes dumped on the floor near a far door, it was more like a workshop than a living space. It smelt of wood and varnish and dog.

Mick unscrewed the vice off the table and put it on the floor out of the way before brushing ineffectually at the surface of the table with his hand. He waved an arm vaguely at the bench seats and returned to the kitchen to make breakfast. While she waited Alex moved along the bookshelves, reading the spines. There were novels: thrillers, mysteries, classics, and books on steam trains, but the vast majority were books on wildlife. On another line of shelving was an old radio/compact disc player and a quantity of discs. On an open magazine on the floor was the finished carving of an oyster catcher, the legs and beak stained to be darker than the light wood of its belly.

'Is the finished carving destined for the gallery?' Alex called through.

There was no reply.

'I've seen those carvings in the window of the gallery,' she continued in a raised voice as Mick clattered the metal rack under the grill. 'They're wonderful.'

Mick ignored her, pulled the rack out, tossed six pieces of hot toast onto a plate and brought them to the table. He went back to get more plates, knives, butter and marmalade and dumped them on the table too.

'Help yourself,' he said shortly and went back to make the tea.

Alex glanced at the dusty bench, tried to brush the dust off it, then sat down with a wince. She gingerly pulled a plate over, took a piece of toast, buttered it and spread a thick coat of marmalade over the top. She'd already eaten half of it by the time Mick returned with two mugs of tea and a carton of milk which he dumped on the table.

'Hungry?' he said and his grizzled face stretched into the suggestion of an amused smile.

He sat opposite her, helped himself to toast and they ate in silence. Alex finished eating and pulled her mug closer. She picked up the carton of milk and smelt it before tipping a little into the tea. As she put it down she realised Mick's dark eyes were watching her.

'Someone else must visit here,' she said. 'The postman obviously calls.' She gestured at the opened envelopes and letters scattered around.

'I collect it.'

'Ah.' She hesitated. 'So what was that bird I heard just now? That sort of coarse clicking followed by a...what would you say...trill?'

He shrugged, still chewing toast. 'Could have been anything.'

Alex fixed her eyes on a point across the room, listening. Mick had left the door open and a whole symphony of different birdsongs drifted in. 'That,' she said a few minutes later. 'That...then. I saw a little bird on one of the reeds the first time I came here. I think that was what it sounded like.'

'A sedge warbler.'

'A sedge warbler,' she repeated. 'Never heard of it. What does it look like?'

Mick put the last wedge of toast in his mouth, stood up and walked across to one of the racks of books. He pulled out a large one, flicked through the pages until he'd found what he wanted, and then brought it back and laid it on the table in front of her. He jabbed the page with one brown index finger.

Alex read the entry and nodded. 'Yes, that could be it. But I didn't get a close look. It flew off when I looked at it.'

'You're better off staying out of sight to watch them,' he remarked dryly. 'They tend to be scared of humans.'

'I dare say. But how on earth can you do that?'

'I've got a hide here. You can see all sorts of things from there...if you stay still and quiet.'

'Really?' She considered him a moment. 'Where is it? Could I use it sometime?'

'It takes a lot of patience.'

'I can do patience.'

He looked at her with raised eyebrows as if the idea was a novelty.

'Don't look at me like that,' she said crossly. 'You don't know me well enough to judge what I can and can't do.' She took the dark glasses off and stared at him directly. 'Well?' she prompted.

He stared into her eyes a moment and then picked up his mug of tea.

‘You’d certainly see the birds better without those on,’ he remarked casually.

‘Does that mean yes?’

‘I suppose so. If you don’t get in the way.’

She smiled, and for a moment Mick looked as if he would too. Then he looked away.

Chapter 8

The brown hare died. It didn't last the second night and when Alex returned the following morning Mick had already dug a grave for it behind the pen and covered it over. Alex said nothing but her distress was palpable. Mick had expected tears but her stony retraction inside herself was worse. In an effort to distract her, and cover his own discomfort, he showed her the hide - a small wooden shed with shallow glassless windows along one side and a wooden bench to perch on in front of them – and then left her to it. Masked on two sides by shrubs, the hide looked out over a shrubby bank to one side, a triangular stretch of open water in front and the beginnings of a wide expanse of reed bed.

He left her to it, sitting in the draughty hide, surrounded by the piping calls of birds, their twitters and squeaks and warbles and the constant whisper of the wind through the reeds. He was sure she had no idea what she was looking for or at, but she stuck it out for over an hour. The next day she returned, wearing thick jeans and armed with an extra sweater. He was surprised and thought it displayed a genuine interest. Mid-morning he joined her in the hide, his old battered binoculars hanging round his neck, and perched beside her on the bench, explaining what to look for and pointing things out. Alex's ignorance was complete so he started from the beginning.

‘This is fresh water,’ he explained. ‘That’s the difference between the Grenloe and the Kella. The bar stops the sea water from getting in. There’s a little bit of brackish stuff down at the bottom where the high tides sometimes wash or seep some salt in – those stones reinforcing the bar are only one course thick. Essentially the water in here comes down from deep water springs on higher ground and from rainwater run off. And that dictates partly the sort of wildlife that comes here.’

‘Partly? So what else dictates it?’

‘The weather, the position, the vegetation, shelter, predators. The Grenloe is slow and shallow, a mixture of marsh and stream. There are some deeper channels and I’ve dug some ditches. The secret to attracting a variety of wildlife is to provide a variety of habitat. You see the reed bed there? There used to be lots of reed bed in Britain, hundreds of miles of the stuff, but it’s been lost to drainage and development so just a few pockets remain and there are certain creatures which need it to survive.’

‘Really? So this is rare?’

Mick nodded almost imperceptibly, staring out over the water.

‘Relatively. It’s not a big reed bed, but big enough to be attractive to certain species like the sedge warbler, Cetti’s warbler, bearded tits. And we’ve even had a bittern here – not to nest. It’s a bit small really. Still…maybe one day.’

‘A bittern? What’s that?’

‘It’s a very reclusive kind of heron.’

‘Is there one here now?’

‘No. I haven’t seen one here since last winter. We’ve had one overwintering here the last two years. I’m hopeful next year…’ He shrugged. ‘Anyway, we’re coming to the end of the nesting period now for most species. Summer can be a quiet time for birds.' He returned his gaze to the water, scanning automatically slowly back and forth. 'You might be lucky. We have water voles too, but they're very shy. You might hear the 'plop' as they slide into the water from the bank but that's probably all.'

He fell silent. Alex stared out across the water. She'd taken the dark glasses off and he could see her eyes sweeping back and forth, trying to spot something move. He noticed how pale the blue of her eyes seemed against the darkness of her hair. But what made her eyes really striking was a ring of darker blue around the pupil. He pulled his eyes away and looked out of the window too.

'Look,' he hissed urgently, grabbing the binoculars and focussing towards the edge of the reed bed. He stared through them for a minute and then thrust them into Alex's hands. 'There. See the willow in the distance over to your right? Now bring the glasses down in a straight line to the edge of the reeds. There's a brown bird there, wading. Pink legs, red bill.'

She waved the binoculars about wildly.

'No. Where? I can't see anything but the reeds. Oh wait a minute. I've got it. Wow. It's got red eyes.'

'That's right. It's a water rail. They feed on insects and molluscs, sometimes the odd vole or even a small bird, dead stuff even. They're scavengers really.'

Alex watched with a rapt expression as the bird prowled through the water, foraging with its long bill. Mick touched her shoulder.

'Turn the glasses to the left,' he mouthed. 'You see the bank over there. There's a low horizontal branch leaning out over the water.'

‘Yes,’ she whispered. ‘It looks like it’s been put there deliberately.’

‘It was. Look…there. He’s back. Near the end of the branch.’ A kingfisher had just shot up out of the water to perch on the stick. A fish was rapidly disappearing down its throat. ‘The kingfishers have nearly finished nesting too. They’ve got their nesting tunnels in that bank over there, out of sight of here unfortunately. But they like a branch over water like that to dive from.’

Alex watched the dancing iridescence of the damp plumage in the sunshine.

‘I’ve never seen one before,’ she murmured. ‘It’s beautiful.’

From that moment on, he could tell she was hooked. Several times over the next couple of weeks Alex appeared in the clearing. Susie became so used to her that she’d run to meet her, bark just once, dance at her side for a bit of attention, and then trot along ahead of her, escorting her to the hide.

Mick was astonished that she kept coming back and he wasn’t sure how to react to this new intruder into his life. He’d reached a point where he thought he preferred solitude; it made him feel safer and he was comfortable with it. So he refused to encourage her, treating her with wary disdain, and yet he’d hear that familiar welcoming bark from Susie, and would know she was back. Irresistibly he found himself going to join her in the hide for a short while, telling her odd things, answering questions, or just saying nothing. It became a strange sort of habit.

*

Theo, sitting in his cabin on the yacht, finished writing the postcard at the tiny fold down table, put the pen down and reread his cryptic message, grinning. It was to Helen, addressed to the gallery, written with his left hand and signed from N.B. A few times, with playful coyness, she'd called him a Naughty Boy for the things he got up to in her bedroom. He'd responded by pointing out that she didn't seem to mind and she'd giggled. He'd been round to her flat twice more since that first visit, armed with champagne, and she hadn't hesitated to let him in. When he promised before he came away that he'd send a card from Italy, she panicked and told him not to. 'Suppose Bob sees it?' she said. 'How would I explain that away?' Theo just teased her, enjoying her fear. 'You'll manage,' he said. 'Be creative. You must know several Theos. How would he guess?'

Of course he wouldn't sign his name but he was sending the card more to give himself the pleasure of running close to the wind as much as anything else, of knowing that he was cuckolding the man behind his back and – near as dammit – broadcasting the fact. It was part of the game and gave him a surge of adrenaline. It was small enough punishment for having his car clamped and making him look stupid. He had to prove a point. But he liked Helen well enough; physically she was just his type and she was keen for diversion so she was anxious to please. He liked that; it massaged his sense of power.

He pulled the next card close on the table in front of him and stared at its virgin surface, popping the biro on and off with his thumb. He sighed; this was an altogether different matter. What to write to Alex? How to hit just the right tone suggesting easy friendship but nothing too familiar? He wasn't sure. He'd thought he was beginning to get a hold on what sort of person Alex was but when he'd last spoken to her before leaving she'd been quite distant and he'd had to check himself. She was confused, he reasoned, which was to be expected after losing Simon like that. But something had happened during her sister's stay which she didn't want to talk about and he wondered if it was something her sister had said which was making her act differently. Now, with her guarded behaviour, he worried a little how much influence the sister had over her and how he would be able to counteract it. Could he win the sister over? And if not, would he be able to get Alex to like him enough to ignore the opinions and doubts of her friends and family? He'd noticed the suggestion of an obstinate streak in her, a reluctance to be dictated to, and, provided he was careful, he thought that could work to his advantage.

He shook his head, surprised at his own doubts and uncomfortable with them. He generally had the assurance of someone possessed of many favours – handsome features, education, ability and charm - and he knew how to temper his confidence with a pleasing hesitation at times or an occasional note of self-deprecation. And it was indeed this easy self-assurance which tended to work in his favour; it made people believe him. He'd learned as a child that if you said something with enough conviction, even adults believed you. So it was important to keep faith in himself. Maybe he'd let the importance of this relationship affect him and he was analysing it too much. He pulled the postcard closer and scribbled a quick message, paused to check it over and nodded approvingly. That was the way to do it: relax; be positive. He signed it and put it on the pile to post.

*

Alex glanced round the sitting room again, smacked a couple of cushions on the sofa and walked to the fireplace. She picked up the postcard propped up on the mantelpiece and smiled. A flash of sunshine and blue waters. Theo had sent it from Sorrento and it had taken a week to arrive. She read it for the umpteenth time.

Weather is wonderful, food is not, company is worse. Amazed to find I remember the decorating with such pleasure – what a laugh we had! Home early August. Let's go wild and do the drawing room!

PS. Don't tell mother about the food – she'll inform the Red Cross.

Did we laugh? Alex wondered. She supposed they had and felt a little guilty for it.

She stared at the card. He signed his name with a huge, flourishing capital T while the rest of the name disappeared into a squiggly line. A surprisingly small hand for someone so outgoing, she thought, though Simon's signature had been similar. It was uncanny that they had so much in common. But Simon would never have been as flippant as that. Where Theo was light-hearted and upbeat, Simon had been temperamental. Loving, tender and charming when things went well, he could be darkly despondent too, sometimes finding it hard to shake off a bad performance for days. Alex suspected Theo would simply laugh about a failure and then forget about it.

She replaced the postcard and apprehensively glanced round the room, checking that it looked as good as she could make it. Sarah Hellyon was coming for coffee. The postcard had been the catalyst for the invitation. A pang of guilt had made her ring the Lodge and offer to return Sarah's hospitality. Alex had half hoped she'd refuse. She couldn't quite put her finger on it but Theo's mother was a little odd. She's all right really, she reassured herself, just give her time, barely acknowledging to herself the faint apprehension that this was what happened to widows who spent too much time on their own. But the prospect of entertaining Sarah in the house she had once called home sat awkwardly on her and when the doorbell sounded Alex perceptibly jumped.

Sarah had her back to the door when Alex opened it, taking in the view down to the harbour. When she turned she was smiling.

'Alexandra,' she said in that light voice, at once innocent and yet suggestive of criticism. She reminded Alex of a school teacher she'd had who'd always smiled broadly whilst telling you how awful your homework was. 'So kind of you to invite me,' Sarah added as she came in, exuding a strong scent of Chanel.

Alex led the way into the sitting room where Sarah paused in front of the fireplace and looked round.

'I haven't managed to decorate the sitting room yet,' Alex said, gesturing towards the peeling wallpaper. 'I'm afraid this room's been badly neglected. It's going to be a lot of work. We could sit in the snug if you'd prefer?'

'The snug?'

'The little room across the hall.'

'Ah, the sitting room. We called this the drawing room. No, this is fine.' Sarah vented the suspicion of a sigh, gazing round again. 'I chose this wallpaper.' She smiled and shrugged dismissively. 'Still, that was years ago wasn't it? You get foolishly nostalgic with age.'

Alex smiled tactfully. 'Please take a seat,' she said, waving a hand towards the mismatched easy chairs. 'I'll go and make the coffee.'

Sarah slowly lowered herself down into one of the chairs and elegantly crossed her legs. She wore seamed stockings, the seams immaculately straight. Walking through to the kitchen, Alex idly wondered where she bought them from.

When she returned with the tray of coffee things, Sarah was still sitting in the chair, straight-backed, staring apparently impassively around the room.

'We used to have wonderful soirees in here once upon a time,' she said with a smile. 'Everyone would come.' She gave another shrug. 'Of course, people don't do that sort of entertaining any more. It is a shame.'

'How long has it been since you lived here Mrs Hellyon?'

'Twenty-four years.' As an afterthought, she added: 'You must call me Sarah.'

Alex smiled her acknowledgment and poured the coffee.

'Do you miss it? It must be strange living so close.'

'No, no, The Lodge is perfect for me. Easy to look after.'

Alex passed Sarah her cup and saucer and saw her hand shake as she took it and then added milk. A little milk spilt in the saucer. 'Silly me,' Sarah muttered, stirred in two cubes of sugar and then sat back, clutching the cup and saucer tightly together as if they might escape. She stared at the top of Alex's head for a second as if trying to remember something.

'Theo is such a restless boy,' she said suddenly.

'Theo? Yes, he likes to travel doesn't he?'

'Yes. I think it's about time he stayed still a bit. He doesn't get a chance to drop any roots.' Sarah carefully extracted the cup from the saucer and lifted it to her mouth. It didn't shake and she appeared to drink with more confidence, replaced the cup and looked at Alex again.

'It's important to put down roots, don't you think? Find somewhere you feel comfortable and settle.' Sarah paused for Alex to answer but after a moment's expectant silence she carried on. 'I think Kellaford Bridge is a perfect place. There's something for everyone here isn't there?'

'Yes, I suppose so.'

'Of course. There's the boating and the beach if you like that sort of thing. But then come a little inland and it's such pretty, quiet countryside.'

'Yes, it's very nice.' Alex was ill at ease. Sarah was different from their last meeting, too chatty. It sat oddly on her. Desperate to find something to say, her eyes fixed on a silver brooch Sarah was wearing, a solid but elegant miniature model of a sailing boat.

'That's a lovely brooch,' she remarked.

'Thank you.' Sarah automatically looked down and fingered it. 'Theo brought it back for me from Paros.'

'I noticed there's some nice jewellery in the gallery in the village.'

'Yes. I did go in there the once. She has an odd mixture of things I must say. I didn't like those bird carvings very much. I found them rather threatening.'

Alex bit her tongue and the conversation died while they both drank a little coffee.

'So have you got more plans for the hall?' Sarah continued a couple of minutes later.

'Yes, a few. More decorating and perhaps a new kitchen and bathroom.'

'Oh, you *will* be busy then. That'll take a while.'

'Yes, probably.' Alex hadn't thought through the timescale. Her ideas and plans still changed from day to day, vague, drifting, reluctant to be fixed. She tried to think of another topic of conversation but Sarah Hellyon was nowhere near as easy to talk to as her son.

'Have you been exploring the area?' Sarah asked. 'Getting to know the place?'

'Yes, a little. I like to walk a bit.'

Sarah nodded. 'And getting to know people too, presumably?'

Alex's mind flitted to the reserve then pushed it away.

'Just the odd person, on nodding terms. Elizabeth Franklin's been very kind.'

'Elizabeth? The woman who does the B and B down at Captain's Cottage is that? I know who you mean but I've never had much to do with her myself.' Sarah paused and then smiled again. 'And I believe you had your sister staying just recently?'

'Yes, Erica. She lives in London.'

'So you don't see much of her then?'

'Not so much at the moment.'

'I had a sister. She was a lot older than me.' Sarah shook her head and her immaculate bob swung side to side. 'She always used to think she could tell me what to do. Of course I completely ignored her. How do you manage?'

'Well my sister's younger than me but she still likes to tell me what to do.' The argument loomed into Alex's mind, the culmination, apparently, of years of seething dissent. 'I'm afraid I don't always fall in with her plans either.'

'Sisters always think they know better,' Sarah said confidingly. 'It's important not to give in too much. Gives them too much power.'

Alex forced a smile as she leaned forward to put her coffee cup down on the table. 'If you've finished your coffee

I wondered if you'd like to look around?' she offered. 'See what's changed, what's the same?'

Sarah's face lit up.

'Yes I would like that very much.'

Sarah put her cup and saucer down on the table and Alex stood up with a sense of relief.

'We'll start with the snug shall we?' she said. 'I'm afraid I can't imagine calling it anything else.'

They walked round the whole of the downstairs. Sarah said little but stared at everything as if she were involved in a game of Pellmanism and was committing it all to memory. Alex made odd remarks about things that had been done, things she might do, tried to keep it light, ease the atmosphere a bit, but Sarah responded little. They went upstairs, looked at the rear bedrooms and bathroom, then moved forward and went into the spare bedroom Erica had used.

'This was our room,' Sarah murmured. She stared round and frowned.

'Is there something the matter?' said Alex.

Sarah turned to face her and the frown instantly disappeared to be replaced with a smile.

'No, no, of course not. You've decorated in here haven't you? It's so different. I was just trying to remember.'

'I sleep next door,' Alex said, leading on into her own room and wondering why she'd thought showing Sarah Hellyon her old home would be a good idea. It had occurred to her recently that she had a tendency to try too hard at the wrong things and never quite got it right.

She pushed the door open and walked in to stand by the chest of drawers, close to Simon's ashes.

'This was Julian's room,' murmured Sarah.

'Sorry?'

Sarah walked past her, across to the side window, and looked out down towards the River Kella.

'This was Julian's room,' she repeated.

Alex suddenly felt very cold again. She thought she was used to it but this time it took her by surprise. She reached out a hand to touch the casket and rubbed her fingers on it shakily.

'Really? Theo never said.' She hesitated, watching Sarah uneasily. The silence in the room between them felt almost tangible. 'But I did ask where Simon slept when he was here,' she added, attempting a bright tone. 'Theo said he used the little room at the back.'

Sarah turned and stared at her, her face slowly falling into a heavy frown. Her eyes strayed to Simon's photograph on the chest of drawers.

'The box room? Did he? Yes, I suppose he must have. It's such a long time ago. You start to forget all sorts of things as you get older.' Sarah turned her eyes away and began to move back towards the door. 'I really ought to be going now. Thank you *so* much for showing me round.'

Alex watched Sarah step out neatly down the path and round the house towards the Lodge. The older woman's behaviour had been even stranger than on their first meeting. She wondered if Sarah had been drinking whisky before she came out. Did Theo know his mother drank so much? *The danger of becoming too reclusive*, she could imagine Liz Franklin saying. *Are you getting out? Meeting people?*

And when Julian's name had come up Sarah's manner had noticeably changed. Alex had avoided discussing Julian's death with Theo so far, but now she made a mental note to ask what had happened to him. It was becoming something she thought she ought to know.

Chapter 9

'You're really brown.'

'And you're much too pale,' responded Theo. 'I'm glad I suggested we go out or you'd spend the whole summer stripping wallpaper and miss the sunshine.'

Alex smiled. She was glad to see him home; happier than she thought she'd be. He exuded energy and good cheer. His hair had grown and with the twitch of the shoulder before he spoke and the set of his mouth when he was concentrating she was immediately reminded of Simon again. He was loading food she'd prepared into a rucksack for a picnic. He'd rung up the day before and even his voice had made her tingle. Perhaps that was it, she thought, perhaps it's his voice that makes me think of Simon most, a frequency of sound which reaches inside me, like a familiar piece of music that runs through your head.

'You're back,' she'd said stupidly when she'd heard his voice on the phone.

'Yesterday. What a relief. Did you get the card?'

'Yes, thank you. Did you have a good trip?'

'No. Yes. That is, it went well but I was bored to death. I must be getting too old for it. It's not the fun it used to be. And what about you? What have you been up to?'

'Oh, nothing special. This and that. Reading. Walking a bit, you know.' When asked, it occurred to her that really she did very little that was worth talking about. The only thing that was interesting was the wildlife she'd seen on the reserve and she wasn't supposed to mention that.

'I was thinking about my suggestion for decorating the drawing room.'

'Yes?'

'Why don't we go out instead?'

'Go out?' Alex said sharply, scared that he'd got her wrong all along and now he was suggesting a date. She tried to think of excuses. 'I'm not sure,' she said defensively.

'I was thinking of going for a walk somewhere, getting some Devon air. I've been at sea for too long and I need my land legs back. Maybe I could show you somewhere you haven't been yet. Or have you been everywhere?'

Alex laughed a little nervously, aware that her mind had been running on ahead of her. A *walk* seemed innocent enough.

'I shouldn't think so,' she replied. 'Where have you got in mind?'

'Nowhere in particular. Throw some sandwiches together. I'll bring something to drink and a rucksack and we'll go exploring tomorrow. I told Patrick I wouldn't be back at the yard till Monday. The forecast is good. I'll see you tomorrow. Ten o'clock.'

And he'd put the phone down, leaving Alex wondering what she was doing.

Now Alex stood watching Theo putting her hastily prepared sandwiches in the rucksack, along with a couple of chocolate bars and two apples. Theo brought excitement with him, a boyish enthusiasm which made the mundane interesting. The kitchen was filled with his presence.

He finished stowing the food and pulled an ordnance survey map out of the back pocket of the rucksack.

'So where shall we go?' he asked, flashing her a smile.

'I've no idea. Where do you suggest?'

'Have you been to the old chapel yet?'

'No. Where's that?'

Theo didn't answer but began to fold the map up again before it was even open.

'I don't need this to go there,' he said. 'I could go there in the dark. And luckily the tide's just right too.' He put the map away and faced her. 'Trust me?' he asked with another smile.

'Of course,' she answered, without thinking.

'Good. Follow me then Alex Munroe. Let's go exploring.'

*

Up close, the stepping stones across the River Kella looked bigger than they did from the bank. Originally Alex had thought they were single huge stones, but they were each made up of several flattish slabs, stacked and mortared into place. There were nine of them, the top of each a little under half a metre square. And Theo had been right about the tide – she supposed it was ingrained in him – for it had gone out leaving just the middle five stones with their feet in water, more than forty centimetres below their upper surface.

Theo stepped nimbly from stone to stone and then stepped down onto the mudflat on the other side. He turned to face her and grinned.

'Now you,' he called.

Alex glanced warily again at the drop down to the water and then stepped across. It was easier than she'd expected and she joined Theo on the drying mud the other side. He led the way onto the farther bank and picked up the narrow track which headed south and west towards the sea. The track wound in and out of the trees, sometimes close to the river bed, sometimes secretive and swathed in greenery. Further inland, the ground climbed steeply, its contours masked by almost unbroken woods.

'We used to come this way all the time,' Theo said over his shoulder.

'Who's *we*?'

'Simon and I.'

'Really?' The path widened a little and he paused, allowing her to come alongside. 'Was this your favourite route then?' She glanced round, imagining the two boys setting out on some sort of adventure. 'Tell me. Tell me everything.'

Theo laughed.

'What is there to tell? We were boys. This was the wild side of the river where there were no grown-ups, no-one to tell us to pull our socks up or not to swear. We were Amazon explorers or archaeologists looking for ancient treasure or soldiers escaping hostile fire. In a place like this, with the imagination of a child, it can be anything you want it to be. Yes, I think it was our favourite route.' He started off again and Alex fell in behind. 'Watch your step,' he called back. 'There are exposed tree roots in places that can trip you up if you're not careful.'

They'd been walking for ten minutes when Theo took a footpath that branched to the left and climbed, steeply in places, zigzagging around trees and rocks, and then suddenly emerged near the cliff edge. He stopped and waited for Alex to catch up and she came to stand beside him, panting. As she caught her breath she took in the view. Over the trees further down the hill, over the river, she could see Kellaford Bridge like a miniature working model. She could see people walking across the quay, could see Ann Darrecott from the pub, clearing out the ash trays from the outside tables into a bin, and Bob Geaton talking to a man on one of the pontoons, waving his arms and pointing aggressively. Turning to look south, over the edge of the cliffs, there was a clear view out to sea and the horizon.

'Wow, what a spot,' she said.

'Worth the climb then?'

'Definitely.'

'This is called Dolphin Point. You can see them out there sometimes.' He turned away. 'And this is where the old chapel is.'

Alex dragged her eyes from the view and looked round. Set back from the cliff face, sheltered by a short run of higher ground and a backdrop of trees, stood a tiny stone building with a round-arched doorway in the near side. It still had a roof of sorts, but part of the west wall had fallen down, taking that end of the roof with it, and ivy and nettles had grown up and through the stonework. Theo was already walking towards it. He turned to wait for her in the doorway.

'What a surprising place for a chapel,' she remarked, joining him.

'I suppose so.' He grinned. 'But this was the ancient forgotten palace where we would find the buried treasure. Or a castle that had to be defended from our enemies…or each other. This was a magical place.' He turned, glanced around and up and then stepped inside. Alex stuck her head in the doorway – the door had long since gone – and then followed him in.

It didn't look much like a church at first glance. The stone floor was cracked and infiltrated with weeds, the walls covered with creepers and lichen. But the arched window facing east still had stained glass in place, some missing, some with holes, but enough to make the sunshine throw rainbow colours across the dusty, leaf strewn floor.

Theo folded his arms and stuck his hands under his armpits, looking around with a rueful expression.

'I haven't been up here for years,' he said. 'It's a shame to see it falling down.'

He moved suddenly and took a couple of steps towards where the altar would have been and then crouched down, sweeping leaves and rubbish away from one of the stones.

'What is it?'

Alex came up behind him and looked over his shoulder. He pointed at the worn chiselling on the surface of the stone.

'Somebody's gravestone. It's too worn to read. Some hermit or priest or something.' He straightened up and he was looking down on her, serious suddenly. 'We used to reckon that there were probably lots of graves around her. These sites are passed on as holy from generation to generation aren't they, going back millennia? We used to talk about digging around here, finding all sorts of grave goods. We never did of course. We always treated the chapel with a bit of respect. Simon especially used to love it.'

'Really?' Alex glanced round, surprised. Simon had never been a church goer. 'Who does it belong to, the Church?'

'Don't think so. No idea really. The chapel dates back several hundred years originally, though it's been rebuilt a few times. It's not been used ever since I can remember. I guess no-one wants the expense of looking after the place so it's just falling apart.'

'Mm. Shame.'

They went outside again.

'It wouldn't be such a bad place to be buried at that, would it?' Theo said softly, sweeping his arm to indicate the tussocky grass. Thrift grew amongst it, the pink flowers rocking in the breeze off the sea. 'Peaceful, great view.' He nodded, unusually introspective. 'No, I think I might put it in my will that I'd like to be buried up here.' He looked up at the sky which was deep blue with white scudding clouds and his mood brightened. 'Looks like the forecast was right for once. Let's move on.'

'What about the tide? How will we get back?'

'If it's too far in we'll cadge a lift from Andy on the ferry. Come on. If we take the coast path there's somewhere along there with a great view where we can stop for lunch.'

Alex glanced back once more at the old chapel and then followed him.

*

'Mother?' There was no answer and Theo walked through into the sitting room. Sarah was lolling in the wing-backed armchair, her head resting sideways on the wing. Her eyes were closed and her breathing heavy. On the small side table sat an empty cut glass tumbler. A book had fallen from her lap to the floor. 'Mother?' he repeated sharply.

He walked across, retrieved the book and threw it down on the coffee table. Sarah woke up with a start as it slapped down on the glass surface. She stared at him blearily and then smiled as she realised who it was.

'Theo. You're back. Have a nice day darling?'

'It went well…mostly.'

Sarah frowned, licked her lips with a dry tongue and straightened up in the chair.

'What do you…?' she began but Theo cut her off impatiently.

'Really mother, you need to be more careful.'

'Careful? What do you mean by that darling?'

'Apparently when Alex showed you round the house you made a big point of talking about Julian's room.'

'I did?' Sarah's frown deepened.

'So inevitably she started asking me all about Julian.'

'Does that matter?'

'It is too soon to be talking about Julian, you do see that don't you?'

Sarah struggled to straighten herself in the chair and glanced at Theo with a frown, trying to clear her head.

'I don't know what you mean. I said all the things you told me to say when you phoned me. I wrote them down on the pad as you were saying them.' She extended one hesitant index finger towards a notepad on the sideboard by the phone. 'I told you already: I talked about you and Kellaford Bridge, who she'd been talking to, her sister, her plans…' She counted off the subjects on her fingers as she went. 'I don't think I said much about Julian; I just mentioned that the end room was his bedroom…and it was.'

'Well something about your manner made her think. She particularly wanted to know how he died.'

'And what did you say?'

'I told her the truth or part of it anyway. I told her that he was crossing the stones when the tide was already too high and he fell in and was carried away and drowned.'

'That's all? You didn't mention Simon?'

'It works to our purpose if she continues to adore Simon. I remind her of Simon.'

Sarah's face crumpled into another frown.

'I really can't think why.'

'Because I make sure I do,' he replied crossly. 'Really mother, you must understand and keep to the plan. If you try to make her think badly of Simon at this point you'll jeopardise the whole thing.'

'All right, all right,' she said huffily, pushing herself carefully to her feet. She reached down and picked up her glass. 'I won't say anything else about him.' She crossed to the sideboard and picked up the decanter of whisky, looking at its remaining contents reproachfully as if they had gone down while she was asleep.

'Don't drink that,' Theo said, coming across to her and taking it out of her hand. 'I'll make you some tea. You should be starting to cook for dinner soon anyway.'

'Are you in for dinner this evening?' she asked, her expression changing to childlike expectation.

'I will be if you'll cook it.' Bob Geaton was going away again this weekend but it was only Friday; Theo could visit Helen the next day. He put his arm round Sarah's waist and squeezed her, unable to stay cross with her for long.

'Come on Sally,' he said, shepherding her towards the kitchen. 'Make me a big dinner.'

'You say it went well though?' she asked, craving his reassurance.

‘Yes. We went up to the old chapel by Dolphin Point. Simon loved it up there remember?’

‘Did he?’ She turned round with a puzzled expression as they reached the kitchen.

‘Of course he did. Don’t you remember? That was one of his favourite places; he said it was really peaceful.’ He paused and made sure he had her full attention. ‘That’s why I knew she’d want to see it: because Simon liked it so much.’

‘Oh.’ Sarah nodded, a light frown still puckering her brow. ‘I see.’

Chapter 10

September already. Alex stood in the middle of the sitting room and surveyed it. Drawing room, she corrected herself. That's what Theo always called it and with its grand dimensions and now freshly decorated, she supposed the title suited it better. It was nearly finished. It had taken three weeks altogether, three weeks of patchy solitary work, helped on odd evenings and weekends by Theo, to transform the dingy, disintegrating décor into something she could live with. All that remained to do was to get fresh curtains made and choose some new furniture. Gone was the blousy pink rose patterned paper which Sarah had chosen all those years before, and the heavy burgundy damask which had hung below the dado rail, to be replaced by a delicate blue-grey bamboo pattern on the upper part of the walls and a fine-striped blue paper below. The woodwork was finished in white satin and the wood-block floor, courtesy of a local company, had been thoroughly sanded and resealed a gleaming honey colour. A couple of rugs set it off nicely.

The grandfather clock which she'd left unwound for weeks had been repositioned again and now ticked reassuringly as if it had never done anything else. She'd consigned the night-time episode of the frozen hands as the result of a bad dream and what Victoria had once described as her 'wild fancies'. 'Too much time spent in that fantasy music world of yours, daydreaming,' her mother had gone on to say. It hurt to admit it but maybe she was right.

In between decorating, when, tired of dust and paint fumes and wallpaper paste, she'd needed a break, she'd walked down to the nature reserve. It was especially quiet there at the moment. The birds had finished nesting, some had gone, a few would be feeding up ready for the autumn migration, and those who would over-winter were yet to arrive. The margins of the ditches rocked with late summer flowers: yellow bur-marigold and purple loosestrife and pinkish-white sprays of water plantain. In response to her questions, Mick had told her all their names.

He was taking advantage of the low water levels and lull of activity to clean out some of the ditches and cut back sections of the reeds. 'Management,' he called it, in one of his more talkative moments. 'Left to themselves the ditches will silt up and the reeds would choke, dry up and slowly become scrub. The birds will look after themselves – any wildlife will - but you have to give them the right habitat and that requires planning and management.' He showed her how, over the years, he'd dug and shifted the earth to form bunds and channels, installed basic sluices to control the water levels and made a couple of suspended board walkways to allow him to cross the water to the far side.

Visiting the reserve was like stepping into another world, with none of the grief-ridden baggage which weighed down her own. On odd occasions Mick was almost amiable and then seemed obliged to compensate by being grumpy or at best distant, but at least he made no attempt to draw her out or ask intrusive personal questions. With her increasing familiarity there, she regularly took refuge in a succession of jobs which, out in the murmuring, rustling wilderness, threw a soothing blanket over thoughts she preferred not to pursue.

She'd kept her promise and not told anyone she went there though she was happy to keep the two existences separate anyway. But disguising what she was doing wasn't always that easy. On her way back from The Grenloe one day, having been helping Mick clean out some of the reed bed, Liz Franklin called her over to the garden where she had just invited Minna and Harry in for tea and insisted that Alex join them.

As they sat down to home-made scones and jam, Alex noticed Liz's gaze rest for a moment on the bits of stem, leaf and earth sticking to her tee-shirt. To avoid comment, she began asking Minna about the time she'd worked at The Hall for the Hellyons. Behind round, strong glasses, Minna's eyes were sharp and bright but she dismissed her memories as 'Not too good any more. It was such a long time ago.' Harry, on the other hand, appeared eager to talk but his speech was fitful and muddled and he became frustrated and then distressed. It was painful to see. 'He's rather tired; he didn't sleep well,' Minna said defensively and took him away suggesting he needed to rest. Not wanting a probing tête à tête with Liz, Alex made her escape too. Walking back up the hill, pulling a stray piece of twig from her hair, she wondered if there was another way she could get down to the reserve without going through the village and being seen.

But none of these activities could fully distract Alex from the increasing awareness that there were choices she had to make. Autumn was coming on and she'd been in Kellaford Bridge five months already. Sooner or later she would have to decide what to do about the house in London. In any case, Erica wouldn't let her forget. Since the awkwardness of their parting in July, they had managed to reinstate a relationship of sorts. They talked on the phone, each on their best behaviour, talking mostly about Ben or items in the news. But recently Erica kept dropping hints. 'I went to a performance of Fauré's Requiem the other day,' she said one evening. 'Quite good but I'm afraid the soprano was a bit disappointing. Her Pie was nothing like yours.' And, another night: 'I bumped into Ros yesterday. She said that people were asking when you'd be back on the circuit again.' Alex refused to get drawn in. Erica mentioned the house regularly too; she would drop it into the conversation, assuming a casual tone. 'Should I get the boiler serviced? With winter coming on, you'll need it seen. It's under contract isn't it?' or, more peevishly, 'There've been a lot of burglaries in your road recently. It's a terrible worry Alex, looking after your house.'

'I'm sorry Erica but I never intended you to have to look after it.'

'What else am I going to do? I'm your sister.'

'When I left I didn't really expect to be away so long. I wasn't thinking straight.'

'Well, now you need to decide what you want me to do about it. I mean it'd be nice to know when you're thinking of coming back.'

'I know. And I appreciate you worrying about the house,' Alex had said, meaning it, but evading the issue. 'But I really don't expect you to do anything with it. Though I suppose it's not wise to just leave it empty and uncared for like that. Perhaps I should get an agency to look after it.'

'Oh no. *I'll* do it.'

Alex felt she was in a permanent revolving loop with Erica. If she allowed her to continue checking on the house, she was exacerbating Erica's sense of grievance; if she used an agency, Erica would feel spurned and inadequate. And clearly this spiralling, confusing interdependence was nothing new; it was just that she had been too blind and swept up in her own affairs to see it like that before. Or perhaps she hadn't wanted to see it. Still she knew it wasn't fair to impose on Erica. She wondered if everyone's sibling relationships were complicated like this.

She put the thought aside but still the issue remained: what to do with the London house? Did she want to keep it? Could she imagine going back to live there? She tried to picture it. London; people she knew; pressure; journalists; intrusion and questions. The Underground. Her stomach turned in knots at the thought of returning. Perhaps she could rent it out while she decided? Could she face letting it out to strangers? And wasn't putting the decision off just cowardice anyway? Surely it would be better to make a crisp decision one way or the other, for while she prevaricated it was difficult to settle in Devon, to make plans or go ahead with renovations. She was effectively preventing herself from moving forward. A voice in the back of her head suggested tauntingly that that was precisely why she did it.

The sound of rain beating against the windows brought her out of her brooding introspection. She went to the window and watched the water streaming down the glass, heard it trickling into gutters and running insistently down the drainpipes. It reminded her of a piece of music Simon had written which was intended to sound like rushing water. It had had a melancholic, even harrowing timbre - all chromatic woodwind sequences and unresolved melodic progressions - and she'd never liked it. It was Saturday afternoon, the weather had closed in and the wind was blowing in off the sea. She would spend the evening in the snug with the curtains drawn tight. She switched on a comforting array of lights to fight the gloom and walked through to the kitchen to open a bottle of wine.

*

Down at the Lodge, Sarah had gone out. She'd said she'd catch the afternoon ferry up to Southwell to do some shopping. Theo went upstairs and into his mother's bedroom. It was immaculate as always and there hung in the air the unmistakeable trace of her perfume. He walked to her dressing table, picked up the bottle of Chanel and put it to his nose. It was her favourite and he bought it for her every Christmas. The shaking of her hands which was now becoming so apparent had started around last Christmas; he'd noticed it for the first time when she was pulling the wrapping off her presents. It had shocked him and the cause was only too obvious but she'd drink less, he was sure, once she was back in Hillen Hall.

He put the bottle down, turned away, crossed the room again, and opened her wardrobe. It was a large, oak construction with intricate carving on the door panels, brought from the Hall along with the rest of the bedroom furniture when they'd left. Theo had known nothing of the decision to sell Hillen Hall to his aunt and move to the Lodge until he'd got back from Harrow at the end of the summer term and his things had already been moved. He'd been furious and upset at not having been included in the decision, aghast that the home he'd known, and the estate which he'd assumed would be his eventually, no longer belonged to them. And then he'd been mortified the following autumn when he'd had to go back to school. Somehow the news had got round the dorm and he'd been endlessly ragged by the boys for coming down in the world. His so-called friends came from wealthy families; they had no need to watch their finances, downsize or manage without servants. He'd never heard the end of it till the day he'd left.

It was all his father's fault. Richard Hellyon had doted on Julian. It had been Julian this and Julian that; Julian will be just the person to keep the family name going and the business. 'He likes antiques,' his father had said, leaving Theo in no doubt that he was incomplete in some way for not doing so. And he hadn't been slow to bawl Theo out whenever he stepped out of line while Julian, of course, could do no wrong.

And Julian had even liked his father's porcelain collection. Theo's mouth curled at the thought. The bloody porcelain figures. Richard had been so devastated at the death of his eldest son that he'd been unable to work for months; he'd just moped around the Hall. When he'd finally gone back to work he'd spent most of his time buying porcelain figures to add to his collection. He'd been obsessed with them. And the blackest joke of all was that most of them were junk. He'd insisted they were a good investment but his judgement, never strong, had been further weakened and he was regularly fooled by fakes and broken pieces, inexpertly repaired. He squandered money and there had been little enough of it in the first place. True, the sale of the Hall had enabled Theo to continue at public school – at Sarah's insistence – but at what cost?

Theo stared unseeingly at the rack of dresses and coats running the length of his mother's wardrobe. His father had been contemptible. Theo had been away on a yacht when the news of his father's death came through and he'd drunk so much in celebration that he'd made himself ill, been reprimanded, and had to spend the next day in his cabin.

He glanced at the clock. Sarah wouldn't stay long in Southwell. She never did, and she'd catch the next ferry back. He turned his attention to the contents of her wardrobe, in particular the plastic sheathed dresses at one end of the rail. These were his mother's most prized dresses, most of which she'd had since she was young and couldn't wear any more; her waist was no longer so narrow, her breasts were too heavy. But he could remember her in them at dinner parties and dances when he was a small boy. They had done a lot of entertaining at that time and, if the boys were good, they were allowed to stay up to see the guests arrive. Julian had showed little interest but Theo used to creep out of his bedroom after they should have settled and slink down to sit on one of the lower steps of the back staircase. From its dark interior space he could sit safely in the shadows, watching and listening.

Now he lifted each dress out in turn, holding it up, turning it, considering it. Each one brought back an image of his mother, looking beautiful and happy. She had been stunning as a young woman with immense poise and a wonderful figure. He'd thought her a princess. He'd overheard men talk about her at the parties when they thought there was no-one around to hear. He vividly remembered being upset by some of the things they said about her. If he'd been bigger he'd have hit them and told them to shut up. She was his mother; they didn't have the right to talk about her like that and his father shouldn't have let them.

He pulled out an emerald green dress. It was a dress Sarah had had made soon after she'd married, made of silk brocade with a tight, shoulder-less bodice and a full, long skirt. Suspended in a separate bag from the hanger was a pair of above-elbow gloves to match. The dress was perfect. Theo laid it on the bed, moved the remaining dresses back along the rail in the wardrobe so that it looked the same as before, and closed the doors. Sarah wouldn't miss it for a while. He picked up the green frock, looked round the room one last time, and took it through to his own bedroom.

*

For the first time Helen had invited Theo round for dinner. It was the gesture, he thought, of a woman looking for something stable from the relationship, a desire to show that she could be more than a mistress. He guessed, from odd remarks she'd made about her husband that she was increasingly disenchanted with her marriage. 'Bob's nothing like I thought he'd be,' she'd complained. 'He was so handsome at first and seemed such fun. Now look at him. *Bor-ing.* But then he was away a lot when we first started dating. I suppose I never knew him well enough.' Theo got the impression she thought he was an altogether better prospect and she'd begun to make plans. He didn't want to encourage her too much but, for now, he was reluctant to disabuse her.

Now he was standing at the top of the stairs which led from the gallery up to the Geaton's living accommodation. They had a large open-plan living and kitchen area, separated by a peninsular unit, with a short passage leading to a bedroom and a bathroom. Another narrow run of stairs led up to the loft which had been converted into an en-suite bedroom. Helen had kept him waiting and forced him to knock twice before she'd let him in. Her apparent lack of enthusiasm was belied by the flush in her cheeks and the evidence of intensive food preparation laid out along the kitchen worktops.

She saw him glancing at all the dishes and bowls.

'We're having oysters to start,' she said. 'Then fillet steak and salad. For dessert I've made tiramisu.' And then she added keenly, betraying her anxiety: 'I hope you like it.'

'Of course I do, though I don't think we'll need oysters.'

He smiled at her, eyebrows raised, and she giggled. She was wearing a strong musky scent and it suited her. She really was a very attractive woman. He was gambling that she was now sufficiently smitten with him to go the extra mile.

'I've brought the wine,' he said, holding up a carrier bag with his right hand. 'Red wine *and* champagne.' He noticed the two elegant glass flutes already taken out of the cupboard and put on the side. 'I see I'm becoming predictable,' he added with amusement and put the bag down in the kitchen.

'What's in the other bag?' Sarah's casual manner didn't mask the excited anticipation in her voice.

'This one?' he said, holding up the bag in his left hand. It was an ordinary supermarket carrier bag containing something soft and folded. There was the crackle of paper as the bag moved. 'I don't know. I suppose it might be a present.'

'A present?' said Helen, smiling foolishly. 'God, I can't remember when Bob last bought me a present…just like that…for no reason. What is it?' She reached out for it but he pulled it away from her playfully.

‘I’m scared you mightn’t like it.’

‘I’m sure I will,’ she said, staring at the bag expectantly.

‘I put it in a different bag…you know…in case someone saw me.’

Theo allowed Helen to take the bag off him and watched her face intently.

She slowly pulled out the tissue-wrapped parcel and unwrapped it to reveal the green dress. Theo had taken it out of the plastic sheath and neatly folded it with the gloves laid on top. Sarah’s heavy perfume drifted out of the bag with it and hung in the air. Helen’s smile became fixed and her brow furrowed.

‘It’s not new,’ Theo said quickly. ‘I got it from one of those vintage dress shops, you know? Those old styles had so much glamour, didn’t they? And I thought, as soon as I saw you, that you’d look wonderful in it. You’ve got just the figure for it.’

Helen put the gloves to one side and held the dress to let it fall.

‘It’s lovely,’ she said doubtfully.

‘Put it on.’

‘But I’ve got a new dress on.’

‘And it’s very nice,’ he said, barely flicking it a glance. ‘Still, put this one on. I’d especially like to see you in it…tonight.’

Theo kept an expectant smile on his face while Helen shifted her gaze hesitantly between him and the dress.

‘All right then…if you want. I won’t be long.’

Barely five minutes later, Theo walked softly into Helen’s bedroom. She had only just slipped the dress on.

‘I’ve brought the gloves through,’ he said, handing them to her. ‘Here, let me fasten you up.’ He edged the dress together and carefully pulled the zip up her back. 'A perfect fit, I knew it would be,' he said, pulling her round and examining her.

They stood for a moment, facing each other, while he ran his eyes up and down her, studying her, checking her appearance against the image in his head. Then he picked her up roughly and carried her over to the bed.

Chapter 11

Mick tipped his head back, shielded his eyes against the sun, and watched five mallards fly over and descend further up the water. September had just tipped into October and the weather, as if trying to compensate for a mixed summer, had settled into a fine spell. Mick wondered what the winter had in store; the seasons seemed to be all to pot. He'd seen firecrests already which wouldn't normally have arrived yet. Did this presage a hard winter or were they just confused by the change in the weather too? He turned back to the huge bag of bird seed he'd just been to collect from a wholesale feeds supplier. Mick drove a clapped out old van which he parked on hard ground the other side of the Grenloe. From there he could access a track which eventually led onto a public road without ever being seen in the village. He locked the van, hefted the bag onto his back and made for one of the walkways. How expensive it all was these days. He'd been muttering about it a few days previously when Alex, helping out, had asked how he could afford it.

'Oh, I'm sorry,' she'd immediately said. 'That's none of my business.'

He'd looked at her directly then. It was rare that she came out with a frank question of that kind, though he suspected that her apparent indifference simply masked her natural curiosity. He assumed that she thought questions from her would only encourage reciprocating enquiries from him and she didn't want that.

'I manage,' he'd said. 'I starve to do it of course but if I get desperate to eat I can always shoot a duck to get me through.'

She'd looked shocked for a second and then tutted. He often said things which she took seriously for a moment before realising he was teasing her. He couldn't resist doing it; she could be very intense sometimes.

'No, but seriously,' she said, 'why don't you open the reserve up to visitors and charge them an admission fee to help cover your expenses?'

'Because it wouldn't be a reserve any more, it'd be a zoo,' he'd answered impatiently. She'd touched a raw nerve. 'It's supposed to be a place of retreat and peace, somewhere the wildlife won't feel threatened, not a place to have cigarette ends and sweet papers thrown down, and people complaining that the birds won't appear to command.' He could have added that it was a retreat for himself too, free from the accusing eyes of humans and their loaded questions and ignorant assumptions.

He was surprised she kept coming. The frequency of her attendance varied but she never allowed too many days to pass without a visit. He knew, though she never talked about it, that she'd formed a friendship with Theo Hellyon. He'd heard the gossip in the village, while he waited in the queue in The Stores or called at the Post Office. She and Theo Hellyon had been picked up by Andy Turner in the ferry from the far bank of the Kella. They'd 'been for a picnic together' it was said, 'spending a lot of time together'. The prospect of romance in the village had caused a buzz of excitement. 'How nice for her,' he'd heard Tess Webber, the hairdresser say. 'After all she's been through. She must be lonely up in that big house all by herself.'

Lonely. He supposed she was or why else would she spend so such time with him getting dirty on the reserve? He knew quite a bit about loneliness himself but he'd found you learnt to cope with it and, having become accustomed to his own company for so long, he still had mixed feelings about Alex's visits. He was scared of what they might lead on to; he didn't want trouble. And he was surprised to find he liked her; she wasn't the vain, overly sophisticated creature he'd imagined a classical singer would be like, all smart clothes and affected airs. On the contrary, she was straightforward, warm, impulsive and even sometimes downright pig-headed. She had a quick temper but had enough humility to apologise if she thought she'd gone too far. But liking her was a problem all its own, a can of worms he definitely didn't want to open.

But he couldn't quite bring himself to tell her to stay away so instead he refused to make it easy for her. 'Well if you're here,' he'd say, 'you might as well make yourself useful and do this for me.' And he'd get her cleaning out the hens or going up the ladder to check on the nest boxes and clear them out, or filling the feeders he had hanging from odd tree branches. He was surprised she never demurred. He watched her sometimes from a distance, meticulously carrying out his instructions, getting dirty and then fastidiously trying to brush herself off. There was almost an air of penance about her, as if, by doing these dirty jobs which she found so distasteful, she was trying to repay some debt. And, to judge from the shadowy sadness which she carried around her like a mantle, it was about as effective as throwing in spadefuls of sand to dam a flowing river.

He usually made them coffee and toast when they stopped to rest, and they'd chat about the reserve, or he'd answer Alex's questions about the wildlife. She rarely mentioned anything personal so he'd been taken by surprise when, on her last visit, she'd started talking about her dead husband's ashes which, apparently, she had in a casket at the Hall.

'The thing is,' she said, stirring her coffee round and round, watching the instant coffee granules slowly dissolving off the surface of the liquid, 'I think I ought to bury them. It's not right to keep them with me. Maybe it's selfish.'

She'd glanced up at him expectantly then but Mick didn't answer. He got the impression that the comment was the start of a much bigger issue, like the first corner of a huge piece of submerged wood which, despite being repeatedly pushed down below the surface, insists on returning to bounce around on the top of the water. He sensed pain and confusion and he was determined not to get involved; he didn't want to be confided in. He found himself wondering bitterly if she confided in Theo bloody Hellyon.

Alex stirred the coffee round again, removed the spoon, sucked the coffee off it to stop it dripping and then placed it down on the wooden table. She rubbed ineffectually with her index finger at a couple of water stains on its surface and pulled a face as the dust smeared at her touch.

'But, if I did bury them, I'm not sure where,' she went on. 'I couldn't face another formal service and, you know, consecrated ground...none of that meant anything to Simon. But there's an old ruined chapel up on the other side of the River Kella...Do you know it?' She looked up at him again. She'd stopped wearing the dark glasses and those very blue and compelling eyes of hers were hard to avoid.

'Sure,' he said. 'Up on the cliff near Dolphin Point.'

'What do you think?'

'I think it's up to you.'

'Well, of course, but as a place?'

He hesitated to answer but couldn't stop the next remark from coming out rather sharply.

'If he didn't care about consecrated ground, why a chapel?'

'Because...someone...told me he liked it up there.'

'Oh, well, if *someone* did. But the cliff's eroding up there.'

'Is it? I didn't notice. But anyway, the chapel's a long way back from the edge.'

'So why did you ask me then if you already know better?' he suddenly snapped at her.

'Hey, which side of the bed did you get out of this morning?' she'd retorted. 'Whatever's rattled your cage, there's no need to take it out on me. I only asked.'

'I'm not here to give out advice. It's nothing to do with me.'

'Oh, excuse me.'

He'd regretted the words almost as soon as he'd said them but he didn't have Alex's facility for apologies and she'd immediately left anyway, abandoning her barely-touched coffee. He'd been bad-tempered for the rest of the day.

Now Mick heaved the bag of seed in through the shed door and slit it open ready to transfer it to metal drums away from the invasive teeth of rodents. He found himself listening out for his unwanted visitor. It concerned him that he thought about her so much. Since that last visit, he'd speculated about her relationship with her late husband and how the man had died; he'd heard mixed reports. And now he wondered if he'd put her off ever coming back again. Then he heard Susie's distinctive welcoming bark and felt the tainted pleasure of knowing that he'd hadn't.

*

'I don't know,' said Theo. 'Perhaps it's too late to be throwing so much money at the old place. It's been starved of affection and attention for so long; maybe the old girl isn't sound any more. You might be wasting your money. I mean…I'm not trying to be nosey…but you can't have money to burn and property can eat it up before you know it.'

Alex looked at Theo in surprise; it wasn't what she'd expected him to say. 'The old girl' was Hillen Hall and she'd just been describing to him her plans for a new kitchen. They were sitting either side of a small table in the corner of The Black Goose, a country pub turned smart restaurant in the nearby village of East Walkham. It was Alex's thirty-ninth birthday and, Theo, back home from a short crewing job round the Isle of Wight, had insisted on taking her out. Her guilt and confusion at the thought of a formal date with him had been quickly overcome by his easy persuasion. 'You can't spend your birthday alone,' he'd insisted. 'And think of all the meals you've thrown together to feed me while we've been decorating. I owe you.'

He'd turned up at the Hall bearing a gift. He'd bought her the carving of the avocet from the gallery in the village. She'd commented on it to him a few days previously, saying how much she liked it, just stopping short of mentioning that she knew the person who had done it. Now it already stood between them, this black hole of evasion, and she backed off from disturbing it, sure it was unimportant, uncomfortable because it was unlike her to be intentionally secretive. In any case she'd promised Mick, and even if he was a moody, awkward devil at times, she didn't want to stop going down to The Grenloe. 'What a lovely thought,' was all she said, taking the bird and putting it to stand on the table and admire it, and her opportunity to mention her visits to the reserve slipped away and disappeared.

She'd taken ages to get ready, trying on outfit after outfit, unsure what would hit the right note. It was such a strange feeling after all these years, getting ready for a date, and she tried to play it down in her own mind, desperate not to feel the weight of the occasion. Now they'd nearly finished their meal and she'd relaxed. There was nothing different about the event; they were just together in a different place. Theo had been the same as always, telling her amusing stories about the people he'd met on his last trip, complaining about the food again, casual and just himself.

'I'm not going to just throw money at it,' she answered him now indignantly. 'But the investment would surely be worth it. And I can't believe you mean that. You don't think a house like that which has survived for so many hundreds of years is just going to fall down, do you? I know it needs work doing on it; the rest of the windows need replacing and there are tiles missing off the roof.' She wondered why she was arguing the point like this when she still hadn't actually decided what she was going to do. Still, it didn't harm to talk it through. She sat back in her chair and grinned. 'Who knows what evils might be lurking in the loft?' she jokingly went on. 'Houses always need things doing to them, especially old ones. But even so I don't think it'll come crashing down round my head.'

Theo grinned too.

'I wasn't suggesting it would. Just that you shouldn't go spending your money without knowing what you're getting into.'

'Maybe I'll get it surveyed. I suppose I should have thought to do that in the first place.' She leaned forward to pick up her glass and drank the last mouthful of wine. 'I'd have thought you'd be pleased to see Hillen Hall smartened up. Or did you hate living there?'

'Not at all. I liked it. But I was a child. What child wouldn't enjoy having all that ground to run around in? And old houses have hiding places. It was fun. But I didn't have to worry about wet rot or dry rot or any other kind of rot.' His face became serious and he stared at the unused cutlery on the table, fiddling with it. 'I guess my father bore the brunt of all that. He was a worrier.' A muscle twitched in his cheek. He looked up at her and gave her a wan smile. 'I think it's one of the things which helped to make him ill.' Alex reached across and touched his hand a second, registering her understanding. Theo flicked her a grateful smile.

'I saw your mother in the village yesterday.' Alex withdrew her hand and sat back. 'She was getting on the ferry for Southwell.'

'She goes a couple of times a week. She's a creature of habit; does the same things week in, week out: same days for washing or cleaning or baking.' He grinned. 'Fish for dinner on a Friday, church on Sunday morning. As far as Southwell is concerned the only thing that changes is the time of the ferry and, much as she'd like to, even she can't control the tides.'

Alex thought of the smell of whisky and the shaky hands but wasn't sure how to bring the subject up.

'I'd never be that organised,' she remarked lightly. 'I generally do things on the spur of the moment. It used to drive Simon crazy.' She paused. 'Is she happy?' she asked suddenly.

Theo's expression clouded.

'Mother? Yes. Why shouldn't she be?' he asked.

Alex shrugged.

'No reason. I just...' Under Theo's baleful gaze she hesitated. '...When she came round to the house, she seemed kind of...wistful.'

His eyebrows lifted.

'Wistful? That's not a word I would ever have used to describe my mother, I must say.'

'Well, preoccupied might be better.'

'Ha. She was probably thinking about all the jobs she'd got lined up to do at home. Or what food she should send me to stop me being starved.'

Alex laughed, relieved at his change of tone. For a moment there she thought he looked almost cross.

When he took her home she invited him in for coffee but he resisted, claiming the need to be up early the following morning.

'Anyway, I mustn't outstay my welcome,' he said, standing outside the kitchen door where she'd let herself in.

'Don't be silly. Of course you couldn't.'

'No?' He put a hand to each side of the door-frame, leaned forward and kissed her softly on the lips. By the time she'd realised what he was doing he'd moved away again and smiled. 'That's good to know. Sleep well, Alexandra Munroe. Sweet dreams.'

She watched him as he walked away, watched him turn as he reached the edge of the drive and blow her a kiss. Then he was gone and the place felt curiously empty. She put a couple of fingers to her lips and smiled.

Later on, sitting in front of the dressing table mirror, brushing her hair, she saw the light from the bedside lamp bounce off her wedding ring. She put the brush down and turned the ring on her finger. Eleven months on and still she wore Simon's ring. She stared at it, turning it round and round, round and round. Then slowly she twisted it up and off and slid it onto the third finger of her right hand.

*

Theo felt his mobile phone vibrate in his pocket and glanced across at his mother who was sitting beside him on the sofa. It was Saturday afternoon and they were watching a DVD of Breakfast at Tiffany's at his insistence. But Sarah had fallen asleep. He'd tried controlling how much whisky there was available to her in the house but it didn't seem to have made any difference to how much she appeared to be drinking. She was obviously keeping hidden supplies somewhere; he just hadn't found out where yet.

The phone vibrated again and he eased himself to his feet, carefully trying not to wake her, walked out into the hall and put the phone to his ear.

'Yes?' he said.

'Theo?' said a low voice.

'Yes. Helen?'

'You can't come over tonight.' A note of urgency coupled with the need for secrecy made Helen's voice fizz at him through the speaker. 'He hasn't gone away. He's got man flu and is draped all over the sofa. He's being a pain in the ass.'

Theo almost laughed. She sounded so scared and so cross.

'Where are you?'

'I'm down in the gallery, in the kitchenette at the back. But you can't come here,' she added urgently. 'God, I'm so miserable not to see you.'

'We'll do it again, don't worry.'

'Yes, but *when*?' Frustration made the last word come out much louder than she'd intended and there was a pause. He could sense her getting herself back under control. 'He won't be away again for a couple of weeks,' she hissed. 'This is an awful way to have to carry on.'

'Are you trying to tell me you want to finish it?'

'No,' she said sulkily. 'Of course not. Oh hell, someone's just come into the gallery. Speak to you soon.'

Helen rang off abruptly and Theo looked down at his mobile with amusement. How ironic that the woman he desperately wanted to throw herself at him was reserved and cautious and studiously platonic, while the woman he would undoubtedly give up as soon as circumstances required it – or when he got bored, whichever came sooner – was as devoted as a puppy. Sarah's green dress had caused Helen a momentary pause - he'd thought, briefly, that maybe he'd pushed his luck too far too soon – but she'd come round under his devoted attention and he thought the evening had been a great success. When he'd left she'd certainly been looking forward to their next meeting.

But there had been further problems, a few days later, when Theo went into the gallery to buy Alex's present. Helen had heard the gossip that he was seeing Alex Munroe, that it was more than just a hand with a bit of DIY, that they'd been seen *out* together. When he asked for the bird carving, Helen guessed who it was for and promptly lost her temper.

'So it's true then? You're buying it for that singer woman aren't you? You're two-timing me with her? *I've* seen her standing staring at that thing. You're a bastard, you know that?'

'Oh come on Helen. I can't believe you said that.'

'It's no good denying it. I know you're seeing her.'

'I wasn't going to deny it. It's true.'

Helen flashed him a poisonous look as she picked up the carving from the window and stalked back to the glass counter with it to wrap.

'Helen,' he said softly. 'You're taking this all the wrong way. I thought you'd be smarter than that.' He went on to stress how platonic his relationship with Alex was - 'Just like a brother and sister; we are related in a way,' - and how minor it was in comparison with the steamy one he shared with her.

She pretended to ignore him while she wrapped the carving but she kept glancing up at him, her eyes showing how desperate she was to believe him.

'I'd bet she'd be really frigid compared to you,' he went on. 'But honestly I'm not that interested to find out.'

'Really?' Helen looked at him big-eyed, like a child being offered a trip out.

'Really. Don't you believe me?'

She pulled a face and stared into his eyes.

'Maybe.'

She'd given in. While he offered her his credit card, they arranged their next date. And now she was miserable because it had had to be called off. Theo shook his head; she was such a fool. But she was a welcome and amusing distraction from his more pressing concerns. He'd already replaced his mother's green dress - 'I'd better keep it safe with me so Bob doesn't see it,' he'd told Helen - and picked out another one for their next meeting. It would be safe tucked away in his bedroom until the next opportunity presented itself.

Chapter 12

The sky over the far hill was lightening, the increasing intensity of the ochrous glow suggesting the rising sun beyond. A white vaporous mist hung wispily over the River Kella as Alex reached the mudflats and hesitated. It was nearly half past seven and the tide had already receded, exposing the rugged columns of stepping stones. Her arrival disturbed the oystercatchers and they shuffled off and then flew further up river, their piping calls of protest echoing back through the mist to her. A heron reluctantly rose into the air and flapped languidly away. It was the twenty-sixth of October, exactly one year since Simon had died, and Alex resolutely picked her way across the stones on her way to bury his ashes.

'How long did it take you to get over Bill's death?' she'd asked Liz Franklin once.

'Get *over* it?' Liz pulled a face, a rare puckering of her brow. 'I'm not sure I ever have dear. You just get used to it. But I think the first year is the worst. You know, getting through all those 'first times' when you have to do something without him, and then there's Christmas of course and his birthday and your wedding anniversary. So many minefields to negotiate. But when you've done it all once you know you can get through it all again.' She nodded her head and her double chin shook. 'Yes, once you pass the year I think it starts to get easier.' She smiled then and added kindly: 'I'm sure it will for you too.'

A dense, pressing dread had insidiously crept up on Alex as the anniversary of Simon's death approached. Torn between marking the occasion in some way and wanting to escape it, the idea of using it to finally bury Simon's ashes had come to her just a few days before, during one wet and windy night. In the early hours of the morning she'd been woken, she thought, by the sound of a voice. In the leaden dullness between sleep and wakefulness it had sounded like someone saying a name though she couldn't make out whose. She'd sat up jerkily and peered into the darkness around her.

'Simon?' she managed to ask eventually. 'Simon? What do you want? Tell me darling, what do you want?'

And there'd been silence; just the whistling of the wind outside and the rain hammering on the window, and a strange lingering resonance of her pathetic voice, high and unnatural. She suspected herself. Her wishes and confusion were breeding this. Deep within her subconscious, when her guard was down, she was conjuring him up. It was as her mother and Erica had so often suggested: her imagination ran wild. Perhaps everything she'd felt and thought she'd seen – all the coldness, the movements, the unexplained noises – could all be explained by her own muddled desire and guilt.

She lay awake, trying to make sense of it all and failing. But as the rain stopped and the first glow of dawn lit her bedroom, it became clear, once and for all, that she needed to finally lay Simon to rest, both in the ground and hopefully in her mind. If she didn't, she was practically inviting him to haunt her forever.

So now, with Simon's casket firmly stowed in a rucksack on her back, she walked the riverside path on the far bank of the river, laboured up the final rise, on and up to the lonely spot on the windswept cliffs where the old chapel bore the brunt of the channel storms. Breathless and hot by the time she arrived, she paused and looked out at the views, hazy and mysterious in the early morning mist.

'I heard someone in the village suggest that the cliff's eroding up at Dolphin Point,' she'd said casually to Theo. 'Does that mean the chapel's going to fall into the sea?'

He'd laughed. 'Eventually maybe, but not for centuries I shouldn't think. One stone falls every ten years and everyone panics about erosion. They make me laugh. Why?'

She shrugged. 'I just wondered,' she said, and dismissed Mick's comment from her head. She wasn't going to tell anyone what she was going to do, not even Theo who had put the idea in her mind in the first place. Certainly not Erica. Having felt so dissociated from the funeral service in London, this time she wanted to be alone to say her goodbyes.

She slipped the rucksack to the ground and took out a trowel. Having carefully monitored the tides for several days, she'd been across the two previous mornings in order to find a suitable spot and to prepare the ground. In a place where the earth was a little softer, she'd loosened it and then covered it with a heavy stone. Now she heaved the stone away and cleared a hole deep enough to bury the casket. She glanced at her watch, retrieved the casket from the bag and carefully laid it in the ground, piling earth and stones back on top and treading it firm. Then she dragged the stone across the top again and stood back, catching her breath.

'Rest in peace darling,' she murmured.

With the sun clearing the hilltop in a burst of orange light, she clasped her hands in front of her and haltingly sang

Ireland's 'Nunc Dimittis', tears silently coursing down her cheeks.

Then she gathered her things and hurried back to the stepping stones before the water rose too high for her to cross back.

*

'If you keep bringing her things to eat she'll get fat. She's a greedy pig.'

Mick shook his head despairingly as he watched Susie gently take the large bone-shaped treat from Alex's hand and trot off behind the carriage with it.

'She doesn't have time to get fat, running round after you. Anyway, you don't mean it. You spoil her to death yourself.'

'No, I don't overfeed her. That's not a kindness.' Mick tried to sound stern but failed and was frustrated with himself. His feeble efforts at keeping Alex away hadn't lasted long and they hadn't worked. He'd even apologised – sort of – for losing his temper about her questions regarding Dolphin Point and had caught himself trying to make it up to her. It was crazy. He felt more alive than he'd done for years and ten times more vulnerable. But it was a friendship which had no future and if he had any sense, he'd tell her to stay away. He reluctantly concluded that he clearly didn't have any sense.

The days were getting progressively shorter as November moved on and the reserve buzzed with activity. The month had begun with a couple of days of cold and frost and then the weather had turned mild and damp. Birds were arriving daily from further north, either stopping to feed on their way south, or to stay for the winter to take advantage of the shelter, mild weather and the food. He'd seen gadwall and a couple of tufted ducks; some whimbrel had passed through on their way to Africa and a few green shank had arrived; that morning a grey wagtail had been bobbing its way along the muddy edges of the water.

Sitting side by side in the hide a little later on, Alex saw a shoveler on the open water, upending itself to feed. She silently pointed it out to him at the same time as wresting the binoculars from his grasp. He raised his eyebrows, amused. She'd learnt a lot about birds recently, even going so far as to buy herself a book about them. She'd also found a way to get to the Grenloe basin without going through the village, cutting across and down the parkland on its northern edge and then coming down into the wooded land which led through to the reed beds and the clearing. The route apparently included climbing fences and a chained wooden gate. The first time she appeared in the reserve through the back of the reed beds, she'd grinned at him and brandished an ordnance survey map triumphantly. 'Seems you've learnt something then,' he'd said dryly. 'Shame you didn't think of doing that in the first place.

He watched her now as she peered out towards the water.

'These binoculars are scratched,' she muttered. 'They're useless.'

He sometimes wondered what went on in her mind. At times her speech was animated, her face and hands remarkably expressive; on other days she was dull and introspective. And her trips to the reserve were similarly erratic. She'd come on successive days and then not come for a week. She reminded him of a nervous bird, wanting to fly in to feed, but too wary to settle for long.

Increasingly they had started to have serious conversations over coffee. They'd discuss music or politics or arts and crafts. They agreed, disagreed and argued, sometimes heatedly. For a professional, independent woman, it surprised him at times that Alex could be so gullible and trusting of what she read in the papers. Her straight-backed, head-high demeanour appeared to mask a deeper-seated self-doubt. But she was intelligent, articulate and well-read. It had been a long time since he'd been able to talk to anyone in this way and he found he was greedy for it.

'You're very well informed for someone who shuts himself away from the world,' she said once after a passionate debate on the environment and global warming.

'I can read. I've even got a radio.'

'But I didn't think you'd even want to know.'

'I could say the same thing about you.'

She let it drop. He'd met few women – or men come to that – who could restrain their curiosity and not pry. And she still never mentioned Theo and neither did he, though he sometimes felt the man's invisible presence hung around them like a dark spectre, conjured up by their pointed evasion. But it was none of his business and never would be.

'If you keep buying dog treats at the shop,' he muttered now, staring through the draughty windows of the hide, 'that nosey Lyn Causey who runs The Stores'll get suspicious about what you're doing with them.'

'I don't buy them there,' she replied, barely moving her lips. 'I get them in Southwell, in a big pack. It's cheaper anyway.'

'You're always saying that money isn't an issue.'

‘It’s not but there’s no reason to squander it. I buy plenty of other things in The Stores. In any case it did occur…even to me…’ She flicked him a scathing glance. ‘…that I didn’t want to have to explain who I was getting the treats for.’

‘Sh, there’s a bearded tit…on that reed over there.’ He reached across to take the old binoculars from her hands.

‘They’re useless,’ she repeated. ‘You should get some new ones.’

‘*I* can see through them. *There’s no reason to squander money*,’ he fluted in a poor imitation of her intonation. He peered through the glasses. ‘Female.’

She frowned and stared towards the bird. ‘How can you tell?’

*

Alex pulled the surveyor’s report out of the envelope and blanched as she read it. She was already aware of some of the issues it raised like the missing tiles from the roof and the leaking gutters, but it brought up a whole catalogue of other problems to address, both major and minor. ‘You shouldn’t rush into redoing everything. I mean you probably won’t be there long enough to make it worthwhile,’ Erica had predictably said during their phone conversation that night, and Alex wondered why she’d told her sister anyway. Theo had been, equally predictably, more upbeat about it. ‘You pay the surveyor to find the problems or potential ones. It doesn’t mean that everything has to be done immediately. You should go through it and prioritise.’ He’d flashed his infectious grin at her. ‘Like you said, the Hall isn’t about to fall down.’ More seriously he added: ‘I know a decent builder who could help out if you want.’

What would I have done without Theo? she often thought; she'd come to depend on him so. When she'd told him what she'd done with Simon's ashes he'd put his arms round her and given her a hug. 'Well done,' he'd murmured. 'That must have been tough.' They'd just finished hanging the new curtains she'd had made for the drawing room and the sudden physical gesture had taken her by surprise. Time had passed since the kiss by the back door and she'd consciously not allowed herself to think about it, unwilling to apportion it too much significance.

It was becoming increasingly clear to her that Theo wanted a more physical relationship with her. She sensed it in the way he touched her and the occasional lingering look, but he said nothing and didn't press. Sometimes, between telling jokes and being flippant, he looked at her indulgently as if he was trying to make it clear that he could wait until she was ready. Her own feelings were confused. She wondered if it were possible for her to genuinely care for another man, especially when so little time had really passed since Simon's accident. And guilt still shadowed her, suggesting that allowing Theo to be anything more than a friend would be an act of betrayal to Simon. But sometimes, lying in bed, she longed for the intimacy of another human body against her own; in the dark hours of the night, alone in the creaking empty house, she dearly missed that warm reassurance.

With Theo about to go away to the Boat Show at Earl's Court he asked her out for dinner again. 'I thought we'd try Chez Jacques, the bistro down by the quay.'

'But everyone will see us together there.'

'Does that matter?' He sounded hurt.

'No, I suppose not,' she replied doubtfully. 'It's just that they'll talk.'

'So...does it matter?' he repeated. 'They already do anyway. People talk because they haven't enough to do. Ignore them.'

He was right; there *was* gossip about them. She could feel it in the air when she walked into the shops; she guessed from the things that were said in her presence containing an implicit assumption that she would know where Theo was or what he was doing at any given time. Elizabeth Franklin, invited over for coffee a few days before, had referred to them as a couple and had only smiled when Alex had tried to correct her.

The restaurant was quiet and Theo was on good form, talkative, teasing. He exhorted her to let him take her out sailing – 'You'd love it,' he said, adding, when she shook her head: 'Sure you would. It's exhilarating.'

She smiled. 'Well, maybe, sometime. How old were you when you learnt to sail?'

He shrugged. Their main course arrived and he paused until the waitress had gone. 'I don't know. Six or seven. But I grew up with boats all around me remember. Then Harry Downes used to take us out in his boat. The lifejacket was bigger than I was. He had an old wooden dinghy. Once I got hooked I asked for proper lessons.'

'And Julian? Did he like sailing too?'

Theo rocked his head side to side thoughtfully, wrinkling up his nose.

'Not so much. But Simon did. He and I used to go out together with Harry in the summer.'

'I didn't know he could sail.' Alex sipped some wine. Something else she didn't know. They ate in silence for a few minutes.

'I see Harry quite often standing watching the ferry or the boats in the harbour,' Alex said at last. 'He looks so lost, as if he'd love to be out there again on the water; it's a shame.'

'Yes, I know. Definitely a sail short of a full rig these days.'

'Mm. He wanders you know. I met him down by the stepping stones the other morning. He must have just walked out of the house. He was wearing a coat over his pyjamas.' Alex remembered Harry's agitated manner. It was the day she'd got back from burying Simon's casket. Even though she introduced herself, it wasn't clear whether Harry knew who she was but he'd talked to her anyway in that disjointed, distracted way he sometimes had.

'By the stones? What was he doing there?' Theo asked, taking the last forkful of food and laying the cutlery down.

'I'm not sure,' she replied.

'What did he say?'

'I can't remember now. I'm not sure I understood what he meant anyway. Why?'

'Sorry?'

'You asked as though there was a reason.'

'Hell, no. I was just curious about what he was doing. But he probably didn't know himself. He doesn't know what day of the week it is any more.' He held up the bottle of Bordeaux. 'More wine?'

They finished their meal with coffee and then went for a stroll along the quay. It was a clear night and starry, the moon three quarters full and casting a flat, silver light. There was no-one else around; the holiday makers had gone home, the second homes stood empty, their windows either shuttered or yawning holes of blackness. The lighted houses lay mostly inland where the prices were cheaper. Kellaford Bridge, like a squirrel, was in semi-hibernation for the winter.

Theo took her hand, looped it through the crook of his arm and drew her to the harbour wall where they looked out on the swelling tide, at the boats which had spun on their moorings as the water changed direction and now all pulled upriver and inland, moonlight bouncing and twinkling off varnish and windows. They stood companionably, Theo with his hand still resting on top of Alex's, listening to the slap of the tide against the harbour wall and the halyards tinkling against the masts in the breeze. Out at sea a tiny pinprick of light marked the presence of a ship at anchor for the night.

It was after eleven when they got back to Hillen Hall. Alex asked Theo in for coffee and, for only the second time, he agreed. 'Why don't we have the shampoo,' he said, already reaching inside the fridge for the bottle of champagne he'd brought with him when he'd arrived. 'To toast my going, and my even quicker return?'

They sat on the floor in front of the wood-burning stove in the snug, opened its vent to flame up the wood and, with their backs against the sofa, sat and drank and chatted. Alex felt drowsy and relaxed, her eyelids occasionally fluttering closed. When Theo spoke – odd murmured remarks about the day, the meal or the prospective work on the house – the timbre of his voice brought Simon to mind, as if he were there again beside her. In the half-world between being awake and asleep, a little euphoric from all the wine, she allowed herself to run with this dangerous fantasy.

Theo came to the end of his last glass of champagne and put it to one side. As he turned to look at her the movement made her open her eyes.

'Penny for them,' he said.

She flushed.

'You'd be paying too much,' she said. 'I wasn't really thinking about anything.'

He reached out to take the glass from her hand and she let him and watched him put it down beside his own. Then he put his hand to her shoulder, pulled her round and kissed her. This time he explored her mouth with his tongue, pulling her hard against him. She could feel the firmness of his body, the warmth of his hands and his face and the heat and wet desire of his mouth. He pulled away leaving her breathless and stunned.

'You look so beautiful tonight Alex,' he whispered, so close to her face she could feel his breath on her skin. 'I think I'm falling in love with you, do you know that? No, don't say no.' He put his index finger up to her mouth and pressed her lips gently, stopping her speaking. 'Don't fight it. You know I am.' And then he pulled her close and kissed her again.

A couple of minutes later he stood up and reached a hand down to her.

'Let's go upstairs.'

Alex saw her hand go into his and he led her out of the room and up to her bedroom. She felt as though she were watching someone else from a great height.

*

'That should see it sorted.'

Mick Fenby hadn't really expected an answer as such but there was no response at all from his companion and he looked across to where Alex was standing, staring out across the water and the reeds, eyes unseeing. They'd been cutting back an elder which had become overgrown and was threatening to invade and choke up one of the ditches. Alex had turned up late in the morning, pale and quiet. On her arrival she'd asked in a false, bright voice if there was anything she could do to help and when he'd suggested she could help him with the pruning she'd fallen in alongside. They'd hardly exchanged a word since. He glanced at her occasionally but she'd been intent on the task in hand, her face shuttered and pinched. When they finished it was nearly two.

'Lunch?' he offered.

Alex glanced at her watch, appeared to have a mental argument with herself, then nodded.

The air was brisk and cold and the Pullman was contrastingly warm and cosy. Mick had made an effort to clean the place up but she didn't comment. He put out bread, cheese, tomatoes, a couple of glasses and a jug of apple juice.

'Help yourself,' he said.

And she did, though once the food was on her plate she ate little.

Mick ate vigorously, glancing at her from time to time. When he'd finished he sat back, the glass of juice in his hand.

'I'm disappointed you haven't noticed.'

'Mm?' Alex raised clouded eyes to his.

'I said I'm disappointed you haven't noticed.' She stared at him, frowning. He pointed at his beard which was neatly trimmed back short against his face. 'You said it looked a mess last time you were here, needed a cut. I looked in a mirror. Nearly cracked it. So I did something about it.' He poked his chin and ran a hand over the short bristles; the sensation was a novelty.

Alex's expression flickered as she took in what he was saying. She looked the beard over.

'Better,' she announced.

'I should bloody think so. It took me ages.'

They lapsed into silence.

'Not hungry then?' he asked.

'Hangover.'

'Ah.'

He drank his juice and said nothing more. Alex tried to eat some more bread but in the end she pushed the plate away with a sigh.

'I went out yesterday evening.'

Mick nodded, silent.

'With Theo Hellyon.'

'Uhuh.' He felt his stomach twist. 'Seems like you had a good night then.'

'Mm.'

'That doesn't sound too sure.'

'I drank too much.'

'Obviously.'

Alex fiddled with the knife on the plate, pushing it back and forth, studying it as if it were a scientific specimen. Suddenly she dropped the knife with a clatter onto the plate and looked up at him.

'Is that all you can say: *obviously*?'

'Hey, don't take your hangover out on me. What do you expect me to say?'

'I don't know,' she said crossly. 'Just show some interest I suppose.'

'I imagine if you want to tell me you'll tell me anyway.'

'Is life really that simple for you?'

'Is that what you think?'

'I don't know what I think.' She sighed, looked wistfully round the carriage and tossed a glance out of the window. 'Life seems a lot simpler here anyway. It's like going into some sort of retreat, like a monk.'

'Except I'm no monk,' he muttered. She allowed her gaze to rest on him a moment.

'Have you ever done something because you were drunk that you wouldn't otherwise have done?' she asked suddenly.

'Oh yes.'

'Really?'

'Of course. Inhibitions down, you do crazy things. I clouted some guy once when I was smashed. Not smart.' He hesitated and then added, in a quiet voice, reluctant to ask: 'And was it so awful, whatever it was you did, whatever you're punishing yourself for?'

Alex leaned back in the chair and threw her head back with a heavy sigh.

'I don't know. Yes.' She shook her head. 'I don't know.' She looked at him intently with a frown. 'Last night I …' She stopped and shook her head again, her ponytail flicking side to side. 'It was too soon. I don't know why… Oh God, I'm so confused.'

She suddenly rose to her feet.

'Thanks for the lunch Mick. I must go.'

He stayed in his chair as she grabbed her coat and left and he heard her speak to Susie before her footsteps faded away down the path. He didn't move at all but stared at the place where she had been sitting.

Chapter 13

Alex arrived back in London late the following day. The traffic had been a shock, a succession of queuing cars and weaving taxis, one way systems, low gears and impatient horn blowing. It had been part of her life for years but after the quiet of rural Devon for so many months it seemed alien. The decision to come back had been taken on the spur of the moment. The night spent with Theo had felt like too much intimacy, too soon, and she needed to get away. She wished she could blame it on the alcohol but she guessed it was more likely the fruit of loneliness. She wasn't sure what she felt for Theo. She was fond of him, she enjoyed his company and she was grateful to him, but his talk of love was both intoxicating and frightening and she was confused.

So, like some sort of Prodigal Daughter, she'd returned on reflex to the comfort of a home she'd recently spurned, telling herself that she'd been planning to come back anyway, that she *needed* to go back, that it had only been a matter of time before she did so. But on the drive east her stomach had tightened with apprehension at how she would react to seeing the house again and a brief and incomprehensible feeling of excitement had rapidly given way to misgivings and misery.

The house which she had shared with Simon sat under a grey November afternoon sky, rapidly darkening into a long winter night. Its windows stared out vacantly. Dead leaves had been blown into the front garden and up against the front doorstep; rain had left them soft, slippery and dank but at least the journalists no longer hung around outside. Despite the constant sounds of traffic and the hums and drones of planes far overhead, the place felt bleakly silent.

She remembered the first time she'd seen the house. Simon had heard from a colleague that it was going up for sale long before it had reached an agent and had insisted that she drop everything and come with him to see it. He was excited. 'We'll have to be quick or it'll go. This sort of house doesn't come up that often.' The area had been known for years as the home to many famous musicians, artists and writers. He was keen to live there. It was the place to be; it projected the right image. Simon had always been very concerned about image. 'It's important,' he'd said to her. 'Even if the music's wonderful, if the image is wrong people won't even bother to listen. That's the sort of society we live in.' They'd argued about it several times, Alex finally acknowledging that maybe she just didn't want to believe that it was true.

But they hadn't argued much about the house, only about whether they could – or should - afford it. She looked up at it now. She had loved the house for itself. It was spacious, light and welcoming and was near to the heath where she liked to walk. It had also been very expensive. They hadn't even sold their apartment when they put in an offer for it and Simon's mother had put up a lot of money to ease them through the purchase. But even if Alex had not been keen, she knew they'd have ended up buying it. Simon had always had a way of persuading her. Withdrawn, hurt silence had been a favoured technique.

Once inside Alex walked over junk mail and a free newspaper on the mat. Piled up on a side table in the hall were more papers and more junk. On one of the work surfaces in the kitchen were yet more. Erica had obviously been in and deposited them wherever a space presented. Normally she would have meticulously put them out into the recycling bin; their presence suggested her sulking rebellion.

Alex drifted from room to room. She'd dreaded coming back and had expected anguish but all she felt now was sorrow. The place was replete with memories, both good and bad, which loomed into her mind unbidden. Everywhere she looked Simon was there: the baby grand piano he used to sit at sometimes to compose; the cherished Hoffnung originals, framed and hung on the wall in his study; his electric razor, still on the shelf in the bathroom and his toothbrush, still in the rack. In the bedroom his dressing gown hung limply behind the door. She hadn't had the courage to part with anything that he had owned before she'd left; she hadn't even considered it. Now, after being away for so long, she felt at a slight remove from it all and it was like looking at an arrested moment in time, a moment that would never come again. She stretched out a hand to run a finger over Simon's watch, carefully placed back on his bedside cabinet the way he always left it. Her eyes started to fill and then a prickle of discomfort ran over her. After her experiences in Hillen Hall, she recognised the danger in keeping it like this; she needed to do some sorting.

She walked as purposefully as she could out of the bedroom and back downstairs. Before going out to the car to get her bags, she went into the sitting room and put a Sinatra CD on to play, turning the volume up loud. The house was all too achingly quiet.

*

'There's no reply.' Theo shut down the call and tried another number. 'Her mobile's not on either. Hell.' He threw down the phone and then glared at his mother as if she were personally responsible.

'I told you she'd gone away,' said Sarah. 'You wouldn't believe me.'

'Of course I believed you. That's why I came back as soon as the show finished. But why would she go away?'

'*I* don't know. But I know she's cancelled her newspaper; Billy told me that when he brought ours yesterday morning. The lazy boy was so pleased he didn't have to do the rest of the hill, he was bragging about it.'

Sarah was crabby. Theo had driven through the night and had woken her up early. When she'd come downstairs she'd gone to the whisky decanter to get a drink and Theo had walked over and taken it off her, insisting he needed breakfast and encouraging her into the kitchen.

'You've done something to upset her probably,' she added now irritably.

Theo thought back to the night he'd spent in Alex's bed before going away. She hadn't seemed upset when he'd left early the next morning; she'd been curled up against him when he'd come to, naked, soft and vulnerable. He hadn't done anything that night which could have upset her as far as he could remember. He'd made love to her thoroughly and attentively and afterwards she'd fallen asleep in his arms. Before getting up to leave he'd whispered in her ear and she'd murmured a reply and reached for him as he slipped out of the bed. She'd opened her eyes as he'd left her and had looked surprised, perhaps even a little embarrassed. Yes, that would be it. He'd half pulled the quilt off her as he'd got out and she'd looked down at herself and seen her nakedness. Ideally he'd have taken the time to reassure her, maybe made love to her again to reinforce their new intimacy, but he'd had to go; he'd been due to meet up with Patrick from the yard at eight.

Theo shook his head and paced round the kitchen.

'You're sure she didn't tell anyone where she was going?' he said fractiously.

'No-one that I know. But how do I know who she knows?'

Sarah filled the kettle, spilling water down the sides of it and dabbing it afterwards with the dishcloth. Theo stopped pacing and brought his fist down hard on the table.

'Bugger,' he said, and threw himself down in a chair by the table.

'Perhaps she's missing London,' said Sarah. 'Still…I'm sure she'll be back…don't you think she'll be back? I thought you said she adored you.' There was a note of reproach in her voice as though he'd told her a lie, as he would when a boy, accused of taking something of Julian's.

'I thought she did.'

'Maybe she's gone to see her sister. You said they were close?'

'*She* said they were, though she hasn't seen much of her recently.'

'Well I hope she comes back.' She paused. 'You slept with her didn't you?'

'Yes. Yes, I did. Everything seemed to be going so well,' he muttered, and ran a hand through his hair.

Sarah came to stand behind his chair and raised a hand to stroke his hair back into position. Then she put both hands on his wide shoulders and massaged into his muscles. Her fingers were so weak, to him it was like the touch of a butterfly.

'I'm sure she'll come back,' she said. 'Who could turn their back on my handsome son?'

Theo leant his head sideways to rest it on his mother's hand.

'I'm sure she will too,' he lied.

*

When Alex turned up at Erica's door later that first evening their reunion was stiff. The weeks of telephone conversations which had apparently soothed the atmosphere between them were as if they had never been. Alex could see in Erica's eyes that, face to face, her sister remembered as clearly as she did those rows at Hillen Hall.

'I'm sorry. I should have told you I was coming,' Alex offered tentatively. 'It was a sudden decision to come.'

'Isn't it always?' Erica said with a tight smile and hesitated just fractionally before coming forward to hug her. 'Come in. I was just about to make supper.'

'Am I disturbing you? It doesn't matter if you're busy.'

'Not at all. It's fine. Ben's staying over at a friend's. Have you eaten? I haven't had anything yet. I'll make something for us both. It didn't seem worth it just for me.'

Erica fussed and busied herself making risotto and opened a bottle of white wine. She talked about her job and about Ben and what he'd been doing; she talked of Alex's house and all the burglaries in the area and 'God, I'll bet it's dusty'; she fretted over Christmas presents and the cards she hadn't even bought yet, let alone written. It seemed to Alex that her sister was intentionally filling the air with sound, determined to keep a check on the conversation, unsure where it might lead.

'So you're back,' Erica at last said, more comfortably, when they'd eaten, had cleared away and were sitting with a second glass of wine.

'Mm, for a while.'

'You're not staying?'

'I don't know yet. I've only just got back.'

'Of course.' Erica clamped her lips together as if she were afraid something might escape them and then managed to stretch them sideways into an unconvincing smile.

'Look, I'm not sure what I want to do,' Alex said. 'I thought it was time to see how I felt back in London, to see if there's any future for me here.' It was little more than a half truth, but Erica looked pleased.

A couple of minutes of silence passed while Erica stared at her wine glass and ran a finger through the condensation on the side of it.

'Are you still seeing Simon's cousin?' she asked casually.

'Now and then.'

Erica nodded and Theo wasn't mentioned again. They chatted idly about other things while they finished the wine. Then Alex got up to leave.

'Do you want to stay over?' Erica immediately offered, jumping up. 'I can easily make up the bed in the spare room.'

Alex shook her head and forced a smile. 'Thanks Ricky but I'd better not. I need to stay in the house. If I don't do it now, I never will. Got to stand on my own two feet, haven't I?' She gave Erica a hug. 'Don't worry. I'll be fine,' she added over her sister's shoulder before pulling away.

'Of course you will.' Erica spoke with the forced cheer of a children's television presenter. 'But you'll come over to eat? Don't eat alone.'

Alex poked her sister playfully with a finger. 'Hey, don't fuss. I've been eating alone for months.'

'Well...yes, I suppose you have.'

*

Back in her own home, Alex tried to settle in and see if she could pick up her old life. She stocked up the house with food and treated herself to new clothes from her favourite shops. She had her hair done, went to the cinema with Ben and Erica, and dodged the bleak November showers to tidy up the tiny garden.

She also made a start on trying to clear away some of Simon's things, and found herself putting back as much as she threw out. 'Letting go' sounded like such an easy thing to do, she thought, but actually involved a lot of pain. She became distracted by old photograph albums and anniversary cards kept and now creased; she intended to throw away old manuscript books with Simon's cramped notation inside but found herself flicking through them to look for familiar work, humming an odd phrase, and then putting them back in the pile. She took a pile of old books to a charity shop but kept back a battered old copy of Prince Caspian which had been Simon's childhood favourite.

The piano in the sitting room stood in silent reproach at not being played. Several times Alex walked up to it and then walked away again. One morning she sat on the stool and slowly opened the lid. She had played quite well at one time - it had been an occasional source of relaxation - but she hadn't played since Simon had died. Even before his accident she'd let it slide. Simon was such a perfectionist about his music that she'd preferred to play when he wasn't around. In any case she tended to prefer to play light music to unwind and, after one cutting remark expressed early in their marriage, it was obvious he thought Cole Porter played on a baby grand a kind of sacrilege.

She allowed her fingers to run along the keys and then tentatively pressed a few notes of a favourite song. How she missed the music and yet how it terrified her too. She couldn't understand how she had allowed herself to lose the thing which she'd held so dear ever since she was a child. Music had grown from an instinct to a passion and then to an obsession which had steamrollered everything else in its path. But had it been love of the music itself or the desperate need to justify her choice to Victoria? Or maybe, she wondered, to herself? But she was aware that the cost of that obsession had been the little time or energy she'd had left for anything else. For some time now, there'd been a growing fear, barely acknowledged, that without the music her life had become pointless.

She fumbled her fingers along the keys again, trying to remember the whole tune. After a few mistakes and repeats, it started to come back and she felt a warm glow of relief. That evening, following hours of deliberation, she raised the courage to ring up her old singing coach. After a brief and taut conversation, they arranged to meet for coffee in town the next day.

Francine Vann, reading glasses perched on the end of her long nose, was installed at a table in the café before Alex had even arrived, leafing through a pile of sheet music. Forthright and uncompromising, she was a well-known singing tutor, as feared as she was respected. She'd spotted Alex's talent early and had taken her under her wing. Without Francine's support, Alex knew she'd never have been able to withstand Victoria's opposition to her career. Now, as she set two mugs of cappuccino down on the table and eased into her seat, it struck her that Francine had aged since she'd seen her last and she felt a pang of regret.

'Why did you want to see me?' Francine asked brutally, dropping her glasses off her nose to dangle pendulously from the burgundy cord round her neck before coming to rest.

'Did there have to be a reason?' Alex said with a smile. 'You're one of my oldest friends.'

'In both senses of the word, true. But not so good a friend that you thought fit to discuss giving up your career with me it would seem.' Francine paused and gave Alex a pointed look, eyebrows raised. 'I heard you'd gone to Devon.' When Alex looked up at her questioningly, she added: 'From that eager sister of yours. I met her a few weeks ago at a charity concert.'

'Ah Erica.' Ever since Alex had become part of the music set, Erica had been vicariously part of it too. She was always bumping into people.

'I'm sorry Francine. I should have told you I was going.' Alex shuffled on the seat, playing with the plastic spoon between her fingers. 'The decision was sudden and then I was too embarrassed to get in touch.'

'I think I've got over the hurt now,' said Francine acidly, and took a long draught of coffee. 'Mm, good.' She put the mug down.

'But you must have heard about…my last concert?' Alex said.

'Yes.'

'Well, that was why.'

'Was it?' The question hung there and then died for lack of an answer. 'So...you're back from Devon then?' Francine added.

'Mm.'

Francine pursed her lips forward ruminatively and allowed her eyes to run over Alex's face. 'You know you could walk back into a job anywhere round here, even now. All over the world I imagine. You were starting to ride high when you walked out. I may not be hurt but I'm not sure I've forgiven you yet.'

'Well I *am* sorry...' Alex raised her chin and met Francine's accusing gaze. '...but you can't sing when you're feeling like that.'

'Can't you?'

'You don't understand,' said Alex bitterly. 'Singing, when you feel so lost...it seems to exaggerate it all, to multiply every feeling you've got until you think you'll be crushed by them.' The plastic spoon in her fingers started to bend under the pressure of her fingers.

Francine took another mouthful of coffee, apparently unmoved.

'Look, I'm sorry if I've let you down,' said Alex fiercely.

'It's not me you've let down. It's yourself. Did it help?'

'Help?'

'The running away?'

'Yes,' said Alex defiantly. 'Yes, it did.' She thought for a moment, running the spoon around the foam on the top of her coffee. 'I think so, anyway.'

'Hm. Well I think you've been wasting precious time. When you're as old as me you'll value your time more.'

'Really Francine, if...'

'I was amazed at you. After all the work you'd put in...To be so single-minded for all those years and then risk throwing it all away. Still, I don't believe in looking back. So you want to get back on board do you?' Francine fidgeted her solid bulk to allow her access to the large handbag which hung on the side of the chair. She pulled out her diary and began to riffle through the pages, talking to herself. 'Of course it's been a long time so first of all we'll have to see how your voice is.'

'Francine, I'm really not sure.' Alex felt deflated suddenly and wondered why she'd arranged this. Had she really thought she was ready to perform again? She could feel herself shrinking inside with panic just at the sight of Francine's diary and all the events and commitments it implied.

Francine stopped turning pages and looked up.

'What do you mean?'

Alex met her eyes and then looked away.

'I'm not sure if I can do it again.' She hesitated. 'I think I've lost my nerve.'

Francine studied Alex's face closely. Then her eyes narrowed and she closed the diary with a snap.

'Look you're too old now to be behaving like a child,' she declared, leaning forwards and tapping one index finger peremptorily on the table between them. 'You never used to be like this – you were focussed. You're not the first person to lose someone, girl. You're letting your emotions rule your head, rule everything. Yes, it's partly those emotions which make you such a good singer but they have to be harnessed and used constructively, not left to run unchecked. You've got just a few short years left to you when you can sing at your best.' She paused and Alex was uneasily aware of people watching them. Francine resumed, uncaring. 'Now if I believed in a God, I'd say he made you to sing. But it doesn't come to you; you have to chase it, grasp it.' She clenched her liver-spotted hand into a fist till it shook with the tension. 'It's up to you. You sing or you don't sing; it's your choice. Simple as that. No-one could say it will be easy but I'm not here to jolly you along into it. Anyway I'm a busy woman.' She drank the remains of her coffee and put the mug down with a clunk onto the table. 'I've got things to do.' She picked up her bag, tossed the diary into it and stood up briskly, throwing her shawl across her shoulder. Then she fixed Alex with the look all her students had learnt to dread. 'You have to make some decisions for your life and stop drifting. And if you want any help from me with your voice, you know my number. But don't ring unless you're serious.'

*

Since soon after arriving in London, Alex had received a succession of voice and text messages on her phone from Theo. She had replied by text early on explaining that she was in London, she was fine and would be in touch soon. It was a holding tactic; she didn't want to talk to him yet. Like Simon, she'd found he had a way of persuading her and she needed space to think.

For a few days after meeting up with Francine, Alex abandoned jobs at the house and wandered round London, trying to see the way forward. She felt like one of Mick's migrating birds which gets blown off course and finds itself in unfamiliar territory. But she suspected that up to now she'd only been playing at living there. She'd been holding the place at arms length as if she thought it might pull her in if she got too close, and that wasn't going to help any decision-making. It was like trying to tell if an old pair of trousers still fitted by looking at them. So she tried to make an effort. She visited a succession of old familiar haunts and made apologetic contact with people she knew but had neglected. She even bought a ticket for a concert at the Barbican but left at the interval and chided herself for her weakness, vowing to do better next time.

But, whatever she did, she couldn't fool herself, it wasn't the same any more. It didn't feel like home. Perhaps I've been away too long, she thought, or maybe I've changed. She'd end up walking by the Thames but thinking of the Kella, so much smaller and more insignificant and yet so much more appealing. Then her mind would slip smoothly to the Grenloe and Mick and Susie and she would wonder what was happening on the reserve. And then of course there was Theo. She hadn't so much allowed herself to drift away from him as consciously run, the same way she'd run away from London when it had all become too difficult. *Wallowing in it,* Victoria had said. Maybe she was right after all. At the very least she now thought her behaviour betrayed some weakness of character and she was ashamed. The time had come to stop vacillating and to do something purposeful with her life.

She announced her decision to Erica a couple of days later.

'You're going back to Devon? Already?' Erica had just sent Ben to bed and poured two glasses of wine. It was obvious she had been expecting a nice cosy evening of chat, just the two of them. 'But you've only just come back.'

'I won't go straight away – it'll be a couple of days. I've got things to sort out.' Alex took the glass of wine Erica handed her and sat down on the sofa. She took a deep breath, let it out slowly and then said: 'I'm going to put the house up for sale.'

Erica was in the middle of drinking and nearly spilt her wine. She put the glass down with exaggerated care and then looked up.

'Oh Alex, are you sure?'

'Yes.' Alex affected more certainty than she felt. 'Simon's not here. You're here of course, and Ben, but you can come and see me often. I hope you will. Ben'd love it in Kellaford.' She shrugged. 'It was time to make a decision, to stop living a split life and I've decided to stay on down there.'

Erica picked up her wine again and drank a large mouthful with a frown. She swallowed, a little ostentatiously, Alex thought. Why was she taking it all on herself still? It occurred to Alex that the time was long overdue when Erica should stop feeling so responsible for her sister's happiness or, indeed, should consider that their lives needed to be so intrinsically and irrevocably linked.

'Is it because of Theo?' Erica blurted out. 'Are you going back for him?'

'Maybe. To be honest I don't know. I really like him. I don't know how far it will go but if I don't make a clean break from London and the house and all the memories, I'm not giving it a fair chance.'

'But you've not really tried it here…' Erica began, but Alex flashed her a warning look and she fell silent.

'I *have* tried it,' she protested, 'and I can't settle. I just can't see me living here again. Not at the moment anyway. I need a fresh start. Try to support me will you? It's not been an easy decision.'

For a moment Erica looked as though she would argue again but then she forced a smile and raised her glass.

'Here's to a fresh start then. I guess that's what we all need sometimes.'

Alex offered her a grateful smile and returned the toast.

'Thanks Ricky. Yes, I think maybe we do.'

Alex spent the next few days sorting through the house, contacting estate agents and her solicitors and steeling herself to get rid of the last of Simon's clothes and the less sentimental of his personal effects. She left keys with the agents, packed up the things she could fit in the car to take back and arranged to have her favourite bits of furniture sent on.

She'd been in Hampstead nearly a fortnight by the time she and Erica parted the following Saturday morning.

'Come for Christmas,' she entreated her sister and was pleased when Erica agreed. 'You can meet Theo. You'll like him. I'm sure you will. Everyone does.' She gave Ben a hug. 'And you'll love Devon. If the weather's any good, we'll go exploring.'

Alex drove away and headed west persuading herself that the flutter in her stomach owed more to excitement than fear at her decision.

Chapter 14

'Did it not occur to you that I might worry?' Theo said when Alex returned home. She'd rung him that same evening, anxious to hear his voice. The trip to London, the enforced absence, had put things into perspective. She had missed him. 'One bloody text to say you were all right and you'd be in touch. That was nearly two weeks ago. No answers to my calls or messages. Nothing.' His voice had an edge she hadn't heard before.

'You're cross,' she said. 'I can understand that. And I am sorry Theo. But I needed to get away and think it all through. I should have told you, explained or something. But I was so confused. Forgive me?'

'I thought we were so happy together. That night we spent together…' He paused and she could hear the emotion in his voice when he spoke again. '…it meant so much to me Alex. I'd hoped it would to you too.'

'It did Theo. But I think that's why I ran away. It was all happening too fast. I was scared.'

There was silence and she wondered if he was still angry but he sounded calmer when he spoke next.

'Alex, this isn't a casual thing for me; you do understand that don't you? But I don't want to get hurt either. Don't toy with me will you?' His voice dropped low. 'We need to cherish each other; cherish what we have together. It's been good so far but we could be so much more yet.' The softness of his voice in her ear was warm and tender. 'If you really care for me, promise me you won't run away like that again. Promise me you'll talk to me if you have worries or anything. There's nothing we can't work out together you know, you and I.'

And she'd promised and meant it, relieved to have made peace with him. The emptiness of the house in London, rendered more stark by the presence of Simon's things, had brought into focus how much she enjoyed Theo's company. She was determined to embrace the decision she'd made and, as Francine had put it, 'stop drifting'.

On the following Monday morning, keen to catch up with what was happening there, she walked down to the reserve.

'Hello stranger,' Mick said, appearing from the sheds at Susie's barked greeting. He looked her over for a minute with his usual inscrutable expression, and added: 'There are jobs to be done if you're stopping.'

Suppressing her perverse disappointment that he didn't appear to have missed her, she followed him round to the sheds to collect bags and secateurs and then they went harvesting seed heads from the reeds. He did it every year he said, so that he could raise new reed plants and expand the reed beds without having to buy them. Mick wore waders while Alex wore his wellingtons which were too big for her and slid up and down as she walked.

'You stick to the edge of the bed,' he told her, wading out a couple of feet. 'Right, you put the bag over the seed head and then pull it in tight round the stem…like this…before you cut it. Do a few then tip them into the drum over there. OK?'

For a while they worked silently to a background bird chorus of chirrups, warbles and trills. A woodpecker hammered at a tree somewhere nearby.

'I went back to London,' she said after a few minutes. 'I had some things to think through, to decide. That's why I haven't been down recently.' She glanced across at him but he was involved in what he was doing; it wasn't even clear if he'd heard her. She felt obscurely rattled by his disinterest. 'Or maybe you already knew? You always seem to know everything anyway,' she added tartly.

He straightened up then and looked at her, eyebrows raised.

'And did you?' he responded.

'Did I what?'

'Think things through and decide?'

'Yes.'

'Good.'

He bent over again and returned to his task.

'I'm going to sell my house in London. I'm going to live here, in Kellaford Bridge.'

'You make it sound like a warning.' He straightened up again with a rare grin on his face and she thought how much younger he looked when he smiled. 'Should we be scared?'

'Perhaps.' She grinned back at him and then became serious as she watched him, long after he'd bent over again, paddling slowly and silently along the shallow stretch of reed bed, apparently absorbed in his task. When she'd told Theo the previous day that she was selling the house in London he'd been thrilled, his pleasure obvious.

She didn't know what Mick thought. He probably didn't care. There again, why should he?

*

Alex's preparations for Christmas made the intervening two weeks pass quickly. Theo helped move some things round the house ready for the visitors, took her out to dinner a couple of times and brought the inevitable bottle of champagne to celebrate her move to Devon. He kissed her and hugged her but made no further sexual advances. She was both relieved and disappointed and aware of the contradiction. He's scared of frightening you away again, she told herself but, unsure of her own desires, felt unable to initiate love-making herself. But if he was happy, she told herself, what did it matter?

She became swept up in the preparations for Christmas, buying decorations and presents, wrapping paper and absurd amounts of food. She stood baking in the kitchen, made extra mince pies for the Christmas Fayre in the village, arranged for a Christmas tree to be delivered, and went out walking, looking for greenery to put round the rooms. She sent out cards, delivered a couple by hand and invited Liz round for lunch, pressing a gift on her before she left. 'Just something tiny to thank you for everything.' And the day before her family arrived for the holiday, she went back down to the reserve and had coffee with Mick and, as she was leaving, left carefully wrapped presents on the table for him and for Susie.

'Hell Alex, I don't do Christmas presents,' Mick said grumpily, frowning.

'I hope you're not going to insult me by refusing them,' she said shortly, offended. 'Just think of all those lunches you've given me. Anyway, it gave me pleasure to buy them. I'm sure Susie will appreciate hers at least.'

She slung her bag back over her shoulder and walked to the door, head high. He caught up with her there and lightly touched her arm.

'Alex?'

She turned, one hand on the door handle, and they stood, face to face.

'I didn't mean it like that. I was embarrassed. I meant I haven't got a present for you. Jesus, you go off like a bottle of pop sometimes. I'm sorry. I suppose I should have said thank you.'

'Don't be,' she said with a smile. 'Perhaps it was selfish of me. I didn't think. Of course I don't expect a present from you. But I'm determined to enjoy Christmas. I want everyone to enjoy Christmas.' She leaned forward and laid the touch of a kiss on his bristly cheek. 'Happy Christmas Mick.'

And she stepped through the door and away.

*

Erica and Ben arrived soon after three on Christmas Eve in Erica's 4 by 4, her only nod at rural life, which was filled with everything she could think of which could make their Christmas complete.

'Why did you bring so much food?' Alex complained when she saw it all being unloaded into the kitchen. 'I told you I'd already sorted all that.'

'I wasn't sure you remembered just how much Ben can eat,' puffed Erica, struggling in with yet more bags. She dumped them down and then laughed. 'Or me. Anyway I wanted to contribute.'

'Can I go and explore?' Ben asked as they went to get the last bags out of the car.

Erica looked around, unsure. It was a miserable, cloudy day and already it was going dark.

'I don't know. It looks a bit gloomy and there are no streetlights here you know.'

'Oh mum,' he groaned.

'He'll be fine if he doesn't go out of sight of the house,' said Alex, grinning.

'OK,' Erica agreed doubtfully, 'but don't go far.' Ben disappeared out of the door. 'It'll be dark soon,' she called to his retreating back.

Erica wandered through to the drawing room.

'Wow, big change since I was here last,' she called back into the kitchen. 'Huge improvement.'

Alex followed her in.

'Haven't you been busy?' Erica looked around appreciatively. 'Or was it Theo?'

'Both of us. But me mostly. Damn, the clock's stopped again. I've been so busy I hadn't noticed.' Alex walked across to the grandfather clock, opened the door and lightly tapped the face. 'And I thought I'd got it sorted,' she muttered to herself. 'That's the first time in ages.' She frowned, staring at the hands which read twenty-past eight.

'So when do we get to meet the mysterious Theo?' Erica asked with a lightness of tone which didn't quite cover the underlying tension in her voice.

Alex turned, forgetting the clock.

'He's coming for supper, the day after Boxing Day.'

'Good.' Erica saw the naked spruce in the corner of the room. 'You haven't decorated the tree then?'

'I thought Ben might like to do it but maybe he's grown out of all that.'

'He's growing up so fast it frightens me. In any case he'd probably complain that it should still be growing in the ground outside somewhere.'

'It's got roots,' Alex said defensively, reflecting that Mick would probably say the same thing. 'I can plant it outside afterwards.'

'Fine.' Erica dismissed the remark without further thought. 'We should do it between us later. It'll be fun: like old times.'

*

In general, Theo tried to devote Christmas Day to his mother; he went to church with her, laid the table for their dinner, got in her way in the kitchen and loved to watch her unwrapping her presents. But when he was in Kellaford Bridge for the festival he liked to spend the evening before in the Armada, drinking and exchanging jokes with the men at the bar. He assumed this year would be no exception. His relationship with Alex, so recently suffering stormy weather, appeared to have reached more stable waters, but they hadn't yet reached a stage where he was expected to be permanently available to her. On the contrary, her sister and nephew had come to stay for Christmas and Theo wasn't apparently wanted at Hillen Hall just yet; he was free.

But there was the small matter of Helen to organise. She had informed him, some three weeks previously, that her husband Bob planned to spend Christmas Eve in the pub as he had done the year before. He'd had a great time apparently. 'If it's anything like last year, he'll probably drink himself into oblivion,' she said, 'and be lucky if he even makes it home. Anyway, the point I'm making is that you'll be quite safe to come round.' Theo had tried to look interested but remained non-committal. That wasn't what he had in mind to do, nor was he happy about her starting to dictate the terms on which he saw her.

'Why don't you go to The Armada too?' he'd asked casually, running a finger round her ear lobe which drove her crazy and always turned her on. 'It's a good place to be on Christmas Eve. Great atmosphere.' He thought it would be quite amusing for them both to be there together with Bob looking on, none the wiser.

'God no,' she said abruptly, and he heard the fear in her voice. The same scenario had obviously crossed her mind. 'That's more of a man's pub really,' she added as an afterthought. 'I never feel comfortable there, especially in the winter when the tourists have gone.' She nuzzled up to him, running a hand over his chest. 'Anyway it's too good an opportunity to miss isn't it Theo? You will come won't you?' She must have felt his hesitation, the stiffening of his back as he'd backed away from being pinned down like that. She added, in a low, pleading voice: 'I'll wear another of those dresses if you bring me one.'

'We'll see,' he'd said, as if to a demanding child. 'I'm not sure I'll be able to get away.' He had no intention of going but then he relented. He wasn't ready to end the relationship yet so he wanted to keep her sweet. In any case he liked the idea of having a drink in The Armada with Bob Geaton, only to slip out and seduce his wife before returning to the pub to watch the gullible fool from the other end of the bar.

So it was just after eight when Theo left the pub. He'd kept a low profile and the place was heaving; he doubted he'd be missed for a while. The harbourmaster was propped up at the bar, already well down his second pint. Theo knocked briefly but firmly at Helen's back door and she opened it, breathless, just a couple of minutes later wearing a slinky knee-length dress.

'I can't stay long,' he said, glancing back down the yard and stepping into the doorway. 'Put the light off; there are people everywhere tonight.'

She kissed him and took him upstairs but she was unusually tense.

'What's the matter?' he asked.

'Nothing.' There was a noise in the street outside and she flicked a nervous glance towards the window.

'He's in the pub. Stop worrying.'

'I'm not worrying,' she protested, without conviction.

'So what is it?'

'He wanted me to go with him. When I said I had things to do here he said he might come back and get me later.'

Theo gave a dismissive shake of the head. 'I doubt it. Why would he do that?'

Helen hesitated and ran a hand along the back of the sofa. She raised anxious eyes to his face.

'He said some of the men had been teasing him saying they never see us out together. And the last few days he's been asking odd questions and looking around. I think maybe he suspects something.'

Theo laughed. 'Oh stop worrying. He's not that smart.'

'He's not stupid Theo.'

'Here,' he said. 'I brought you a present.'

He handed her a long thin box, a bottle of perfume, casually wrapped in gaudy paper. Helen immediately disappeared into the bedroom and brought one back for him, thin and flat, expensively covered in gilt paper and finished with a ribbon rosette.

'Sorry, it's a bit crumpled,' she said. 'It's been buried at the back of my wardrobe.'

He thanked her but threw it down on the sofa unopened and reached forward to pull her to him. He began to kiss her urgently, one hand holding her to him while the other ran down the curve of her buttock and then round her hip to stroke inwards along the scoop of her groin. Helen groaned and Theo released her, turned her round and slowly undid the zip down her back. He'd just reached his hand inside the dress and worked it round to the front, caressing down the soft flesh of her rounded belly, when they both heard heavy footsteps on the street outside stop outside the gallery. Helen shrugged herself away from Theo's probing fingers and ran to the window, parting the curtains a crack and peering down to the street.

'Oh God,' she breathed. 'He's back.'

She immediately began adjusting her dress while Theo picked his present up from the sofa, ran across the room and stepped lightly down the stairs into the back of the gallery. He kept to the back wall away from the security lights and slid through the door into the kitchenette, just as Bob, fumbling with his key in the front lock, managed to get the door open.

'Helen,' he called thickly. 'I'm back.' Theo heard him tread heavily across the gallery to the stairs and then call up as he climbed: 'It's a great atmosphere at The Armada tonight. All lit up and decorated and everyone's there. I think you should come. You'd like it.' Theo waited until Bob was at the top and then slowly moved himself across the kitchenette to the back door and turned the key as silently as he could. He eased the door open and let himself out into the dark. The door clicked as he closed it to and he slipped quickly up the garden path to the rear gate just as Bob Geaton's voice spilled out of an open window.

'What the hell was that? Helen? What was that downstairs?'

Theo was out of the back garden gate and the other side of the wall by the time he heard the back door open and Bob's voice again.

'This door wasn't locked Helen,' he shouted up. 'Did you know that?'

'Why would I know? I must have forgotten to lock it. I do have a lot on my mind too you know.'

Theo smiled to himself as he carefully moved away, keeping to the shadows, admiring the righteous indignation in her voice. He'd almost have believed her himself. He stopped in a dark place at the back of one of the boatyards and peeled the paper off the cashmere scarf she'd given him. He glanced around to check there was no-one nearby and crossed the back of the car park to a bin. He threw the scarf and the paper inside and then made his way back towards The Armada, the adrenaline coursing threw his system still making his pulse race with excitement. He pushed his way to the bar and ordered a pint.

*

'I can't believe you didn't tell me when you came to London. We spent so much time together and yet you never said anything about it.'

Alex sighed. She'd just told Erica that she'd buried Simon's ashes and the reaction had proved why she hadn't had the courage to mention it before. In any case, Erica and Simon had never been exactly close.

'Look, I'm sorry if you're offended but you were there for the cremation service. This time I wanted to do it alone.'

There was a strained pause before Erica replied in a small voice; 'Well I can see that but I think you might have said.'

Ben was in bed and Erica and Alex were finishing decorating the Christmas tree in the drawing room. It was nearly midnight and they were nearing the end of a bottle of wine. Until Erica had gone up to Alex's room to get some presents, they'd worked in companionable silence, hanging baubles and chocolate novelties, spreading tinsel and throwing icicles over the tree with childish abandon. But on her return she'd immediately asked about the missing casket.

'Can we at least go to see where he's buried?' she said now.

'Of course, if you want. But we have to fit it in with the tides so that we can cross the river when the water's not too high. We'll keep an eye on the weather and plan round it. I had thought Ben might like to go over that way anyway.' She stepped back from the tree to consider it. 'I think that'll do don't you? Lets put the presents round now and call it a day.'

They finished up and sat down with the last of the wine split between them.

'So I'm going to get to meet your Theo at last,' remarked Erica.

'He's not *my* Theo.'

'No? You're sure?' she teased. 'It's OK Alex, I'm not going to make a big thing out of it. Actually I'm getting really curious to meet him. What's he like?'

Alex looked at Erica suspiciously but her sister looked genuinely interested.

'Well…he talks too much,' she said with a grin. 'But it's usually interesting. He's fun.' She paused, considering. 'You know he looks like Simon and some of his mannerisms are the same too but his passions are very different: he loves boats and the sea. And he's more physical…'

'Oooh.'

'No, not like that. I mean he's not a sitting down sort of person. He likes to be up and doing.'

'Is he musical?'

Alex smiled.

'Not really. And he prefers pop music to classical. Actually,' she confided, 'he can hardly hold a tune.'

'And you like him.' It was a statement more than a question.

'And I like him.'

'So why isn't he coming for dinner tomorrow?'

'Because I didn't ask him. Anyway he wants to have dinner with his mother because she's alone and I didn't want to invite her here.'

'You didn't want to invite his mother? Why, what's *she* like?'

Alex shrugged.

'She's all right.'

'What does that mean: *all right*? You don't like her?'

'I didn't say that.' Alex sipped her wine. 'She's very distant – well sometimes she is. Sometimes she's almost too friendly. I can't make her out.'

Erica was looking at her disbelievingly.

'OK, OK, she's really odd if you must know,' Alex added with a grin and they both laughed. 'The problem is she likes her whisky too much if you ask me.'

'Really?'

'Yes, but don't tell Theo I said so,' Alex added quickly. 'He doesn't talk about it. Anyway, as far as Christmas is concerned I wanted it to be just the three of us. And inviting them both over would make the whole thing too…significant.'

They both fell silent and Erica sighed and settled herself more comfortably into the chair. She looked round the room, at the newly decorated walls, the billowing curtains, and the fire burning brightly in the grate.

'This room looks great. I'm beginning to understand why you might like it here.' She paused and appeared to consider whether to say anything else, before adding: 'And you do seem happier at last.'

Alex nodded. 'I am. Now will you stop fretting over me?'

'When I've seen Theo.'

Alex smiled and then hesitated. 'I'm sorry Ricky for…you know…all those things I said back in July. I was cruel and I didn't mean to be. I was…I don't know…' She shook her head, unable to explain how she had felt. 'Really there's no excuse. Forgive me? Anyway I *am* happier now, so please don't worry over me so much.'

Erica nodded, looking sheepish.

'I'm sorry too. I said some terrible stuff as well. I don't know what got into us. But I've been…' She shrugged and forced a smile. 'Oh never mind. It's nice to be together again. Let's just put it all behind us shall we?'

'Sure.'

They both drank some wine, looking thoughtful.

'By the way,' said Erica, 'I know you've had a lot of work done on the house but is there still some problem in your room?'

Alex frowned. 'What do you mean?'

'When I went up there just now it was incredibly cold. I checked the radiator and it was hot but in one place I stood it was icy. I wondered if there's something wrong with the window or something. Why are you looking at me like that?'

Chapter 15

For years Christmas Day for Mick had been the same as any other day; Susie didn't know the difference, no more did the birds or the hens or any other living creature he was likely to meet that day. But this year Alex's present still sat where she'd put it on the table, beautifully wrapped in shiny paper, tied with a red ribbon and finished with a bow. He passed it several times a day, eyed it up, wondered about it. He'd picked it up once or twice, prodded it, turned it over and put it down again. It was something in a box, that much was obvious. But what was she thinking, buying him a present?

He tried to ignore it and got on with his chores. When he'd finished, he made himself a bigger lunch than usual, cleared up, let Susie in and poured himself a beer. He handed Susie her present and smiled as she pulled the paper off with her teeth and retreated to a corner with the huge bone-shaped treat. Then he picked up his own parcel and slowly pulled the paper off to reveal a smart new pair of binoculars.

Pulling them out of the box, he turned them over, took the lens caps off and held them up to his eyes, focussing them at places around the room. Then he got up and walked to the window and directed them outside. They were good, sharp lenses, quality; expensive he guessed. He threw himself down into the chair and held them on his lap while he finished his beer, thinking. Susie came to lie beside his chair and he stretched a hand down to stroke her silky head.

He got up and put some music on then poured himself another beer. Back in his chair, he kept the binoculars on his lap and studied the compact disc case. It was a recording he'd bought the previous week, made some four years previously, of Schubert songs by Alexandra Munroe. He examined the list of contents and then flipped it back to stare at the photograph on the front. It was unmistakeably her and yet not the Alex he knew: a little fuller in the face, immaculately made up and groomed, her long hair cleverly coiled and fastened up. Her blue eyes looked directly at the camera, her lips bearing just the suspicion of an amused curl at the corners. He recognised the gaze but he preferred her when she was dressed in jeans, her hair loosely plaited, mud on her face where she'd pushed the errant strand out of her eyes.

He put the case down, drank some beer, and then leaned his head back and closed his eyes. Her voice was magical: spine-tinglingly clear and yet warm and vibrant. It wasn't his kind of music but he could listen to her all day. It sounded so effortless, so pure. You stupid, stupid girl, he thought. What are you doing holing yourself up here with me? A voice like that ought to be out there, being heard.

But she's not with you, his inner voice replied. She's with Theo Hellyon.

His eyes snapped open and he sat forward restlessly, picking up his beer. He downed the remains in one and got up to get another but Susie began to bark, a deep, warning sound, and Mick went cautiously across to the window and peered round the edge of the curtain. His view was obscured by rainwater streaming down the glass. He went to the door and opened it, releasing Susie who threw herself down the steps. By the time he got out himself she'd circled the intruder and was barking at him excitedly. It was Harry Downes, the old man who lived at the end of Harbour Row with his wife Minna. Mick sometimes saw them walking together, in the village or along the beach. Minna was one of the few people who made eye contact with him and exchanged a greeting while Harry sometimes spoke and sometimes looked right through him. Now here he was, wandering up to his door. After years of solitude, Mick kept having visitors.

'Susie. Quiet,' he commanded and she fell silent, panting. 'Hello Harry. What are you doing here? You're a long way from home. You'll get soaked out there. You'd better come in.'

*

For Alex, Christmas didn't work out the way she'd planned. Erica fell ill. There had been a stomach bug going round work apparently, but she'd come away thinking she'd escaped. Instead, she was running a temperature, had spent half the previous night in the bathroom and couldn't get out of bed Christmas morning.

'Better not come too close,' she said to Alex who kept trying to help. 'I'll be OK.' She rolled on her side, eyes closing. 'I'm really sorry to mess everything up like this. I just need to sleep. Leave me to it and go and enjoy yourselves.'

Back downstairs, Alex made an effort for Ben, admired his presents, helped him find somewhere to set up his new microscope – a gift from Erica – and fielded a phone call from Victoria who was off on a cruise somewhere, saying as little as possible before handing the phone on to Ben. She and Ben ate dinner together - turkey for her, nut roast for him - at the little table in the snug while watching a documentary on dolphins on the television.

In the afternoon, after checking on Erica, they went down to Longcombe beach. Alex collected shells and Ben skimmed stones and they both scrambled over rocks and peered into pools for signs of life. Further up the beach they found a dead crab which Ben insisted on taking back to examine under his new microscope. By the evening Erica was less giddy and drank a little but stayed in bed while Alex and Ben watched Toy Story 2 and the Doctor Who special, eating tomato sandwiches and Christmas cake.

On Boxing Day, Erica was better but still couldn't face getting up. In desperation to do something with the day which she knew Ben would think special, Alex cut some meat off one of the turkey legs and wrapped it in foil, told Ben to wear something warm and took him down to the reserve, explaining all about the Grenloe and its wildlife as they cut across the fields. It wasn't until they reached the clearing that the first shadow of doubt crossed her mind and she wondered if she was doing the right thing, but she shrugged it off as Susie came to greet them, sure that Mick wouldn't object to her own nephew visiting. And her decision felt vindicated when she saw how much pleasure Ben was already getting from playing with Susie; he'd always wanted a dog.

But it was obvious from Mick's expression when he first saw them that he wasn't happy. Alex he treated stonily as if she were someone he once knew but had fallen out with. For Ben he raised a taut smile and made an effort to be pleasant, explaining the nature of the place and then taking him to the hide and indicating what sorts of things to look for. 'Your aunt knows all about it herself anyway,' he said, flicking her a baleful look, 'so she should be able to answer your questions. Excuse me, I've got things to do.' Alex watched him go, frustrated and cross. She would have preferred frank annoyance to this forbidding resentment; at least she would have had a chance to argue the point.

A few minutes later, she left Ben staring out over the water and went to look for Mick. He was in the shed filling feeders with seed.

'What's the matter?' she demanded.

'What do you think's the matter?'

'Because I didn't ask you before I brought him?'

'Because you promised you wouldn't tell anyone you came here or anything about it. Now you're doing guided tours.'

'But he's my nephew, for God's sake, not someone I dragged in off the street. And he's obsessed with wildlife. He'll love it here.'

'I've got nothing against the boy. It's you. I knew when I let you come that this would happen.'

'You're being absurd. What difference does it make…?'

'Aunt Alex?' Ben's voice drifted through to them. He'd returned to the clearing. 'Aunt Alex?'

'I'm through here Ben.'

'I've seen a bird with red legs,' he said, joining them. He hesitated, glancing between them uneasily, a light frown puckering his brow. 'Can you come and tell me what it is?' he asked her.

Alex gave him a smile which she hoped suggested calm reassurance. 'I'll try. I should have brought my book.' She waited for Mick to offer one of his own from the carriage but he said nothing and she began to follow Ben. She turned at the door, leaving him to go on ahead. 'I brought some turkey for Susie,' she said to Mick in a chill voice. 'Is it OK to give it to her?'

Ben was barely out of earshot when Mick replied.

'Would it make any difference if I said not?'

*

That evening, Erica finally got up and managed to eat a little. At the sight of her sister struggling to eat a boiled egg and a piece of bread, Alex suggested putting off Theo's visit for the following day but Erica wouldn't hear of it, insisting she'd be fine. 'I want to meet him,' she said indignantly. 'Don't you dare stop him coming.' Then she wanted to know what they'd been doing and where they'd gone. Alex was relieved. This was more normal; she was obviously getting better.

'A nature reserve?' Erica said, when Ben told her all about it. She looked at Alex with a puzzled expression. 'You never said anything about a nature reserve before.'

'It's not a public place. The man who owns it keeps it private. He likes it that way.'

'But you've been there before?'

'Now and then.'

'Aunt Alex knows it really well,' said Ben, and then glanced at her suggesting he'd realised too late that he might have said the wrong thing. He quickly added, with a note of admiration: 'I didn't know she knew so much about wildlife. Really cool.'

Erica's eyebrows nearly hit her hairline.

'Neither did I. So what's he like, this man? What's his name?'

‘Mick Fenby.’ Alex affected disinterest to stem her sister’s rising curiosity. ‘The locals call him The Birdman because he’s obsessed with birds.’

‘Yes, but what’s he like?’ Erica looked at Ben.

Ben glanced at Alex again. ‘Well he’s really old,’ he said. ‘He’s got a grey beard and he’s a bit grumpy. Naturalists often are,’ he added sagely. ‘They spend a lot of time alone. It’s a great place and he said we can go back. Is that OK mum?’

‘We’ll see.’

‘Look Ben,’ said Alex. ‘I’d rather you didn’t go telling people about the reserve. Mr Fenby likes to keep the place a secret. He doesn’t want people just turning up there.’ Even as she spoke she realised the futility of her words. It was as if she’d wilfully drilled a hole in a dam and then belatedly realised the mistake and was now pushing her finger to the hole to keep the water back.

‘But he did say we could go back.’

This was true. As they were leaving, Ben had asked if they could go again and Mick had agreed with what she had considered to be thinly-veiled irritation and reluctance. Alex was relieved that Ben didn’t appear to have noticed.

‘Yes, but that was just us,’ she said, ‘because you were so keen. He wouldn’t want it to get out that people visit. Too many people would disturb the birds.’

Ben nodded, weighing the argument over.

‘OK.’ He turned to look at Erica. ‘The dog there was great mum…a collie…really well-behaved. Do you think I could have one like that? She’d be no trouble.’

Erica gave a long-suffering sigh.

‘No Ben, we’ve been through this a thousand times.’

When Ben left the room a few minutes later, Erica came back to the subject.

'So how come you know this old guy on the nature reserve if he's so private?'

'I wandered in there by chance one day. It's no great mystery Erica. I'm not sure I could say that I really knew him.'

And when she thought about it later, Alex reflected that, in many ways, it was the literal truth.

*

But Ben didn't go back to the reserve. The next day Erica had made a big improvement and she wanted to go out so Alex took them in the car for a drive along the coast. They stayed out for a light lunch and then went home to prepare for Theo's visit.

He arrived bearing gifts as he so often had before. Alex was used to this; it would be flowers or a gift-wrapped present, or Belgian chocolates or of course champagne. 'You spend far too much on me,' she'd complained once. 'Hey, I'm well paid, I can afford it,' he'd replied. '*And* I like to.' This time he brought Christmas presents: perfume for Erica, an interactive computer football game for Ben and, for Alex, a stunning necklace of multi-coloured semi-precious stones intermingled with tiny drops of gold. She was both pleased and embarrassed and purposely avoided catching Erica's eye. And there was the inevitable champagne.

He also brought with him a buzz of energy which their Christmas had so far been lacking. Erica had taken ages getting ready and was clearly flattered when he immediately complimented her on her dress. He showed concern at her recent illness and was sympathetic to her ruined Christmas; her cheeks began to look rosier than they had for days.

The meal went well and Alex started to relax. The much anticipated – and dreaded - meeting between Theo and Erica was working out all right. Afterwards, Erica suggested they played Monopoly and Theo opened the champagne.

'So your mum's obviously been too ill to do anything much so what have you been doing?' Theo asked Ben, sitting back, having just bought Regent Street. 'It's your first visit, right?'

'Yes,' said Ben, watching his mother take her turn and land on Piccadilly. 'That's mine,' he said quickly, checking to see how much rent she owed him.

'Weather's been a bit mixed,' Theo remarked. 'Still I hope you've been down to the sea.'

Ben was busy with his turn. Alex glanced at him uneasily. All those evasions she'd made to Theo to hide her knowledge of the reserve and Mick Fenby danced through her mind. And when she'd taken Ben down to the Grenloe, hadn't it occurred to her that the subject was bound to come up tonight? How stupid was that? What was Theo going to think? You're blowing it out of all proportion, she told herself without conviction. It doesn't really matter either way; he'll understand. But the thoughts gave her no comfort and she willed Ben to say nothing.

'We went to the beach on Christmas Day,' she said, wondering if her voice sounded as odd to everyone else as it did to her. 'It dried up in the afternoon. It was quite nice down there.'

Ben moved his counter and passed the drum with the dice in to Alex.

‘Then yesterday we went to the nature reserve.’ There was silence and Ben frowned and looked towards his aunt. ‘I’m sorry Aunt Alex. But it was all right to tell Theo wasn’t it?’

Theo frowned and looked at Alex, then at Ben and then back at Alex.

‘The nature reserve? What nature reserve? Tell me what?’ he asked with a strained laugh.

Ben still looked at Alex, waiting for her reply.

‘Of course,’ she said, giving him a quick, brittle smile.

‘We called at the nature reserve down by the river,’ Ben went on. ‘It was great. There’s a huge reed bed there and the man who looks after it showed me round. All sorts of unusual birds visit there. I’m going to be a naturalist you see so I’m really interested.’ No-one said anything and Ben looked uneasily at the adults round the table, then abruptly stopped talking.

‘What? You want to be like David Attenborough and talk all the time as if you’ve lost your voice?’ joked Theo and proceeded to mimic his breathy, sotto voce speech pretending he was describing an elephant in the bush. The atmosphere broke a little and Erica and Ben laughed. ‘But still I didn’t know we had a reserve as such in Kellaford Bridge.’ Theo looked at Alex and she flushed.

‘Down on the Grenloe,’ she said. ‘It’s not a proper reserve really. Just a quiet place where the birds congregate.’

‘Fancy,’ said Theo. ‘And to think I never knew. I thought it was just wild down there.’ He gave Alex another penetrating look and then took the tumbler with the dice.

It was after eleven when Theo left and Ben, tired and quiet, went to bed.

Back in the drawing room, the last of the wood burning in the hearth, Erica threw herself down on the sofa.

'I've only just realised,' she said. 'I've been trying to place him all evening. I was sure I'd seen him before. He was that guy I saw fleetingly at the funeral, remember?'

'Is he?' remarked Alex without apparent interest, picking up the poker.

'But you are a dark horse,' Erica continued with an arch smile. 'You didn't quite conjure up for me just how charming he was. Good-looking and charming; a fatal combination.'

'Yes.' Alex poked lugubriously at the remaining wood sending sparks shooting out to be sucked up the chimney. 'Isn't he?'

'Oh yes. To be honest, if I hadn't seen him with my own two eyes, I've have thought he was too good to be true.' She flashed Alex a look. 'I didn't believe you, you know? About him being like Simon. To be honest I thought you just *wanted* him to be. But you're right, the resemblance is striking in some ways: mannerisms, tone of voice…' Her voice trailed off and she forced a smile. 'It's rather weird actually.'

Chapter 16

Erica and Ben left on the thirtieth of December and Hillen Hall gaped without them, suddenly echoing and vast. Erica's recovery had been brisk in the end and they'd gone out every day, making up for lost time. They didn't visit Simon's grave however; one look at the water coursing round the stepping stones had changed Erica's mind. But, despite her illness, it had been a good visit. Alex thought normal relations between them had been resumed at last and hoped the friction over Theo was finally at an end.

To mitigate her despondency at their departure, Alex turned her attention to the New Year's fancy dress party at The Armada. Theo had invited her to it before he'd left that night after the meal.

'Fancy dress?' she'd queried as he stood outside the back door, his face half in shadow, and she'd been immediately unsure. 'What sort of fancy dress?' she asked.

'The theme's pirates,' Theo said with a flatness of tone she hadn't heard before. 'Will you come?'

'Of course,' she'd responded, trying to sound keener than she felt. She'd been expecting him to say something more pointed about the mysterious nature reserve and why she had never mentioned it but Erica was in the kitchen behind her, moving around, clearing things away. It wasn't easy to talk. Now the issue had been left untouched between them and she didn't know how to bring it up, whether even she *should* bring it up. Maybe that would just make it all appear more important than it was.

The pub was full for the party though Alex knew less than half the people there. She'd made an effort, shopping specially to make up an outfit. She wore tight cropped trousers and a full sleeved low-cut blouse, a long red and white scarf tied round her waist and high boots to finish the look. Theo's brown chest was exposed by a shirt slashed to the waist and his muscular legs showed through tight, fraying jeans. A piece of cloth was tied round his hair and somewhere – she guessed he'd done this before - he'd found an eye patch. He appeared to know everyone and all evening, to her ears, his bonhomie and laughter sounded unusually forced. She noticed that his way of speaking changed too, his public school accent modified to a soft Devon burr. Alex, however, felt uncomfortable and out of place. She had always felt awkward at big parties whereas Simon, given the right mix of people, had always been able to circulate for hours. She tried chatting to a few acquaintances but the music was loud and conversation difficult.

Walking back up the hill in the early hours of the morning, Theo was short, morose and sullen. He'd been much the same before the party. Only in the pub had he affected attentiveness to her. Back at the Hall, Alex let Theo into the kitchen first and then flicked the lights on, closed the door and leant her back against it.

'So what's the matter?' she asked crisply.

Theo, fingering the virginal New Year's calendar she had ready on the wall, had his back to her.

'Matter?' he said, turning. 'What do you mean?'

'You've been acting odd all evening. Is this about the reserve?'

'If you ask the question you must know why I'm upset.'

'I don't *know* why you're upset. I'm guessing. But if that's what it is, you're not being fair.'

'*I'm* not being fair.' He paced the length of the kitchen and turned at the end again to look at her. His expression suggested sadness, his eyes glinted with a mixture of anger and hurt. 'Why didn't you tell me you'd been seeing that man on the Grenloe?'

'I haven't been *seeing that man.* It's not like that. I've just been down to visit the reserve.'

'First I've heard of it being called a reserve. I thought the guy was just a gypsy, living in a filthy railway carriage.'

'He does live in a railway carriage. He's not a gypsy though.' She turned away. She had a sudden memory of Simon cross-questioning her about where she'd been one night when he'd come back unexpectedly from a cancelled talk. She'd been asked out at short notice to a friend's and wasn't there when he got back. Simon always liked to know where she was though it never occurred to him to account for all his own movements. At first flattered by the concern and affection it suggested, over the years it had begun to make her cross. It made her cross now; she didn't press Theo about everything he did. 'I suppose you could say he's a friend,' she said now firmly, lifting her head and turning back to look at him.

'A friend? And yet you never mentioned him to me.' A light of comprehension suddenly glowed in his eyes. 'He's the chap carves those bloody birds in the gallery, isn't he? That's why you like them so much.'

'No. I mean he does carve them but that's not why I like them.'

'So how old is this guy?'

'*I* don't know. I've never asked him. It's not important. Why did you wait till now to ask me all this?'

'It didn't seem an appropriate conversation to have in front of your nephew,' he remarked sourly. 'In any case I was waiting for you to tell me yourself. And I didn't want to spoil this evening. Though for all the pleasure I got out of it I might as well have asked in the first place. I'm beginning to see that I've been a fool over you while you've been running after another man.'

'Oh for God's sake, Theo, it's not like that. I've not been *running after* anyone.' She paused, trying to suppress her anger. 'I've only been there a few times, on the reserve. I've just watched the birds, helped him with a couple of jobs. It all happened by accident and it did me good to just get away, to be somewhere completely different. Don't you see?'

'Just you and him, alone there. Yes, I think I do see Alex.'

'No, no.' She thumped the nearest worktop in frustration. 'You're being ridiculous and making it into something it's not.' She took a deep breath and exhaled slowly, stretching out a hand towards him, fingers spread as if holding back something pressing in on her. 'Look, I'm sorry I didn't tell you but I didn't do it intentionally…Well I did, because Mick – that's the guy that runs the place – asked me not to tell anyone. He doesn't like visitors and likes to keep the place quiet. I didn't mean anything by it. I took Ben there because I knew he'd love it. Simple as that.'

Theo looked at her fiercely as if trying to look inside her brain.

'Really?'

'Yes really.'

'And this Mick…what's his name?'

'Fenby.'

'He means nothing to you?'

'Of course not. I told you: he's just a friend…sort of. I don't really know anything about him.'

He suddenly strode across the kitchen and wrapped his arms around her and hugged her hard and long.

'Oh Alex, don't ever keep anything like that from me again. I've been tortured, thinking I'd lost you.'

She leant her head against his chest and closed her eyes with a sense of relief. But she found herself wondering what this relationship she had with Theo was exactly, a relationship from which he seemed to expect so much. She'd been on the point of asserting that it was all about trust and clearly he didn't trust her. But that suggested that she was tied to him in some way, that she had made some longstanding commitment to him, and she suppressed the remark. Whilst she had no desire to deceive him, she wasn't sure she wanted to be fixed in that way yet. She wanted to be with him but it had all happened so quickly; it had too much momentum. Should she try to explain that to him, she wondered? But by doing that, wasn't there a risk that she would merely intensify their relationship all the more, like using water to try to quench burning oil? She bit back the words, certain the whole thing would blow over.

*

'Ten days initially but the trip might be extended,' Theo told Alex before leaving her. 'It depends on how well it goes.

They've taken an option to run on for a further ten days. The yard's quiet so Patrick's not fussed.' He'd been very careful in his choice of words, not wanting her to question what he was doing or where he was going. The crewing job was true enough; only the timescale was a fabrication. He knew he'd be back in Britain well inside the fortnight. 'The Caribbean'll be lovely at the moment,' he continued, 'but I'd rather stay here with you.' It was the beginning of the second week of January and he'd kissed her goodbye while she still lay half asleep, the second time he'd shared her bed since their New Year spat.

Back at The Lodge, throwing clothes and personal necessities in bags with the speed and assurance of someone who'd done it often enough to make thought unnecessary, he wondered how far his relationship with Alex had progressed since her return from London before Christmas. *Had* it progressed? He wasn't sure. They had slept together again but it was he who had initiated their love-making not her, and though she'd responded, he felt her commitment was still uncertain. Despite his concern to avoid her questioning, it occurred to him that she actually displayed little curiosity about his movements and, paradoxically, he found that worrying. Previous girlfriends – and certainly Helen – liked to try to pin him down. Alex appeared happy in his company and she was affectionate but not effusive. He'd persuaded himself that she was falling in love with him or at least that she wanted to think she was. What her true feelings were was anyone's guess. She'd never appeared jealous of time he spent away from her. And then there'd been that row. What significance had that had?

The news that she'd been visiting the man on the Grenloe had come as a shock. But for the innocence of the boy he might never have known anything about it and that worried him. It wasn't so much that he thought that she was having any kind of affair with the man – he'd seen the Birdman a couple of times skulking through the village and the idea was laughable - but that she'd consciously not told him about her visits. He'd thought Alex easy to read, open, that she wore her heart on her sleeve, but now he'd seen a side to her character which made him less certain.

And he wasn't sure now whether he'd played it right with his tight-lipped anger and frosty indignation. He'd sensed that, even in her apology and relief at their reconciliation, she still held something back. It was as though she were protecting the Birdman in some way, as though she cared what people thought of him. It was both extraordinary and worrying. Who was this Mick Fenby anyway? In the early hours of New Year's Day, feigning genuine interest as well as a lover's concern, Theo had asked Alex all about the reserve and the man who ran it, what happened there and what she did. Her answers had given him a picture of the place but not the man. Without wishing to make a big issue out of it, he'd suggested to her that she would be wiser not to visit the reserve if she knew so little about the Birdman but she'd dismissed the idea without apparently giving it any thought. He'd even detected an obstinacy in her response suggesting that the more he pursued it, the less likely she would be to heed him and so he'd backed off.

The following week he'd made a few discreet enquiries in the village but it seemed the guy had been around for years without anyone really registering much about him. Nobody appeared to either care or to want to know who he was or where he came from. But Theo cared and when he got back from his trip he was going to spend a bit of time finding out.

He knew he had a short window of opportunity to nail this relationship with Alex and time was passing all too quickly. And he wasn't prepared to let other friendships – whatever form they took – put his plans at risk.

Chapter 17

The first week of January had been unseasonably warm and wet. Then just as suddenly as it had started, the rain stopped, the thermometer fell and Kellaford Bridge succumbed to rare sub-zero night-time temperatures. For several mornings in succession the thin winter sun rose over a frosted landscape and glinted off trees made white with frozen raindrops. Beyond the harbour and the sweep of the Dancing Bears, the sea twinkled like diamonds. Inland there were heavy falls of snow. When Mick turned the radio on he heard of people being stuck in their cars on the A38, children rescued from a school trip on Dartmoor and shops running out of food because there'd been no deliveries. *A normal winter at last,* the radio presenter declared. *Global warming? It's just a cycle we've been going through. I always thought there was no need to panic.*

Mick turned the radio off in disgust. Next week the temperature would probably swing up ten or fifteen degrees, the wind would howl and in some sleepy suburb somewhere there'd be a tornado. 'There's none so blind as them that will not see,' his mother used to say. He'd laugh but he found it all rather depressing. *In a few years' time we must cut our carbon emissions*, the politicians kept saying, affecting concern, as if they were in a charity relay race, holding a flaming baton which they were determined to pass on before it burnt them.

He'd had a similar conversation with Minna Downes just recently. It seemed she was a sort of latter day 'wise woman', obsessed with the seasons and making home made remedies. When he'd taken Harry back home on Christmas Day, Minna, grateful and relieved, had invited him in. Feeling unusually keen for company that afternoon, he'd surprised himself and agreed, joining them in their tiny two up, two down house for tea and sponge cake. Before he left, seeing him with a cut on his arm, Minna had thrust a jar of calendula cream on him, a mix of her own concoction. Given the barely-disguised poverty of the house, he'd found their hospitality touching. The next day, late in the afternoon when the sun had gone down and everyone was back inside with the curtains drawn, he pulled a trailer of logs and kindling round to their yard and then unloaded and stacked them. It had created a bond of sorts and he'd seen them again since, checking they were all right in the cold weather, moving wood inside, talking to Harry to divert him a little. Harry Downes was obviously ill and Minna, though she masked it as best she could, was struggling to cope. It was a novelty to find someone in a worse condition than himself whom he was in a position to help. He found it humbling and grasped the opportunity with wary enthusiasm.

Now, after several days of freezing weather, the ground had become solid and areas of still water disappeared under a thin layer of ice. Mick went round gently breaking the parts he could easily reach and then took a sack full of empty feeders back to the shed to refill with seeds and nuts, his cold hands clothed in fraying fingerless gloves. Desperate for food, the birds were emptying them faster than he could fill them.

He'd been doing the same thing when Alex had turned up a couple of days before, wearing a heavy coat, thick boots and a soft-brimmed fleecy hat. After his reaction to her visit on Boxing Day, and his clear objection to the presence of the boy, he'd wondered if he'd finally gone too far. Her obvious attachment to the boy had perhaps proved the tipping point. It was clear she'd been offended and upset and after she'd gone it had brought him up short. He found himself thinking back over the time he'd known her and all the time they had spent together. He'd be fooling himself if he didn't admit that he'd be gutted if he didn't see her again. But why, he couldn't help asking himself, would she bother to keep coming? He saw himself suddenly as she must see him and the impression shocked him. What had he become? Fear, resentment and bitterness had made him both cynical and irrationally defensive. Why she had ever visited more than once was a mystery to him. So she'd told her nephew about the place and brought him to see it. So what? Maybe enough years had passed now anyway; perhaps it was all behind him and it was time for a fresh start. And then he'd promised himself that, if she did come back, he simply wouldn't mention the Boxing Day thing; he would behave as though it had never happened and that it wasn't important; he would show he didn't mind.

So when Susie's ears pricked and she barked and then ran whining from the shed, he tried to look casual. Alex found him there a couple of minutes later.

'Happy New Year,' she'd said, guardedly, as she walked into the shed.

He glanced round at her, gave her a smile and returned his attention to filling a feeder.

‘Same to you…and thanks for the binoculars, by the way. I forgot to say when you came before.’

Alex bent over to stroke Susie’s head and run a finger behind her ears; Susie loved that. ‘My sister was ill over Christmas,’ she said, still bending over the dog. She straightened up suddenly and he could feel her eyes drilling into the side of his head. ‘I would have told you on Boxing Day but you never gave me a chance to explain. I’m sorry that...’

‘Is your sister better?’ He turned briefly and saw her frown at the unexpected question.

‘Yes…thank you. Much. By the next day she began to improve quite quickly. And fortunately, whatever it was, she didn’t pass it on to Ben or me.’

Mick nodded.

‘Smart boy, Ben. Close are you?’

‘Yes…yes. We get on really well.’

‘Good. How old is he?’

‘Eleven.’

‘Interesting age.’

He turned again to look at her properly and smiled.

‘Are you all right Mick?’ she asked, frowning.

A deep, booming call echoed across the reserve. The air still vibrated long after the sound had gone.

‘What was that?’ Alex asked, jerking her head round and listening.

‘It’s a bittern.’

‘*That’s* a bittern. What an amazing sound. So they’ve come back.’ She hurried across to the shed door to look out.

‘The male’s back, that’s who you can hear booming. But you’ll be lucky to see him. They’re very shy birds. That booming’s his way of trying to attract a mate. But he’s too early – the damn weather's got them all confused.' He picked up three feeders in each hand and nodded at the three left on the table. 'Bring those will you? We'll put these up and then I'll make some coffee.'

And they hadn't mentioned Christmas again. Alex seemed reluctant to revisit it too.

Now, as he filled the last of the feeders, Mick heard the bittern call again. It was a sound which carried well beyond the confines of the reserve and it had sounded just before he'd left the tiny house on Harbour Row a couple of days before. Minna Downes had lifted her head at the sound and frowned.

'I haven't heard that since I was a child,' she'd said and then turned her sharp gaze on him. 'That means bad luck. That's what my grandmother used to say – something bad will happen.'

Mick had grunted something non-committal and left before it occurred to her to blame him for it, dismissing the idea from his mind as so much superstitious nonsense.

*

How easily she'd slipped back into her routine of visiting the reserve, Alex thought, a few days later. *You're doing it just because Theo said you shouldn't*, Erica would probably have said. Her sister had asked about Mick in one of her telephone calls. 'Have you seen any more of the Birdman?' was how she'd put it, and Alex had said as little as possible about it, knowing Erica would never understand anyway. 'So what did you tell Theo about him?' Erica had asked archly. 'I saw the expression on his face when you mentioned the reserve. He didn't like it did he? He must have brought it up again. I'll bet he could be a jealous man, your Theo,' and she'd laughed suggestively as if that made him more appealing. Alex was surprised at her sister's insight into Theo's character. She'd never shown that much insight into the men she'd chosen for herself.

Alex didn't see why she shouldn't continue to visit the Grenloe. It wasn't just a strike for independence or rank stubbornness; she liked to go there, she always had. It had gone from being a place of refuge to somewhere she genuinely enjoyed for its own sake. And she'd truly come to regard Mick as a friend. Even so, when Theo rang her from London she didn't mention her visits. He didn't ask...so she didn't say. She had no intention of going through all that again.

With Theo away, she'd taken to going down daily, keen to see the rare and elusive bittern. With spring coming on, the reserve buzzed with activity. And since Christmas Mick had become easier to talk to; he seemed more relaxed.

'Have you ever been married?' she asked him one day. 'Years ago,' he'd said shortly. 'It all went wrong.' And he was coming up fifty, she'd found out. He'd cut his hair too, she noticed, and he'd cleaned up the carriage, with his possessions put away or neatly piled up. 'Welcome to civilisation Mr Fenby,' she said dryly.

Now it was nearly nine in the evening on a balmy late January night. As Mick had predicted the spell of cold weather earlier in the month had been relatively brief, to be replaced by a protracted spell of dryness and surprisingly mild temperatures. Alex walked into the snug and across to the front windows, sneaking a furtive glance into the glass at the mirror image of the room over her shoulder, checking there was no-one there. She quickly drew the curtains against the blackness outside and turned back to face the room, and then did the same with the curtains to the side window. She'd come off the phone with Theo just a few short minutes before but, just as she rested the handset back on its stand, there'd been the unmistakeable sound of footsteps. She was sure they'd come from upstairs and she'd had to go up to look, just to be certain. There'd been no-one there of course. She'd lost count of how many times she'd been through this before.

So back in the snug, her hands nervously clumsy, she slipped a CD of Prokofiev's Romeo and Juliet into the machine to play. She'd brought a pile of CDs back from London before Christmas and had only recently started listening to them again. Then she walked to the sofa, sat down a little stiffly and crossed her legs, waving a defiant foot in time to the music. She forced herself to lean back more heavily into the seat and let her head fall back, trying to relax. Her eyes closed, she tried to focus on the music, but before long a conversation she'd had with Mick that morning drifted back into her mind.

'I hear Theo Hellyon's gone away,' he'd said, not looking at her. 'I suppose that's why I'm being graced with your presence so much: you're bored.'

'You know that's not true.' She'd leaned back and pointedly looked out of the window behind her. 'Do you know you can hear the booming of the bittern all over the village? It's quite eerie.'

There was a pause before Mick spoke again, quietly then, almost as if he were addressing the question to his coffee mug rather than her.

'Is it serious with him?'

'Serious? With Theo?' She'd forced a laugh. '*I* don't know.' She'd immediately changed the subject.

Serious? she thought now, as the music filled the air around her. She really didn't know. She'd sometimes asked herself the same question, at times like this, alone in the evening, usually after one of Theo's calls. When he was with her it all seemed clear; he was a perfect partner: affectionate, interesting, reassuring and supportive. When he was away it was as if a spell was broken; though she thought about him often he didn't seem to hold her in the same way. When he rang her, she loved to hear his voice. When she put the phone down after talking to him, she nearly always had a smile on her face. He had that effect on her. So why did she hesitate to respond when he said: 'Miss you,' as he so often did?

There was a noise again and she opened her eyes with a start. This time, it came from outside: the shrill, rasping bark of a fox and she gave a wry smile. She really shouldn't be so jumpy. A few times recently she thought she'd seen something out of the corner of her eye, only to find nothing there when she turned to look. Then there were the doors which seemed to close or open at will.

Her mind was playing tricks on her again. Maybe she'd feel better when Theo came home after all.

*

It was the twenty-ninth of January and Theo still hadn't come home. Alex filled the filter coffee maker, primed it with coffee grounds and switched it on. She was expecting Elizabeth Franklin.

They'd met in the gallery in the village, the first time they'd spoken since Christmas. Alex needed a birthday present for her sister and Liz had followed her in soon after in search of one of the pretty hand-made greetings cards.

‘Don’t see you passing much these days,’ Liz had remarked affably though sounding a little disappointed. They chatted, watched over with barely disguised curiosity by the woman behind the counter. Helen Geaton reminded Alex forcibly of a younger version of Sarah Hellyon. It was disconcerting, as was the woman’s habit of staring at her and then suddenly looking away when Alex turned. It made for stilted conversation and, before she left, Alex invited Liz up to the Hall for coffee the next morning.

It was Elizabeth’s third visit to Hillen Hall and, as usual, she came bearing an offering from her garden, this time a plastic pot of daffodil bulbs, their green tips already well sprouted.

‘They’re coming up early this year,’ she said. ‘It’s been so mild. Oh and isn’t the house looking lovely,’ she added, wandering into the drawing room. ‘You’ve made *such* a difference here.’ Over coffee, Liz chatted about her plans for her garden, pressed Alex again – with undimmed enthusiasm but no more success - to join some club or other, and remarked on Theo’s absence gently, as one might bring up the subject of an illness in the family, curious to know more about it but reluctant to cause upset.

‘He’s back next week,’ Alex replied. ‘He got back from a cruise and then met up with an old friend in London. Someone he went to Cambridge with. They’ve been doing some catching up apparently.’

‘Oh good.’ Liz was clearly glad that there had been no rift. ‘By the way,’ she added, delving into her capacious leather handbag. ‘I’ve been doing some clearing out of boxes in the attic and I found these.’ She pulled out four old-fashioned school exercise books, trapped into a bundle with an elastic band. ‘These were Bill’s notes for his local history.

He had grand plans for writing up a book on the area some day but of course…' Liz smiled and offered them to Alex. 'I thought you might be interested to have a look through them - if you can understand his writing, that is. It's terrible. I just glanced through – you know how you do – and I noticed Hillen Hall mentioned a couple of times so I thought, since you're thinking of restoring the old place, there might be something relevant in there. Anyway, they're no good to me. Do what you want with them when you've finished with them. I keep far too many things as it is.'

'Thank you,' said Alex, taking the bundle and pulling the band off. She flicked through one of the books at random. The script was cramped and sloping with crossings out and occasional notes crammed in the margin or the text. 'They'll be interesting, I'm sure,' she said politely.

It was evening before Alex picked up the books again and began to idly glance through them, doubtful of finding anything of real interest. The word 'history' conjured up for her boring lessons at school and mind-numbing repetition of kings and queens, battles and dates and the ultimate tedium of the industrial revolution: 'Spinning Jennys' and Watt's steam engines. But Bill Franklin had at least interspersed the dry information with the occasional anecdote, comment or story though his notes were haphazard and illogical, information on the region in prehistoric times rubbing shoulders with medieval land husbandry, tin mining up river alongside the first power boats on the Kella. Information was scribbled down as he came across it with additions crammed into odd gaps on the page and asterisks or other marks to indicate cross referencing elsewhere. Over successive evenings, Alex picked through them, trying to find items of interest.

Hillen Hall, she found, was actually a corruption of the name Hellyon. The Hellyon family had lived there unbroken since the sixteenth century but the name Hillen had developed because it was easier to say and quite simply because the house stood on a hill. The estate, it seemed, had once been far more than just the house and garden with the Hellyons owning everything in the village which didn't belong to the church. Bill had added this caustic comment in the margin: *The Hellyons, with unbounded wealth, access to education and contacts with other people of note in the realm, would have been the equivalent of our modern day celebrities, highly regarded and imitated, and treated with a respect which their behaviour didn't always justify.*

By the third night, yawning, she'd become bored with the detailed information of tenancies and social unrest, shipwrecks and land laws, and was on the point of putting them aside when another reference to Hillen Hall caught her eye.: *The Hellyon family was undoubtedly brought to its lowest point when Julian, the eldest son and heir of Richard and Sarah Hellyon, was tragically drowned in the River Kella when he was just fifteen years old. It is said that he was playing with his younger brother and his cousin one evening when some stones gave way on the famous Stepping Stones across the river. As the tide comes in and mingles with the Kella, difficult underwater currents and eddies are set up. Julian was quickly washed away and out to sea. It was a tragedy from which the Hellyon family struggled to recover. They left Hillen Hall a few years later.* In the margin, Bill had scribbled an extra note: *Julian's cousin is Simon Brook, rapidly rising in the classical music world as a conductor and composer of note.*

Alex stared at it, amazed and shocked. Simon had been there when Julian had died? But he'd never once mentioned it.

Chapter 18

Susie was a good early warning system but Mick had never thought of her as a guard dog. She was wary of strangers but never nasty, circling them, growling, preventing any movement until Mick told her to stop. To a stranger she was convincing but he suspected that she looked on these encounters more as a game than anything else. Susie, intelligent and easily bored, liked to have a challenge.

But the snarl Mick could hear this morning contained a note he hadn't heard before and it set the hairs up on the back of his neck. The noise was punctuated by a man's voice shouting. He left the shed where he'd been oiling his tools and, still with a scythe in his hand, cautiously circled the carriage. The man standing in the clearing, kicking out at the dog, was tall and muscular, and wearing the kind of casual clothes that came with a fancy price tag. As Mick straightened his shoulders and stepped forward, the visitor called out again.

'Hey you, call this bloody dog off.'

'Suse. Here.' Susie didn't move and Mick was obliged to call her again. When she was back at heel, still growling under her breath, the man brushed himself down, swearing like a trooper in a smart, public school accent.

‘I could have you prosecuted for keeping a vicious dog,’ growled the man. ‘They’d have her put down like that.’ He snapped his fingers crisply. He was flushed and sweating.

‘She’s not vicious,’ Mick said quietly, jaws clenched tight.

The man smirked and took a few steps closer, glancing down warily at the dog whose growl got louder.

‘Quiet Susie.’

The smirk grew.

‘No? That’s not my impression. And who do you think the authorities would believe? Respected member of society of longstanding local family, or itinerant tramp living in a railway carriage? Mm? I’m Theo Hellyon by the way. Mr Hellyon to you.’

‘I know who you are.’

‘How do you know?’

‘Lucky guess.’ They stood square on, staring at each other, neither giving ground. ‘What do you want?’ Mick asked coldly.

Theo slowly surveyed the ground around them before transferring his gaze back to Mick. He swept his eyes up and down Mick’s wiry frame with a look of contempt.

‘I understand that you’ve been encouraging Miss Munroe to help you out on this patch of wilderness I believe you call a reserve. It doesn’t seem appropriate to me to expect her to soil her hands by helping you.’

Mick frowned and continued to stare Theo out, the muscles in his cheeks twitching.

‘Alex does what she wants to do,’ he said. ‘I haven’t encouraged her to do anything.’

Theo took a step nearer, glancing down at the dog who rose to her feet again. Mick, his right hand still holding the scythe, took hold of her collar with his left. Theo smiled superciliously. He stood four or five inches taller than Mick and was significantly broader. He looked down on the older man and slowly nodded.

'Miss Munroe to a shitty ex-con like you.'

Mick paled and pulled harder on Susie's collar as her growling got louder again. His hand clenched on the handle of the scythe too, his knuckles turning white.

'Oh yes, I know,' said Theo softly, his face close to Mick's. 'I know all about you.' He glanced towards the scythe. 'But you're not going to touch me are you? That would really make the shit hit the fan wouldn't it? And let me tell you this: if you don't stop Miss Munroe coming here – God only knows what you were thinking of doing with her; it's disgusting to think about – I'm going to make sure that everyone else round here knows all about you too.'

Theo took the time to stare at Mick one minute longer, raised his eyebrows meaningfully, and then slowly turned and walked away.

Mick watched him go and then stared after him long after he'd moved out of sight. He'd heard about Theo Hellyon - he'd made a point of listening out for anything he could pick up about the man – and what he'd heard had been mixed. The man was smooth, he'd gathered, charming even and always generous, quick to buy a drink or lend a hand. Someone had warily described him as sometimes devious and a bit of a bully. Andy Turner usually kept his own counsel but was thought to dislike him. Mick had wondered what to believe but now he'd seen for himself. Did Alex have any idea what the man was really like?

Susie still growled, long and low like background thunder, but Mick barely heard her. It started to rain and the dog finally began to whine. She twisted her head in the collar which Mick still held and managed to touch her tongue across his hand. He came out of his reverie and let go of her.

As he walked back to the shed with the handle of the scythe now sticking in his clammy hand, he bellowed at the sky in frustration and then kicked out at the leafless stalks of a young willow, swearing. He'd been waiting for the right moment to tell Alex all about his past himself. Now he knew he'd left it too late. Theo Hellyon hadn't come to warn him, he'd come to score points and scare him off. There was no doubt he'd tell Alex the whole sordid story…and then the rest of the village too. So much for a fresh start.

*

'Darling.' Theo hugged Alex hard, then kissed her long and tenderly. He pushed her away from him and scrutinised her. 'Hell, I've missed you. And you look lovelier than ever.' He hugged her again. 'I'd have come round last night but…well…you know mothers.'

He raised an eyebrow in a comical expression and she laughed and leant in against the reassuring warmth and bulk of his body.

'It's wonderful to see you too.'

'Good.' He stroked her back fondly. 'Have you seen Mother?' he added.

'No.' She frowned and pushed away from him to look at his face. 'I thought I saw her from a distance at the shops the other day, that's all. Why? Isn't she all right?'

'No, she's fine. Fine. I just thought you might have seen her.'

He took her to dinner at The Black Goose. He was relaxed and funny, full of anecdotes from his trip.

'I've had an offer on the house,' she told him as two bowls of soup were put in front of them.

'Really? A good one?' Theo took the pepper mill and ground black pepper over his soup.

'Not bad. But I refused it. The agent said she thought they'd offer more yet. And I was glad to have an excuse to put the decision off really. Well...you know...there's no rush.'

Theo gave her a sympathetic smile as he picked up his spoon.

'Of course. You're bound to feel odd about it. But it'll all work out, you'll see.'

While they ate she prompted him to tell her more about the Caribbean; and she told him about the new bathroom she'd ordered and the plumber whom she'd been unable to pin down as to when he might fit it. She wanted to bring the conversation round to the delicate subject of Julian's accident but wasn't sure how to start. The soup dishes were removed and there was a sticky silence.

'Theo?'

'Mm.?'

'Liz Franklin gave me some notebooks...'

'Who's Liz Franklin?'

The waitress appeared again with sirloin steak for Theo and Dover sole for Alex. Theo shook salt and vinegar liberally over his chips, glancing up at her expectantly as he did so.

'The lady from Captain's Cottage...the B and B?'

'Oh yes, I know.'

'Her husband was a local historian and kept notes.'

Theo had started chewing a large mouthful of steak and nodded, watching her face.

'There's a reference in one of them to your brother's accident.'

Theo finished his mouthful, swallowed and picked up his wine glass.

'So?'

'It said that Simon was there. That all three of you were together, playing on the stones. Is that true?'

He sipped some wine and put the glass down.

'Yes. Why?'

'You never told me.'

Theo lightly shrugged. 'It wasn't relevant.'

'Simon never mentioned it either.'

'Hardly surprising is it?'

He picked up his knife and fork and took another mouthful of steak. Alex started on her fish, frustrated but not sure what else to say. Usually Theo was so easy to talk to; at the moment she felt he was stone-walling her.

'You mean because he wanted to block it out?' she prompted.

'Maybe.'

A couple of minutes later, Theo laid his cutlery down against his plate, picked up his wine again and cradled it thoughtfully.

'You know, Simon and Julian didn't really get on.'

Alex looked up in surprise.

'I never had that impression from you.'

'I wasn't sure you'd want to know. But they used to argue and fight. Maybe Simon just didn't think about Julian any more. It's not as if they were close.'

Alex frowned but let the subject drop. They ate on in silence.

Theo finished first, leaned back in the chair, picked up his glass of wine and drank the last of it with evident satisfaction.

'I hope you didn't mind me staying over in London?' he said. 'I bumped into James at the airport. He asked me over to dinner at his house and insisted I stayed on there a couple of nights. We were big friends at Cambridge.'

Alex finished her fish and pushed the plate away.

'Yes, you said on the phone.'

'You didn't mind then?'

'Of course not. Why should I?'

Theo looked at her quizzically but she couldn't read his expression.

'He's married with two kids,' Theo continued. 'Seems really happy. He's a lawyer. He came from Lancashire originally but he works in London now.'

'Oh?' Theo's tone was light but a prickle of apprehension suddenly ran over Alex's skin. She had the sensation that the speech had been rehearsed, that there was a more serious point to this apparently casual conversation.

'He used to live near a big nature reserve though and he misses the wildlife. It was a bit of a hobby with him. I was telling him about the reserve down here and the chap who looks after it.'

Alex said nothing but kept her eyes fixed intently on Theo's face.

'Well, when I told him what you'd said about this Mick Fenby guy, James said he thought the fellow rang a bell, he wasn't sure why.'

'In what way?'

‘I’m telling you: he didn’t know. Not then. But he remembered what it was the next day and looked it up to check. It had been a big story back where he used to live. There was a chap just like this man except that his name wasn’t Mick Fenby, it was Martin Foster, and there was a good reason why he might have changed his name.’

‘Go on.’

‘He’s an ex-con. A paedophile.’

‘A what?’ She shook her head. ‘No,’ she mouthed, though she made no sound at all.

‘I know. Shocking isn’t it? I stayed on a bit to look into it. I thought it was important to know but I didn’t want to say anything to you until I was sure. It seems he was a secondary school teacher originally – taught biology. Then he went to work as the education officer on this reserve near James. Among other things he took school parties round, things like that. Anyway the next thing a sixteen year old claimed he sexually abused him at the school when he was eleven. He’d been the boy’s form teacher in the first year and had befriended him and kept him behind sometimes to ‘give him extra help’. You can imagine. He’d threatened the boy that, if he said anything, he’d suffer for it and the kid was too scared and ashamed to say anything at the time.’ Theo’s expression suggested distaste. ‘Then another boy came forward and said the same thing had happened to him. So Martin Foster was arrested, tried and sent to prison. I suppose when he got out he wanted to move a long way away and ended up here, God help us.’ Theo reached for the wine bottle and then let his hand drop. ‘Wait a minute, I’ve got a picture of him here so you can tell me if it is the same guy.’ He patted the pocket of his jacket hanging on the back of the chair, withdrew a folded piece of paper and handed it to Alex. ‘Is that him?’

Alex slowly unfolded the paper. It was a copy of a newspaper article with a photograph at its head. A clean-shaven young man, wiry and dark-haired, glared at the camera, his arms apparently pulled behind his back, his expression angry and accusing. She stared at it. Even given the passage of time, there was no mistaking that it was Mick Fenby.

She nodded and carefully folded the paper up and laid it on the table, repeatedly smoothing it over with her hand as if she could obliterate the information it contained in the action.

Theo watched her closely.

'Thought so,' he said. 'So I was obviously right to be worried about you going down to that place by yourself. The bloke's a pervert.'

Alex picked up her glass and took a large mouthful of wine. Her face was white and her hand shook slightly so the glass bounced a little on her lips. She emptied the glass and put it down, catching the edge of the plate as she did so. Theo reached across and took her hand.

'Are you all right? Is it that much of a shock?'

'Yes. I'm…' She shook her head. 'I keep thinking of Ben. I took him there didn't I? And to think what might have happened. I'm…' She took a deep breath and exhaled slowly. 'But then I can't quite believe it either. Mick's so gentle really. Difficult certainly, a loner, yes but there's nothing about him that would make me think…' Images of Mick flitted across her mind and she shook her head again.

'Loners,' remarked Theo mildly. 'They're always the ones you have to look out for. And these people often seem quite harmless, otherwise they wouldn't be able to get away with it.' He shrugged and raised his eyebrows, expressive of the unpredictability of human behaviour.

The waitress reappeared to ask if they'd finished and began to clear the plates.

'So now we know why he's hiding away in a railway carriage in the wilderness,' Theo continued. 'Shall I top you up?' he asked, picking up the wine bottle. She nodded. 'Don't be too upset will you? I mean… you didn't know him that well did you?'

'No, no, of course not. Obviously not.' She frowned, unable to stop shaking her head. 'I'm disgusted…but I just can't believe…'

'No…well. People can be amazing. I certainly don't think you should go there any more.'

'No…absolutely not. God.'

'Good. I'll feel better.' He reached over and squeezed her hand again. 'Now, how do you fancy one of their delicious desserts?'

*

For three days after Theo's return dinner, Alex moped round the house or wandered round the grounds and garden. Confused, disgusted, cross; her mind flitted at random from one emotion to the other leaving her drained and heart weary. She was angry with herself. It was ridiculous to let someone she knew so little upset her so much. But she *had* thought she knew Mick, if not in details at least in essence, and she had considered him a friend. She'd liked him. When Theo rang and spoke of coming round after work, Alex put him off, pleading illness. 'I'm fighting something off,' she said. 'Just sleeping all the time. I'm better left alone.' She didn't analyse why she felt unable or unwilling to talk to Theo about it or to seek his comfort, blaming her own embarrassment at the half truths she had told about her visits to the reserve and therefore her inability to explain properly to him why she should be so upset.

She thought of ringing Erica to talk it through but knew that Erica, more like her mother than she cared to think and more naturally suspicious by nature, would say how she'd expected it all along. *You're such a soft touch to these ne'er do wells*, she'd say. *You're the only person I know who regularly gives a fiver to street beggars. They see you coming.* It was a conversation they'd had in one form or another many times over the years.

Despite telling Theo she wouldn't go, she even toyed with stalking down to the reserve and challenging Mick about his past and then felt a rush of distaste and a crush of confused guilt for even considering it. Her feelings of anger towards him were always followed by an awareness of her own gullibility for not guessing the truth and a sense of humiliation. But what would the signs be of such a perversion and how would she have known? He had steadfastly refused to tell her anything much about his past; that alone should have rung warning bells for her. But then she'd remember the way he'd sat and patiently explained the birds to her, how he'd prepared coffee and food for her, how gently he treated Susie and how they'd laughed. But, of course, all that was meaningless, held against the nature of his crimes. She was just fooling herself, trying to find an excuse not to believe something that there was no reason to doubt - she'd seen it in black and white.

On the Friday evening, Theo turned up at the door. When she opened up to him he stood there with a huge bunch of flowers in one hand and a bottle of champagne in the other.

'I've come to rescue a damsel in distress,' he said, with his infectious grin. 'I *have* come to the right house haven't I?'

She had to smile.

'Yes, I think you have,' she said and let him in.

'Are you better?'

'I'm OK.'

'Are you eating?'

'You sound like Erica.'

'That's not the right answer.'

He put down the flowers and the bottle on the hall table and gave her a hug.

'I think I'll have to risk this terrible disease,' he said and bent over to kiss her, long and warm. 'There. The princess will now get better.' He took hold of her hand and led her through to the drawing room. 'No fire?'

'The stove's lit in the snug.'

'Oh, OK. Well suppose I cook for us. You didn't know I could cook? You'll be amazed what I can do, Miss Munroe. You have got food I assume?'

'Yes, some.'

'Good.'

He made Spanish omelettes and Alex washed salad and cut bread. He told stories and made her laugh. She thought she'd been a fool to keep him away; she felt better already. He cheered her up; he was reassuring - a solid point of reference in a shifting world. They ate from trays sitting in front of the stove in the snug, and then cleared up together in the kitchen, washing and drying like an old married couple. Then Theo insisted on opening the champagne he'd brought – 'no-one's ever too ill for shampoo' – and they sat on the sofa and stared at the fire companionably, talking little.

'You've been fretting over that bastard down on the Grenloe,' he said eventually.

'I have.' She glanced at him, a little surprised at his understanding. And grateful too. 'It's stupid of me. You read about these people in the papers and wonder how no-one guessed...You don't think you'd be daft enough to believe them yourself.'

Theo, his arm stretched around her shoulder, gave her a squeeze.

'People never fail to amaze me,' he said. 'It makes me feel bad to even think about you being alone with him. I want to protect you from people like that.' She started to protest but he put a finger to her mouth to stop her. 'No, hear me out darling. It's not just jealousy, though I do admit to being jealous of every man who's around you. But I care about you and I want to look after you. This business has made me see it even more clearly.' He paused and turned his head to look at her. 'You do see what I'm saying don't you?'

'Theo...' she said warningly.

He pulled his arm away and eased himself to his feet. Then he slid down onto one knee on the floor in front of her.

'Don't be silly Theo. What are you doing?'

His expression had become solemn, his eyes fixed on hers. He was compelling her to look at him.

'Marry me Alex, please? You know how much I love you. Please make me really happy and marry me.'

'Don't Theo.'

'Why not? I know it's probably too soon, that I should wait, but I can't. Ever since I met you I knew that this is what I wanted. I've never felt like this before, truly. And life's too short isn't it, to take a chance on leaving things? Marry me and marry me soon. I'm an old-fashioned guy at heart and I want to call you mine. And then I can look after you properly, the way I want to. Please? Say yes.' He took her hand and kissed it. 'Please Alex. We could be so happy together.'

'I don't know Theo. I need to think about it.'

'Don't you love me…just a little bit? You said you did. It'll only get better in time you know. We'd make room to let it grow.'

Alex gave a nervous laugh but held his gaze. She *had* said she loved him before, in moments of intimacy, when he'd said he loved her and seemed to be waiting for her response. She'd thought she meant it. When she'd been younger relationships appeared so much easier and more black and white; love was an overriding emotion, seemingly obvious to identify. These days the word 'love' conjured up a breadth of feelings; she recognised more shades of grey in it.

The decision appeared to hang in her mind for ages, just out of reach. But Theo was pressing for an answer. And then she heard herself say yes.

Chapter 19

'Engaged? Gosh.'

Erica laughed a little nervously and Alex could imagine the expression on her sister's face. She thought she could even sense Erica wondering how to accept the news, what line she should take. It had taken Alex a couple of days to pluck up the courage to ring up and tell her, determined to plan a few things first and have a chance to think everything through before she faced the inevitable questions.

'We're having an engagement party at the Hall,' she said. 'I've booked a local caterer. It's a sort of house-warming too. It's all been a bit of a rush. It's two weeks on Saturday. Can you come?'

'Two weeks? Blimey Alex, that's a bit tight.'

'I know, but please say you'll come.'

'I might be able to arrange it.'

There was a short silence.

'Is that it?' prompted Alex, defensively. 'Aren't you pleased for me?'

'Of course I'm pleased for you. Congratulations. Of course…it's wonderful.' She hesitated. 'It's just…are you really sure Ali? It seems so quick. You're sure it's not a rebound thing?'

Alex rolled her eyes heavenwards and took a deep breath. She'd known this would happen and had promised herself she wouldn't react.

'You've met him. You know how well we get on. And I've known Theo since last summer. It's not that sudden is it? Anyway I thought you liked him?'

'I do. I just want you to be happy.'

'I *am* happy Erica, really…' Alex paused, checking herself, and then added: 'You will try to come to the party won't you? You won't stay away in protest?'

'Would I?' Before Alex could reply, Erica added: 'I thought you didn't like parties?'

'Well, no, I don't, not normally. But it's nothing too big and this is a special occasion.'

As if by tacit agreement they both went on to talk about other things: Victoria's latest campaign; the new bathroom which was finally scheduled to be fitted at the Hall the following week; Ben going on a trip to Paris with the school.

When the call finished, Alex put the phone down and wandered to the front window of the snug, looking out to the hazy, grey sea in the distance. If she were honest she too was surprised that she'd accepted Theo so quickly. And yet not, for wasn't that the way she'd always lived her life, riding on the impulse of the moment, driven by emotion. She'd protested to Erica many times that some of her best decisions had been made that way, that she'd taken job offers which had proved huge successes and good career moves when initially they appeared to have little to recommend them. And she'd known Simon a much shorter time before taking what she considered the big step of moving in with him and had gone on to accept his proposal of marriage less than a year later. Impulse decisions could work; she'd proved it.

Having said that, her thoughts of Simon and their time together were more confused these days. These last few months had been painful. Picking over their relationship with the thoroughness of a doctor doing an autopsy, she had to reluctantly accept that all had not been right between them. The problems hadn't started immediately; their early days had been good: she a relative novice in the classical music world, unsure and happy to take advice; Simon, apparently self-confident, flattered to play the expert. When had it gone wrong? When she became successful and his regular unsought advice became clearly unwelcome? Or when she began to spend so much time away from home? Despite his own success did he resent hers? She would never know. The truth was that she was rarely around latterly to know what he thought and, when they were together, too often she had her mind on work. And so did he.

Not, perhaps, a good endorsement of a hasty decision after all. And yet, for all their rows and unhappiness, she'd still loved him. She was convinced the relationship could have worked if they'd done things differently. She could blame Simon easily enough for all sorts of character faults: he'd been dogmatic, pompous and moody – secretive even; he had not always been easy to live with. But she'd been no angel either, wrapped up in her own ambitions, not prepared to give the relationship the time it needed, quick to fly off the handle and storm off. And when Erica mentioned the dispute over children, she'd touched a sore point; Alex knew it had driven a wedge between them.

She turned away from the window and walked back to the table and her collection of lists for things to do and buy before the party. She sat down and looked them over: invitations to write and send, jobs to do in the house, furniture to move, a new outfit to buy. It was Theo who had suggested the party - he'd been very keen - and, after an initial reluctance, she'd agreed. Regarding it more as a house-warming had won her over; she thought maybe the house deserved a joyful gathering of friends and family. It would make the place come alive after years of unloved neglect.

How would Simon feel about her doing this? She wasn't sure. She hoped he'd be happy with it; she thought he'd understand. Theo was good for her. With his support and help she was nothing like the mess she'd been when she'd first come to Kellaford Bridge. It wasn't all down to him of course but he'd been there when she'd needed him. Mick too...No. she pushed that thought away. Perhaps something had sent her to Hillen Hall especially. It was appealing to think that it was part of a bigger plan, that there was some order to the otherwise apparent chaos of life. But whatever the bigger picture, she was grateful to Theo and she thought she could make him happy. She was determined to try. She hoped she'd learned from her mistakes and was aware, though she barely acknowledged the thought, that she saw it as a chance to get it right the second time around.

*

Helen was starting to cause Theo problems. She was getting restless and troublesome. She'd begun to moan repeatedly about the 'vintage dresses' and the stale perfume they exuded. Then she complained that he was getting heavy-handed in his love-making, leaving her with bruises she had to explain away to Bob, that the things he wanted to do with her sometimes were 'weird'. 'That hurt Theo,' she'd whined recently. 'I don't think you even see me when we make love.

You're all wrapped up in some world of your own. It could be anyone, couldn't it? Well, couldn't it?' He'd laughed the idea away dismissively but then she'd started talking about how she should never have started with him in the first place, that she felt bad about cheating on Bob. 'He's boring and a bit bossy sometimes but he's not bad at heart,' she'd said. 'He means well.' It might have been genuine remorse, Theo thought, but if she was hoping to make him feel jealous, she was wasting her time.

But the news of the engagement seemed to be the final straw. Word had passed around Kellaford Bridge very rapidly; Theo made sure that it did. Once everyone knew about it, Alex would find it harder to change her mind and their betrothal would have taken on an unstoppable momentum. She might have preferred to keep the party small but Theo knew it needed to be a very public event and he was determined to fill the Hall with people. It was inevitable that Helen would hear about it.

'You're engaged,' she blurted out crossly when he went into the gallery to arrange their next meeting. He'd never seen her quite so angry before and he had to stop himself from smiling.

'News travels quickly,' he said.

'So you admit it?'

'Of course I admit it,' he'd said. 'I was just coming to tell you.'

'You've got a nerve.'

'It doesn't make any difference between us though,' he said easily.

'You must be *joking.*'

He looked at her. She spent so much time complaining these days that her pretty face seemed to be permanently twisted into one angry grimace after another, nothing like his image of his mother. On his last visit to her flat, with a beautiful dress of sapphire blue – one of Sarah's favourites - she'd suddenly asked him where the dresses came from. 'Some old flame?' she'd demanded. 'Someone who jilted you?' It had been a struggle to hold his temper and she was rapidly spoiling the illusion he'd worked so hard to create. He was getting bored with it all. Perhaps it was finally time to kick her into touch after all.

'I've seen Alex Munroe,' she said now when Theo didn't speak. 'She's been in here. Actually she seemed like a nice person. I feel sorry for her. Do you get her doing kinky things too? I don't suppose she has any idea what you've been getting up to. She can't have or she'd never have agreed to marry you would she?' She looked up at him slyly through her eyelashes. 'Perhaps someone should tell her.'

He grabbed her arm then, glanced out of the shop window to check there was no-one around and forced her into the kitchenette, out of sight.

'Threats?' he said, twisting her arm up painfully till she squealed. 'That won't work with me Helen.' He pressed his face close against hers. 'Just say one word,' he said slowly, menacingly, 'and I'll be back to teach you a lesson. Remember, one word. Understand?'

She nodded, eyes wide with terror, face ashen, and he let her go. She backed up away from him and rubbed at the marks his fingers had left on her wrist, glancing up at him warily, and he left, satisfied that she'd hold her tongue.

*

There were still three days to go to the party when Theo found the note. He had come to from a deep sleep, unsure what had woken him, struggling to remember where he was. Then he heard Alex's slow, even breathing and remembered. He was in her room at the Hall and she was curled up, her back to him, fast asleep. He grimaced in the dark. He really didn't like sleeping in this room. To him it was Julian's room and always would be. It brought back too many memories.

He rolled over to peer at the luminous fingers of the clock on the bedside cabinet. Ten past one. He wriggled himself into a more comfortable position and was slowly drifting to sleep again when he heard something. He was sure of it this time. It sounded like the gate at the end of the front path. Wide awake now, he slipped out of bed, careful not to disturb Alex, and walked to the window, shivering a little as the cold air hit his naked body. He pulled the curtain aside a fraction and stuck his head into the gap. The sky was banked with cloud, the garden and parkland a series of black shapes on darkest grey. Then a shift in the cloud allowed a little moonlight to filter through and he spotted a dark figure moving away in the parkland beyond the garden wall, indistinct and head down, the occasional sweep of a torch beam visible by its feet.

He quickly slipped on his fleece and jeans, crept silently out of the room and ran barefoot down the nearest stairs, adrenaline pumping his heart. He'd obviously been woken by something that person had been doing at the house and he had to know what it was. Down in the hall he paused; there was no sign of anything: no damage, no fire, not the slightest spark. Then he saw the note, still sticking in the letter box. He eased it out, holding the spring with his other hand to stop the flap banging.

The envelope was addressed to *A. M.* He walked quietly through the drawing room to the kitchen, put the light on and stared at the letter. His lip curled and he turned it over, inserted a finger in the end, ripped it open and pulled out the single sheet of A4 paper. It read:

I think you should be aware Alex that the man you have agreed to marry is not everything he seems. You are not the only woman he has been seeing these last few months. I know for a fact that Theo Hellyon has been having an affair with a married woman in the village. I don't wish to disclose the woman's name for fear of what might happen to her but please believe that what I say is true. If you doubt me, think back to these nights. There followed a list of dates. *Theo wasn't with you on any of these nights because he was with her.*

Please pay attention to this letter – for your own sake. Believe me, Theo may seem gentle and kind to you now but really he is a cruel man. You should get away from him as soon as you can.

A friend.

Theo shook his head, gave a brief laugh and then glanced up at the ceiling and hastily quelled it. He looked down again. The letter was typed and printed but the initials had been handwritten on the envelope. What a foolish oversight. He had recognised Helen's handwriting immediately. He shook his head; she clearly wasn't to be trusted after all. It was a shame really; she'd given him a lot of pleasure.

He walked back through into the snug where the dying embers in the wood-burning stove still glowed red. He flicked open the vent, opened the door, and threw the letter and envelope inside. He nudged them with the poker then closed the door and watched them both burn, small flames licking slowly across them until the paper was thin, crisp and black.

'Is that you Theo? Is there anything wrong?' Alex's voice from the landing brought him into the hallway.

'Yes, it's me,' he replied, as he started back up the stairs. 'Nothing wrong. I just came down to clear my head. I couldn't sleep.'

Chapter 20

Over the days leading up to the party, Alex was busy and content. She found herself humming snatches of music while she touched up the décor in the new bathroom; she picked over CDs to play and accepted Theo's offerings of pop and rock with a generous, if doubtful, smile; she oversaw the catering plans and happily left Theo to sort out the drinks. One day, she even stood in front of the mirror in the bathroom and did some vocal exercises, stretching her facial muscles and vocal chords, filling the echoing space with reverberating sound. She'd been uncertain how she'd react after all this time but her rusty voice made her more appalled than emotional and she resolved to do some practice. She went to Plymouth with Theo to choose her engagement ring, arranged to have it resized, and Theo collected it and made an occasion of presenting it to her. He helped her move furniture, and then she changed her mind and they moved it again, amid a lot of laughter. He continually teased her and, after a mock battle one afternoon, they made love on the rug in front of the stove in the snug. They were good days and she was convinced she was happy.

But the party didn't turn out the way she'd intended and afterwards she wondered if that had been the start of everything changing. Or had the party been blighted? Two days beforehand, the woman who ran the gallery in the village had been found dead at the bottom of the stairs which led up to the flat. Her neck had been broken in the fall it was said; a tragic accident but she'd probably died instantly.

'Perhaps we should cancel the party?' Alex had said to Theo when she heard the news.

'Cancel it?' Theo said with surprise. 'Why would we do that? We didn't know her very well did we? Or did you?' he added, eyebrows raised.

'No, hardly at all. I'd just exchanged the odd word with her when I was in the gallery. But it seems frivolous to have a party after such a tragedy.'

'Nonsense. People are looking forward to it. They'll be glad to have something else to think about.'

'I suppose you're right.'

Alex quelled her disquiet, unsure if it was born of some sort of foolish superstition, or the product of her concern that the 'small celebration' appeared to have grown out of all proportion. Originally Alex had invited her sister, three old friends from her music college days and their partners, and a number of people she'd got to know in the village; Theo had invited his mother - 'she *loves* parties' - and 'a few friends'. Then, on the last minute he told her that he'd invited some extra people.

'Who?' she'd asked, trying not to sound as irritated as she felt. 'How many?'

'I'm not sure. Just some more people from the village and some sailing friends. It came up in conversation and I didn't want them to think I'd excluded them. It's OK isn't it?'

'But it's very short notice to inform the caterers.'

'That doesn't matter. They won't be bothered about eating. I'm sure there'll be enough anyway. I'll get in some extra drink.'

Come the night, her fears were realised. Though Erica had been forced to cry off at the last minute because Ben got tonsillitis and only Catherine, one of her old music friends, could come, Hillen Hall seemed to be full of people, many of them people she barely knew or not at all. Alex forced herself to tour the rooms, smiling, exchanging a few words here and there, fingering the diamond cluster engagement ring on her finger occasionally as though surprised to find it there. She marvelled at all these people Theo knew and, for the first time, wondered a little what he did when he wasn't with her. Saturday nights he had often kept to 'have a night with the boys', he said; sometimes other nights too. Quite honestly happy to have the time to herself, she'd never quibbled. She'd realised he was more gregarious than her; she just hadn't realised how much.

As she circulated now she could hear local people exchanging their amazement and disgust about the revelations regarding 'the Birdman'. He'd been banned from the Stores, they said. Word had travelled quickly it seemed. They spoke of Helen Geaton's death too, still speculating on how it had happened. 'Probably been drinking,' she heard someone say to Liz Franklin. 'Apparently she smelt of alcohol. They found an empty bottle of champagne in the flat.' Far from distracting local attention, the party only seemed to have allowed the story to be discussed and spread with more relish. She thought some of the conversations had a ghoulish quality.

Sarah had come, wearing a dress of grey silk, set off by a necklace of pink diamonds and matching drop earrings.

She'd had her hair done, freshly highlighted, looking almost pearly in the artificial light. She was still striking, Alex had to admit, but she watched her arrival with some misgiving and then found herself constantly checking to see what she was doing. She caught a fleeting sight of her at intervals, glass in hand, nodding to people as she drifted regally from room to room.

There was constant music; some people danced. Then the food was served and there was a brief lull before the dancing started again. Alex saw little of Theo. Wasn't that always the way at parties, she thought: you arrange them to celebrate something of significance and are then too busy to spend any time together? By eleven thirty, all the people Alex had invited had gone. Even Catherine, though offered a bed for the night, had left too, claiming the need to be back in Winchester for early the next day. The caterers had cleared up, sorted out the food residue and dishes, and gone.

Alex wandered into the hall, away from the increasingly rowdy conversation and the drunken laughter, and then made for the refuge of the snug, expecting it to be empty. But Sarah was in there, a glass of neat whisky in her hand, standing studying a painting on the wall. Alex stopped short.

'Mrs Hellyon,' she said, rather stupidly she thought.

Sarah started and turned to look at Alex, seeming to take a moment to remember who she was.

'Ah Alex. Hello. Lovely party dear.' The words ran together a little and she paused as if vaguely aware that they hadn't come out the way she'd intended. She turned back to the painting. It was a bold, impasto oil painting of Kellaford harbour with the tide in, the view out across an assembly of colourful boats towards the Dancing Bears and the sea, done perhaps from one of the jetties. 'Charming picture,' she added, speaking more slowly. 'I don't remember it.'

'I bought it in the gallery in the village last month.'

Sarah nodded, staring at the picture mistily. 'The gallery,' she murmured and then took a mouthful of whisky. 'Where that woman died last week.'

'Yes. It's very sad, isn't it?'

Sarah turned, glancing round the room regretfully.

'You've done a lovely job here. But there's nothing much left that I recognise now.' She looked at Alex and smiled wanly. 'There's the grandfather clock in the drawing room of course. I'd hoped to take that with me when I moved to the Lodge but I couldn't fit it in anywhere. In any case it hasn't worked for years.'

'I've managed to get it to work,' Alex said, sounding more defiant than she'd intended. 'I had a man out to look at it. He suggested moving it to get it more balanced.'

'Oh?' Sarah's expression and tone suggested disbelief. 'But it's stopped now, isn't it?' She hesitated again and then nodded. 'If I remember correctly it was Julian who broke it; he was always playing with the thing. Fascinated by it he was.' She took another mouthful of whisky, her eyes increasingly hazy.

'What was Julian like?' Alex asked suddenly. He'd been on her mind a lot lately.

'Julian?' Sarah thought for a moment before speaking. 'He was a strange mixture, really. He was quiet sometimes, studious, like his father; he shared his father's interest in old things too. But then he was a stronger character than Richard. Richard could be high-handed but it was born of weakness, you see. Yes.' She nodded thoughtfully. 'Julian was a stronger character; stubborn at times. Whereas Theo, you see,

Theo always knows when to give in gracefully.' Sarah finished the last of her whisky, licked a dry tongue over her lips and looked regretfully into the glass before looking back up at Alex. 'Still, he was a good boy, Julian.'

Alex left a respectful silence, her mind drifting to Bill Franklin's notebooks.

'It must have been terrible for Theo and Simon,' she said. 'I gather the boys were all playing together on the stones when it happened.'

'Playing? Who told you that?'

'I read it...in someone's local history notes. Why, isn't it true?'

Sarah fingered her empty glass and appeared to be thinking it over.

'Well, yes, I suppose it must be,' she said slowly. 'Of course I wasn't there.'

'But Theo was, wasn't he? He said so. Not that he ever talks about it. It was me who brought it up.' Alex paused but couldn't stop herself adding: 'Simon never talked about it either.'

'No, well he wouldn't would he?' Sarah rejoined quickly. 'After what happened. I mean, he was an intense boy, difficult sometimes, but I wouldn't have thought he'd...' She frowned and stopped quite suddenly, looking uncomfortable as if she'd spoken out of turn. 'It was a long time ago,' she added. 'He was very young when it happened.'

'Yes...I suppose... ' Alex hesitated, wondering what Sarah had stopped herself from saying and why.

'I think I'm going to get another drink,' said Sarah, already treading a careful path to the door. She turned on an afterthought with her hand on the handle and put on a smile. 'Can I get you anything?'

'No, I'm fine…thanks.'

Alex walked to her favourite chair by the fire though the stove wasn't lit – she hadn't expected the snug to be used that evening. She sat down, her eyes resting on the avocet carving by the hearth which she'd thought several times she ought to get rid of but couldn't bring herself to move. She pulled her eyes away. Mick came into her mind often enough anyway, unasked and unwanted; she certainly didn't want to think about him now. She changed her position in the chair and found herself glancing up at the painting Sarah had commented on.

Unable to settle, she got up again and went back out into the hall. Someone had left the front door open and she walked across to close it and then changed her mind, grabbed a jacket from the rack behind the door and stepped outside. She slung the jacket over her shoulders and walked down the front garden path. With March still several days away there was a brisk chill in the air. A quarter moon occasionally masked by thin, wispy clouds, threw a pearly light on the ground. In the distance, she could hear the faint roar of the waves breaking against the cliffs and the call of a tawny owl, hunting in the valley.

She paused and looked down at the shadowy bundles of the lavender plants which bordered the path on each side. She'd planted them herself, carefully measured their distance apart, then lovingly firmed and watered them in. She was looking forward to watching them grow and to their scent filling the garden on sunny summer days. There were other plants and shrubs she'd put in too. There was a lot to look forward to. Alex walked slowly to the gate at the end of the path and rested a hand on the stone gatepost. She loved it here. What a shame Simon had never talked about it with her. How wonderful it would have been to have shared it with him. She opened the gate and stepped through. She'd had a slatted wooden seat put the other side of the wall, facing the sea and she moved round to sit on it, shrugged the jacket on properly and pulled it tight around her.

Why had Simon never talked about Hillen Hall? It was a question which refused to go away. Was it all about Julian's accident? And if so, why exactly? If he'd forgotten about it as Sarah had suggested, it didn't explain why he wouldn't have spoken otherwise of Devon and his childhood holidays there. And, in any case, he was fifteen when Julian died; he wasn't a young child. Alex remembered a great deal about her teenage years – all those rows with her mother among other things. Was Simon so traumatised by a freak accident that he'd preferred not to ever mention it? But no-one talked about it, did they? Everyone who spoke his name did it as if they were lifting a dust sheet to reveal a picture, always letting the fabric fall before anything could be seen. And there was something about Sarah's comments which didn't feel right. Sadness and grief over the tragedy was understandable, but, twenty-five years on, there was an edge to her remarks which suggested rank bitterness.

Her thoughts automatically shifted to the stepping stones. She'd been down to them just the day before. In an effort to clear her mind of its clamour of nervous activity in advance of the party, Alex had walked along the footpath on the near bank of the Kella. The tide had started to come in and she'd watched, fascinated as always, at the way it crept back up the river bed, insidious and surprisingly fast. The bubbling sound of a curlew rang lingeringly in the air somewhere up river. Then, as she approached the crossing she'd seen Harry Downes, out on the mudflat near the stones. He was looking down intently at the sandy mud where the water was already lapping the bottom of the nearest stone column.

'Have you lost something?' she called to him, stepping down onto the damp ground to join him. He turned and stared at her face blankly. 'Hello Harry. It's Alex. Sorry, did I surprise you?'

He'd grinned then, a flash of a smile which lit up his eyes for a moment and spoke of mischief and humour, a glimpse of the man he had once been. He put a finger up to his cap and nodded. One of his good days, she thought. Liz had said that he hadn't been sleeping well lately and sometimes disappeared from the house at night prompting Minna to hide the key after locking the door in an effort to stop him. He looked fresh-eyed this morning though.

'Have you lost something?' she repeated.

'No, no. Not me…the boy.' Harry stepped closer to the stones, looking down, and then lifted his head up to look to the far side. 'But it was on the other side,' he muttered and his face crumpled into a frown. He looked intently to the other side of the river and raised a hand to point a thin finger towards a large rock on the far shore. 'Over there. It's behind that rock.' Then he shuffled his feet towards the first of the stone steps and she thought he was going to try to cross. She put a hand out to touch his arm.

'Don't go over will you Harry? The tide's coming in. The water's too far in to cross.' He turned to stare at her and she wasn't sure if he understood what she was saying. 'It's not safe,' she added.

Harry continued to stare at her as if he'd seen a ghost.

‘That’s what he said,’ he murmured.

‘Who?’ When Harry didn’t reply, she said it again. ‘Who?’ But he didn’t answer, his expression full of confusion. But then he suddenly turned and shuffled away, back along the mudflats in the direction of the village. Was he safe to be left to wander like that, she wondered, or should she go after him? She watched him as he headed to the bank further down river and he stepped up purposefully onto the footpath where a procession of feet had worn it down low. Confident he was on his way home again she’d turned away.

Standing now, looking out over the park, Alex pushed the memory away as little more than a distraction. Irresistibly, fragments of Sarah’s conversation came back into her mind instead:

... ‘I think Julian broke it; he was always playing with the thing. Fascinated by it he was.’ ...

... ‘Playing? Who told you that?’ ...

...‘No, well he wouldn’t would he? After what happened...I wouldn’t have thought he’d...’

She felt like she was listening to a piece of orchestral music where a discordant note kept sounding. She couldn’t place where it was exactly and she had to keep listening to it to try to work it out. Behind her, up by the front door, she heard voices as a succession of people left. Eventually she got up and made her way back towards the house. There had clearly been a major exodus; there was only a handful of people left in the drawing room when she went in. Theo was standing in front of the fireplace.

‘Darling,’ he said, quickly coming across to her. ‘I’ve been looking everywhere for you. Where have you been?’ He put his arms round her and gave her a hug then pulled away from her. 'You're cold.' His voice was a little too loud, slightly overblown. She'd never seen him drunk before.

'I went outside...to get some air.'

The last stragglers came over to say their farewells and left. Only Sarah remained, sitting in one of the armchairs, head back and eyes closed. Alex glanced towards the clock. Sarah had been right: it *had* stopped again. At twenty past eight.

I think Julian broke it; he was always playing with the thing. Fascinated by it he was.

Alex moved away, towards the kitchen.

'I'm going to make some coffee,' she said over her shoulder. 'Do you want some?'

'Coffee? Sure.' Theo followed her.

The kitchen was a mess. Alex cleared some space, moving glasses and bottles to one side. She could feel Theo watching her.

'Are you all right?' he said. 'I'm sorry, I'm afraid I neglected you this evening. I got talking to some old friends and lost track of time.' He laughed, a little self-consciously, she thought. 'I've drunk too much.'

Alex filled the coffee maker with water, primed it with coffee and turned to look at him, leaning against the unit. He'd eased himself down into a chair by the table.

'You had a good time,' she said, more by way of a statement than a question.

'Yes.' He ran a hand through his hair and then stretched his eyes wearily. Alcoholic fatigue was setting in. 'You didn't?'

'You know I'm not a great party animal,' she said coolly. She shifted more glasses from the table, took a cloth and wiped it off and sat down opposite him. 'I thought we'd agreed it wouldn't be a big affair? Who were all those people anyway? To be honest, I found it rather oppressive; that's why I went outside.'

'Then I'm sorry too. I should have been looking out for you. I should have introduced you to everyone. Stupid of me.' He smiled at her and reached a hand across the table to take hers in a now familiar gesture. She returned a brief smile, squeezed his hand and then pulled hers away, leaning back in the chair.

'Theo, was there anything...*wrong* about Julian's death?'

'Wrong? What on earth do you mean? What a strange thing to suddenly say.'

'Is it? Mm.' Under Theo's cool scrutiny, she faltered, doubting herself. She shrugged. 'Forget it.' The water had gone through and she got up to pour the coffee. But still she couldn't shake the idea away. 'Your mother did say something odd though.'

'What?' Theo laughed, rather too brightly. 'About Julian? What on earth did she say that's worried you so?'

Alex tipped some milk into each mug, spooned sugar into Theo's and brought them back to the table.

'I asked her about Julian – what he was like – and then we spoke about the accident. I said how awful it must have been for you and Simon to have been there but that Simon never said anything about it. And she said that he was intense and difficult...' She paused.

'So...?'

'I don't know.' She ran a finger round the mug, frowning. 'I got the impression she blamed Simon for Julian's accident. And *you* said they fought a lot, that they didn't get on.' She met Theo's now sharp-eyed gaze, needing to know the answer but dreading to ask the question. 'Was there anything suspicious about Julian's death? Was Simon responsible in any way?'

Theo laughed again but this time it definitely sounded forced. He shook his head.

'I can't imagine where you've got that idea from. It's ridiculous.'

'Theo, I'm being serious.'

'Well, you shouldn't be. There was nothing suspicious about Julian's death. It was a horrible accident. I should know.'

'Really?'

'Of course. What are you thinking of? You haven't been reading creepy crime thrillers late at night have you?'

'Don't make fun.'

'Well, you shouldn't pay too much attention to what my mother was saying. She's drunk far too much – like me – and probably has no idea *what* she's saying. She's not used to late nights like this. I ought to take her home.'

Alex wrestled with her conscience and it finally won.

'She could stay in one of the guest rooms if you like,' she offered reluctantly.

'Do you think? That's a kind thought. Still maybe it would be better if I take her home this time.' He drank some coffee and then got up. He moved round the table and bent over to kiss her. He peered into her eyes. 'Will you be all right alone?'

'Of course.' She hesitated. 'Theo?'

'Mm?'

'Your mother seems bitter about Julian's accident. Was there something about it that could have been prevented?'

He straightened up with an impatient sigh.

‘For God’s sake, no. It was bravado. I told you. He was running over the stones - we all did it, all the time, showing off. But Julian got it wrong and the tide was too far in. Why on earth are you so obsessed with Julian’s accident? Forget about it Alex. Please. *I* want to. Hm?’

Alex nodded but when she followed Theo into the drawing room to say goodbye to his mother, she couldn’t stop herself glancing uneasily across at the grandfather clock.

Chapter 21

March stormed in windy and mild with a succession of squally showers which buffeted Kellaford Bridge and sent white spray up and over the quay at high tide. Children hid beneath the harbour wall waiting for the next big wave and then ran away squealing with delight, trying to stay ahead of the water.

But the tide was far out and the harbour quiet when Theo left The Armada and wandered across the quay on the first Saturday of the month. It was lunch-time and he'd had just one pint of bitter before coming away. Today most of the men at the bar had been heavily involved in a discussion about football, a subject which left Theo cold. It had been Eric Ladyman who, hoping to cadge a drink, had manipulated Theo into the conversation, commenting conversationally that he often saw Alex out walking.

'Do you?' Theo had responded, and quickly seized the presented opportunity. 'I know she likes to walk – all weathers.' He'd laughed wryly then. 'Fortunately she doesn't always expect me to go along too. Not that it stops me worrying about her. She goes over the stones and up to Dolphin Point sometimes and there's a couple of nasty-looking cracks forming in the cliff up there. I think there'll be some more rocks down before long.'

'You should tell her then,' Andy Turner had said, tersely. 'Perhaps she doesn't realise how dangerous it can be up there.'

'Hell, I've told her often enough,' he'd returned, affecting frustration. 'But if Alex has set her mind on doing something, she won't be swayed. She's incredibly stubborn. Anyway, you know women: they won't be told.'

There'd been nods and mutterings of agreement then and he'd let the subject drop. Now he wondered if he'd been too heavy handed. Andy Turner was no fool and could be an awkward bugger at times. All he'd wanted to do was to sow the next seeds of his plan. But suppose Alex got talking to Andy on the ferry and the man brought up the subject of Dolphin Point himself? Was he starting to lose his hold on this whole project?

Theo walked to the harbour wall and looked out on the wet, sandy bowl and the gulls which strutted across its surface, looking for food. One of them noticed his arrival and flew up to land on the wall a couple of metres away, eyeing him speculatively with one pale impertinent eye, and he chased it away with an impatient wave of his hand.

He was unusually ill at ease. Just over a week had gone by and the mistakes of the party still preyed on his mind. In retrospect he'd invited too many people. Instead of making Alex feel the pressure of so many witnesses to her engagement, the crush of people appeared to have alienated her, rendering the event perhaps too impersonal. And then he'd drunk too much himself and had carelessly neglected her. After months of hard work, it had been a brief but dangerous lapse in concentration. And he'd allowed his mother to drink too much and to roam too freely. How had that particular and awkward conversation come up between her and Alex? He wished he'd pursued what had been said exactly but didn't want to bring it up again. He'd treated the whole thing as absurd and couldn't afford to alter that impression.

But now, though Alex still treated him the same way, still wore her engagement ring, still talked in vague terms of their future together, there was something about her which worried him. He had long been aware that she held a part of herself back but he had only lately realised how deep she ran. Grief and vulnerability had given him a false impression of her shallowness and compliance; he was beginning to see a steelier side to her character. When he'd tried to pass all the cost of the party onto her, she'd stood her ground, pointing out that the party had been his idea and it had mostly been his friends who had consumed all the drink; *and* it had been she who had had to clear up afterwards. He'd been obliged to give in with good grace rather than cause a rift. He knew she wasn't bothered about the money as such, that it was a matter of principle for her, and he was concerned about what significance that had. It suggested an independence of thought which was worrying. And though she responded to his love-making she still did so perfunctorily, without any real passion. There was something inside her which he couldn't reach. He'd thought he had the measure of her which put him in control; now he wasn't so sure. He was scared that she would slip out of his grip before he'd worked his plan through.

The morning after the party, he'd tried talking to Sarah again, explaining how fragile Alex's compliance might be, how careful they both needed to be about their behaviour towards her and what they said. 'Of course darling,' she'd immediately responded. But the party at the Hall had embedded the prospect of living there so firmly in her head that it was getting harder and harder to quell her enthusiasm, made worse by the news that Alex had accepted an offer on the Hampstead house and that there would soon be money to spend on the Hall. Sarah kept talking about how she'd like the annexe refurbished for when she moved in. He didn't want to encourage her to think about it yet but, if all his plans worked out, her stay in the annexe wouldn't need to last long.

But in the short term he needed to look for another well-paid crewing job. He left the harbour wall and walked back up the quay, shoulders hunched against the spatter of rain in the wind. The job at the yard paid little and Theo was prodigal. In any case, courting Alex was expensive and it was important he kept up the right image until the wedding. Perhaps working abroad wasn't ideal but giving Alex a bit of space for a week or two was no bad thing; it had become clear she wasn't someone he could afford to crowd.

*

So Theo had gone away again. 'This chap I met last year got in touch to ask if I'd crew for him,' he told Alex. 'I couldn't say no. He's been let down by someone at short notice and he's already had the deposit for the charter. Patrick said it was OK. It won't be for too long. Then I promise I won't go away again for ages. I'd rather be with you.'

The night before he left he'd persuaded her to set a date for the wedding. 'Maybe late April?' he'd suggested. 'It would be a great time for a honeymoon. And I know just the place we should go. Let me arrange it all. It'll be a surprise.'

Now that he'd gone, Alex remembered being flattered by his enthusiasm and desire – who wouldn't be? – but wondered a little that she'd agreed. April seemed so soon. There again, why not April? she thought. Why wait? Time was marching on after all; her fortieth birthday loomed at the end of the year. She should embrace her decision and run with it. She tried to recapture the happy, careless mood of those days before the party, when it had seemed easy for a while to seize the moment and look forward to a new beginning. Now it felt harder to do. Something had changed.

The conversation with Sarah Hellyon had stayed with her, like the bad aftertaste of a meal not enjoyed. Before Theo left, Alex had tried to bring Julian's accident up with him again but he'd brushed off the subject impatiently and said he couldn't remember much about it now anyway. But she hadn't told him about the clock stopping, or the icy columns of air which moved around the house, or the voice she sometimes thought she heard calling, always falling silent before she could grasp the words. When Theo had found his wallet thrown casually in the waste bin and had accused her of a strange sort of humour, she'd tried to suggest that there might be some sort of restless spirit in the house, hoping he'd give her a chance to discuss it with him. He'd been unusually abrupt then, dismissing her 'wild imaginings' rather savagely and she'd let the matter drop. She couldn't cope with the friction. And perhaps he was right anyway. Julian was beginning to haunt her dreams and it was time she tried to put him out of her mind; she was letting the eccentric sounds and movements of a creaking old house develop a life of their own. And now she wanted to give them a name.

So Alex made some phone calls, exploring possible dates for the wedding, searching for suitable hotels which had a civil wedding licence and facilities for an informal reception. Then she rang Erica to tell her the news and check when she'd be available. Her sister clearly had someone at the house, someone she wasn't prepared to talk about and didn't want to leave for long. Her reaction was therefore necessarily subdued and Alex was relieved to be able to obtain Erica's promise to come without yet more warnings and advice. When the call ended, Alex held the phone for some minutes, arguing with herself before ringing her mother's number. It was Erica who'd persuaded Victoria to come to Simon's funeral, Erica who'd negotiated their mother's invitation to their wedding so many years before. This time Alex was determined to seize the nettle and do it herself. A few minutes later, after a mutually guarded conversation ending in Victoria's promise to attend, Alex put the phone down feeling a small glow of weary personal triumph.

A couple of days later she drove to Plymouth to look for something to wear for the wedding, ordered a dress and bought some accessories and then drove home questioning her choice. When she got home, she found Theo's mother sitting on the sofa in the drawing room, a fire burning up brightly in the grate of the inglenook. As she walked in Sarah looked up at her coyly.

'Ah, Alex. I hope you don't mind? It was a bit chilly so I put a match to the fire.'

'No, of course not.' Alex trotted out the form reply without thinking and then frowned. 'Did I forget to lock the door?'

'No, you gave Theo a key to the front door didn't you? He left it at the Lodge.'

Alex stood, staring. In the face of this blatant intrusion, she couldn't think what to say.

'Didn't Theo say I might call?' Sarah added, shifting edgily in the chair. 'I thought he said he had.'

'Not that I remember. But you should have rung before you came, Mrs Hellyon, to check I'd be here. I might not have got back for ages.'

'Do call me Sarah dear. Mrs Hellyon always makes me feel so old. And we'll soon be related after all.'

'Sarah,' Alex repeated, tight-lipped. 'Was there something you came here especially to see me about?'

'No Alex. Just a visit. You know.'

'Of course…' Alex tried to smile. 'Right.'

She offered Sarah tea and then drifted into the kitchen to make it. She didn't remember Theo saying anything about his mother calling. Or did she? She'd had a lot on her mind lately. Or did he forget? Or had Sarah dreamt the whole thing up in some whisky-induced alcoholic haze? Sarah's drinking was obviously becoming an issue which could be avoided no longer. She needed to speak to Theo about it though it wouldn't be easy; he could be very protective and touchy about his mother. And then there was the issue of Sarah letting herself into the house. Why did it bother her so? Sarah was going to be her mother-in-law after all. But still this was Alex's home and she couldn't shake off the disturbing suspicion that Sarah had come to the Hall knowing that it would be empty. She regularly saw the woman's face watching at the window when she drove out past the Lodge.

Over tea, Sarah talked endlessly about the wedding. She wanted to know what Alex would be wearing and what outfit her mother would have. The dress and silk jacket she described as having chosen for herself sounded worryingly grand. An image of her at the party floated into Alex's mind. Then she wanted to know all about the reception.

‘I thought we might have it here,’ she said. ‘Hillen Hall would make a perfect backdrop for a wedding reception. It’s convenient for the church and we could have a marquee out on the park.’

Alex finally dug her heels in. She didn’t like the sound of this ‘we’.

‘But I don’t want the reception here, Sarah,’ she said. ‘In any case, as I thought I’d made clear, it’s going to be a small wedding and very informal. A marquee would be quite unnecessary. We’re not having a church wedding anyway. You can get married in lots of places these days.’

‘I suppose so.’ The smile froze on Sarah’s face. ‘Well, it seems a shame, but if that’s what you want.’ Soon after, she made her excuses and left.

Clearing up after she’d gone, Alex made a mental note to bolt the front door in future. She usually used the kitchen door anyway. There would be no more uninvited visits while she was out.

*

Theo’s mother might be kept at bay but Alex found Julian harder to keep out of her mind and Sarah’s visit rekindled all the old questions. Later in the afternoon she picked up Bill Franklin’s notebooks again and read through his brief account of the tragedy several times over, willing it to give up more information. She began to flick through the books hoping to find another reference to it but the notes were such a succession of infuriatingly haphazard scribbles that in the end she threw them down in frustration and went to make herself a meal.

That evening, curled up in the chair by the stove in the snug, she picked them up again and steeled herself to restart from the beginning. After a while, getting nowhere, she went back to the original account and read it through. At the bottom of the piece there was a squiggle, as if Bill had caught the paper by accident or was testing out the pen. She'd seen it before and hadn't apportioned it any significance. But then it occurred to her that it might indicate a cross-reference to another relevant note and she began to search again. It was two in the morning when she finally found the matching mark and another reference to Julian's accident. It was brief but contained the particular information she'd been looking for:

It is difficult to get eye-witness accounts of the accident after all these years. Most reports now are second or even third hand. Apparently Julian, his brother Theo and their cousin Simon were playing by the river in the evening. Julian's parents were entertaining guests to dinner up at Hillen Hall. The boys were often seen out in the village together in the evening; their sometimes boisterous behaviour had caused comment. Some said they weren't being controlled enough. Around dusk someone reported hearing shouts. It is believed that around eight fifteen Julian was trying to get over the stones when one of them gave way and he fell in. The cousin ran back up to the Hall. The brother stayed by the river but Julian disappeared from sight. It is assumed he drowned almost immediately. It was a couple of days later when his body was washed up on Longcombe beach.

Around eight-fifteen. It was just as she'd begun to suspect: Julian had died at twenty-past eight. Alex shuddered involuntarily and glanced at the clock on the mantelpiece. It was after eleven o'clock. She walked through to the drawing room, put on every light, and crossed to the long case clock. After a few minutes she managed to get it to run again and closed the door. She stared at it and then looked round the room, unsure in what way the clock stopped or when, or if, indeed, there was any pattern to it at all. But since she couldn't stay there constantly, watching, she reluctantly abandoned it for the night and went to bed. This was going to be a waiting game.

Thereafter, each successive evening, soon after eight, Alex walked into the drawing room and positioned herself in front of the clock. For three nights the clock chimed a quarter past the hour and then ran through, uninterrupted, and chimed the half hour. It ticked on and eventually Alex gave up and left the room. When she checked in the morning, it had run through the night. By the fourth night, standing there again around ten past eight, watching the dial slowly move round, she began to think her obsession with the death of a fifteen-year old boy she'd never met was sending her crazy. This was a stupid idea. What on earth did she think she was going to achieve? She shuffled her feet restlessly and yet couldn't bring herself to leave.

The clock chimed the quarter hour and ticked on. She glanced around the room, checking to see if anything had moved, for anything abnormal at all, but there was nothing. Her gaze irresistibly returned to the clock. The minute hand was virtually on the four and she was trying to convince herself to leave when it juddered the last millimetre into position and she felt a creeping chill sweep through her. She stared at the hand; it was frozen. The ticking had stopped. She glanced around again. Her chest felt tight and she realised she was holding her breath and forced herself to breathe out and inhale again. There was nothing to be scared of, she told herself. Nothing. Looking back at the clock, she jumped as an owl hooted outside and then laughed nervously. She lifted a hand to open the door to the clock face but stopped short of touching it and then moved her hand up and down either side of the case instead. She felt nothing but what, in God's name, did she expect to feel? She slowly turned round and addressed the empty room.

'Julian?' she said softly, in a voice that shook. 'Is that you?'

Chapter 22

Mick wrapped up the carving in an old canvas bag and then, glancing out of the window and seeing light rain starting to fall, he put it inside a large bin bag and knotted the top. He stood a moment, gazing down at it. He had argued with himself for weeks before resolving to do this – a host of compelling reasons for going almost always counteracted by equally cogent ones for staying away - and yet he was still unsure if he was doing the right thing. He glanced across at Susie who was standing by the door watching him, waiting patiently to accompany him wherever he intended to go. Since Theo's visit he'd made a point of bringing her in to the carriage with him rather than leave her outside unattended. He didn't like her out of his sight these days, didn't want to give the man any excuse to carry out his threats.

'What do you think?' he asked her and she tilted her head to one side, listening, flop ears pricked. 'Should we go to see Alex?' At the woman's name Susie tipped her head the other way and her tail thumped the floor.

Still undecided, Mick stretched out a hand to stroke Susie's head and then sat down again. The dog lay down too, stretched out one front leg and rested her head on it with a pointed grunt. Mick looked round his tiny sitting room and sighed. It was a shambles; he hadn't cleared up properly for weeks. He'd intended to, had even made half-hearted attempts to do so at first, but then he'd realised that Alex wouldn't be coming any more and he couldn't be bothered. On the outside of the carriage, someone had sprayed obscene words in paint and tails of the paint trailed across the window and he hadn't done anything to clear that up either.

Would she listen to him if he turned up at her door? There again, what did he have to lose? There were so many reasons why he wanted to see her. He swore and stood up again. He'd been through this a million times. He should just do it.

*

Pushing open the wrought iron gate which gave on to the front garden of Hillen Hall, Mick glanced warily around and then flicked a glance towards the Lodge. He'd heard that Theo had gone away for a couple of weeks but he couldn't be sure. It was two-thirty. The man would probably be at work anyway but Mick was both nervous and angry with himself for his cowardice. Still, he was on alien territory, unknown; he felt more confident when he was on his own patch. He called Susie close to heel, stepped up the path to the front door, hesitated and pressed the bell-push. He could hear it ring inside and waited, heart thumping, for the door to open. When there was no response he was considering trying again when Susie twisted round and whined. He turned to see Alex standing just inside the gate, watching him. She appeared fixed to the spot but eventually walked slowly towards him. She wasn't wearing a coat and her hair was flattened against her head in the rain. He thought she looked lovelier than ever; he'd forgotten how luminous she was, how she radiated warmth. When she got close to him she stopped, square on, hands rammed in the pockets of her jeans. She said nothing but her blue eyes challenged him and she waited.

'Hello Alex,' he said. Susie moved to her side and Alex bent over to give her a fuss. The rain was getting heavier by the minute and when she straightened up he could see it running down her face onto her neck and then down to her sweater. She ran the back of one hand under her chin to wipe it away. 'I've come to tell you all about it,' he said.

'I don't want to know,' she said, and stepped forward to pass him but he put a hand out and gripped her arm.

'Please…Alex. I can't believe you don't want to hear my side of the story. The Alex I used to know was always fair. I can't believe you've changed that much.' She looked down at his hand and he let go of her but still she didn't move. She ran her eyes over him and he could sense her disapproving appraisal. He'd made a weak attempt to tidy up his beard and his hair before he'd come out but he knew he didn't look good. He wished he'd taken more trouble. 'I should have told you everything long ago,' he continued. 'I know that. And I'm sorry. I'm sorry you found out from someone else.' He hesitated. 'Look, I'm not sure what you know exactly but it isn't…wasn't…what it seems. Won't you let me explain?' He waited but she said nothing though neither did she move. She just looked at him. He thought he could see evidence in her eyes of some sort of internal struggle. 'Please?' he pressed her softly.

'You'd better come in,' she said. 'You'll have to come round to the kitchen door though. This one's bolted.' She walked off and he followed her round the corner to the back. She turned at the door and caught him glancing down towards the Lodge. 'Theo's away,' she said, and then turned the key in the door and pushed it open.

‘I know. All the same I’d better not come in. I’m dirty.’

‘Of course you are. But you’d better come in anyway. I’m not going to stand in the rain talking to you.’

‘I don’t want to leave Susie outside.’

‘She can come in too.’ Alex looked down at the dog and smiled. ‘Come on Susie. Let’s see if I’ve got a treat for you.’ She stepped inside onto the doormat, kicked her muddy shoes off and called the dog again. Susie followed her in and immediately shook her rain-sodden fur all over the kitchen. Mick hesitated and then stepped inside too.

*

Mick stood in the middle of the kitchen and glanced around. It was old and worn, dingy even. He was surprised perhaps, though in truth he hadn’t known what to expect. He’d rehearsed this moment so many times but now his witty opening gambits felt clearly out of place and the more sensitively considered sentences deserted him. He stood there, feeling foolish. Susie was in the corner, already demolishing the chewy treat Alex had given her. Alex had grabbed a towel from behind the door and was dabbing it over her face and neck.

‘Take your coat off,’ she said. ‘Here,’ she added, passing him the towel. ‘You’re soaking too. Have a seat.’ She nodded at the chairs by the table. He dumped his bag on the floor and rubbed the towel briefly over his face. He glanced down at it to see if he’d made it dirty, then pushed it back onto the hook. ‘Coffee?’ she said, without looking at him and was already picking up the coffee jug to fill with water.

‘Yes…thanks.’ Mick carefully removed his waxed coat and put it round the back of a chair before easing himself down onto the seat.

Neither spoke while Alex filled the filter with coffee and set it running. Susie patrolled the kitchen, nose to the floor in search of crumbs, her claws clicking on the stone floor. The rain pattered against the window and could be heard gurgling insistently down the drainpipe outside. Eventually, and reluctantly it seemed to Mick, Alex had nothing left to do and she slid into a seat opposite him. She lifted her eyes to his.

‘Well?’

‘I see you’ve already judged me.’

‘I don’t need to do that. You were judged years ago and found guilty. How do you expect me to react?’

‘I expect you to keep an open mind.’ He could see distrust in her expression. ‘I didn’t do it – whatever version of the story you’ve heard.’ Mick checked himself. He hadn’t intended to be so confrontational. He could understand why she might be upset and confused but defensiveness was ingrained in him.

Alex stared at him and then got up and walked out of the room. She came back a couple of minutes later with the press copy Theo had given her. She passed it to Mick without a word. He looked down it and then lifted his eyes to look at her.

‘Is this all you’ve seen?’

‘Isn’t it enough?’

Mick tossed the paper down on the table.

‘No.’

‘So, it’s not true? You haven’t been to prison for sexually abusing children?’

'Yes, of course,' he said. 'That bit's true.' Alex pulled a pained face and turned her head away. '*And* some of the rest of it,' he pressed on. 'I *was* a biology teacher and then went to work on a nature reserve but there was no abuse...ever.' Alex turned back to look at him and he could see how much she wanted to believe him. This was probably his only chance to make her understand and he hesitated, desperate to choose the right words. 'I never did anything inappropriate with any child. That's not to say there weren't a few I wouldn't have liked to slap at times but I never touched any of them...ever. Alex? It's true.'

'So? Go on.'

'The school I used to work for began to run regular school trips to the reserve, three or four times over the term, and I was responsible for showing them round, organising projects for them to do. There was one lad – a fifteen year old - who was a troublemaker. He kept throwing things at the nesting birds, trying to get to the nests to steal eggs. He was a complete pain in the ass. I remembered him from the school and he'd always been difficult when I was teaching him. In the end I caught him actually stealing eggs one day and gave him some grief. I said I was going to report him. He was cocky and aggressive and made a load of threats. I didn't pay any attention. I'd heard stuff like that before.'

He paused. 'That evening I had the police at my door. They were arresting me for supposedly molesting this lad when he was in the first year at the school. I couldn't believe it. I knew I was innocent so I tried to stay calm. I assumed that it would all be sorted out over an interview and that would be the end of it. But I was wrong; it was just the start of a god-awful nightmare. The next thing one of the boy's cronies came forward to claim the same thing. So much time had passed that there was no chance of doing DNA tests or anything to prove it one way or the other. It was my word against theirs.' Mick shook his head, feeling the throat-thickening emotion he still had every time he thought about it. 'I didn't have a hope. I was remanded. It took ages to come to trial and then I was sent down for six years. That was hell on earth. You know what they do to child-abusers in prison? Well, you don't want to.'

Alex was watching every move of his face as he spoke. Then the sound of hissing from the coffee-maker prompted her to get up. She opened a cupboard, took out a packet of biscuits and tipped some onto a plate. 'Here,' she said, putting them in front of him. 'You're thinner than ever.' She turned back to pour the coffee and then brought it to the table.

She sat down but this time didn't look at him and sat fiddling with a spoon, as he had so often seen her do before.

'I did three years Alex. But then I was released early on appeal.' She looked up at him then.

'What? Why?'

'Some new evidence came up. My defence team found another boy who said he'd heard my two accusers laughing and joking about how they'd stitched me up. He was prepared to testify.' Mick paused. 'It was bloody brave of him.'

'So what happened?'

'To cut a long story short, after much debate and argument, the appeal court overturned the verdict, said that I was innocent after all and I was released.'

Alex leaned forward onto the table then with an earnest expression.

‘I don’t understand. So, if you’re innocent, why did you end up here? Why the carriage thing? Why do you behave as if you’re guilty, hiding away?’

Mick leaned back in the chair and rested his wiry hands flat on the table, trying to look calm.

‘Because once you’re convicted of a crime like that, everyone doubts you. A lot of people think that a successful appeal means that you’ve just got away with it, not that you’re innocent.’ He sat forward again, drank some coffee and then picked up a biscuit. He shot a glance towards Alex’s face. She was frowning.

‘I didn’t know. That was the only report I saw,’ she said, looking towards the newspaper article.

‘How did you see it?’ he asked, though he knew the answer.

‘Theo showed it to me. A friend of his brought it to his attention.’

‘There’s an unlucky coincidence,’ he said casually. ‘Well, there *were* other reports. Of course there were pages of it when I was convicted, column upon column of spurious evidence and hearsay. When my appeal was upheld, it was crammed into one paragraph inside. If you look, you’ll find it somewhere. Have a look on the internet. You can find everything there these days can’t you?’ Mick grimaced. Try as he might, he couldn’t keep the bitterness out of his voice. He picked up the mug of coffee again.

Alex was quiet for a few minutes. He waited. Susie had come to lie down near his feet and he reached a hand down to rub the top of her head.

‘I’m sorry,’ Alex said eventually. She lifted her eyes and looked at him directly. ‘I’m sorry it happened and I’m sorry I didn’t come to give you a chance to explain. I found it hard to believe but…' Her voice trailed off as her eyes came to rest on the news copy and then added: 'It seemed impossible to deny.'

'After seeing that report, I can see why. And it's my fault for not telling you in the first place. Silence suggests guilt, doesn't it? But at least you're listening to me now which is more than most people would do, believe me. Once you've been accused of doing something to a child, no-one wants to know you. That's it – the end of your life as you know it. I can understand why people get so worked up about it – it's a filthy thing to do - but when you're innocent…' He left the sentence hanging. 'Well I had to move away. In any case there was no job to go back to.'

'Family?' Alex asked tentatively.

Mick shook his head.

'My wife divorced me and moved away when I was put in prison. I've got a son somewhere but I haven't seen him since. He was very young. It's probably kinder for him, though I'd love to see him. I'd like him to know the truth.' He took another mouthful of coffee. 'I tried living in a few different places – I even changed my name - but each time someone would find out and then life would become impossible and I moved on.' He paused but Alex was listening keenly now and the words seemed to be tumbling out of him, the release of pressure pushing them out.

'Then I received some money as compensation for my wrongful imprisonment and I found out about the marshy Grenloe land. Felicity Brook had been told it was good for nothing and more of a problem than an asset so she let it go cheap. It was just the sort of place I needed: no-one knew me and I could keep my head down and set up my own reserve. A loyal friend helped me get the old railway carriage down here and I made it over to live in. I wrote a few articles for nature magazines under yet another name, did some carving to sell…' He shrugged. 'I was doing OK.'

'And then I came along and spoiled everything.'

He shook his head.

'I wouldn't put it like that. Not at all.' He looked down and ran one callused finger along a knotty piece of wood in the table top. 'I loved to see you.'

She watched him, frowning.

'So why didn't you tell me?'

He shrugged again. 'I was used to people not believing me.' There was a moment's hesitation before he added, 'I was scared you'd stop coming.'

'And then I did anyway.'

'And then you did anyway so I was a fool.'

'No.' Alex drank some coffee. It had gone cold and she pulled a face and put the mug down. 'You've been having a rough time in the village haven't you? It wasn't me that told them, you know. But I'll certainly tell them the truth now.'

Mick shook his head. 'There's no point. It won't make any difference. People won't believe you. They don't want to believe. I'm marked for life. That's it. I'm the man who exploits children.' His gaze fell on the diamond ring on her left hand. 'So you're engaged?' He tried to sound careless.

'Yes.' She automatically glanced down at the ring. 'You hadn't heard?'

'Oh yes. I still hear odd things. So…have you fixed a date for the wedding?'

'April 25th. A small one.'

'It's all right,' he said dryly. 'I wasn't fishing for an invitation.' He smiled at her, allowing himself the luxury now of studying her face. He opened his mouth to say something else then closed it again. 'We've got a bittern nest,' he said instead. 'I was hoping to show it to you.'

'That would be good.' She smiled. 'How many eggs?'

'Not sure. Don't like to get too close in case I scare her off.' He finished his coffee and they were silent again but it seemed to him that the air was charged with things unsaid. He wanted to talk to her about Theo but didn't know what to say or how to say it, reluctant to spoil the pleasure of the moment.

'So you're Martin Foster,' Alex said in a forced, flippant tone. 'We should be introduced.'

He shook his head. 'Nope, I'm Mick. Martin was a previous life.'

She nodded and hesitated, playing with the spoon again.

'You'll think I'm crazy,' she said suddenly and looked up at him. 'But what would you say if I said I'd got a ghost here?'

It was the last thing he'd expected her to say and his first reaction was to laugh.

'I'm serious Mick.'

'OK, so I'd say: what makes you think there's a ghost?'

'All the usual things people joke about: icy columns of air, creaking boards, doors which seem to open and close at will. But then I can feel him too.' She looked up and glanced round and he automatically did the same and then found himself grinning.

'Don't laugh,' she said.

'I'm sorry. You said 'him'. Why do you think it's a him?'

'Because I think it's Julian.' She shook her head. 'I can't believe I'm saying this. But I can't deny it any more. That's what I think.'

'Julian Hellyon?'

She nodded. 'You know about him?'

'A little. He died in the Kella when he was young. Why do you think it's him?'

'Things first started happening in his bedroom – that's the room I sleep in. And sometimes the spirit seems young. It's…' She frowned as if trying to find a suitable word to describe it. '…playful. And then there's the clock. The grandfather clock in the drawing room keeps stopping at the same time. Over and over again. Twenty past eight. And the thing is: that was the time Julian Hellyon died in the river. Twenty past eight in the evening.'

Mick leaned forward onto the table, all thoughts of humour now gone.

'That's…weird.'

She laughed nervously. 'Don't you think I know that?'

He sat back again, running a hand over his tatty beard.

'You believe me then?' she asked.

Mick pulled a face. 'Yes. If you're so sure. What does Theo say about it?'

'It's difficult to talk to him about it. He thinks I'm imagining things.'

'I see.'

'Don't say 'I see' like that,' she said defensively. 'I can't blame him. And I don't like to pursue it anyway. It's his brother for God's sake. That would be really odd, wouldn't it?'

Mick nodded.

'I suppose so,' he said slowly. 'So does it scare you, this ghost?'

'Yes and no. He did to start with but now I've got used to it, up to a point. I don't feel threatened by him. He's just there. Not in any sinister way. It's just uncomfortable. I feel as though he follows me around. Not all the time...' She looked into her mug at the cold, scummy remains of her drink. 'Do you want more coffee?' she said, getting up abruptly.

'Yes...thanks.'

Alex took the mugs to the sink and began to recharge the machine.

'What really bothers me,' she said carefully, with her back to him, 'is that I don't know why he's here.'

'Does there have to be a reason?'

'Maybe not. I know very little about Julian. Theo's reluctant to talk about him. His mother says a little and then clams up.' She paused while she rinsed out the mugs and then dropped her voice so quiet he had to strain to catch what she was saying. 'Apparently Simon was with Theo and Julian when the accident happened. And yet he never even mentioned it to me.'

'And so now you're wondering why?'

Alex dried the mugs off and turned round to face him, her expression strained and intense.

'Exactly. I'm wondering what happened that stops everyone from talking about it.'

'You could ask Harry.'

'Harry Downes?' She looked at him sceptically.

'I take wood now and then to Minna and Harry,' he continued. 'I get talking to Harry sometimes. One day he stood watching me stacking logs while Minna was inside. I think Harry was on the river when Julian died. If you want to know what happened, he might know.'

'But Harry can't remember anything. He's muddled and confused.'

Mick shook his head.

'He can't remember things that are going on now; but he remembers things from the past, sometimes very clearly. It depends on the day or the hour. If you give him time, it's surprising what he comes out with.'

'Why, what did he say?'

'Nothing much. Bits. Something seemed to be troubling him. When I got there, Minna said they'd just been up to the shops and then walked round by the quay so he could watch the ferry. When she'd gone inside he said something about having been out in the boat, fishing; he mentioned the stones and Julian's name. "He drowned and I couldn't do anything," he said, and then repeated it, getting really agitated. Minna came out to say that the tea was ready. I said that Harry seemed to be talking about Julian's death and I asked her if she knew anything about it. She got cross, said no, she didn't, and they never talked about it. It was years ago and only made Harry upset. But Theo's protracted return to the village seemed to have set him thinking about it again. "And you'll just make him ill," she said quite angrily, "getting him to talk about it. I'm sure that accident's what made him ill in the first place. He doted on those boys." I didn't stay after that. She gave me some home-baking the way she always does as her payment for the logs, and I left.' Mick leaned forward onto the table again. 'It's no good asking him direct questions because that throws him; you have to come at it from an angle. But if you really want to know about Julian's death, Harry's the person to ask.'

*

Walking home from the Hall, Mick kept to the side of the park and then slipped over the gate into the neighbouring field, unsure if he felt better or worse for having seen Alex again. He was heart-heavy and reluctant to consider why. Susie dropped a stick near him as he walked. He ignored it and she brought it closer, almost dropping it on his feet. He picked it up mindlessly and slung it across the grass. He stopped for a moment to watch her as she pounced on the stick and then trotted back to him with it hanging out of the side of her mouth. While he noticed, for the thousandth time, that she always carried a stick by one end and never in the middle, he wondered why he hadn't told Alex about Theo's visit to the reserve and his threats; he'd intended to. Would she have believed him? It wasn't likely. Look how defensive she'd become over his question about Theo's reaction to the ghost. So he'd said nothing, scared of alienating her again.

He picked up the stick, threw it and started to walk again. And maybe Theo's protectiveness towards the woman he loved was to be expected in the circumstances. Mick would be the same. He wondered if all his resentment of Theo was after all simply the result of jealousy, if all his suspicions were coloured by his own desire, his reasoning poisoned and unsound.

He stopped for a second with a sick feeling in his stomach as if he'd been winded. The 25th April. Hell. When Susie next dropped the stick, he picked it up and then swung it heavily against the nearby hedge in bitter frustration, sending twigs flying.

Chapter 23

The wooden bittern sat next to the hearth in the snug; Alex's eye fell on it as she sat trying to read, waiting for Theo to arrive. She thought of the way Mick had thrust the canvas-wrapped bundle at her before he'd left, hastily in the end as if he couldn't wait to be gone. She'd protested that he had no reason to give her anything. 'Look on it as a wedding present,' he'd said. 'I thought you might like a bittern. Best chance you've got of seeing one. Ugly as hell but we can't all be beautiful, can we?' On the opposite side of the hearth was the avocet Theo had bought her. Theo, freshly returned from his trip, was due to take her out to dinner. She'd spoken to him several times during the week on the phone but had avoided mentioning Mick's visit. She added it to the list of things that she preferred to talk about face to face. She wasn't sure what his reaction would be. Theo was usually equable, easy-going, but as she'd got to know him better she'd seen occasional flashes of his temper, quick to flare, rapidly dampened. But she'd had time to think and there were things which needed to be said, issues which needed to be resolved whatever Theo's response might be.

With the wisdom of hindsight, she knew that she and Simon should have talked more; major problems were hotly argued about but not often resolved, trivial disagreements were ignored or brushed aside only to grow disproportionately with time to seem important or foolishly irritating. She wasn't going to make that mistake again. Now she listened out for Theo's arrival whilst her eyes mechanically scanned the lines of text in her book. It was a Saturday night. It occurred to her that Theo wasn't so protective of his 'nights out with the boys' any more. She supposed that was a good thing.

'Hello-o. I'm back.' Theo now called out, as he always did, in that sing-song way he had as he let himself in. The manner of it held an assumption that she would be waiting on his arrival. And I usually am, she thought. Should I be?

'Hello. I'm in the snug,' she called back, and to her own ears her voice sounded tense.

'Darling.' He swept in, she stood up and he embraced and kissed her. 'It's been ages. God, I've missed you.' He squeezed her tight again then eased away from her and looked round. She'd noticed that he always did this when he came in too, as if checking to see what had changed. Now he frowned, lightly.

'That's new, isn't it, that bird? Odd thing – what the hell is it?'

'Yes. It's a wedding present… Early. It's a bittern.'

'Oh? Who gave us that?'

She hesitated a fraction of a second, just long enough to make him look at her more closely.

'Mick Fenby,' she said. 'Or Martin Foster I suppose I should say but apparently he prefers to be called Mick.'

Theo's face darkened. 'You went to see him? I thought you said you wouldn't?'

'He came here.'

'The hell he did, the bugger. I'm sorry Alex, but he's got a nerve. I told him to stay away from you.'

'Did you? Really? He didn't say.' She frowned and then crossed to the stove, opening the door to put another log in. *That's an unlucky coincidence,* Mick had said. It came back to her now though it hadn't struck her especially at the time. Did he mean anything by that? She kept her back to Theo and bent to poke the fire. 'You didn't tell me you'd seen him.' She felt anger rise inside her, a flame of heat which she was determined to control. They were not going to argue about this; it could be sorted out.

'No.' He shrugged. 'Well I didn't want to upset you.'

She stopped poking the fire and, still crouching, turned to look up at him.

'So I suppose it was you who told everyone in the village too.'

'I thought people had a right to know.'

'He told me he was innocent Theo.'

He snorted derisively. 'Well he would wouldn't he?'

'But apparently the verdict against him was overturned on appeal Theo. And I checked on the internet and he was telling the truth. It took some finding but it was there. It was reported.'

'Really? But that doesn't mean he was innocent Alex. It just means he had a good lawyer and they found a way round it.'

'He said that's what people always say.'

'Because it's true.'

'Well not in this case. There was a new witness. Did you know about the appeal?'

'No. No, of course not. Why are you asking me all this?'

She stood up, the poker still in her hand.

'You seem to have taken his case very personally: going to see him, warning him off, then telling me not to go to the reserve.' She waved the poker as she spoke and gave it a last flourish. 'I don't understand why.'

Theo took the poker from her hand, joked that she was looking dangerous with that thing and surely she wasn't that cross with him. He laid it down on the hearth. She waited, watching him expectantly. She got the impression that he was buying time. Perhaps he, too, was choosing his words carefully, anxious not to cause a rift. When he faced her again, his expression was calm, reasonable.

'I heard about him from that friend I told you about. Obviously I only heard half the story. But it doesn't change the way I feel about him. I have taken it personally as you put it. I was jealous to know you spent time with him alone. And it worried me that you hadn't told me. I suppose I've overreacted. I suspected he was up to no good. I can't say that what you've told me makes me feel any better about it. To be honest I don't trust the guy, but I'm sorry if you think I was out of line.'

'You didn't need to feel jealous. I told you: it wasn't like that. Anyway, we've been all through that before. And I don't see why you can't trust him; you hardly know him. *I* trust him.'

'Fine. That's all right then.' Theo gave her a hug but she barely responded. She was still taut with things yet to be said. She turned away, bent over to close the stove door and then wandered across to the window to draw the curtains. Theo went to the fireplace and put one hand up on the mantelpiece, gazed down at the stalking bittern and then looked across at Alex and smiled. 'In any case I imagine he probably won't stay here now. Things have got a bit hot for him. It's difficult to shake off a past like that, whatever the truth of what happened.'

She registered the persistent suspicion in his words but decided to let it go.

'Well I've been telling everyone I know in the village about his appeal and that he was declared innocent,' she said. 'I hope it'll get easier for him soon. But in any case Mick said he had nowhere else to go, that he had no real money and that no-one would buy that land back; it's too water logged to do anything else with.' She gave the curtains one last twitch and turned to look directly at him. 'I thought I could probably buy it from him with some of the money that's going to come in from the house. But I'd rather he stayed…if that's what he wants to do, wouldn't you?'

Theo raised his eyebrows. A flash of surprise crossed his eyes.

'Mm?'

'Wouldn't you rather he stayed?'

'If that's what you want.'

'I don't want to think that anyone is hounded out of a place, especially when they haven't done anything wrong.'

'Of course not. But I wouldn't exactly…'

'And I assume you wouldn't mind if I went to the reserve again to help out? There's no reason to stay away now. We're not going to have the kind of marriage, are we, where you have to vet everyone I see?'

He looked offended then and she wondered if she'd gone too far. Was she being unfair? She recognised that from Theo's point of view Mick would seem dubious company.

Theo crossed to her and put his hands on her shoulders.

'Of course you can go to the reserve if you want to. I'm sorry. I was just being too protective. You can do whatever you want.'

Alex leaned forward and kissed him, then moved away again.

'Good. I thought it was just a misunderstanding. Let's forget about it.' She turned her back to the hearth. 'But there's something else that I need to talk to you about and it's better we do it now, isn't it? Clear the air?'

'Hell, Alex, what next?' His tone was teasing but she thought he sounded worried – or perhaps cross? 'I've just got back and now all this.'

'It's about your mother Theo.'

'Ye-es. What about her?'

Alex hesitated.

'She used the key I gave you to let herself into the house while I was out.'

'Did she?'

'Yes. She was sitting in the drawing room when I got back, with the fire blazing.'

'OK. Er, sorry, I don't see the problem.'

'You don't?' Alex was thrown. To her, the issue seemed quite clear: it was an invasion of her privacy. 'It's a very uncomfortable feeling having someone let themselves in without you knowing it.' Or perhaps, she thought suddenly, it's just because it's Sarah and she's so odd. Not sure what to say, she added: 'I mean I hardly know your mother…' She'd intended to bring up the drinking, the incessant smell of whisky on Sarah's breath, but Theo was looking at her stonily. She felt her courage waver and she abandoned it for another time.

He shrugged. 'Well, perhaps that's the problem: you don't know my mother well enough. Give her time, you'll get used to her. She doesn't mean anything by it; she's just trying to be neighbourly. I take it she didn't do anything she shouldn't?'

'No, of course not.'

'Or say anything to upset you?'

'No, no. We mostly talked about the wedding. I'm afraid she thinks it's going to be a much bigger, grander affair than it is.'

'She's very excited about it. That's probably why she came over. But I'll talk to her about it again if you like and explain how intimate the wedding's going to be.'

'I wish you would.'

'Fine. But hey, enough of this. You're looking beautiful as always. Let's go out and you can tell me more about what you've been planning and all about your dress.'

'Absolutely not.' She smiled tentatively. 'You can't know anything about it. It's bad luck.'

'No, no, I'm just not allowed to *see* it.'

'Says you.' Alex laughed and took his arm as they went out, relieved to have got the conversation over without a row. Of course it would all sort out.

*

Sarah was in the bathroom when Theo came home the next morning. A brief knock at the door signalled his entry and, as usual, he didn't wait to be invited, but walked straight in. She was standing naked in the bath, drying herself with a large cream towel as the water drained away. He said nothing and sat down on the little wicker chair in the corner, watching her as she rubbed the towel over her sagging flesh and then bent to dry each leg and foot in turn before carefully stepping out of the bath onto the cork mat. He had done this ever since he was a child and she had never objected. Theo liked the intimacy of it, the feeling that he had this special privilege of being with his mother at her most vulnerable. As a child he'd considered himself her guardian against intruders and always moved the chair so that its back was to the door. No-one else would be allowed in, not even his father who, to Theo's surprise and relief, had never shown any interest in sharing his wife's bath time anyway.

Jealousy had always haunted Theo's relationship with his father. As childhood moved into adolescence, he became convinced that his father didn't treat Sarah well. There was no physical abuse as such but Richard Hellyon didn't cherish her enough. Surprise turned to disappointment and then to frank scorn as Theo watched his father obsess over his china and pots instead of his wife. Ironically, he was also pleased and saw a kind of justice in it. He didn't want to share his mother with anyone.

Now, watching Sarah, he remembered how pretty she'd been in her youth with her curvaceous figure, her smooth soft skin and her sleek blond hair. He didn't really see the change in her: the slow corruption of her flesh as she aged. She would always be the same for him. Without success, he felt he'd spent his whole life looking for a woman who would compare with her. Every time he stole a woman from her husband, it was a notch in the tally against his father but the satisfaction was always incomplete.

Now, with her long satin dressing-gown tied and trailing out softly behind her, Sarah left the bathroom and Theo followed her through to her bedroom where she sat down in front of her dressing-table mirror and picked up her hairbrush. Standing behind her, Theo reached for the brush and, catching his eye in the mirror, she let him take it and sat while he brushed her hair.

'Alex has seen that Birdman again.' Theo brushed slowly and rhythmically as he talked. It was soothing, almost mesmeric. 'He actually came up to the house. If I'd only been there…'

'What did he want?'

'He brought us a wedding present – one of those carvings of his. It's as much as I can do to stop myself throwing it on the fire. But Alex seems to love them.'

'Dear me, I can't understand her letting him in.' Sarah smoothed the satin gown out over her dimpled knees. 'Especially after what you told me about him.'

'I know. I went down to where he lives not long ago. It's a filthy place.' He brushed a little faster. 'And he's got a dog. A brute. You know how I hate dogs.'

Sarah reached up a hand to lay it on his.

'Darling,' she said soothingly.

Theo smiled at her reflection in the mirror but his expression masked his anxieties. Alex was becoming difficult to manage and her determined and controlled display of the previous evening had worried him. He hadn't expected her to stand up to him in that way and it was proof, he was sure, of the bad effect Mick Fenby had upon her. He'd spent the rest of the evening attempting to smooth it all over and put it behind them. She'd seemed keen to do the same but still he was concerned.

'I'm not sure what to do about that man.' He stopped brushing her hair, laid the brush down and came to kneel down on the floor beside her. 'I think he's got some sort of hold over her. He influences her.' He ran a hand up into his hair, leaving his curls sticking out at angles. 'He bothers me.'

'He should have had the decency to leave when all that information came out about him.' Sarah reached across and patted his hair down and then ran her hand down his cheek. 'Perhaps he still will. What on earth does it take to make someone like that realise they're not welcome?'

'Mm.' Theo picked up a lipstick from the dressing table and repeatedly twisted it out and back. He smiled suddenly and Sarah smiled back at him indulgently.

'That's right darling,' she said. 'I'm sure it'll all be all right. It's not long till the wedding. There's no time for anything to go wrong, is there?'

Theo lifted himself up off his haunches, leaned over, and kissed her.

'I won't let it.' He patted her hand. 'I promise you. I know what I can do about Mick Fenby.'

Chapter 24

It was the first Thursday in April when Alex visited London again. Completion was due for the house in Hampstead on the Friday and she told Theo she wanted to take all the keys back in person, check the place out and have a look round one last time. It didn't feel right to dispose of somewhere which held so many memories without a personal witness to the parting. Theo had offered to come too, 'to give you moral support', but she'd insisted that it was something she needed to do alone. In any case, she'd rung in advance and arranged to stay with Erica, a chance for them to spend a little time together again before what her sister insisted on describing as 'the big day'.

The visit to the house was a good excuse for a break anyway. The wedding was little more than three short weeks away. The arrangements, slow to get going, now seemed to have taken on a momentum which felt unstoppable. Alex recognised creeping cold feet, passed it off as wedding nerves, and was pleased to distance herself for a few days to clear her head. She stopped at Winchester to have lunch with her friend Catherine, and then idled her way on to London, a welcome distraction from the pressures of home.

Theo had already moved a few of his things into Hillen Hall, taking over one of the spare bedrooms as his study. 'Somewhere to keep all my clutter out of your way,' he'd said. He'd chosen the room he'd had as a child and had moved an old desk into it from one of the other rooms along the corridor. 'My father's,' he'd declared, and had appeared particularly pleased to be using it. He'd brought books to fill the shelves, pictures for the walls and a pile of file boxes. 'Paperwork. Things I need to keep on top of.' There was a lot of it. Theo was a hoarder; he kept mementoes: tickets, receipts, wine foils, beer mats, leaflets – she'd seen him pocket them all. She viewed it as an engaging eccentricity. But it did seem strange to suddenly have Theo's belongings in the Hall, a house she had come to regard as her own territory over the preceding year, and she recognised a deep-seated nervousness about sharing again and the threat to her independence.

Scared of another commitment would be more like it, she thought, as she negotiated the hectic traffic round London and wondered why she hadn't come by train. The good times with Simon had been wonderful but she didn't want a repeat of all that conflict, the jostling for position and petty jealousies. She'd convinced herself that there was no risk of that this time; there could be no clash of musical egos or artistic temperaments. *And* she had learnt from her mistakes. But with his personal belongings in the house, she'd already seen another side to Theo: possessive of his own space and not a little defensive of his privacy, character traits she hadn't realised he shared with Simon. And there was something in his attitude to the house which occasionally jarred with her, something which seemed to have changed though she couldn't quite say how. She reminded herself that it would shortly be his home too which made his behaviour only natural, but it was, perhaps, a warning sign of things to come. She remembered Erica once declaiming: 'Compromise, that's the key to a good relationship.' Maybe, thought Alex with a wry smile, but, considering Erica's success with men, the advice seemed out of place.

She turned into 'her' road for what she knew would be the last time, opened the gates to the house and drove in to park. She looked up at the house she'd shared with Simon and felt the familiar assault of a host of memories. With a deep breath, slowly exhaled, she grabbed her bag and got out of the car.

*

'What's happening down on that nature reserve?' Ben asked, pouring lavish amounts of ketchup over his veggie burger. 'Have you seen anything rare there?'

It was the Friday evening. Alex had handed the house keys over to the estate agent first thing that morning and had then done a little shopping. She'd met Ben from school and had taken him swimming while Erica took advantage of her freedom to have her hair done after work. Now they were in his favourite burger restaurant while Erica went to her weekly Italian class.

'We've got a bittern,' Alex said, and then wondered at her choice of pronoun. She'd only been back down to the Grenloe once since Mick had called at the Hall and it had been a strange visit. She'd been keen to catch up on the place and desperate to see the bittern's nest. She'd done it too to prove that she wouldn't be put off by Theo's pointed disapproval. But it hadn't felt easy the way it had before. She'd hoped to pick up her friendship with Mick – seeing him up at the Hall had emphasised for her just how much she'd missed him - but they were stiff with each other, a little polite perhaps. The prospect of her forthcoming wedding loomed in both their minds it seemed and couldn't be ignored.

'What's a bittern?' asked Ben, breaking into her thoughts, and she went on to describe the shy bird and its little cup-shaped nest built in the reeds. Her nephew was animated and unusually chatty, excited at the change to his routine – he usually spent Friday evening at his friend Jake's house.

'You like Jake, don't you?' she enquired.

'Yes. He's OK. But his mum *always* gives us fish fingers.' He pulled a face. 'Disgusting.'

Alex laughed.

'So why don't you tell her you've become a vegetarian?'

'People can be funny about it. Mum still insists on giving me fish too.'

Alex's thoughts inevitably turned to Erica.

'I was surprised to hear she was taking Italian,' she said. 'She's never been into languages much before.'

'It's beginners.' Alex drank some Coke. 'She thinks we should go to Italy some time and get some culture. You know: galleries, monuments, Roman amphitheatre.' Ben hesitated, picked up his fork, and then added, casually: 'If that's what she's really doing of course.'

Alex, chewing a mouthful of burger, stared at Ben's face, her brow puckering into a frown.

'Why? Where else would she be?'

Ben shrugged his narrow shoulders. He was a little small for his age. He would never be a big man, she thought, but what he lacked in stature, he more than made up for with mental acuity. But he'd taken her by surprise with this one.

'Maybe she's got a date,' said Ben. 'She had her hair done and she said she might go for a drink with some of the class after.'

'Because I'm here with you.'

'No, she's done it before.'

Alex thought of the mysterious visitor Erica had been entertaining when she'd rung about the wedding.

'But why wouldn't she tell you?'

'I think she's scared of upsetting me with another man – 'a father figure'. And she's scared of putting off a boyfriend by introducing her difficult eleven-year-old son.'

'You're not difficult.'

'That's not what she says. In any case,' he remarked, in that studiously poised way he had, as if he didn't care, 'she's probably right. I guess a man might be nervous about taking me on too.' Ben worked his way through some more chips. 'Maybe I'm wrong, but I haven't seen her doing much homework. Anyway, she's done it before. Only last time she said it was a book club. I don't think it was; I think it was a boyfriend – they kept changing nights – but of course I couldn't be sure.'

Alex grinned. Ben was maybe too smart for his own good.

'So would you like 'a father figure' then, or not?'

'I'm not bothered. I like things the way they are.' He finished his burger and pushed the plate away. 'Will we still be able to do this when you're married?'

'Of course. Didn't we do it before?' She smiled ruefully. 'No, well maybe not often enough, I suppose; I was always too busy. But it'll be different this time. And you can come down to stay with us in Devon too.'

'You don't think Theo would mind?'

'Good Lord no. Why should he?'

Ben didn't answer but drank the last of his Coke while Alex finished her meal.

'I'd like to come,' he said eventually. 'I'd like to see the reserve again.' A couple of minutes later, he added: 'Are you planning to have children with Theo?'

Taken off guard, Alex hesitated. She'd asked Theo if he wanted children not long before coming away and he'd looked surprised, as though the idea had caught him unawares. 'If *you* do,' he'd said, flashing his smile, 'I do too. Yes, why not?' It hadn't been the considered response she'd hoped for.

'I'm not sure I'd cope if they were as smart as you,' she said now, teasingly. 'Have you finished? Shall we go home?'

'Yes. Let's go and look up bitterns on the internet.'

*

Alex was staying till the Tuesday. On the Saturday morning she had a lesson with Francine which she'd arranged by phone the week before, though by the time she arrived she was a bundle of nerves and nearly turned away. Francine lived and worked in St. John's Wood in a small, quirky detached house set back from the road. Alex rang the bell and fidgeted on the doorstep. It brought back so many memories: arriving as a child, excited but awestruck; coming in her mid teens, often after a row with her mother, looking on it as a refuge and a way out; coming for last minute practice before exams; and, more recently, coming to fine tune a performance, to work on particular technical issues or a difficult piece of music. There had always been something to learn from her old tutor. When Francine answered the doorbell and Alex followed her through the house, it felt like she was stepping back in time.

Francine's home was warm and lavish, with an eclectic mix of art and antiques and mementoes from her travels. Francine had never married though occasional comments had suggested a passionate love affair in her youthful past, but her home showed no record of it; it was hers alone. Her music studio was in a room at the rear of the house where a baby grand piano stood near the patio doors out to the garden. On the shelves each side were books on music, musicians and singers, and photographs of people Francine had taught: in concert, collecting awards, alone or posing self-consciously by her side. While Francine went to get a glass of water for Alex – a routine that never changed – she glanced along the photographs. There were two pictures of her: one of her receiving the prestigious Kathleen Ferrier award and a second of her singing at Cadogan Hall, her hands unconsciously raised in an eloquent gesture to confirm the thrust of the song.

The session went surprisingly well. It was like putting on an old and comfortable sweater. Vocal exercises, old songs she knew by heart – Francine cajoled her and shouted at her, pushed and chivvied. There was no time for conversation – there never had been. 'Stand straight; stop slouching and lift your head up. Feet apart Alex, come on, feet apart. Now…' She'd play a chord. '….again please.' Everything was reassuringly the same. Alex left feeling tired but invigorated and nervously excited. She'd forgotten just how exquisite the singing could make her feel, deep inside. It touched a part of her nothing else ever had.

The rest of the weekend was for the family. It stayed fine and dry and Alex went out with Erica and Ben. They went for a boat trip on the Thames, visited the Natural History museum and had a picnic up on the heath. On the Monday, Alex had another gruelling lesson with Francine and parted with her promising to get in touch when she got back from her honeymoon. On her arrival back at Erica's house, while the wind was still beneath her wings, she rang Ros and asked her to start looking into possible singing engagements.

That evening, her last in London, with Ben already in bed and the sisters getting ready to go up too, Alex finally mustered the courage to offer setting up a trust fund for Ben.

'Would you mind?' she ventured, wary of Erica's reaction but keen to do it anyway. 'I'd like to help. He can use it for his university fees or whatever you both think.' Erica said nothing, biting her lip. 'You're offended?' Alex went on. 'Please don't be. I've just got money enough to spare, especially now I've sold the house, and it'd be my way of saying thank you for all your support – to both of you.'

'I'm not offended Alex.' Erica sounded quite emotional. 'It would be brilliant – obviously. It's just...' She shook her head. 'No, it's nothing. Take no notice of me. If you're sure? Have you discussed it with Theo?'

'With Theo? No.' Alex was surprised at the suggestion; that hadn't crossed her mind. 'It doesn't affect him,' she added dismissively and then smiled. 'Good, that's settled then. I'll get on and set it up. I'd like to get it sorted before the wedding.' She walked to the door but before she could open it Erica joined her there, put her arms round her and gave her a long hug.

'Thank you,' Erica said huskily. 'Whatever I've said, I'm sure Theo's a great guy. I hope you're going to be really happy with him. You deserve to be happy Ali.'

*

Alex had been back from London more than a week when Francine's letter landed on the doormat. The violet envelope was instantly recognisable. Francine, who never used a word processor and still used a fountain pen, refused to use electronic mail, declaring it an abomination. Frowning, Alex returned to the snug, edging her finger under the flap to rip the envelope open.

My dearest Alex, it began in the familiar sloping writing. *Good to start getting that voice of yours back into shape again. I was pleased with your progress in such a short time last weekend; you hadn't deteriorated as much as I thought you might have done.* Alex raised an amused eyebrow; from Francine this was praise. *I hope you'll keep at it now and not let any more time go to waste.*

You know I don't like talking in lessons – it's so distracting – but there has been something on my mind I've been wanting to say to you and I thought I'd prefer to write to you. You know I don't find the personal things easy to say. Alex frowned, a knot of irrational foreboding forming in her stomach. She read on: *I never told you that I saw Simon on the day he died.*

Without taking her eyes off the letter, Alex eased herself down to perch on her favourite armchair.

We'd met by chance coming out of Chappell's music shop. We discussed the concert by the Berlin Symphony Orchestra the previous week. I thought he'd been there – I knew he was expected – but he'd missed it. I remarked that he'd missed a few things lately and it occurred to me that he was looking a bit pale so I asked him if he was feeling quite well. He insisted he was fine but that he was supposed to be meeting someone for lunch at Leone's Bar, someone he hadn't seen in a long while, and he was feeling a bit pressed as he was running late.

Anyway I'm telling you this because there was all that nonsense in the newspapers when Simon died suggesting that he'd been depressed, that your marriage was on the rocks, and that he had killed himself. I didn't think he looked depressed at all, just preoccupied – which as we both know was only normal for him. I'd asked him if he was going to be conducting the Christmas Oratorio this year, and he'd said quite cheerfully that certainly he would be; he wouldn't miss it.

Doubtless I should have told you before but I thought the last thing you needed was yet more speculation and discussion. Perhaps more honestly I didn't know how to bring it up when you were so upset. With your forthcoming marriage, it seemed the right time now to tell you and hopefully clear your mind so you can start afresh.

Good luck Alex. I hope I'll see you again soon.

Alex reread the letter and then sat staring at it. Simon hadn't been to the BSO concert, had 'missed a few things lately'? She shook her head, staring at the paper. 'No,' she murmured. She automatically tried to think back and then stopped herself; she'd relived those last few months too many times already. However kind the impulse behind the letter, she couldn't bear to go over all that ground again now. 'No, Francine,' she said more loudly. 'No. Not now.' She didn't want to feel all that pain again. She tossed the letter in the basket by the hearth to burn later.

Chapter 25

With the rain finally stopped and the sky clearing, Alex let herself out of the house and picked up the footpath down to the village. It had rained at some point every day since her return from London and the ground was sodden. Taking the ferry up to Southwell the day before, the Kella had been pregnant with muddy water, overstepping its banks in places, the fast and powerful current forcing the tethered boats to tug dangerously at their moorings.

The path down the hill was wet and slippery but Alex stepped out as briskly as she dared, relieved to be moving. The wedding was now just five days away and she was desperate for it to happen. All the arrangements were in place: the venue all organised, dress and accessories checked and rechecked, the guest list completely up to date. All that remained was the waiting and she'd never been good at that. She found she couldn't settle to anything. Even the vocal exercises she'd taken to doing every day lacked what Francine would have called 'commitment'. It was impossible to concentrate.

A couple of days before, whilst cleaning her bedroom, she'd moved Simon's cello and then, on a whim, had opened the case and fingered the instrument inside. Suddenly she'd burst into tears, a convulsing and violent spasm of emotion which afterwards had left her feeling spent and miserable. It had taken her completely by surprise – she hadn't cried like that for months – and so close to the wedding, she'd found evidence of such enduring acute grief unsettling and had quickly tried to shrug it off.

And the same afternoon, she'd been invited down to Captain's Cottage for tea. Liz wanted to give her a pretty antique hair comb set with sapphires – 'something blue to wear for the wedding, my dear' – and she had been determined to relax and let Liz's cosy chatter wrap around her. But over tea and cake, the conversation had turned to Bob Geaton. Liz was concerned that he'd lost a lot of weight and blamed the police who apparently kept questioning him, suspicious of his involvement in Helen's death.

'But I thought it was an accident,' said Alex.

'Well I'm sure it was,' Liz responded, 'but there are suggestions Helen might have been having an affair. Bob regularly went away on weekend fishing trips you see and yet there were reports of someone coming and going at the flat on Saturday nights. And, it seems...' Liz paused for effect. '...there were other marks on the body. I suppose the police think he was jealous.'

Alex didn't want to know. She found the information irrationally threatening as if it affected her in some way and she wished Liz would drop the subject. In the end she couldn't wait to go and she thought it betrayed just how frayed her nerves had become.

Reaching the village square, Alex cut up the path to the quay and turned right towards the beach. When she reached the bar she turned inland and negotiated the winding track through to the reserve. She could have come the back way but she didn't want to hide anymore; there wasn't any point and she thought it sent out the wrong signals. When she arrived in the clearing, it was obvious Mick had been busy: the graffiti had gone from the carriage and it had a freshly painted look; the windows sparkled. The reserve was much the same though – just wetter.

Mick showed her round and brought her up to date; she cleaned a few feeders out and refilled them and then they stopped for coffee and toast. Inside the carriage Mick's living space looked recently cleaned and tidied; a fresh, light scent hung in the air. She got the impression he had been expecting her. She examined his latest carving – a snipe – and they chatted fitfully. It wasn't an easy meeting but when she told him of her intention to start her singing career up again he was obviously pleased.

When she stood up to go, Mick accompanied her to the door.

'I'm afraid I won't be coming again,' she said, rather stiffly, determined not to show too much emotion. She'd rehearsed saying it which hadn't helped at all. She avoided Mick's eyes and stared fixedly at her hand poised on the door handle.

'I know,' he said.

'*How* do you know?' She raised her eyes to look at him.

He shrugged.

'Don't know. Maybe I'm telepathic. Does Theo know you're here?'

'Yes. I told him last night that I was going to call.' She remembered it well. Theo had asked her why she was going and she'd told him she wanted to find out how Mick and Susie were and to see what was happening with the bittern. 'Thank you for telling me,' he'd responded coldly and looked away.

'And he asked you to stop coming?' said Mick.

'No. It's my decision.' She'd been fretting over what she should do for ages, knowing what the result would have to be but reluctant to accept it. She'd almost hoped that Theo would ask her to stop visiting the reserve; then she would have defended her right to go. But he'd said nothing and she thought she owed him this, determined to start this marriage the right way. Not that she'd told him her decision though and she recognised her small-mindedness in letting let him sweat on it. Alex took her hand off the door handle suddenly and thrust it at Mick.

'Thank you for everything,' she said. 'It's been wonderful…well, you know. Thanks for letting me trespass. And…if you ever need anything…' Her voice trailed away.

Mick looked at the hand and frowned then slipped his own hand into it.

'We're very formal this morning,' he remarked, looking down at her pale, smooth hand in his weathered, scratched one. His flesh was warm against hers.

'Yes. I suppose we are.'

He smiled sadly, lifted her hand up and kissed the back of it. Then, abruptly, he let go of her as if she were burning him.

It was for the best, she reassured herself as she made her way back home. She'd only recently understood how fond Mick had become of her. To keep visiting him would be unfair. And then of course there was the realisation that she was fond of him too, an affection whose depth she preferred not to examine too closely. Since his visit to the Hall and her renewed pleasure in his company she'd found herself occasionally wondering what it would be like to be held by him, to feel his intimate touch and share his passion. She found the thoughts disturbing and tried to put them aside.

They had no place in her plans; they were deeply inappropriate.

*

On the Wednesday night, Theo, moving stealthily and dressed head to toe in black, his face darkened to stop any reflected light, took the same path Alex had walked the day before, inland to the reserve. It kept raining intermittently but now and then the burnt out remnant of a waning moon appeared between the clouds and cast an eerie light over the burgeoning trees shrouding his route. There was the constant sound of trickling water and the occasional piping call of a bird or a scuffling noise in the scrub. It made his flesh creep. When he got to the clearing he paused and watched the carriage warily for a few minutes, virtually holding his breath. Dangling from one hand was a heavy piece of fresh red meat. It was two in the morning and the place was in darkness. He could see the dog's kennel but it appeared to be empty. He cautiously glanced around but there was no sign of the collie and he relaxed and allowed himself a moment to get his bearings, to remember what Alex had told him about the layout of the reserve.

The week before, on a dark night when the tide was out in the early hours, Theo had stood in the harbour basin and used a chisel and a rubber mallet to loosen some stones in the supporting wall of the bar. He'd pushed the chisel deep in to make penetrating holes, sure that once the sea got her fingers in the cracks, it wouldn't be long before the wall crumbled, allowing the high spring tides to wash the bar away. With the bar gone, the reserve would be at the mercy of those same tides, its low, flat ground awash with insistent, damaging salt water. Theo anticipated that the final push of water which dislodged the wall and bar would be quick and would therefore take the occupants of the reserve by surprise, leaving them to fall victim to the swell of the sea as it rushed inland. Theo dearly wanted Mick Fenby out of the way.

But the deterioration of the bar was progressing more slowly than he had expected and Alex's recent visit to the Birdman had made him panic. She wasn't in any danger from the sea yet but he hated to think of her continuing her visits down there. And yet he risked alienating her if he tried to stop her and there was too much at stake. He felt like he was walking a tightrope which had started to sway dangerously; he could see the other side, he was nearly there in fact but was still several tricky footsteps away. Lately he'd found himself trying harder to identify himself again with Simon in Alex's mind but from her occasional expression he wondered if that tactic was now exhausted. He desperately needed to get this marriage solemnised and take control. But, even so, he didn't trust Mick for a second. The marriage had to last long enough before Alex's 'tragic accident' to quell any idle speculation about her death. A fall from the cliffs too soon and people would ask questions, especially with Sarah moving promptly back into the Hall. Or suppose Mick made Alex suspicious and she started watching him or being wary of where she would go with him? No, he needed to get rid of Mick and he needed to do it soon.

Theo remembered Alex telling him how Mick had installed simple boarded sluices to control the water levels through the ditches. When he'd asked her the night before – contritely, as if penitent for his intransigence – about the reserve and the bitterns, Alex had mentioned that the Grenloe was running high, the ditches full and boardwalks almost submerged. 'Mick's concerned about the nests in the reeds,' she'd said, clearly pleased at his interest. 'He thinks they'll be vulnerable if it gets much higher. He's opened up the side channels as much as he can to spread the water around.' It had occurred to Theo then that, if he were to close all the sluice gates, the outer ditches would be starved of water while the main channel would flood and as the sea water leaked in too, the reserve would be destroyed. It would take a few days before it happened he reckoned and they'd almost certainly be away on their honeymoon. It would look like a freak accident which no-one would be able to trace back to him.

'And if there's any justice, Fenby'll drown in one of his own sodding ditches,' Theo muttered now. He allowed himself a humourless smile; it would be a perfect wedding present.

Using a tiny torchlight to keep a check on his footing, he skirted the edge of the clearing and worked his way deeper into the reserve. He left the poisoned meat on the ground where he was sure the dog would find it, and then moved further inland in search of the sluices.

Chapter 26

On the Friday morning Alex came to slowly, as if being pulled out of a deep cocoon, unsure what, if anything, had woken her. She rolled over and tried to go back to sleep but shivered and pulled the quilt closer against her shoulders and neck. She felt a prickling of unease but was at a loss to know why. Rain pattered insistently against the window; it had started again early the previous evening and had rained on and off ever since. Sleep rapidly evaporating, she turned over and peered at the clock: twenty-five past five. There was no need to be up for hours yet. She rolled onto her back, closed her eyes and pulled the quilt up to her neck again.

A couple of minutes later she rolled over again. Her mind felt crowded and preoccupied with persistent and yet pointless thoughts; sleep felt a million miles away. Theo had taken her out for dinner the previous evening and snatches of the conversation kept running arbitrarily through her head. He'd been excessively jovial, telling jokes and fooling around. She remembered him pretending to struggle reading the menu, holding it at arms length, and then saying it must be a family weakness and he'd need reading glasses soon like Simon. Then he'd started a string of frantic impersonations capped by a terrible imitation of Jimmy Cagney. He was completely over the top. 'Well, I'm excited,' he'd said when she'd commented on it. 'Aren't you?' Actually she'd been feeling nervous and she guessed he was too, and that accounted for the way he was behaving. After bringing her home, he'd left early. 'Work tomorrow,' he'd said. 'Last day too, thank God. Then next week we'll be on our honeymoon.'

Then her mind flicked to Erica. She would be arriving early that evening with Ben, having had permission to take him out of school early. It would be wonderful to see them again. And then there was the wedding: had she forgotten anything she ought to have done? Should she have done anything differently?

She opened her eyes again and tried to clear her head. It had gone quiet; the rain had stopped. As her eyes adjusted to the gloom, she could see the first glow of sunrise brightening in a broad panel between the fall of the curtains opposite. She eased herself up onto her elbows, frowning, for surely she remembered drawing the curtains tight shut the night before?

She reached over to click the bedside lamp on and got up, picking up the dressing gown slung across a nearby chair. She pulled the gown on and flicked her hair out from underneath it as she padded across to the window and then looked out.

The sun was still hidden behind the hill the other side of the valley but the clouds were rapidly clearing northwards on a scudding breeze and the sky glowed amber and apricot merging into deepest cerulean blue. Even with the window closed the River Kella was audible, funnelling its way down the valley to the sea. She looked down through the gap in the trees towards it. Down in the bottom of the valley it was still dark but the river showed light against the heavy blackness of the banks and trees.

On the near side of the river a shape moved, a man, slow and slight. She stared harder – she thought he looked familiar – but he disappeared again behind a stand of trees. When he reappeared she recognised him; it was Harry Downes.

When she'd seen Mick, on that last unhappy visit, he'd asked her if she'd spoken to Harry yet. She hadn't. It had proved impossible to see him without Minna's defensive and protective presence and, with the wedding so imminent, she'd decided to put it off. But Mick had been insistent. 'I think you should speak to Harry,' he'd said. 'I think it's important. Promise me you'll try to speak to him?' And she had finally agreed.

So now Alex took one last glance down out of the window, then quickly dressed and left the house, heading down towards the river.

*

Getting close, the noise of the river was frightening, like a living thing, shouting and groaning in its effort to chase on down to the harbour. Alex was taken aback at the violence of it. In her route over the park and footpath, she'd been able to see the harbour and the tide was still far from fully in, yet the river level was already high, swirling and nudging at the banks precariously, its surface strewn with twigs, branches, even logs. And the water itself was heavy with mud, brown and thick. Alex pulled her raincoat protectively tighter round herself and advanced cautiously towards the bank. Harry was still there, standing facing the water where the stones lay, now deep and invisible beneath its surface.

'Harry?' she called. He was wearing pyjamas with a thick grey overcoat slung unfastened over the top, his thin, naked ankles rammed into carpet slippers. The noise of the river caught his name and pummelled it into nothing; he didn't hear her. 'Harry,' she repeated more loudly, coming closer and reaching out a hand to take his arm. He was standing too close to the edge of the bank; the river drummed powerfully a few inches from his feet. At her touch he flinched and turned to look at her, his feet shuffling precariously closer to the edge. 'Harry,' she bellowed, trying to make her voice carry over the roar. 'It's me, Alex. Be careful. Come away from the bank. It's dangerous there.'

Harry stared at her without recognition and then looked back down at the water. For a moment she thought he was going to step into it and be dragged down to its slimy depths but then he turned back to her, still staring, and after a moment stepped towards her. He gave her a weak, troubled smile.

'Let's get away from the river Harry,' she shouted, attempting a reassuring smile. She pointed at the water and then put her hands to her ears. 'I can't hear myself think.'

He let her take hold of his arm and he placed his other hand down onto hers and pressed it. Perhaps he recognised her after all. She led him away, up the path, till they reached a wooden seat, high and safe from the river, the water's bellow muted by the intervening shrubs and trees. Since Harry appeared reluctant to go any further, she suggested they sit down to catch their breath and they sat, side by side, facing the river as the sun finally cleared the hill opposite, flooding the valley with lemon light.

'You're out early,' she said, close to his ear. 'Couldn't you sleep?' He didn't respond so she added lightly: 'Me neither.'

He stayed silent, staring out towards where the river roared beyond the trees. She realised now just how many times she'd seen him standing, watching the stepping stones across the river. And he watched it like a haunted man. *I think Harry was on the river when Julian died.* Was Mick right after all? *Did* Harry know what had happened the night Julian died? And would he be able to tell her if he did? Was this a good day or a bad one for Harry, she wondered, given that he'd clearly wandered out of the house in the dark, undressed? His eyes looked alert enough though his gaze seemed distant.

'I've heard that Julian Hellyon fell in the river,' she said to him, as casually as she could. '...a long time ago. They say he fell from the stones and drowned. It was a terrible accident.' She waited, looking intently at his profile, wondering if he knew what she was talking about. Could he even remember who Julian Hellyon was?

Harry slowly turned his head to look at her. He shook his head.

'It wasn't an accident,' he said, so quietly that she could only just hear him over the noise of the river. Her heart almost stopped.

'Wasn't it?' *It's no good asking direct questions.* She checked herself, and then added: 'I thought he overbalanced and the tide was too high. He was carried away.'

Harry was staring back towards the river again. The muscles of his face twitched and pulled, seemingly at random.

'I was on the river,' he said suddenly. 'I heard them shout'n. Those boys were always fight'n. Damn stupid it was.'

'Which boys?' said Alex. It seemed very important all of a sudden to know who was fighting. Harry turned to look at her again and she could barely breathe, waiting for his answer.

'Julian and Theo,' he said slowly, as if it were obvious.

'The brothers?' she said, stunned. 'I didn't know they fought. I thought it was Julian and Simon – his cousin – who fought.'

Harry shook his head.

'Julian and Theo,' he repeated and then looked away and fell silent.

'So you were on the river, and you heard shouting…?' she prompted.

'I was on the river,' he repeated, as if he were talking to himself, his warm West Country drawl stronger than ever. 'I'd been out fish'n and was bring'n 'Puffin' in to tie up. But those boys were fight'n, mak'n a hell of a noise. Sound carries over the water. I thought maybe I ought to break it up. So I skulled upriver to find out what was goin' on.' His voice dropped even lower. 'I was too late.'

Alex had a mental image suddenly of Harry by the river, all those weeks ago, before the party. The boy had lost something, he'd said. And it was behind the rock on the other side. She wondered what relevance that had, if any.

'And something of Julian's was the other side of the river,' she said. 'He'd lost something, hadn't he?'

'I was too late,' he said again.

Alex touched his hand and repeated her question. This time Harry shook his head.

'Theo had put it there. Julian kept shout'n at him. He loved that old stamp but Theo had taken it and put it over the other side. Julian was furious.'

'The old stamp? What stamp Harry?'

Harry looked at her impatiently.

'You know. The stamp.' He mimed his fist coming down sideways onto the palm of his other hand. 'The old stamp.'

Light dawned.

'Oh, Theo's seal.'

Harry shook his head again in exasperation.

'No, Julian's seal.' Harry's eyes glazed over again. 'So he goes to cross the stones, and the other boy…' He pulled a face, trying to remember the name but failing. 'The other boy shouts at him not to. Water's too far in, he says. It's not safe. But Julian carried on anyway. He gets up on the first stone and on he goes. And then the next stone falls away and he goes with it.' Harry stopped talking and covered his face with his hands. 'And I could've stopped it,' he moaned and began to shake, racked by dry, violent sobs.

Alex put her arm round him. He was so thin she could feel his ribs through the fabric of his coat.

'No-one could have stopped Julian falling, Harry,' she said in an effort to console him and looked round helplessly. It was cold, sitting so still, with the chill of the teeming river nearby. 'Come on Harry,' she said, standing up and pulling on his arm. 'We ought to get you home. Minna'll be worried about you.' He wouldn't move and looked up at her blankly, as if she hadn't spoken.

'You see the stones had been loosened,' he said. 'But I didn't think till after.' Alex stopped pulling on his arm and sat down again, watching him.

'And I saw him do it,' he went on. 'I didn't realise though, not then…' He shook his head. 'I couldn't believe he'd do that. But then…afterwards I remembered. And I knew. I'd heard the hammer'n at the mortar early that mornin' at low tide and saw Theo runn'n back along the path.' He turned his eyes away from her to look back towards the river. 'And when I saw Julian fall…that's when I understood. But then I didn't know what to do. I loved those boys. I couldn't say could I? I thought he'd tell himself. I thought perhaps it was some horrible joke that went wrong. But then he didn't tell. So I didn't know what to do.'

Alex stared into Harry's face, transfixed. Odd conversations crossed her mind: Theo telling her how grief-ridden he'd been at Julian's death, how little the seal had meant to Julian, that there was absolutely nothing suspicious about the accident. Surely this couldn't be true? Could this frail, muddled little man truly remember…?

Harry's face had gone very pale; he swayed a little as he sat. Alex got to her feet again and took his hand; it was frozen.

'Come on Harry,' she said firmly. 'We must get you home. Minna will be looking for you. Come on.'

This time he stood up and allowed her to lead him on along the path towards the village. He was silent as if all his words were burnt out and she wondered if he had told anyone this story before or if he'd been storing it up all these years. Perhaps Minna was right and it was Julian's death which had made him ill, that and Harry's deep and lingering sense of guilt. Alex wanted to ignore the story as the nonsense of an addled brain but it hung in her mind, numbing it with its deadening implications. Her thoughts felt stupefied by Harry's astonishing revelation, like eyes exposed to bright light left temporarily blind, dazzled into confusion.

They reached the quay, passed the chandlers and Bob Geaton's hut and, as they looped round the back of the Armada, Minna was walking towards them, her head wrapped in a scarf, her coat thrown loosely over her workaday clothes. She broke into a trot when she saw them and scurried, limping, across the quay.

'Harry, there you are,' she called and came up, dragging her breath. 'Where've you been? I've been look'n everywhere.' She took his free hand. 'And you're cold. Going out like that and not dressed for it neither.'

'He was by the stepping stones,' said Alex dully. 'He was upset.'

'The stones had been loosened, but I didn't think till after,' Harry repeated, like a refrain. 'That's when I understood. But I thought he'd tell.' He looked into Minna's face imploringly. 'Should I have said?'

Behind the thick glasses, Minna's eyes opened wide in alarm and she glanced quickly at Alex.

'He's been talk'n about Julian again hasn't he? He doesn't mean it, you know. He has bad dreams and he gets upset and he says these things. But he doesn't mean it. Don't go tell'n anyone what he's been say'n, will you, Alex? Because it's not true and it'll get us into trouble. Theo'll say he's crazy and not fit to be at home. Please don't say anyth'n.' She peered desperately into Alex's face as she spoke, then patted Harry's hand, muttering something consoling, and began to lead him away.

Alex stood and watched them go. Then she began to walk slowly across the village and up the hill towards home. Her brain began to work again, jumping at random through all the things she'd been told. She remembered Theo's glib descriptions of the boys' idyllic childhood holidays together; thought of how Sarah had carefully chosen her words; how little she'd actually said. Did she know what Theo had done? Do I really believe it myself? She tried to push it away but it kept coming at her, insistent and compelling; this story possessed a frightening ring of truth.

Could it have been a game that went wrong? But if so why didn't Theo say? Desperate to excuse him, she argued with herself: he was just so scared by the reaction there would be; he was covering his tracks. But then there'd been his lies about Simon and Julian fighting, and about the seal. However hard she tried, Alex couldn't keep the doubt out of her mind. What was the truth? And if Theo had lied about those things, what else might he have lied about?

She was half way along the final stretch of footpath now, walking up the hill, the bottom of her jeans sodden from the rain-soaked grass. Supposing, she thought, just supposing Theo had done it deliberately, could it have been done from pure malice? But Theo wasn't like that, was he…? She thought of his recent flashes of temper; she thought of his possessiveness and his pride in the old seal. She marched on, thinking furiously now. She couldn't imagine him doing anything so terrible without a real motive. What would he have stood to gain? She paused as she reached the gate to the front garden and looked up at the house. Hillen Hall. It was like working out the answer to a cryptic clue. It seemed so obvious when you got it that you felt it couldn't be that easy. With Julian dead, Theo would have expected to inherit one day. But then it had been sold and Simon had inherited instead. Then Simon had conveniently died too and Alex had inherited it and Theo had courted her single-mindedly for months…

Alex shook her head and walked through into the garden. Her mind was running away with itself on some fantasy trip. It was preposterous and she was ashamed for even thinking it. But then she thought of Erica's endless questioning of Theo's motives in marrying her. And she remembered her sister saying: *I'd have thought he was too good to be true*. Perhaps it was Erica all along who had been the more astute. Alex couldn't wait to get back inside. Had she really been that stupid? She had to think; she badly needed time by herself to think.

Chapter 27

Alex showered and changed, barely aware of what she was doing, Harry's story running round and round in her head. Pulling on fresh jeans in her bedroom, her eye fell on the photo Sarah had given her which had fallen down. She leaned down to pick it up off the floor and, glancing at it as she went to put it back, she saw something she'd noticed but never registered before: Julian with the seal proudly hanging round his neck. Julian's seal, not Theo's; proof that at least part of the story was true. But that didn't mean the rest of it was, she reasoned desperately. Or if it was, the loosening of the stones had just been a prank that went tragically wrong. It must have been.

But, in spite of herself, things began to click into place in Alex's mind, small things she'd ignored at the time, comments or behaviour she had willingly excused. Theo loved Hillen Hall; that had become increasingly clear quite recently. Despite his earlier assurances that it meant nothing to him, she could tell it from the way he talked about it, the way he sometimes reached out and affectionately touched a wall or would look round admiringly at the fireplace. He adored the place and regularly talked now of his plans for it. And the other day he'd referred to Hillen Hall as 'our house' and had then gone on to include Sarah in his next remark as if his mother were the other owner of the Hall. At the time

Alex had passed it off as a slip of the tongue, a simple mistake. And it was plain Sarah loved the Hall too. A thought came to the surface which Alex had been suppressing for weeks: Theo's devotion to his mother, thinly veiled in dismissive sarcasm and wry wit, was obsessive and unnatural. She could feel it when she was with them together. There had been times, she could admit now, when she had felt like the gooseberry in the party.

Alex sat down heavily on the side of the bed. Could she really imagine Theo courting her just to get Hillen Hall? After all, they'd started out as friends and he hadn't pushed her into the relationship; he'd never pushed her. His first visit had been casual – it was she who'd taken him up on his offer of help.

She still held the photograph of the three boys and stared at it now bleakly. How alike Theo and Simon were. But when she thought back to those early days she remembered how Theo had cultivated that resemblance. No, he hadn't pushed himself on her, he'd insinuated himself, and she, desperate to have Simon back again, to make good all that had gone wrong, had virtually thrown herself into his arms. That Theo was something of a chameleon, she'd noticed a long time ago. She had seen how he could change to fit in with whomever he was with and she'd labelled it affability and good nature. Now she wondered if it had a darker, more devious side. It had never occurred to her before that he wasn't himself with her. So what was he really like, under all the changing masks?

She threw the photograph onto the bed and stood up, unsure what to do, where to go. She wandered down to the kitchen, vaguely thought of making breakfast but wasn't hungry and drifted out again with just a mug of coffee in her hands. She glanced at her watch. Ten to nine. Theo would be on his way to Dartmouth now. She had all day to think.

She walked into the snug, drank the coffee and then paced up and down, rubbing her hands together, flicking her hair back, ramming her hands in her pockets and then taking them out again. Her glance caught the log basket and she remembered Francine's letter, tossed carelessly into it so many days before. Suddenly she was down on her knees, pulling logs out of it and dumping them on the hearth, riffling through the odds and ends of paper that she regularly threw in there. Then she found it, straightened it out and brushed the dirt off.

...he was supposed to be meeting someone for lunch at Leone's Bar, someone he hadn't seen in a long while... she read. So who was Simon meeting for lunch that fateful day? She frowned. Something sat out of reach in her mind, something Theo had said which had struck her as odd. She felt a cold clutch at her stomach. Of course, it was the joke about the family weakness: he'd be needing reading glasses soon like Simon. But Simon only got reading glasses a couple of weeks before he died and Alex had never thought to mention it to anyone. There was no way Theo could have known unless he was the 'someone' who'd met Simon in London the day he died. Alex shook her head. No. Surely not...

The sound of the front door bell intruded on her thoughts and she jumped. Alex folded Francine's letter, forced it into the pocket of her trousers, and walked into the hall. Through the upper glazed panels of the door she could make out Sarah's head and shoulders. The bell rang again. Then Alex heard the key being put in the lock and turned, but the door wouldn't open. The bolts had been thrown across.

Alex's body froze but her mind ran feverishly on. Were her fantasies grounded in any truth or was her brain just running panic-stricken and wild? How much did Sarah know? And would she say anything if she did? Perhaps it was worth trying though. Alex forced herself to step forward, threw the bolts back, and opened the door. Sarah was just turning away.

'Sarah,' she said, trying to keep her voice calm and mild. 'You're out early.'

Sarah turned back and smiled sweetly.

'Alex…dear. So you *are* here.' She glanced expectantly over Alex's shoulder into the hall. 'I thought I'd just call…on my way down to the shops. Everything ready for your big day tomorrow?'

Alex nodded. Sarah had done this regularly in the last few days – 'just calling'.

'Come in,' she said, letting Sarah pass. Irresistibly she found herself glancing out of the door nervously towards the path. 'Theo's not here is he?'

'Theo? No dear. He's gone to work. Last time for a while. Just one more day to the wedding. How exciting. I've got everything laid out ready.'

Alex closed the door and turned to find Sarah had already walked through into the drawing room. She followed her.

'I won't keep you,' said Sarah, sitting down with her coat still on. 'I'm sure you must be busy.'

'Yes. My sister arrives tonight.' Alex hesitated. 'Actually, I'm glad you've come.'

'Really?' Sarah looked both puzzled and a little suspicious. She sat pertly on the edge of her chair, hands on the handbag resting on her knees.

'Yes. I'm rather nervous. I know it's early but how would you feel about joining me in a little drink? I believe I've got some whisky somewhere. Will you keep me company?'

Sarah smiled, uncertainly. 'Of course.'

She put her bag on the floor and watched Alex expectantly as she walked across to the drinks cabinet in the corner of the room and returned with two tumblers half full of amber liquid. Alex was aware that her hands were shaking slightly but Sarah didn't seem to notice, took her drink and immediately swallowed a large mouthful.

Alex sat down on one of the sofas and tried to look relaxed, occasionally tipping her glass to let the whisky touch her lips. While Sarah drank, she chatted about the wedding and asked Sarah about how she'd do her hair; she talked about the honeymoon and how she didn't know what to pack for it. She chattered as she had never done before to put Sarah at ease. When Sarah's first drink had gone, she gave her a refill. As Alex sat down again, she glanced across at the clock, their silent witness. Then she transferred her gaze to Sarah who was sitting back in her chair now, looking comfortable and mellow.

'I was thinking the other day,' Alex began, 'that it's such a shame Julian didn't live to see his brother married…or get married himself.'

'It is,' Sarah agreed. She smiled sadly. 'But then if he had lived, Theo wouldn't be marrying you now.'

'Oh?'

Sarah frowned deeply and swallowed hard.

'I mean we'd probably have stayed here in the Hall,' she stammered, 'and you wouldn't be here…like this. That's what I mean.'

'I see. No, I suppose Simon wouldn't have inherited Hillen Hall then, would he.' Alex paused. 'Actually I'd got the impression that Simon was involved in Julian's accident. That's rather ironic then, isn't it?'

Sarah stared at Alex as if trying to work out if there was some hidden meaning behind the comment, but Alex's face was expressionless and Sarah nodded. 'Well, yes, that's true. Simon and Julian were fighting down by the river, you see. Simon wouldn't stop even when Julian tried to get away from him over the stones. Theo said the top couple of stones must have shifted in the fight, but Simon virtually pushed Julian into the water anyway. Of course he always denied it...' Sarah shook her head and sighed, running a finger round the rim of the glass. 'Poor Julian. You can't imagine how difficult it is to lose a child, especially like that. Though it brought Theo and me much closer together of course.'

'I'm sure it did,' said Alex, more tartly than she'd intended. 'And I suppose that was why Theo didn't bother with his cousin again. I mean, they never met again did they? Even when they were older and had put it all behind them? I don't remember Simon ever mentioning meeting Theo.'

'Oh no,' said Sarah emphatically. 'They never met again. Simon stayed away you see. Well of course we didn't invite him again. Not after that.' She finished the last of her drink and looked at her watch. 'I'd better get off to the shops,' she said, putting the glass down on the table and standing up carefully. 'Let you get on.'

Alex watched Sarah walk away, closed the door and locked it again. She leaned against it, thinking rapidly. She was sure Sarah was telling what she thought was the truth; but Sarah only knew what Theo had told her. Alex needed proof. Driven by suspicions she could barely even think about, she went upstairs to Theo's study.

*

But for a couple more boxes, little had changed since the last time Alex had been in Theo's private domain. Nothing had been put away, she noticed. It looked more like a storeroom than a study, a holding area for his belongings until he could move them elsewhere.

She walked to the desk and began pulling out the drawers and riffling through piles of paper: Theo's hoarded mementoes. She worked her way through details of boats, menus and entertainment lists from cruises, old press cuttings which mentioned his name, old photographs from his student days and work. She found a photograph album full of pictures of his mother: old photographs of her as a young woman in a succession of glamorous dresses, photographs of her on the beach in a swimming costume, photographs of her with Theo both as a child and as a youth. There were no pictures which included Julian or his father. Alex leafed through it all quickly, her lip curling in dismay. It was disturbing proof of his obsession with his mother. How had it taken her so long to notice? But it was becoming obvious that Theo practised a smooth and insidious deceit. She willingly slipped the album back in the drawer, out of sight.

In a box file, on the floor by the side of the desk, was a huge sheaf of bank statements going back more than three years. She kneeled down, looking through them without expectation. All they told her was more proof of his lies; Theo was badly overdrawn. In another box she found his credit card statements. Now she paid more attention; Theo used a credit card to pay for everything – she should be able to map his life by where he used his cards. She wanted to know where he was and what he was doing on the day Simon died.

She leafed through the pile of statements for one card, each one a litany of his mounting debt, going back through the months, looking for the account for a year the previous October. She found it and pulled it out. There were a few local bills on it; one was an entry for the off-licence in East Walkham. From the amount she guessed it was for a bottle of champagne. How Theo loved to turn up with champagne. There was nothing else of interest. Abandoning it on the floor, she started with increasing desperation on the returns of another of his cards and came to the same October. Scanning down the sheet she found it: Theo had paid for a meal at Leone's on the day Simon died.

She stared at it, gripping the sheet till it started to buckle. So it *had* been Theo whom Simon had gone to meet for lunch that day. And a few hours later Simon was dead. *There was one witness who said she thought he'd been pushed,* the policeman had said.

She pulled her eyes away distractedly and her gaze fell on the statement for the other card she'd left beside her on the floor. Champagne. She thought of Helen Geaton 'accidentally' falling downstairs after drinking champagne and the talk of her secret weekend lover. She remembered how Theo had suddenly become more available on Saturday nights after her death. It was all so clear now. But why, she wondered, did Helen Geaton have to die? What part had she played in any of this? Or did the killing just get easier, more pointless? She felt a sudden deep blood-chilling fear. If her worst imaginings were true, it was pointless to look for any sense in what he was doing. The man's obsessions with his mother and the Hall had made him completely deranged and frighteningly dangerous.

Then she heard Theo's voice, calling from downstairs. She must have forgotten to lock the back door when she came in. Now he was climbing the stairs and calling out again, bright and cheery, the same as usual: 'Hello-o? Alex? Are you up here?'

Chapter 28

Alex was on her feet, still bending over the file box on the floor, fumbling to put everything away, when Theo pushed the door back and walked in. She straightened up and looked directly at him, the desk half between them, the credit card statement still in her clammy hand and her heart thumping painfully in her chest.

'Alex,' he said lightly. 'I didn't expect to find you in here.' He took in her ashen face. 'What's the matter? Are you all right?' His gaze dropped to the paper in her hand.

'Theo,' she stammered. 'I thought you'd gone to work.'

'I couldn't get through. The River Kella's broken its banks. It's pouring like a bloody torrent down the lane to the village. It was hell just trying to turn round and get back up the track. I wouldn't want to be one of the poor buggers down the bottom at the moment.'

He took a step towards her, his eyes not leaving her face, and she automatically stepped back, catching her foot on one of the boxes on the floor and having to touch the desk to steady herself. He reached out and took the paper from her hand. He glanced down at it and nodded.

'Thought you'd just check me out did you Alex?' he said softly, sounding hurt and reproachful. 'Scared I didn't have the means to marry you? Surely that isn't a big issue for you? You said all along that money meant nothing to you.' He threw the statement dismissively onto the desk like so much waste paper. 'Of course that's easy to say when you've got a lot of it. OK, so I'm not quite as well off as I make out but that's because I like to spread my money around. I've spent a lot of money on you haven't I? You have to admit that.'

Alex opened her mouth to speak but her mouth was so dry, her throat so tight, that nothing came out.

'My God, Alex, you didn't have to go snooping through my things like some grubby private eye. You could just have asked me. We don't want to have any secrets from each other do we? So I owe a little money…'

He'd taken a step closer round the desk as he spoke and she stepped away from him round it, and finally found her voice.

'It's not about money Theo. You met Simon in London.' She pointed at the statement on the desk with a finger that shook. 'You paid for lunch at Leone's.' She fumbled in the pocket of her jeans and pulled out the folded letter. She waved it at him as if it were some sort of protective weapon. 'Francine told me she met Simon the day he died and that he was going to Leone's to meet someone he hadn't seen in a long time. It was you wasn't it?' Adrenaline kicked in and her voice was rising now, unsteady and bright. 'No secrets?' She laughed. 'You didn't tell me that Theo, did you? Didn't tell me you'd seen Simon? What a coincidence that you should meet him the day he 'accidentally' falls under a tube train.'

Theo's brow furrowed in a heavy frown.

'What's that supposed to mean? Good God, What are you suggesting?' He sounded indignant but his eyes shifted restlessly from Alex to the letter in her hand.

'Why didn't you tell me you'd met him?'

'I didn't. It all went wrong. I'd *intended* to meet him. I knew I was going to be in London and I gave him a ring to see if we could meet up. It had been so long that I felt guilty, thought it was about time we caught up. I offered to buy him lunch and he said he'd love to see me. But he never made it.' Theo gave her a soft, sympathetic smile. 'I thought it might bring back too many memories for you if I talked about it…' He shrugged. 'So I didn't.'

Alex looked at him stonily.

'I want to know what happened.'

'Nothing happened,' he said impatiently.

'But you paid for lunch at Leone's. Why do you keep lying to me?'

'I'm not. For God's sake, Alex. What's got into you? I went there and waited for a while, tried his mobile, but got no reply. So I had a quick lunch and left.' He looked down at the statement for a moment. 'I know the amount seems a lot for one but the prices there are crazy. I was going to try to speak to him later but then – well, you know what happened. I couldn't very well mention it after that, could I?'

Alex stared at him, eyes narrowed, and then shook her head slowly.

'But you did meet him Theo. You talked about Simon's reading glasses the other day. He'd only just got them before he died and I never told you.'

Theo hesitated for just the blink of an eye.

'You did Alex. Don't you remember?' He smiled indulgently. 'You've had a lot on your mind lately. It's not surprising you've forgotten.'

She shook her head again.

'I never told you Theo. Stop pretending that I'm losing it. You saw him in London and you kept it secret. What did you do to him Theo?'

'Do to him? Nothing. What the hell are you accusing me of?'

'So it was just lucky for you then?'

'What do you mean?' He'd lost the cool, measured tone now and his voice was hard and menacing.

'That Julian died in an accident on the river soon after you'd been seen loosening the stones of the walkway? That the man who owned Hillen Hall should die a few months after inheriting it, and that you should be hellbent on courting his widow soon after? What plans did you have for me after the wedding: another push down the stairs like Helen Geaton? Another slip into the river off the stones? Is that why you wanted me to scatter Simon's ashes on the other side? Surely Hillen Hall isn't that important to you?'

Theo stared at her as if trying to come to a decision, then his mouth stretched into a mirthless smile.

'So you've worked it out have you? Even Helen? Very good. Well done. I'd like to know what made you realise. Did I make a mistake?' He nodded. 'Of course, the thing with the glasses – that was careless. But something else must have started it off. Where did the information about the stepping stones come from?'

Alex hesitated, determined not to involve Harry. She didn't answer.

'Why didn't you just ask Simon for Hillen Hall Theo?' she said instead. 'You could have come to some arrangement. He didn't want it.'

'I did ask him. That's what the lunch was all about. I tried to persuade him to give me the Hall since it should rightly have been mine anyway. Tried to appeal to his better nature. But he refused. Did it just to stop me having it I imagine, the bugger. We'd never got on you see. He was big friends with Julian. He told me he'd guessed what I'd done. Admitted that he'd been too cowardly to say anything at the time. Not that anyone would have believed him of course. I'd made certain of that.'

'So what happened?'

Theo ran a finger along the desk in a careless, disinterested way.

'I followed him. When I saw him go down to the underground I knew it would be easy. It was so crowded down there. I just had to time it right to push him as the train was pulling in.'

His frank admission pulled her up short for a moment and the image he'd created took her breath away.

'You're mad,' she said without thinking. 'Completely mad. You *and* your mother.' She saw his expression harden and realised her mistake. She shuffled a little towards the door, talking as calmly as she could to try to mask her movement. 'You can't keep killing people who are an inconvenience to you Theo,' she said desperately. 'It'll start to become noticeable. There are a lot of people who'll start asking awkward questions if anything happens to me. You'd never...'

'Have you seen my mother?' Theo demanded. 'She wasn't at home when I got back. I thought she might have come up here.'

Alex felt a bubble of hysterical laughter rise in her which she failed to quell. This was all so unreal.

'It's really all about Sarah isn't it Theo? I've been so stupid. You were never in love with me. There's no room for anyone else, you're too obsessed with your mother.' Alex backed away another step. The door still looked a long way away. She felt the laughter rising again and thought she was going to be swamped by it. She knew she needed to get out of that room as soon as she could but she felt light-headed, giddy…crazy even. It was all so sick and yet so horribly *funny.* 'And the saddest thing of all,' she went on in a voice choked by something between a laugh and a sob, 'is that she has no idea really, does she? She's more interested in the house than she is in you. Don't you…?'

'Shut up,' Theo bellowed as he crossed the space between them in a couple of long strides, drew back his hand and hit her hard across the face. Alex fell heavily sideways, catching a glancing blow from the desk to her temple as she went, and landing with a thump as her head banged the floor. He stood over her, bent down to grab a handful of hair just below her crown, and pulled it hard till her head and shoulders were lifted forward off the ground. He pushed his face close to hers and she blinked at him, dazed, a trickle of blood running from her mouth and from a deep cut near her eye.

'I'll ask you once more,' he growled. 'Have you seen my mother?' She blinked again and he shook her. 'Hm? Well?'

'Yesh.' Alex thought her voice seemed to be coming from the other side of the room. She tried to lick her lips and tasted blood. 'She was here.' She swallowed painfully.

'Where is she now?' He shook her again and she could feel the hair ripping at her scalp.

'Shops. She's gone down to the shops…'

'Oh my God. The river.' Theo stared at her in horror and then dropped her with another thump.

Alex heard him run across the room and out onto the landing but the world was getting rapidly blacker and soon she heard nothing at all.

*

Alex slowly emerged from oblivion, almost reluctantly, as if someone had been shaking her. She felt bitterly cold and her ears were ringing. When she cautiously opened her eyes she was alone. The room was moving around her; she felt sick and closed her eyes again. After a few minutes lying still, she tried once more. The world was still moving, but more slowly; it had a disturbing undulating quality.

She took a deep breath and tried to move, easing herself up onto one elbow. She felt a wave of nausea, closed her eyes again and stopped moving. It passed and she managed to sit up. She leaned against the back of the desk and waited, eyes half closed, while the room steadied around her. There was a pain in her right shoulder and elbow and a gnawing ache in the side of her head. The events preceding her blackout slowly washed back into her brain. She put a hand tentatively to her face and felt the swelling around her cheek bone and the dried blood on her lips. Theo would come back, that much was certain; she needed to get out of there. She tried to move again but the world immediately shifted and she was forced to wait while Theo's words kept running through her head: *The River Kella's broken its banks…I wouldn't want to be one of the poor buggers down the bottom at the moment.* She thought of all the people she knew in the village, being washed away in the flood. She thought of Mick. Would he be safe on the reserve?

By the time she felt strong enough to get to her feet, she thought it must have been hours since Theo had left her but a glance at her watch suggested, as far as she could work out, that it was nearer forty minutes; she hadn't actually been out that long. She used the desk to steady herself and stood up, taking more deep breaths to stem the faintness. It passed off and, feeling a little better but with legs that felt like jelly, she edged her way to the door and looked out warily into the corridor. There was no-one there. She tried to move purposefully down the landing; she needed to get down to the village.

*

It was obvious to Theo what had happened as soon as he'd seen the foaming brown water blocking the road: all the recent rain had forced the Kella to break its banks up river, uprooting bankside trees and shrubs and carrying them downstream to lodge against the arched Roman bridge. With the bridge blocked, the water had shunted sideways and then been channelled, in a seething, bubbling frenzy, down the sunken narrow lane to the village. He remembered being told about something similar happening once in the nineteen twenties. Then it had been considered a freak 'act of god', a one-off. Five people had died.

Now, scrambling his way as fast as he could down the muddy hillside, he could hear the river's deafening roar as it thundered down the road to his left, the sound magnified as it echoed back and forth across the valley. He was only dimly aware of it, his mind too full of Sarah. Where would she be now? How long had she been gone? He should have asked Alex but he'd been panic-stricken and not thinking straight.

But he would find her; he had to. The village wasn't that big. He tried to recall which way he'd been told the water had run the last time but of course there'd been a lot of building in the village since then. Much had changed. He tried to calm himself; Sarah would probably be safe in the Stores and the river would just spill down harmlessly and out to the sea. She'd tell him how scared she'd been and he'd hug her and make her feel better.

But when he reached the Village Hall he was momentarily frozen. Looking down on the square he could see nothing but a swirling cauldron of water. Sea water was pumping in over the lowest ground of the village to his right, flooding the new housing estate and suffusing the village centre. There it met and fought with the incoming river and the battle churned the water, spinning it round and round. The bar protecting the Grenloe must have finally given way and he felt a searing and unfamiliar twist of fear. The water would rise higher yet: high tide wasn't due for another twenty minutes or so.

He looked around, trying to take it all in, dread numbing his brain. The water had already risen to first floor level and there were people stranded at upstairs windows and on rooftops; a couple of men had clambered up trees. The people who had managed to get out of homes and shops in time had collected nearby on the higher ground in and around the village hall where temporary shelter and aid were being given. Across the bubbling water, the higher ground round the Armada and the hotel stood proud, as unreachable as an island. There were boats, torn from their moorings, being tossed about and thumped against house walls; cars lifted from the ground and carried away into the harbour; bits of garden furniture and fences floated and circled before being dragged out into the bay. And over and above it all was the noise of the water.

Theo began to search frantically through the crowd of helpless onlookers but Sarah wasn't among them. He grabbed people at random, shouting at them, demanding to know if they'd seen her. They all shook their heads, looking at him, white-faced and wide-eyed, before their gaze returned to the frantic muddy water destroying the village below them.

'I think I saw her on the other side of the square,' Tess Webber finally told him.

'What? When? Which way did she go?' He took hold of her and she grimaced as the ends of his fingers dug into the flesh of her upper arms.

'I'm not sure. Twenty minutes ago maybe. She was heading for The Armada. She was already thigh deep in the water so it was the nearest dry ground.'

'Did you see her get there?' He began shaking her. 'Did you see her get there?' he bellowed.

'No. I don't know. I started watching someone else. Let me go.'

Theo dropped her and stared across to the pub and hotel. There was no-one left outside there now. He could see faces at the upper windows, bleakly staring out. It was difficult to make out who they were but they all looked male. He ran down to the waters' edge and gazed into it, trying to gauge its depth but it was frothing and filthy with rubbish; it was impossible to tell.

Uncaring, he kicked off his shoes and lunged forward into it. He had to get across to find Sarah; he had to be sure she was all right. He took a few steps till the water level rose to his hips, then he was lifted off his feet and he started to swim. A plank of wood careered towards him and he swerved, managed to avoid it, and pushed on. He'd always prided himself on being a strong swimmer – he didn't doubt himself for a minute – but the currents kept taking him by surprise; they were strong and unpredictable and he found he couldn't fight them. Suddenly he was being spun round and then dragged under. He surfaced again, gasping for air but he couldn't keep any control and he was buffeted and tossed and then he was rolling and going down again, way down into a black, suffocating darkness.

*

It was Saturday when Alex came to in hospital. It should have been her wedding day but she emerged from a nightmarish dream to find herself in bed with something strapped to her arm and Erica sitting nearby. Opening her eyes to see her sister there, she thought she was imagining her. Erica looked like an angel, hazy as if clothed in mist, and tentatively smiling. Poorly edited memories loomed into her mind, vague at first but slowly coming into focus and she closed her eyes again, willing them away. She waited a couple of minutes before cautiously reopening them.

'Hello sleepy head,' she heard Erica say.

Alex moved her lips but nothing came out.

'Hold on, I'll get a nurse.'

The nurse helped to get Alex sitting up, propped her up with pillows, allowed her a few sips of water and withdrew. In the harsh fluorescent light, the bruises on Alex's face and where her shoulder showed above the sheet, looked livid and painful. Erica, sitting close now, seemed to be trying not to stare at them, or at the crusty blood on the cuts round her mouth and eye.

‘So…’ began Erica. Alex cautiously moved her eyes sideways to look at her sister and then fixed them back on the wall opposite. Erica tried a smile; it lacked conviction. ‘…I hope the other guy looks worse,’ she finished.

Alex found her sister’s hand on the bedspread by her side and covered it with her own.

‘Thank you,’ she muttered with a mouth that felt like she was using it for someone else.

‘Thank me?’ Erica gave a short embarrassed laugh. ‘What for?

‘For being here.’

‘Oh.’

There was a silence before Alex spoke again. ‘How did I get here?’

‘You were wandering round the village apparently, looking wild and scary, talking nonsense. Then you passed out and you were airlifted out here.’ Erica hesitated and then added, off-handedly: ‘The things some people’ll do to get noticed.’

‘So you’ve been to Kellaford Bridge?’

‘How do you think I found you? I heard about the flood on the news just before we set off. I managed to leave Ben with a friend and came hot wheel down to find you. The village is in a terrible state.’ She paused. ‘Do you remember about the flood?’

‘Yes,’ Alex murmured. ‘Some. I remember Theo said…Never mind. Go on…about the village. What happened?’

‘Well,’ said Erica,’ studying Alex’s face anxiously, ‘everyone’s in shock but there’s no shortage of people keen to talk about it.’ Alex cautiously rolled her head a little to look at her sister again. ‘You look shocking too. So what happened to you?’

‘I don’t remember exactly. I fell.’

‘Which is it: you fell or you don’t remember? The staff told me it looked like you’d been hit.’ She winced as she looked at Alex’s swollen, purple skin. ‘I think it looks like that too.’

‘Tell me about the village,’ Alex persisted. ‘Is everyone all right?’

‘It can wait Alex…’

‘Tell me.’

Erica recounted what had happened as it had been told to her. Alex, it seemed, had already missed most of the drama by the time she had staggered down the hill. Apparently Mick Fenby, noticing the sea water seeping in from the direction of the bar, had gone to investigate, to find that the bar was rapidly collapsing and the rising tide was going to make short work of finishing the job. Aware of the vulnerability of the lower village, he’d carried on into the centre to warn people. By then the first of the river water had already made it into the square and was rapidly rising. With most people collecting near the village hall, ‘the woman from the shop’ had been hysterical about her son because she didn’t know where he was. Mick waded back and found the boy clinging to the top of the climbing frame in the playground. He got him down and just managed to get him back to drier ground before the deluge really hit.

‘I heard his mother was sobbing all over the guy, saying he was a hero. That’s that odd, secretive chap from the reserve isn’t it?’

Alex said nothing, her head resting against the pillows, her eyes fixed on the wall ahead of her again.

‘Well,’ Erica continued. ‘Seems like his credit rating has shot up now anyway.’ There followed an awkward pause.

‘Where is he now?’

‘Mick?’

Alex nodded her eyelids for answer. Her head ached too much to move it much voluntarily.

‘I don’t know. Like everyone else, I imagine, looking to see what can be salvaged from the mess. It’s awful down there Alex. I mean, the water left as quickly as it came they say but the sludge and the debris, not to mention the damage and the smell…It’s gruesome. Anyway, fortunately Hillen Hall is fine of course – that’s the advantage of being on a hill.’ Erica was probably trying to be flippant but it came out sounding fatuous.

‘And what about Theo,’ Alex said. She’d closed her eyes again and had spoken so quietly that Erica had to lean forward to hear her. ‘Where is he?’

Erica swallowed and squeezed Alex’s hand.

‘He’s missing,’ she said gently.

‘Missing?’

Erica passed on the most coherent version she’d been told, how Theo had been beside himself when he’d got down to the village, searching for his mother, desperate for any news of her. In a crazy attempt to swim across the seething waters to find her, he had gone under and not been seen since.

Erica squeezed her sister’s hand again. Alex said nothing. She had such a confusion of thoughts and emotions going on in her head, she felt like she was spinning herself. She could have been in the water too, going round and round with that roar in her ears…

'Are you all right Alex?' Erica stroked her thumb across her sister's hand. 'I'm so sorry. I wasn't going to tell you yet. I mean…he still might be found but…well, it was like a whirlpool out there they said. I spoke to the police. They said that the helicopters would keep going over for a while, looking. Theo wasn't the only one unaccounted for.'

Alex felt tears start to roll down her cheeks. She lifted a heavy arm and brushed them away.

'Who else?' she murmured.

Erica automatically straightened the sheet again as she answered.

'I don't know, some old guy…confused, they said.'

'Not Harry Downes?'

'Yes, that was it. And some young girl who'd been out playing; from one of the holiday cottages. Are you sure you're all right Alex?'

'I don't know. How awful it all is.' Alex opened her eyes and rolled them towards Erica. 'And Sarah Hellyon?'

'Ironically, she's all right. She was sheltering with a few others at the hotel. The water never quite reached it. Theo didn't need to risk his life like that. I mean…it was a wonderful thing to do…very brave but…'

Alex stared at Erica and started to laugh. The laugh grew and swelled until she was half-laughing, half-sobbing, her body rocking, shoulders heaving, her hands to her head to support it, pulling at the drip attached to the back of her right hand.

Alarmed, Erica went for a nurse who immediately called a doctor.

'She'll give her something to help her settle,' the nurse said firmly to Erica. 'I think you should go now.'

Chapter 29

Alex remembered reading that Julian's body had washed up on Longcombe Beach a couple of days after he'd been swept away by the river. 'Everything ends up there,' the locals said, 'It's the way the currents pull. Sooner or later, anything that goes into the sea round here will come up on Longcombe Beach.'

And so it was that on the day Alex was allowed home from hospital, forty-eight hours after going in, Harry Downes body was washed up on Longcombe Beach. The next day, the little girl's body returned too. When Sarah had been told that Theo had gone missing and to expect the worst, she had become so agitated that the doctor arranged for her to be taken somewhere where she could be supervised; she was apparently making little sense. So when, another two days later, Theo's body came ashore, Alex was asked to identify him. When she saw him, Theo, having been in the water for several days, battered, eaten and decomposing, was almost unrecognisable; he was most readily identified by his remaining clothes and the seal on the chain around his neck.

Erica had stayed over and accompanied her. She'd made a lot of phone calls, extended the arrangements for Ben and taken a week off work. Alex was still badly bruised and shaken and rested a great deal. She said little. The deluge of conflicting emotions washing through her in the aftermath of the flood had drained away to leave her feeling numb. She preferred to leave it that way, reluctant to revisit the events or conversations of that day, and rebutted all Erica's attempts to get her to talk.

When Erica had to leave to go back home, she suggested that Alex should come back to London with her. 'The doctors don't think you should be alone,' she urged her. 'You've had a bad concussion. You might get a reaction yet.'

To Erica's obvious surprise, Alex agreed. She felt lethargic and dazed and irrationally scared; she didn't think she could cope alone. Nor did she feel strong enough to put up any resistance.

Before leaving for London, she insisted on having the locks changed. But when Erica asked why, she didn't answer.

*

During Alex's first week in London she did little. Her bruises slowly turned yellow and her cuts healed. Her joints and muscles were stiff and weak; she felt like an old woman. She began to go out, did a little shopping and cooking, went off walking by herself, took Ben out after school or sat playing games with him. Her nephew's company was therapeutic. He teased her when she played badly, persuaded her to help him with his new tropical fish tank and even went to the cinema with her to see a romantic comedy. He made her laugh and, with a sensitivity he clearly hadn't inherited from Erica, he asked nothing. Alex began to rally.

As she recovered, Alex found that the emotion which surfaced most forcefully was anger. That Theo had wilfully killed both Julian and Simon in pursuit of his sick obsessions left her feeling impotent and bitter. The only emotion which mitigated it was the relief of knowing that Simon had not taken his own life and that there had been nothing she could have done which would have saved him. It was little compensation. She couldn't shake off the regret of knowing that their relationship had ultimately been so distant that he had never mentioned Hillen Hall and the tragic event which had happened there; nor had he spoken of Theo's prospective visit. Perhaps, like Harry, he blamed himself for Julian's death. Sadly, she would never know.

It occurred to her that she felt no sense of loss for Theo. She wondered fleetingly how a man possessed of so many gifts and advantages had turned into someone so evil but personally, despite the anger, she felt nothing. She was surprised; she'd expected to hate him. She concluded that she'd never loved him, that there had been no emotion there strong enough to transmute into either grief or loathing. And it wasn't simply a reaction to his crimes. Looking back she recognised that she had never really loved him; she had simply wanted to. She was mortified that she had fallen so readily under his spell, blind to his weaknesses, duped because – and she couldn't avoid this painful conclusion – she had wanted to be duped. His apparent love and support had been a heady mix and she had arrogantly ignored all hints, warnings and advice. How deeply, deeply foolish she had been. It had been a lucky escape and the realisation of how close she had come to losing her own life helped to galvanise her mind and make her focus again.

Her thoughts began to turn to home. She'd left Hillen Hall willingly but, as the days went on, she desperately wanted to go back. 'All those people in Kellaford – their homes ruined. I feel guilty at having left them all to it,' she said to Erica one day, only to have her sister snort and ask what she thought she'd have been able to do for anyone, 'the state you were in.' But Alex insisted she was now ready to return and she wanted to go back to help. She'd been in London nearly two weeks.

Erica didn't try to hide her disappointment.

'But I thought you'd be looking for a house back in London.' Erica adopted the hurt expression Alex knew all too well. 'Near us maybe,' Erica added. 'I thought you were going to start your career up again.'

'I am. But I *can* do that from Devon too. It's not the end of the world. Living there'll help me keep things in perspective, make me keep a sense of balance.'

The night before leaving, she finally steeled herself to tell Erica about Theo and what he had done.

'You don't believe me?' she said at the end, watching Erica's sceptical expression. 'I can hardly believe it myself now but it was you who told me to doubt him, remember. You were right and I was stupid.'

'Of course I believe you,' said Erica, though her voice lacked conviction. 'I *thought* you'd been hit.' She paused. 'But all the rest…Did he actually admit to it?'

'Yes, I told you. Just before he hit me.'

Erica winced and automatically glanced at Alex's scars again.

'I've been thinking that I should go to the police and tell them,' Alex said. 'They should know.'

Erica frowned, half smiling and shaking her head.

'Alex, you can't be serious. You've got no proof, have you? They'll just think you're crazy. Or still concussed. Believe me, I've seen the way they think. And what's to be gained?' She gave her sister's arm a sympathetic squeeze. 'Just let it lie Ali. He's gone. It's over.'

*

Getting on the train at Paddington, Alex had been keen to get home; by the time she arrived at Totnes station she was feeling less certain, unsure how she would react to being back in the house again. She had pre-arranged a hire car and drove the last few miles nervously. Passing the Lodge on the way up the lane to Hillen Hall, she automatically glanced sideways, expecting to see Sarah at the window. There was no-one there.

Once inside the Hall she walked slowly round, room by room, making absolutely certain it was empty. Having been away, the last few days at the Hall already felt unreal, like something from a bad dream. Even though she'd seen Theo's body she pushed each door open with a nervous hand, imagining him appearing round a corner, or bounding up the stairs behind her. 'Julian?' she called several times too but the house was warm, the doors still. There were no footsteps on board or stair. If he ever had been there, he wasn't now. In the drawing room she paused in front of the grandfather clock, untouched and silent since before the flood. She wound it up and set it going again. It ticked reassuringly.

She took a couple of days to sort herself out and got Tim Prentice to help her remove Theo's belongings to one of the outbuildings till they could be sent back to the Lodge. 'Or wherever,' Alex muttered. With the remaining suspicion hanging over Bob Geaton in mind, and despite Erica's warnings, she went to the police and told them her story. They listened politely, asked after her health and looked pointedly at the marks on her head. 'They'd make some enquiries,' they said, and she left them to it. It was their problem now.

Sarah hadn't returned to the Lodge. Local opinion had it that she would never leave care; she had already been moved to a home intended for long stay residents. Talking gibberish, it was said; doesn't know what day of the week it is, keeps asking for Theo and gets agitated every time she's told again what happened. So why bother to tell her, thought Alex. Why not leave her in the fantasy world she's been living in for years already? Alex didn't bother to go to visit her; she didn't even consider it.

But she did visit Minna and took her flowers. Harry's widow looked shrunken and grey. 'I should have kept a closer eye on him,' she kept saying. 'I don't know how he found the key. And I didn't think he'd go off again that day. I thought he'd sleep.' She had a lost air and kept glancing at the door as if she thought Harry might walk in at any moment. Not Harry as he'd been in recent years, but the Harry of old, vigorous and cheery, who would come in from a day's work, pop his cap on the hooks near the door, and grab Minna by the waist to give her a cuddle before asking what she was cooking for dinner. Alex could read it all in her face and knew better than to give false cheer. She sat with her a while, promised to call again, and left.

The River Kella now bubbled peacefully back down its own channel but the village still bore the ravages of the flood. Mud was caked over gardens and roadsides and piles of ruined carpets and furniture were thrown in heaps outside houses. Many were uninhabitable for the foreseeable future, businesses ruined. The necessary work to restore them would be a project of months and years rather than weeks. The Stores had been scrubbed out, its substitute shelving sparsely stocked, its ruined fridges and freezers removed and temporarily replaced by one new chiller cabinet. Behind the synthetic air-freshener scent a rank, damp smell still hung in the air. 'Only just got this place usable,' Lyn Causey said bitterly. 'Had to throw everything. Be months before any insurance comes through…' She snorted. 'If ever.'

The place Alex most wanted to visit however, she left till last, scared of what she would find, unsure what her reception would be. Mick was still living in his carriage by the Grenloe, Liz Franklin had assured her. 'But I don't know what the state of his home is. The carriage was washed up by the water and dumped on its side. The rescue services brought some lifting gear to try to move it for him but I hate to think what it must be like there.' There was suspicion that the bar had been interfered with, Liz went on to say, which had made the whole tragedy so much worse. 'But who'd do a thing like that?' she asked, incredulous. Alex was sure she knew.

The tide was out on the morning Alex went to see the reserve for herself. She went the long way round, walking the quay to the bar where engineers had put up temporary barricading to prevent the sea causing further damage, and turned inland on the familiar path. Twice she had to change her route. The old track had been made soft and unstable by the pounding sea water and had disappeared in places. She could still smell the salt in the air and see the sand and seaweed that had been deposited in its wake. Shrubs and small trees had been completely uprooted and now lay haphazardly abandoned by the retreating water. She kept expecting to hear Susie's bark and to see her coming towards her, her tail wagging a welcome. But Susie didn't materialise and Alex wondered if Liz was wrong and Mick had left after all. She wished she had never gone away; she should have stayed.

When she reached the clearing, the carriage was back in the same place. And it all looked much the same, even to the washing on the line. She shouted Mick's name and went round to the sheds but he wasn't there. She shouted again, louder this time and hurried back to the clearing, wondering which way to go to look for him.

Then she saw Susie walking slowly towards her and Mick following close behind, a spade in his hand. The dog reached her first and Alex bent to pet her. Susie was thin and frail; clumps of her fur had fallen out. Alex looked up at Mick who was standing a couple of feet away, watching her. She straightened up.

'Susie looks ill. What's the matter with her?'

'She *has* been ill. You'd be ill too if you'd been poisoned. But she's getting better now.' Mick dragged his eyes away from Alex and looked down fondly at the dog. 'I thought I was going to lose her but she's a tough girl.' He looked back at Alex with the suggestion of a smile. 'No greeting then? And I notice you ask after the dog before me. I suppose that's to be expected.'

'So how are you then?'

'I'll live.' He studied her face, his gaze settling on the scars. 'How are you?'

'I'm fine.' She looked back at Susie. 'How did she get poisoned?'

'Some bastard dropped all the sluices a couple of nights before the flood. I saw the main channel running high and went to investigate. Whoever it was left some meat out for Susie to find. She'd already started on it when I found her. I took her straight to a vet – just in time apparently. It was more than a week before I could bring her home. Though at least she missed the flood.'

Alex bit her lip and gave Susie's head another pat. 'Poor girl,' she said. She looked round the reedbeds. 'It's a mess.'

'It is.'

'So how much have you lost? Are the bitterns still here?'

Mick shook his head. 'Nest got washed away at high tide. Most of the reed nests have gone but there are a few things have survived.' He studied her face and then lifted a hand to gently touch her cheek with the back of his fingers. 'I didn't think I'd see you again,' he said.

'I couldn't stay away.'

'So are you staying?'

'Certainly am. You'll be needing a hand to get this place sorted out.' She hesitated and then met his gaze. 'I'm sorry Mick. I've been such a fool. I'm sure the bastard who dropped the sluices and poisoned Susie was Theo.' She pulled a face. 'And he really was a bastard Mick.'

Mick raised his eyebrows and slowly grinned.

'Now, there's something we can agree on. I'll make coffee and you can tell me all about it. You did want coffee?'

'Of course I want coffee.'

*

Erica finished the conversation with Alex, walked into her bedroom and tossed the phone on the bed. Ben was out and she was alone. Her sister had been back in Devon a month already. She missed her but on the phone Alex sounded happy; happier than she had been in a long time and Erica was glad.

She wandered to the window and stared out over the long, narrow back garden, its tiny concrete patio, the patchy, worn lawn and Ben's wildlife pond. For some time a weight had sat heavily on her mind and she wondered sometimes that Alex had never realised that there was anything wrong. Perhaps she'd put Erica's moodiness down to her succession of failed romances. And then, of course, Alex had been so upset by Simon's death that she had blocked everything else out. But it occurred to Erica, with a pang of remorse, that Alex would never guess the truth; she was too naturally trusting as the recent past had proved. In her defence, Erica consoled herself, she had tried on several occasions to tell her sister what had happened but she'd never known quite how to phrase it.

After all, she hadn't intended to have an affair with Simon; it had all started quite innocently. There had been a party after one of his performances and Alex had been away in Europe doing some concerts and couldn't go. Ben had been staying with Jake so Erica had gone alone and it had been a good night. Simon had drunk too much - which for him was rare - and it had made him unusually talkative. She'd offered to drive him home and then she stayed, just talking. Simon's naturally introspective nature had been exaggerated by the alcohol and he was full of self-doubt. Erica was shocked; it was a side of him she hadn't seen before, quite unlike his public persona. He said he loved Alex but they seemed to have grown apart and he found it hard to talk to her. Then he thanked Erica - rather emotionally - for listening. They arranged to meet again - just to talk, they both agreed. She hadn't meant for it to develop the way it did but she couldn't help being flattered by his attention and his confidences. The whole thing had just got out of hand. They'd been seeing each other for nearly three months when guilt had set in and she told him it had to stop. There was no row, no scene. He'd agreed. He was torn up over Alex too.

That had been just a couple of days before his accident. She'd persuaded herself that it *was* an accident but she'd never quite shaken off the fear that the end of the affair had upset him more than she'd realised. What a relief to hear from Alex that he hadn't killed himself.

Ironically her guilt had made her even more protective of her sister. She had to make it up to her, had to be sure she was all right. And then Theo had come along and she thought it was too soon and, in any case, he was too like Simon. There could be no future in the relationship. *It didn't work with Simon,* she had tried to say in various ways. *You shouldn't go that way again.* For, after all, she convinced herself, if she hadn't had an affair with Simon, he'd only have had one with someone else, sooner or later. It wasn't just her jealousy and frank admiration that had drawn him into it, she was sure. It was that Simon and Alex were never right together. Not really.

Erica sighed, left the window and picked up a photograph from the top of her chest of drawers. It was a picture of her with Alex when she was just nineteen and Alex twenty-one. They were on holiday together, laughing. A stranger had taken it. But Alex was happy again now, Erica comforted herself. There was no point in telling her about the affair after all this time. Theo was gone; Alex had moved on. And now they were on good terms again, she didn't want to spoil her relationship with her sister. She idolised Alex.

Notes

Kellaford Bridge is not a real village in Devon though it has many of the characteristics of the lovely seaside villages of the county with their steep banked lanes, river cut valleys and picturesque harbours. Its particular mix of features I put together for my story, but on any trip to the Devon coast you might find – and fall in love with - just such a place. KS

Lightning Source UK Ltd.
Milton Keynes UK
UKOW04f0617111014

239938UK00009B/73/P

9 780992 832711